A CONFLICT OF INTERESTS

Claire Gradidge was born and brought up in Romsey. After a career as, among other things, a nurse and a school librarian, she went to the University of Winchester, where she graduated in 2009 with a first class honours BA in Creative Writing. In January 2018, she was awarded a PhD in creative writing and *The Unexpected Return of Josephine Fox* was written as the creative element of her PhD study, which went on to win the Richard and Judy Search for a Bestseller competition.

Also by Claire Gradidge

The Unexpected Return of Josephine Fox
Treachery at Hursley Park House

A CONFLICT OF INTERESTS

CLAIRE GRADIDGE

ZAFFRE

First published in the UK in 2022 by
ZAFFRE
An imprint of Bonnier Books UK
4th Floor, Victoria House, Bloomsbury Square, London WC1B 4DA
Owned by Bonnier Books
Sveavägen 56, Stockholm, Sweden

This is a work of fiction. Names, places, events and
incidents are either the products of the author's
imagination or used fictitiously. Any resemblance to
actual persons, living or dead, or actual
events is purely coincidental.

A CIP catalogue record for this book is
available from the British Library.

ISBN: 978-1-83877-664-0

Also available as an ebook and an audiobook

1 3 5 7 9 10 8 6 4 2

Typeset by IDSUK (Data Connection) Ltd
Printed and bound in Great Britain by Clays Ltd, Elcograf S.p.A.

Zaffre is an imprint of Bonnier Books UK
www.bonnierbooks.co.uk

For Romsonians, past and present. Especially remembering Mum and Dad, who gave me the gift of being able to claim Romsey as my home town

Prologue

The night of Sunday 4ᵗʰ June 1944

FROM HIS POST HIGH ON Romsey Abbey's clock tower, Jim Fox raises his binoculars as a pinprick of light appears towards the south-east. A pinkish glow, it might almost be the first touch of dawn, except dawn doesn't come in Hampshire at 3 a.m., even in midsummer.

The light strengthens, the pink streaked with gold, quickly eclipsed by it, a growing haze somewhere off in the direction of Southampton. It reminds him of the way the sky would brighten at the start of an air raid back in 1940 or '41. But though he can see flames now, flickering into the night sky, they don't spread the way they had done then, eating across the horizon.

The fire's not as far off as he first thought. He stares, trying to work it out. Something domestic, perhaps? A hayrick? Except it looks as if it's burning too hot for that. There haven't been any bombing raids, and though there have been plenty of their own aircraft over, there's been nothing untoward. No hint of a concussion that would signify a downed plane: that

1

deep vibration of sound that shakes the belly more than the eardrums.

He reaches for the field telephone, turns the handle to alert his colleagues in the ARP post below. Whatever it is that's burning, it needs investigation. Tensions are high: rumours everywhere about the sudden emptying of the army camps, the disappearance of the lorries and tanks from the lanes where they've been parked for so long. Whispers in every pub, on every street corner. It's the invasion of France, our soldiers are on their way at last.

The first firemen to reach the scene find a vehicle burning in a ditch. The leaping conflagration that alerted Bill Fox has been fanned by the blustering wind into a blaze that has set the hedgerow alight, despite last night's rain. There's an acrid stench of chemical combustion: petrol and rubber, the flammable materials from the car's interior. Overlying that, woodsmoke from the hedge, and something other, more sinister. The unsettling whiff of roasting flesh. With horror, they make out the shape of someone slumped in the driver's seat, but there's nothing they can do. The heat's too intense for heroics. Whoever the poor bastard is, he's a goner for sure. All they can do is try to control the flames, keep the fire from spreading into the crop of ripening wheat beyond the hedge.

1

Monday 5th June 1944,
early morning

I T'S JUST GETTING LIGHT WHEN I wake, haul myself out
of bed. Though my weekend bolt-hole, the little shepherd's hut at Oliver's Battery, faces east, the sun won't
rise over the spine of the downland for a while yet. But the
birds in the woodland behind are singing fit to burst, and
I can hear the first sounds as my friend, Sam, the old goat
farmer, begins to move about in the yard below. It's not the
early start that bothers me, only that it's Monday. Another
week to get through.

I don't dislike my work as assistant to Bram Nash, Romsey's
coroner. It's an interesting job. My employer calls it standing
for the dead, but for me, it's more like detective work, picking up clues as to why someone died. The pain in the chest
they ignored; the toadstool they mistook for a field mush-
room; the lorry driver doing an extra shift, falling asleep at the
wheel; a depressed farmer with a loaded shotgun. We've had
all of them, and twice in the three years I've worked with him,

there's been a murder. A real investigation, tracking down a killer and seeing some kind of justice done.

It's Bram at the heart of my troubles. My feelings for him: the complicated history between us that stretches back to our childhood, when he was Captain Abe, leader of the gang, and I was a bastard girl-child nobody wanted. Despite the years we were apart, the facial injury from the Great War that had turned him inward, afraid to make relationships, and the ridiculous marriage I'd made and regretted, there was no escape for me once I'd come back to Romsey. It wasn't love, I'd tried to tell myself, just animal attraction. But whatever it was, I couldn't turn my back on it. Eighteen months ago, during our second murder investigation, it seemed we had come to a place where we could admit deeper feelings for each other at last. And then my estranged husband had turned up out of the blue. Richard Lester, not dead as I'd come to believe, but escaped from the POW camp he'd been in since Dunkirk.

Since then, it's been stubbornness and a kind of pleasure-in-pain that keeps me working at Nash, Simmons and Bing; that won't let me be a minute late arriving or a second early leaving. I do the job as thoroughly as I can, whatever I feel. It's not as if there's anything I'd rather be doing, anywhere I'd rather be. Only that I wish things could be different.

And this morning, something is definitely *very* different.

From the start, it's the quiet I notice. On Friday when I'd come this way, there had been bustle, a sense of something about to happen. Now, there's a silence that's almost eerie. All the way from Hursley to Romsey, the only sound is the wind in the trees and the putter of my Cyc-Auto's little engine. The military vehicles that have been parked along the roads for weeks, filling every lay-by and lane, have gone. All that's left are the muddy scars of innumerable tracks on the grass verges, the occasional broken branch where some large vehicle has emerged from its hideaway.

There's not a sign of the soldiers who've been billeted in the woods: not a single tent or campfire left. This time last week, my ride to work had been punctuated by good-natured catcalls from the troops in their encampments, but today there's no one to see me pass. The only comment comes from a gaggle of rooks, pecking at something unspeakable on the road.

A spatter of rain blows in my face. This year, June's been a disappointment as far as the weather goes. It should be warm, but these first few days have been as cold as March. I'd hoped to help Sam cut the meadow for hay this weekend, but it's rained every day so we couldn't get it done. There'd been no point in mowing the grass in the wet.

I worry about Sam trying to manage alone in the week. It's a lot of work for one man, cutting and turning the grass, forking it up into stooks. He's no spring chicken, and the ankle he broke when I first made his acquaintance eighteen months ago still gives him trouble. I know his neighbours will lend a hand if they can, but they're busy themselves. If the weather clears up, I'll have to try and go back to the farm one evening, see what I can do.

I owe Sam so much. He says it's the other way round, but it doesn't seem like that to me. He gives me a place to be quiet, never asks questions or passes judgement. A tall order for anyone these days because I know I'm obnoxious, short-tempered and sharp-tongued.

Sam's calm acceptance has been so important this weekend, after the filthy uproar with Richard on Friday. I'd thought I'd never get away from his cajoling and threats, but at least when I did, I knew he wouldn't try to follow me to the farm.

Sam has hated my husband right from the first time they met. Not that he'd ever said it in so many words, but I'd known from the way his sheepdog behaved when-ever Richard was around. Lady's the kindest animal in the world to anyone her master takes under his wing, I'm proof of that. But cross him, and she's most certainly not your friend.

At the office, I greet Fred, the caretaker, and hang up my raincoat. It's still early, and it seems I'm the first to arrive. But it's only a brief respite. They'll all be here soon: Aggie, Bram's secretary, nearly as prickly and bad-tempered as me; Cissie, the typist; and old Mr Simmons who should have retired years ago, but stays on to do his bit for the war effort. And Bram.

He's the one it all falls on, of course, this bitter bloody-mindedness that's been growing in me for the last year and more. I shouldn't blame him, it's not his fault. He's been behaving like a perfect gentleman, but that makes it worse,

6

somehow. I want to see him angry over the whole messy business with Richard, to show he's upset, but there's no sign. He's retreated behind the unyielding reserve that's been his defence ever since he was wounded in 1917, when shrapnel sheared away flesh and bone and his left eye. The physical mask he wears, the painted metal plate behind his spectacles, is nothing compared to the mental barrier he puts up against the world. For a few days, all those months ago, he'd let me in. But now, I'm locked out again. What he feels – how much he feels – is a mystery. I know I'm being unfair, but I can't help it. I hurt, and it makes me want to hit out, make sure someone else shares my pain.

I've hardly sat down at my desk when Fred brings me a mug of tea. It's stewed black, milk- and sugarless, but I'm grateful for its warmth.

'First in again, then,' he says to me. 'Couldn't you sleep?'

'I'm always up early at the farm.'

Fred sucks air through his teeth, a juicy sound of disapproval. 'Maybe you should've gone off to the Land Army,' he says, 'instead of eating your heart out here.'

I bite my tongue not to snap at him. 'Maybe I should. It's a bit late now, though.'

'You reckon?'

'Something's definitely happening out there. All the soldiers have gone. It's got to be the invasion, surely?'

He shrugs. 'I wouldn't hold your breath.'

'You're a cynic, Fred. Surely we can hope?'

'You know what they say. Live in hope and die in despair.'

I laugh, I can't help it. He's always so determinedly miserable, he makes even me seem optimistic. But then, who am I to judge? I don't live in two rooms in a semi-subterranean basement with no company but a cat. 'Let's hope not. The dying, I mean.' But if there's going to be an invasion, there will be deaths. It sobers me up, thinking of all those young soldiers camped along the roads till today.

It's not quite eight when the telephone begins to ring. The office doesn't open till half past, and I haven't heard anyone else arrive, so I get up and go through to the front office, where Aggie usually presides. If someone's ringing at this hour, they're most likely to be wanting Bram in his capacity as coroner, rather than on routine solicitor's business.

When I get there, I see Aggie's arrived. She can only just have come in because her coat, dewy with raindrops, is uncharacteristically dumped on a chair, and her hat's still firmly on her head as she picks up the receiver and identifies herself.

She's more than capable of dealing with any enquiry, and I'm about to go back to my desk when she puts up a hand to stop me.

'I don't believe Mr Nash has arrived yet,' she says, with a questioning look at me.

I shrug, shake my head.

'Oh.' She looks surprised at something the caller has said. 'Are you sure?'

A pause while she listens. 'Of course. As soon as he comes into the office.' She puts the phone down, frowning.

'What's wrong?' I ask. 'You look worried.'

'That was the chief fire officer, wanting Mr Nash. Trying to track him down to look at a body, but they can't seem to find him.'

'There's been a fire?'

'Apparently so.' She sniffs as she takes off her hat. 'A car blaze last night, down in Lee Lane. Crew got there too late for the driver.'

I shiver at the thought. 'They've tried Basswood House?'

'That was the first thing they did. Mrs Stewart was surprised; told them he'd been on duty with the ARP last night.'

Fan Stewart, Bram's housekeeper, is totally reliable. She keeps a closer eye on him than a mother hen on her chick. If she says he should have been on duty, she'll be right.

'And he wasn't there either?'

'He can't have been, can he? Otherwise, he'd have known about the fire.'

'Yes.' A chill runs through me. 'It's not like him to be out of touch.'

'Don't get yourself in a state,' Aggie snaps, and I know she's having the same thoughts as me. It's become instinctive to fear the worst these days. 'It can't be him, can it? No car for a start.'

'That's true, but . . .'

'I thought you might have had some idea.' She stares pointedly at me.

Blood rushes to my face. If I'd been cold before, now I'm boiling. I must look as guilty as sin. The penalty of having a redhead's thin skin.

'Why would I? You must know how unlikely it is, these days.'

She raises her eyebrows in a look of profound scepticism. 'Never sure of anything,' she says. 'Not with the pair of you.'

I want to protest. I want to say we're not a pair, not anymore. We can't be. Not since Richard came back, but she's talking again without waiting for my reply.

'It'll be one of his headaches, then. Ten to one he'll be upstairs in his office, too sick to move.'

It's something he never talks about. No one's supposed to know about the incapacitating migraines that are another legacy of his war injury. But every now and again something will trigger one and he'll shut himself away in a darkened room till the worst is over. Which usually means staying here in his office at the top of the building, out of everyone's way. A habit that caught me out way back when I first started working for him. I'd been taking a chance, trying to find out who my father was. Making an illicit late-night search through the office records. I hadn't realised Bram was upstairs, sleeping off a headache. Embarrassment all round, and it turned out I hadn't even been looking in the right place.

Aggie sighs. 'He won't thank me for it, but I suppose I'd better go and see if he's fit to come down.'

'You put the kettle on. I'll go.' Though she'd never admit it, the climb up to Nash's office makes her breathless these days.

My heart is in my mouth as I take the narrow stairway that leads to the top floor. Let him be there, let him be safe.

Beneath my feet, the wooden stair treads have been worn hollow by the passage of feet over the two centuries since the building was new. There's no way I can approach stealthily, the iron-hard oak creaks and groans like a ship at sea.

I reach the landing. Once I stop moving, it's silent up here. Though I hold my breath, tilt my head to listen, the door to his office is also oak, so thick it effectively blocks out any sound from inside. I knock softly, wait a moment.

Knock again. No response.

Taking a deep breath to steady myself, I lift the latch and push the door open. Still no sound, so I step gingerly inside, making sure to avoid the creaky floorboard by the door. The room's chilly, a breeze blowing in through windows that have been opened as wide as they'll go. Despite the movement of air, there's still the taint of sickness in the room.

He's here. Asleep. Huddled into a cumbersome old leather armchair that someone, once upon a time, must have seen fit to wrestle up the stairs, and which no one since has bothered to take away, though it's donkey's years since the house was converted to office use. His face is gaunt-looking, grey, but he's safe, and that's all that matters. I stand a minute, listening to his quiet breathing. His glasses – and his mask – are off, and the way he's turned away from the light means his old injury is hidden. Down beside the chair there's a bucket, the source of the sour smell, though as I get closer, I can see it's scoured out and clean now. He must have tidied up after himself before he went to sleep.

11

My heart jolts with pity and grief. If it weren't for Richard, I could have been there for him, been able to help. But there's no point thinking *what if*. Unless my husband changes his mind about a divorce, this is the way things have to be.

I begin to make a stealthy retreat. Now we know where he is, I can at least let him sleep. The fire chief can wait. A body that's been in a fire isn't the sort of thing that's going to improve a sick headache.

I'm almost at the door when a misstep makes the treacherous floorboard groan. He wakes at once, reaching for his glasses in what I know is a reflex action to protect the unwary from the sight of his scars. 'Jo?' he says in an unguarded moment. And then, as he struggles into a sitting position. 'Mrs Lester? Am I wanted?'

'Afraid so, Mr Nash.' Again, that pang of regret goes through me. It's only in my head I call him Bram these days. 'I'm sorry to have woken you.'

'What is it?'

'Chief Fire Officer White just called,' I say.

'White?' He rubs a hand across his face. 'What does he want?'

'They found a body in a burned-out car early this morning. He says he wants you to have a look.'

'Oh, joy,' he says wearily. 'Whereabouts?'

'Somewhere in Lee Lane.'

'Lee?' It hardly seems possible, but he looks even more drawn, greyer than before. 'Any details?'

'Sorry, that's all I know.'

'All right.' He sighs. 'Give me a minute to get myself sorted out.'

I turn to the door, but in my peripheral vision I see how he has to push himself up from the chair, the small stagger as he stands.

'Can I bring you anything? Coffee? A cup of tea?'

'Just water,' he says. 'I'm thirsty as hell. But there's no need to wait on me. I'll be down directly.'

Polite, I think, as I make my way down the noisy stairs, but the message was clear enough. He might as well have said *get lost*.

Downstairs, Aggie's waiting anxiously.

'OK,' I say. 'You were right. He looks awful, but he's coming down.'

The door closes behind Jo. Nash waits till the sounds of her retreat down the staircase fade away before moving. Every step jangles an echo in his head, despite the aspirin he was finally able to keep down at dawn.

The last few days have been vile, events accumulating in an avalanche of trouble. The situation in the office on Friday, the news he'd had from London on Saturday. And then yesterday when he'd thought to banish his worries with a long walk, there'd been no peace to be had anywhere. Noise and movement wherever he went: vehicles starting up, convoys of lorries and jeeps inching along even the smallest lanes. The stink of exhaust fumes, shouted orders, marching footsteps. Nowhere to go to escape the war and his thoughts. By the time the worst of the hubbub had died down, the headache had begun. If he'd been able to take something for it right at the start, he might have escaped the worst. But he'd been miles away from home and had nothing to hand.

Then he'd had to go crashing into that . . . row. He'd been crazy to let himself be drawn in. But what else could he reasonably have done?

He shudders. He has to get a grip, pull himself together. Get on with the job.

He uses the handbasin in the lavatory to splash his face. Yesterday's walking gear isn't quite the thing for the office, but it will do to inspect a body. Swap the jumper for the jacket that's been hanging on the back of his door, half-forgotten, for months, put on the sober tie he keeps ready for unexpected visits to the bereaved. Good enough.

Downstairs, Jo and his secretary are waiting for him. Despite what he'd said to Jo, there's a tall glass of water standing ready for him on Aggie's desk. He picks it up, drains it in one. Though the women are trying to pretend they're busy with other things, he can tell by their sidelong looks they've been talking about him.

'So,' he says, as briskly as he can, 'what do we know about this fire?'

'The ARP warden up on the abbey roof spotted it around three o'clock,' Aggie says. 'They couldn't work out the exact location, so by the time the fire crew got there, the car was well ablaze.'

Three o'clock, he thinks. A good long while after. No earthly reason to suppose . . .

'Lee Lane, Mrs Lester said?'

'That's right. The chief fire officer wants you to view the scene as soon as possible.'

'The body's still in situ?'

'So I gather.' She shakes her head. 'Not very nice.'

Nash forces himself to concentrate. The headache's come back with a vengeance, pounding in time with the pulse of his blood. 'An accident, I suppose? There was a lot of military activity down that way yesterday.'

Aggie shrugs. 'I wouldn't know.'

'Would you let White know I'm ready whenever he is? I'll just fetch myself another glass of water.'

Jo starts forward, hand outstretched. 'Let me.'

He shakes his head, regrets it immediately. Snaps, 'I'm perfectly capable, thank you.' Out in the little kitchen, he fills the glass and gulps down more water, regretting his tone even more than the headshake. There'd been no need to take his bad temper out on Jo. With a sigh, he refills the glass once more, then returns to Aggie's office. His secretary has the telephone to her ear, obviously waiting for some response, but Jo is nowhere to be seen.

2

Monday, morning

WHEN I'D FIRST COME TO work at Nash, Simmons and Bing, I'd been somewhat put out to find my desk tucked away in a dead-end back corridor, wedged in between filing cabinets and surrounded by shelves heaped with mouldering files. In the time since, I've tidied the shelves and dealt with the files, but the bulwark of the tall cabinets gives me a private place; a space of my own away from the rest of the office where nobody comes unless they're looking for me.

This morning, I'm even more thankful for my privacy than usual. I've got time to get my face in order before anyone sees how upset I am. I busy myself with mindless tasks, checking the diary for appointments, ruling up a new page in my note-book ready for the day's work. All too soon, I hear footsteps approaching. Not Aggie, not her brisk heel-tap, nor Fred's soft shuffle. Bram, of course. I take a breath to fortify myself, stand up, notebook in hand. 'Mr Nash,' I say, as he appears in the dog-leg turn of the passage.

'Jo.'

I feel my colour mount at the sound of my name on his lips. Another breach of the unspoken covenant we entered into so many months ago, in the wake of Richard's return. 'Please, don't.'

He frowns. 'I came to apologise.'

I fake a smile. 'You don't have to do that. What's the gen?'

'No more than you already know. White's picking me up in a couple of minutes. There's no need for you to come if you'd rather not. It sounds pretty grim.'

It's a sort of fencing match. He offers me a way out; won't say he'd rather go alone. I pretend not to understand, advance my own challenge. He'll have to tell me outright if he doesn't want me with him.

'Of course I'll come. You'll want a note-taker.'

A sigh, not so much conceding the skirmish as impatient. 'If you're ready, then. White will be here momentarily.'

I follow him to the front office, grab my coat just as the chief fire officer comes in. He greets Bram, looks askance at me. 'Is Mrs Lester coming with us? It's not really—'

'Oh, for pity's sake. It's not my first dead body, you know. Not even the first burned one.' I stalk out of the door to the waiting car. If these men think I'll take one look and fall in a heap on the ground, they're very much mistaken.

But it is grim. When we arrive at the site, on a lane that apparently sees little traffic on a Monday morning, the fire officer's car pulls up well clear of a blackened heap of metal. I get out quickly, not wanting another battle about whether I should be here or not. As I approach, I can see the front of the vehicle has been shielded from the worst of the heat by the engine block. Though the whole forward part of the structure – headlights and radiator grille, bumper and number plate – has tipped skywards because of the collapsed chassis further back, the number plate is still surprisingly legible. A local registration, not a military vehicle. Behind the car, several yards of hedgerow are blackened, and the grass underfoot is sodden with water from the fire engine's pumps.

There's a sullen smell hanging in the damp air of metal and organic matter fused together, as if someone has boiled a gigantic saucepan dry. After the first unwary breath, I turn my head aside, but then I see White watching me with a told-you-so look on his face and turn back. Beyond the wreck of the car, a miserable policeman stands. On the ground at his feet, a huddled shape is covered with a green tarpaulin.

Bram looks around. I've never seen him look so bleak. 'How long do you estimate the fire burned before you were able to get it under control?'

'A quarter of an hour, maybe? We got the call from ARP at five past three this morning. The fire must have been going a few minutes before they spotted it, so I'd estimate it started around three o'clock. We arrived on scene at quarter past. We'd have been quicker if we'd known the precise location, but you can see why no one else reported it. Must be half a mile or more to the nearest house, and there'd be no traffic that time of night. The one time all the blessed soldiers who've been about might have come in useful, and they were gone. Soon as we got here, we saw the body, but it was obvious there was nothing we could do for the fellow. Far too hot to extract him, no point in our chaps getting hurt. He must have been dead before the ARP called it in.'

'You think it is a man?'

'Just my manner of speaking, Mr Nash. To be honest, I don't think anyone could be sure as things stand. We'll need the medical chappie to take a look, but I'd say by the general build it's more likely to be a man.'

'Driver's seat, or passenger?'

'Driver's. We've got the number plate, so we should be able to make a presumption of identity once we get information from the registration office.'

'Unless the car's been stolen.'

'If that's the case,' White says, 'could be anyone.'

'As you say. And with all the movement around here in the last forty-eight hours—' Bram takes a deep breath, nods at the policeman. 'Better have a look. The sooner it's done, the sooner we can move the body.'

The police constable grimaces, a complex twitch of his facial muscles that's hard to interpret before he bends and, with a theatrical gesture, sweeps the covering from the victim.

The body's been laid on its side on the grass, still in the kind of position he – or she – had been in, sitting in the car. The blackened skin and fused-on clothes, the arms drawn up into a boxer's defensive pose and twisted legs are no surprise. As I'd said to Bram and Officer White, this wasn't my first experience of seeing someone who'd died in a fire. I'd been in London in the autumn of 1940 when the Blitz was at its height, seen bodies then that had been burned in the bombing. But I'd never seen anything quite as bad as this. My stomach clenches, and for a moment, I wish I'd listened to what the men had said and stayed behind.

It's shocking and yet somehow almost impossible to look away from this ruin of a human being. The hands have gone completely, and no vestige of the victim's features remain. One foot is still attached, but the other, in its charred boot, has fallen away. If this isn't the car's owner, it's going to be a hell of a job to identify who it is.

'All right,' Bram says to the policeman, his voice tight. 'That's enough. Get the body covered up again, for God's sake. I'll speak to Sergeant Tilling about moving it to the mortuary, but I don't want anything else touched until we have photographs of the site. We'll need a full record before you disturb the rest.'

'You'll want an expert to look at the car, too,' White says. 'I can tell you now, there's no sign it was involved in a collision, nothing serious enough to start a fire, anyway.'

I see Bram rub the left side of his face where the metal mask meets the flesh of his cheek. It's a gesture I know so well, betraying more feeling than his impassive expression suggests. 'What if someone was careless?' he says. 'Filling the tank from a can with a cigarette on the go?'

'It's a possibility.' White moves across to the wrecked car, circles round. As Bram and I follow, I can see there's a more intense area of burning on the ground towards the back of the car, a trail of ash where the fire had spread to the hedgerow.

'There are definite signs of pooling of an accelerant here,' the fire officer says. 'And that' – he indicates a ragged metal shape lying where the scorching is worst – 'might once have been a petrol can. But if you'd been that foolish, you wouldn't get back in the car, would you? You'd try and run, surely?'

'Suicide, then?'

Listening to their discussion, I can't help feeling it's more upsetting than the sight of the body. They seem so dispassionate, so matter-of-fact. It's almost as if they've forgotten they're talking about a real person, someone who's lost their life in a hideous way. The policeman, standing over the shrouded bundle, casts a sideways look at me, rolls his eyes. We're probably thinking the same thing. The obvious answer's staring them in the face.

'Who'd commit suicide like that?' I blurt out. 'It's murder, it's got to be.' A shudder engulfs me. 'I just hope the poor bugger was dead before the fire started.'

Jo's outburst breaks Nash out of the cocoon he's built for himself, the intellectual detachment that's protected him from the reality of what's before him. The sight and smell of the pathetic remains. His head reels. It's an effort to draw breath, to stop himself from gagging. An effort not to blast her with anger for shattering his calm. He can't speak.

White cocks an eyebrow at him, waiting. But when he doesn't reply, the fire officer turns to Jo, clears his throat.

'Well now, Mrs Lester, it's a possibility. But as you'll know from your work with Mr Nash, it's a case of taking it step by step, considering every line of enquiry.'

She blows out a long breath. Through the buzzing in his head, Nash catches a muttered '. . . patronising git', hopes the fire officer hasn't heard it too. He looks at his watch, forces himself to speak calmly.

'I'll have to ask you to run me back to the office, White. I have a meeting booked for ten and I can't see that I can usefully do any more here at the moment.'

'Of course, Mr Nash.' White leads the way to the car, opens the rear door to usher Jo in.

Nash climbs into the front, frustrated by the delay before White finally gets in and starts the engine.

As the vehicle moves off, Nash is aware without having to look at her that Jo's fuming. With him, and with White. He'd turn, but he's afraid that the movement would set off the nausea again. Instead, he pitches his voice to reach over the engine's noise, speaks to thin air in front of him. It will make things between them ten times worse, but he can't help that.

'Mrs Lester, make some notes for me. There's a lot to be done today, I don't want to waste time.'

'Yes, sir.'

As he expected, there's resentment in her tone. He has to ignore it. She, of all people, mustn't know what he's thinking. Not yet anyway. 'Contact Sergeant Tilling. Tell him we need a full panel of photographs before they move the body to the mortuary. And we'll have to put in a request for a specialist pathologist to do the PM, someone with experience of bodies in this kind of state.' He stops, wishing he could be somewhere else, anywhere else; could shut it all out till the agony in his head abates. 'Tow the car,' he goes on with an effort. 'Police mechanic to look at it, search for any defect . . . anything that might have contributed to the blaze. Sift . . . the ashes, every bit. We need every . . . last . . . fragment . . .'

In the back seat of the car, hunched over my notebook and straining to hear his voice, I suppose it's a moment before I realise Bram's stopped speaking. When I look up, I see he's slumped forward, chin against his chest. White's concentrating on the narrow road ahead and doesn't seem to have noticed anything.

'Mr Nash,' I say urgently, touching his shoulder. But there's no response.

At the sound of my voice, White glances across. With a muttered 'Bloody hell,' he pulls the car to such a sudden stop that I nearly slide off the slippery leather of the seat. And it's only my hand on Bram's shoulder that stops him crashing forward against the windscreen. I leap out of the back seat, tug the passenger door open, vaguely aware of White leaning over.

'Nash? What's wrong?'

But I can see what's wrong. The thing White can't. The jolting of the car, the inertia of Bram's unconscious head and body has shifted his mask out of position, skewed it so there's no longer a perfect seal along his cheekbone. And from beneath the dislodged edge, there's a dark trickle of blood sliding down his cheek.

'My God.' I don't know whether I say it aloud. 'Bram . . .'

'What's wrong?' White says again. 'What's going on?'

'We need to get Mr Nash to hospital,' I say, as calm as I can, though my heart is beating so fast it's making me breathless. Blessing the designer who gave the front of the car a flat bench seat, I slide in beside Bram, supporting his body against mine. With one convulsive effort, I manage to pull the door shut behind me without letting go. 'For God's sake, Mr White, get us on the road. Quick as you can. Not Romsey hospital. It will have to be Southampton.'

At last, he seems to understand. 'Hold tight,' he says, and starts the engine. I brace myself as best I can as he swings the car round to face the way we've come and puts his foot down. A flick of a switch, and the siren blares out. I worry that the noise will hurt Bram, but there's no flicker of response. He's a dead weight against me, head lolling on my shoulder. Only the slow rise and fall of his chest tells me he's still alive.

3

Monday, late morning

WHEN WE ARRIVE AT THE front entrance to the hospital, White sprints inside, leaving me alone with Bram. In my head, the words, *don't die, don't you dare die*, go round and round. After what seems like an eternity the fire officer returns, accompanied by two young men in short white coats who are wheeling a stretcher between them. I'm frantic with impatience to get him inside, under the care of a doctor. But now, as they hurry to open the passenger door and gather him up, I want to cling on, not let him go.

I should say something, give him the words I never have, however many times I've thought them. *I love you.* But I can't. Instead, the encircling words from the merry-go-round burst out. 'Don't die. Don't you dare die.'

I press myself back into the seat as they struggle to manoeuvre him out of the car and onto the trolley. As soon as they're clear, I try to follow. But my right leg's numb from the way I've been sitting, and I can't feel where my foot is on the ground. I stagger, have to lean against the vehicle. All I can do is watch as Bram is wheeled away.

'You all right, Mrs Lester?' White says. It must be one of the most ridiculous questions I've ever heard, and I don't bother even to try to answer it.

'Give me a hand. I have to go with him.'

'But—'

'Just do it,' I say. Measuring the impossible-seeming distance to the entrance, I take a hobbling, impatient step. 'I'll need my bag.'

Another step, two. White is beside me, one hand under my arm, my bag dangling awkwardly from the other.

'What do you think—?' he says. 'I mean, what happened?'

'I don't know. His war injury, I suppose. Something like that.' We're through the door, into a waiting hall with rows of benches, people turning towards us curiously. 'Where do I go?' I say to White.

'The receptionist's over there,' he says, nodding towards a desk on the far side of the hall.

'I don't care about that.' Close at hand, there's a set of double doors flapping to a standstill, a sign which says EMERGENCIES – STAFF ONLY. 'That way,' I say. 'They must have taken him through there.'

'You're not allowed—'

I grab my bag, pull free from his restraining hand on my arm. 'Don't wait for me.'

'How will you get back?'

I ignore his call, push through the doors. Beyond, I find myself in an empty corridor with shining pine flooring, white tiled walls striped with dark green. All very aseptic, but where, for God's sake, have they taken Bram?

Ahead, there's another set of swing doors, this time with porthole windows. Peering through, there's a bustle of activity beyond, a doctor in a long white coat bending over a stretcher, one nurse beside him while another hurries across with a trolley laden with equipment. I'm about to go through when a hand on my arm pulls me up short.

'You can't go in there,' a woman says. She's grey-haired, wearing tortoiseshell glasses and a badge that says 'Miss H. Scott, Almoner'. 'Come away, now. You'll have to wait like everyone else.'

'I came with a patient,' I say. 'Mr Nash. I think that's him in there . . .'

'That man?' She looks me up and down. 'You'd better come with me.'

Back along the corridor, into the waiting area. Curious faces again, but to my surprise the woman doesn't deposit me in one of the seats but leads me to a cubbyhole office, takes me inside.

'Sit down,' she says, busying herself at a handbasin. What does she have to wash her hands for? I think dully. I'm not that dirty. She looks back over her shoulder at me. 'We can't have you sitting in the waiting hall looking like that.'

'Like . . . ?' I glance down, notice the smear of blood on my coat for the first time. 'Oh.'

She comes towards me, a damp flannel in her hand. 'Your face,' she says, tapping her cheek in illustration.

As I reach for the flannel, I see my hands are bloody too, the same dark reddish-black stain that had seeped from beneath Bram's mask. 'I didn't realise . . .'

I scrub my hands and face. There's nothing I can do about the coat, so I take it off, fold it with the stains inside. 'Now can I go to him?'

'Are you his wife?'

'No. He's . . .' How am I going to describe it? Employer, ex-lover, friend? 'I work for him.'

She shakes her head. 'In that case, perhaps you can tell me who we should inform? We'll need to speak to his next of kin.'

It strikes home. Who *is* his next of kin? I think of Fan Stewart, his housekeeper, Aggie Haward at the office. Myself. Perhaps we three women are the nearest thing he has to family. The closest friends he has. 'I don't know,' I say at last. 'But I expect I can tell you most of what you want to know.'

She sits at her desk, pulls up a form. 'Right, now.'

We go through the details. Name, age, address. Profession. Though I'm bursting with impatience, she won't be hurried. I explain what happened out at Lee, why we were there. Tell her what I know about his war injury, the migraines he suffers. That he doesn't smoke but does drink whisky. That he takes long bicycle rides and solitary walks, and as far as I know hasn't seen a doctor in years. Miss Scott tuts sympathetically in all the right places, scribing my answers carefully into a multitude of pre-printed boxes. I'm half mesmerised watching the way her pen scratches over the paper, the blue-black trail of ink as she writes. It's only when she turns the sheet over to blot it that I come back to myself, the trance broken. Anxiety floods back, worse than ever. '*Now* can I see him?'

'I think it's unlikely yet,' she says. 'But I'll go and find out. You'll need to wait in the hall.'

She takes me out to the waiting hall, sits me down on an empty bench under a sign like a bus stop that carries the letter 'D'. 'You'll be all right here,' she says. 'There's no one in gastric clinic this morning.'

I sit down reluctantly. 'You'll tell them I'm here?'

'Yes, dear,' she says. 'Just you sit tight.'

I wait.

Names are called. Bodies move along the benches under signs A, B and C. Faces change, but the queues hardly seem to grow shorter or longer. A kind of stasis, in which I'm the only fixed point.

I wait.

A nurse brings me a cup of tea, sets it down on the bench beside me. I think I thank her, but the next time I'm aware of it, the tea's grown cold and a brown scum has spread disgustingly over the surface.

I wait.

My whole being is focused on the forbidden doors. Every time someone comes through, I half stand, hoping this time they'll call for me, but each time, I'm disappointed.

At last, I can't bear it any longer. I cross to the reception desk, wait some more, till it's my turn to speak to the harassed-looking woman behind it. 'If you're not here for an appointment,' she says exasperatedly when I finally get to the head of the queue, 'I can't help you. I don't know anything about casualties.'

'Who *do* I need to ask, then? I've been waiting ages.'

A hand taps me on the shoulder, and I turn, ready to snap. If someone's about to complain they can just pis—

'Josephine Lester,' a man says. 'It is, isn't it? Richard's wife? Whatever are you doing in this neck of the woods?'

I look up, way up. A tall man, looming a little too close. Instinctively, I step back, out of the queue, wanting more space. Should I know him? Good suit, good shoulders under it. Tanned skin, blond close-cropped hair. Keen grey eyes, the watered-down colour of an overcast sky. The picture of health if it weren't for the fact his right arm is in a sling. For the life of me, I can't place him, and my blank incomprehension must be obvious. 'I'm sorry, I . . .'

'Corby-Clifford,' he says, with a little laugh. 'You remember, surely? Richard and I were colleagues at the Royal Infirmary.'

The penny drops. Like my husband, Alec Corby-Clifford is a surgeon, though I can't remember what his speciality was. It's years since we last met. I knew he'd gone with Richard on that ill-fated mission to Dunkirk, assumed he must have been captured too. But my mind's too preoccupied with what might be happening to Bram. I can't be bothered to try and work it out now.

'Alec. Of course, I'm sorry.'

He puts his good hand on his chest, adopts a hurt expression. 'Ah, my wounded heart. Never mind, you can make it up to me another time. Don't tell me you're here waiting for Richard? I've lost track of the old rogue. It'd be good to see him again.'

'No. Richard and I ... Look, it's too complicated to explain right now. I came in with a friend. My employer. He collapsed. I'm waiting to see ... to hear ... They seem to have forgotten about me.'

'Surely not.' He winks. 'How could anyone forget you?'

I remember now what he's like, smooth as silk. Once upon a time I might have found it charming, but right now it's a distraction I don't need. Yet I can't just turn and walk away. 'What happened to you?' I make myself say. 'Your arm's not broken, I hope?'

'Thankfully not.' He smiles, a rueful quirk of the lips. 'Just a little mishap.'

'Oh?' I try to make it sound as if I'm interested, but it feels as if I'm operating on two different levels. The superficial part of me is having a conversation, trying to be civil, while the other, deeper, is turned inward, completely focused on what's happening to Bram.

'Most inconvenient. Mustn't say too much, but I was due to take a little trip in a few days. You know, going along with the chaps in a supporting role.'

By which I suppose I'm meant to understand he's been waiting to go overseas when the invasion begins, called up like Richard and so many other doctors to serve with an army casualty unit.

'So, what happened to your arm?' It seems polite to ask, though I'm not really all that interested.

'Hand,' he corrects me, and I remember how precise, not to say pedantic, he always was. 'Thundering nuisance. Moment of inattention, you know. Such a bore, especially since I'll need to have to have it dressed every day.'

'Sorry to hear it.' But my eyes are on the emergency doors, where Miss Scott has appeared. 'Excuse me.'

I don't hear what he replies. I don't wait to see whether the almoner is actually coming to find me but thread my way across the hall to accost her.

'Ah, Mrs Lester,' she says, looking uncomfortable. 'I'm sorry, but they won't let you in.'

'How is he?'

'Well, dear.' She looks around as if afraid of being over-heard. 'I shouldn't really say anything, but he is a rather sick man, I'm afraid. They'll admit him, observe him overnight. There's a possibility he'll need surgery.'

'An operation?'

'I can't go into details,' she says. 'Really, dear, the best thing you could do for him is contact his next of kin. Get them to contact us.'

32

4

Monday, afternoon

FRUSTRATED, SICK AT HEART, I make my way out of Casualty. I'm torn between wanting to stay and knowing I have to get back to Romsey. There's a lot to do to make sure Bram's instructions are carried out without delay. I haven't been thinking about time, but now I see it's already past one o'clock. I wish I had the bike with me . . . I'll have to catch a bus, and heaven knows how long that will take. Better find a telephone box, let Aggie know what's going on.

'Josephine,' a voice calls. 'Josephine! Hold on a minute.'

It's Corby-Clifford again, hurrying after me. I don't want to be bothered with him, but he seems determined.

He starts by suggesting we go for a drink together for old times' sake. Catch up with all the news. I cringe. Even if I didn't have anything else to do, I wouldn't want to spend half the afternoon talking to Richard's old friend about the state of my marriage.

'I've got to get back to work,' I tell him truthfully.

'Oh, come on,' he says. 'What's another half an hour? Who's to know if your boss isn't there?'

'I'll know,' I say shortly. 'I'm sorry, Alec, but I really must get back to Romsey.'

'Romsey?' He grins. 'Perfect serendipity. We can share a taxi.'

'You're going to Romsey? How come?'

'It's a long story,' he says. 'I'll tell you about it on the way. Come on.' He lifts his free hand to flag a taxi parked at the front of the hospital. As the vehicle moves towards us, I concede defeat. Though I'm not keen to spend time cooped up in the back of a taxi with him, it has to be a more efficient way of getting back to Romsey than trying to find a bus.

'You'll have to let me pay my share,' I say as the driver opens the door.

He shrugs, laughs. 'Quite the emancipated little woman,' he says. 'Tell me about this job of yours. What does Richard think about having a working wife?'

His patronising tone sets my teeth on edge. Even this late on in the war, it's annoying how many men still think a woman's place is in the home. And I'd have thought he would have remembered Richard and I are separated. We'd been living apart for two years already when he and Corby-Clifford had gone off adventuring to Dunkirk. But I haven't the energy to challenge him, and besides, I don't want to spend the next twenty minutes shut up in a taxi wrangling about it. It was to avoid that kind of hassle I'd left Richard. So I dodge the question, divert him with some carefully selected details about life as a coroner's assistant. Nothing about our current case, of course, and nothing identifiable from the past. I think I probably manage to convey the impression that what Bram and I do is only one step more hands-on than proving a will: a last duty towards the deceased that's utterly dull. Even so, Alec seems fascinated by what I'm saying, asking all kinds of questions to keep me talking. Or perhaps, I find myself thinking, it's not so much that he's interested, as that he's trying to make sure I don't get a chance to question him in return.

We're almost back in town before I finally manage to ask him how he happens to be in Romsey at all.

'To tell the truth,' he says, 'I'm at a bit of a loose end. I was all set to go to France, leaving in a few days, but this unfortunate injury means I've had to step back. And with my flat in town let out in anticipation of going away' – he lowers his voice as if he's telling me a state secret – 'it's been useful for me to be in Romsey. I've taken a room at the White Horse. A bit primitive, of course, but it'll do for the time being.'

Primitive? I think. It's way above my mark. Ironic, then, that when the taxi draws up in Market Place, he doesn't quibble when I offer him my share of the fare but accepts the cash almost eagerly.

'We must keep in touch,' he says, and I agree absent-mindedly, say a token goodbye before I start off down the street.

I'm so busy working out what to say to Aggie, that I've practically forgotten him by the time I reach Timothy

White's, the chemist's shop on the corner. I break into a jog, seized with a sense of urgency. For all my unthinking abandonment of work this morning, now I just want to get back to the office as quickly as possible.

Aggie must have been lying in wait for me. I only just have time to push my coat, still folded inside out to hide the bloodstains, into a dark corner by the coat stand before she darts out of her room to intercept me.

'What's happened to Mr Nash?' she says. 'Where is he? Officer White said—'

'Hang on a minute,' I puff. 'Let me catch my breath.'

She tuts, taking hold of my arm and pulling me into her office. She shoves me down on the straight-backed, uncomfortable chair she keeps for clients and unwelcome visitors. 'Cissie,' she calls out, 'fetch a cup of tea for Mrs Lester.'

The tea appears in suspiciously short time, a pot on a tray with three cups and saucers, a plate of Rich Tea biscuits. When Aggie eyes what she's brought, Cissie colours up defensively. 'I want to hear what Jo has to say too,' she mutters. 'I'm as worried as you are.'

Aggie sniffs. 'Oh, very well. Find yourself a chair. But if anyone comes in, you'll have to make yourself scarce.'

'Are we expecting someone?' I ask as the typist whisks away to the kitchen, comes back with a rickety stool. 'Did Mr Nash have many appointments in his book?'

Aggie shakes her head. 'Only Mr Hollis this morning. Mr Simmons was here dropping off some papers, so he dealt with it.'

'Is he still here?' I ask.

'Mr Hollis?'

'No.' I try to keep the exasperation out of my voice. 'Mr Simmons. If he is here, shouldn't we let him know what's happened?'

'He went fishing,' Cissie pipes up. 'Soon as he'd sorted Mr Hollis out. He told me this damp weather was perfect for getting a trout.'

'Then I think . . .' I get up, go out to the front door. Move the sign in the window from OPEN to CLOSED, pull down the blind. Turn the key in the lock. Aggie looks ready to argue, but I forestall her. 'Call it an executive decision,' I say. 'No one will disturb us now.'

'All right.' She sighs, picks up the teapot. The soft purr of tea as she pours makes me realise just how thirsty I am. I almost snatch the cup from her, take a scalding sip.

'Come on, Mrs Lester,' she says. 'Tell us. The way you're putting it off, I suppose it's bad news?'

'It's . . . I don't know. What did Officer White tell you?'

'Only that Mr Nash collapsed, and you went to the hospital with him.'

'That's it,' I say. 'Pretty much all I know. I waited as long as I could, but no one would talk to me. They just kept saying they could only speak to his next of kin.'

'That's bad,' Cissie says, 'isn't it? If it's like that?'

'A formality,' I say, hoping against hope that I'm right. 'You know what hospitals are like.'

'But what *happened*?' Aggie persists. 'I mean, I know he had one of his headaches.'

I take a breath, think of my coat. The stains will never come out. 'It must have been more than that. There was . . . blood.'

Cissie lets out a little shriek, but Aggie's intent on information. 'Blood? How could there be blood?'

'I don't know. It was coming from somewhere under his mask. Maybe . . . one of the old scars had broken down? They said . . . the woman who spoke to me said he might need surgery.'

Aggie purses her lips and a muscle tics in her cheek. 'And you're sure that's all you know?'

'Of course.' I nod miserably. 'What about it, Aggie? Who *is* his next of kin?'

'I don't know,' she says. 'Even though I've been here so long. Over forty years now, ever since I left school.' Another sigh. 'Our Mr Nash can't have been more than three or four then.' She reaches for my cup. 'Give me that, I'll top you up.'

I recognise a delaying tactic when I hear one. Leave a silence for her to fill. If I say anything, I think, she'll clam up. I just hope Cissie will have the sense to keep quiet too.

'Do you remember old Mr Nash at all, Mrs Lester? You'd have been a child, of course. He was a lovely man, but for years it seemed he'd be the last of the family line. No one thought he'd ever get married. He was over fifty when he went off to London to deal with a client's estate, came back engaged to the Mrs.' She pauses. 'Whirlwind courtship, it was. Before my time here, of course, but it caused a lot of gossip around town. A foreigner, and Jewish, and our Mr Nash born barely nine months after the wedding. Honeymoon baby, don't they call it?'

'At least they *were* married,' I say.

Aggie flushes scarlet. 'I didn't mean . . .'

'It's fine,' I say. 'Don't worry. I've got good memories of them both. I used to hang around with Bram . . . with Mr Nash and his friends when we were kids.'

'I remember that.'

'Mr Nash's father was always so calm and kind.' I think of my own upbringing, my grandfather who was anything but. 'And Mrs Nash, she seemed so . . . exotic, somehow. She used to make me think of a parrot.'

'A parrot?' Aggie is scandalised.

My turn to blush. 'Oh, you know. She used to wear bright colours, scarves and beads and . . . there'd be paint on her fingers most of the time.'

'She was an artist.' Aggie sniffs again. 'Leastways, that's what she called herself.'

'I liked her,' I say. 'She smelled of roses.'

'That's all very well,' Cissie interrupts. 'But I don't see what—'

I kick her ankle.

'Oh!'

'For all that,' Aggie says, ignoring us both, 'she never had another child. Just our boy.' Her features soften, and she blinks. 'Poor lady died in 1918, in the flu epidemic, only a few months after Mr Nash was wounded. It was touch and go with him, but it was her that died after all. So quick, they said she went out like a light. My belief is, she gave up. But old Mr Nash kept plugging away though he was getting on a bit by then. He was determined to keep the firm going till our Mr Nash was fit to take over.'

A long pause. Her gaze lengthens, fixes somewhere in the distance, far into the past. Cissie fidgets, and even I begin to think I need to say something.

'Anyway' – Aggie takes a deep breath, refocuses – 'the long and the short of it is, there's no one I know of who's kin to our Mr Nash. No one in Romsey, for sure. The Mrs must have had people, I suppose, up in London, but I don't know who'd be left now. You could try asking Mrs Stewart. She's been with him for years, she's as likely as anyone to know.'

'You've told her what happened this morning?'

She shakes her head, avoiding my eye. 'Not yet. I didn't think there was any point fussing her till we knew what was going on. I thought Officer White must have the wrong end of the stick, that it was just another of his headaches. Maybe a bit worse than usual, but . . .'

'I know. Me too.'

'I suppose I'd better go and see her.' She stands up, a heavy movement that betrays her reluctance.

'Don't worry. I'll do it.' I stand myself, fish my notebook out of my bag. 'Before he collapsed, Mr Nash gave me a list of things he wanted done about this body in the car. The people he wanted to contact.'

Aggie looks at the open page, my scribbled notes. I'm expecting a sarcastic comment about my handwriting, but none comes. 'I'll see to it,' she says. 'It's all routine stuff.'

'Leave the office closed until we can get in touch with Mr Simmons, though. And . . .' I steel myself to say it '. . . Mr Nash . . . he must have made arrangements, surely? Power of attorney? A will?'

Aggie frowns ferociously and her eyes fill with water. 'It's never that bad, surely?'

'I hope not.' It's more than hope. I want it to be a mistake more than anything I've ever wanted in my life. But the evidence is all the other way: that fleeting glimpse of him, pale and bloodied, unconscious as they wheeled him away; Miss Scott telling me what a sick man he is; the insistence I need to find someone who can stand kin for him soon.

There's a fire somewhere. He can hear the crackle of flames, feel the heat on his skin. Somehow, he can't manage to open his eye to see, though there are voices calling to him. 'Mr Nash, Mr Nash.' And once, bizarrely, 'Abraham?' But though he listens as best he can through the conflagration, the voice he wants to hear is missing. No one calls to him in her voice. No one says 'Bram.'

I'm nervous, standing on the front doorstep of Basswood House, waiting for Fan Stewart to answer my knock. Instinct and the class taboos of my childhood suggest I should be round at the back door. A feeling ingrained in me by my grandfather: I was a pariah, the lowest of the low. Not fit for ordinary company, let alone the big houses of my social betters. But I'm not a child anymore, and since then I've called a house not so different from this one home when I was Richard's wife.

I've never been sure what Fan thinks of me. A Romsey native, she knows all my disreputable past and she's fiercely protective of Bram. The news of his collapse is going to hit her hard.

The sound of footsteps. The glossy black door opens.

Bram's housekeeper is a neat little woman, who favours monotone colours in her clothing. Today's no exception. Her grey pleated skirt and cream rayon blouse don't quite amount to a uniform, but it's a close-run thing. There's a faint look of anxiety on her face which deepens when she sees it's me. 'Mrs Lester,' she says. 'Mr Nash isn't here. I told Miss Haward.'

It's symptomatic of her state of mind – or perhaps it's more to do with her assessment of my role – that she keeps me standing on the doorstep. But I can't tell her like this, the threshold a barrier between us.

I step forward. 'I know. Can I come in?'

Her look of alarm deepens, but she moves back so I can enter. 'What's happened?' she says. 'Something about Mr Nash?'

'It's a bit of a story,' I tell her. 'Why don't we go and sit down?'

She hesitates, conflict apparent on her face. It's obvious she's trying to decide where to take me. 'Ah . . . the morning room? I suppose we could—'

'Why don't we go through to the kitchen? We'll be more comfortable there.'

'All right.' She leads me down the hallway to the door beneath the turn of the stairs. The kitchen beyond strikes warm as we enter, and though it's June, I'm glad of it. I've got so cold in all the hours of waiting.

'Excuse the mess,' Fan says. But there's none to speak of, just the signs of a woman at work. There's an old Aga, sending out its lovely heat. A big deal table scrubbed immaculately white, a basket of laundry on a chair. An ironing board stands under the window, a half-ironed shirt spread out across it while an electric iron ticks ready on its asbestos stand. The homely smell of starch and scorch takes me back to my childhood, Granny busy with seemingly endless piles of ironing, holding the flat iron next to her cheek to test the heat.

'Sit down.' Fan moves the basket of laundry off the chair, flicks a switch to turn the iron off. 'Shall I make tea?'

Though I've had more than enough tea already, I nod, watch her push a kettle over the hottest part of the range. She stays standing, avoiding my eye, arms wrapped defensively around her waist. 'Go on, then,' she says. 'Tell me.'

So I do. From finding Bram in his room first thing this morning to the moment I had to leave him at the hospital. It seems to take a long time, but the kettle has only just started to whistle when I finish by explaining that the hospital has asked me to find his next of kin.

Fan Stewart shoots a horrified look at me, flops down in a chair by the fire. Before I can say or do anything, she puts her head in her hands and bursts into noisy tears.

I scoot out of my chair, put my arm round her shoulders. Feel them heave under my hand. 'Come on now, I'm sure it's not that bad.'

She sobs. 'You don't know,' she says, shrugging me off as she straightens up. 'You just don't know.'

'Know what?' Rather than having her shun my touch again, I occupy myself with finding the things to make tea.

'There was only one person left in this country,' she says. 'An old aunt of Mr Nash's. He hadn't seen her for years, but Saturday, he got a telephone call. They'd called because he . . . he was *her* next of kin. She'd passed away, dropped dead in the street from a heart attack.' She sobs again, a harsh sound. 'Queuing for her meat ration. He was supposed to be going to London sometime this week to sort things out.'

'That's so sad,' I say as I pour a cup of tea, lace it with sugar. 'Was she . . . I mean, I suppose she was his mother's sister?'

'That's right. Maude, her name was. She was a lot older than Mrs Nash would have been. Nearly ninety. Stayed in London all through the Blitz. Never turned a hair.'

I think of an old lady of nearly ninety having to queue for food, and it makes me angry. 'She didn't have a family in London? No one who could have helped her?'

44

She shakes her head. 'She never married. Stubborn old lady. I know Mr Nash tried to get her to come down here at the beginning of the war, but she wouldn't have it. Said Romsey was too quiet, she'd be bored. There was a companion woman, though. Irene. Nearly as old as the aunt. She was with her when it happened. It was Irene got in touch with him.'

'There's no one else?'

Another shake of the head. She grabs a tea towel hanging over the rail by the Aga, scrubs harshly at her face. 'No one,' she says. 'Just me and young Billy. We're the nearest he's got to family.'

'I don't think the hospital—'

'Look,' she says, turning fiercely to me, 'Mr Nash couldn't have done more for me if we'd been kin. Years and years, I've been with him. Ever since my husband died.'

'I remember him,' I say, to fill the pause she leaves. 'He was one of the gang, went off with the rest of them when they all joined up. He and my uncle Mike, and Jem, and Bert. Bram. All in the same company.'

'Bloody fools,' she says. 'Look where it got them.'

'I know.'

'What you don't know,' she says, 'is how Mr Nash came looking for me after he got out of hospital. When my husband came home first, I was so grateful. But he had these nightmares, shell shock it was. Used to try and hurt himself. It got so I couldn't cope. I was pregnant, and they packed him off to the asylum at Netley. I had nothing when he died, just a load of debt and a baby. I was stuck in a horrible little room over a pub at the back end of Southampton, working as a cleaner in lieu of rent, trying to make ends meet. It got so I thought I'd have to give up young Billy or let him starve, but Mr Nash . . . he and his father gave me a job, a home. The means to bring up my son in a decent place.'

I put my hand out, touch her arm. 'It's all right. You don't have to justify it to me. But the hospital, for them it's all about rules. Official designations.'

'Huh.' She stands up, in control again. 'Rules.'

'Fan . . .'

'Now then,' she says, ignoring me. 'What will he need? It's a mercy I've just done the laundry.'

I'm vaguely embarrassed, though I don't know why I should be, watching her sort through the basket of clean linen, selecting Bram's underthings: pants and vests, stacking them on the ironing board.

'Fan . . . ?'

'Yes?' She's busily matching socks now.

'*Fan.*'

'What?'

'I wondered . . . I know it's tricky, but . . . you'd be the one to know.'

'Know what?' She doesn't look at me, but there's a tension in the way she's standing that makes me think she might guess what I want to ask.

'Well, if he was seeing someone? I mean, since we . . . You could tell me; you wouldn't be betraying him.'

She stares at me now, a striped pyjama jacket in her hands. 'Are you stupid?' she says, as she snaps the jacket straight. 'There's no one. How could there be? You know what he's like.'

I know what he *had* been like, I think. The boy who'd been the natural leader of our gang, full of bravado and kindness, the man whose war wounds had damaged more than his face, left him averse to any kind of emotional commitment. When we'd first met by chance as adults in the height of the London Blitz, we'd each been alone, each looking . . . not for commitment, not that. A brief respite from the bombs, the threat of death. Sex had seemed like a solace, and we'd spent the night together, believing we'd never meet again.

And then when I'd had to come back to Romsey after all, we'd denied the attraction between us. Pretended for so long that it was just physical: an itch to scratch, a hunger to assuage. It was only when the business at Hursley Park House separated us last year that things had changed. We'd reached a place where he'd . . . where we'd both been ready to admit there was more. That it wasn't just lust between us, but love. Then Richard had come blundering back and it was all over.

'Right.' There's an ache in my chest. It's not as if I wanted to hear there was someone else in his life, but the idea he's as lonely as I am, knowing it for sure, is crushing. I feel heavy as I get up, as if lead's been poured into my bones. 'Well, I suppose I'd better speak to Mr Simmons. Perhaps he'll know what to do.'

'No need to go off in a huff,' Fan Stewart says, huffily.

Despite everything, the irony makes me grin. I'm not offended. At least she's feeling better.

'Give me a minute,' she says as she scurries towards the door. 'Someone will have to take his things into the hospital for him. You can do that, can't you? With that bike of yours?'

'Of course,' I say to her retreating back. It'll give me a good excuse to visit the hospital again. Not much use trying tonight, though, while the staff I've already failed to convince to let me in are still on duty. I'll try again first thing in the morning, hope for more success then.

Restless, I fidget round in her absence. Straighten the shirt on the ironing board. Check the time by the clock on the dresser against my watch. Pick up the unwanted cup of tea from the table, pour it away down the sink. Hang the discarded tea towel back over the rail. Touch the pile of clothes she's selected for Bram, fingers lingering over the fabric, a surrogate caress.

He's wandering in endless corridors, looking for something, though he can't remember what. Walls, floor, ceiling, all the same liverish brown. The light grows dimmer the further he walks, but he knows he must go on. He has to find . . . what?

He comes to a place where the corridor he's on widens into a circular bay. There begins to be a sound, muffled and directionless, like the thrum of an unsteady engine. He turns, turns again. Three, four, five featureless openings confront him. Which way to go? He can't remember now which was the corridor he came in by.

He must go on.

He picks at random. As he moves forward, the heat intensifies. The way angles down, darker, deeper. His feet slide. This is a mistake, but he has to go on.

5

Tuesday 6ᵗʰ June 1944, early morning – D-Day

A RESTLESS NIGHT SEES ME AWAKE well before six. Though wartime regulations have put us on double summer time since April, which means we're two hours ahead of the sun, the sky is beginning to get light. It had been hard enough to sleep last night for worrying about Bram, and I know it's no good trying to drop off again now. On weekdays, when I'm staying at my lodgings in Romsey with Dot and her nephew, Alf, who works at Wills' nursery across the road, I'm usually last to wake. But this morning, I'm first up and about, the house beyond my room silent as I creep to wash and dress.

Outside, the light is pearly bright. The blustery wind of the last few days has eased, and for once, it's not raining. I get the Cyc-Auto out of the shed, push it down Tadburn Road and onto Botley Road before starting it up. I tell myself it's a wholly rational decision to go back to the hospital to deliver the bag Fan packed for Bram, but I know in my heart it's an excuse. I'm no more likely to be let in this morning than I was last night. Futile as it is, I'm going because I have to, because I need to be near where he is.

At first, there's no other traffic on the roads, no other travellers but me. When I get to the top end of Southampton Common, though, there's a subdued sense of bustle and expectancy. While it's nothing like the military presence of even a week ago, there are plenty of men in uniform, vehicles buzzing up and down the Avenue. But the road branching down towards the Royal South Hants Hospital is clear, and as I make my way through the rows of terraced houses, I find myself back in the early morning silence I left behind in Romsey. The puttering engine of my motor bicycle seems rudely loud, so as soon as the entrance to the hospital comes in sight, I park the bike up on its stand and walk the final hundred yards, bag banging briskly against my leg.

All quiet here, too. None of the twenty-four-hour activity that I'd expect. A couple of men in porters' brown coats are sitting on a bench near the Casualty entrance, smoking cigarettes. They look up as I approach, and the older of the two grins chummily at me.

'You all right, love?' he says. 'Up and about early, aren't you?'

I shrug. 'I suppose. Couldn't sleep. Do you mind if I . . . ?' I put down the bag, take out my own pack of cigarettes.

'Make yourself at home. Budge up a bit, Cess.'

I sit, and the one called Cess offers me a light. Not the customary match, but a shiny brass capsule that flares obediently at the first flick of the wheel.

'Thanks. Nice lighter.'

'Yank service issue,' he says. 'A GI gave it to me.'

'Mm.' For a moment, we sit smoking peacefully. I'd bet we're all thinking the same thing, wondering where all those GIs we've taken for granted with their presents of chocolate and cigarettes have disappeared to. Hoping they're OK, wishing them luck wherever they are.

'Not busy?' I hazard at last. 'That's unusual, these days.'

'Too right,' the older man says. 'Never been this quiet. Lull before the storm.'

'You think?'

'Yeah.' He nods. 'Day before yesterday, they cleared out most of the patients, anyone who could be moved got sent off somewhere else. Practically empty wards back in there, but no staff leave. Ready for the big event, I reckon.'

I'm alarmed, thinking of Bram. 'I brought in a friend yesterday morning. He was really sick. Unconscious. Someone told me they might have to operate. Would they have sent him somewhere else later on, do you think?'

'What's his name, this friend of yours?'

'Nash,' I say. No use telling them Bram, they won't recognise that. 'Abraham.'

'That's the fellow went up to Theatres last night,' Cess says.

'The one with the scars?' the older man asks. When I nod, he pats my knee. 'He's on Cowen. He'll be getting the best care, don't you fret. Only four or five patients left on the ward, and all the usual staff.'

'You wouldn't know . . . how he is?'

He shrugs. 'Flat out, love, or at least he was when we brought him back from his op.' He pulls a watch out of his pocket, consults it. 'Half past six. They'll be right in the middle of the early morning work. They won't let you in now, not a chance. But if you like to wait a bit . . . I 'spect Cess and I could make you a cuppa, find you a bit of summat for your breakfast. You look as if you could do with it.'

'It's good of you, but I don't think they'll let me in however long I wait. Ow.' My cigarette's burned down to my fingers, and I jerk it onto the ground, grind it out. Pick up the stub, look for somewhere to get rid of it.

'Here.' Cess puts out his hand. 'Give it to me, I'll lose it for you.'

Feeling awkward, I hesitate. 'I can't do that.'

'Go on.' Cess laughs. 'Got to do ours, haven't I?'

It's true, there's a litter of stubs around the bench. 'All right.' I drop the end into his hand, follow it up with the half-full pack. 'Better take these too. I've given up, really. I only got them last night because . . .'

'Helps a bit,' the older man says. 'But I reckon you're better off without them.'

'I expect so.' But I'm already wishing I hadn't given the pack away. 'I wonder, could you to do me a favour? This bag, it's my friend's. His night things and stuff. Would you be able to get it to the ward for me? Cowen, I think you said.'

'Course we can.'

'Thank you.' I fumble my purse out of my pocket, bring out a half-crown. 'Perhaps you'd have a drink on me . . . ?'

'You put your money away, love. No need for that.'

Behind us, beyond the entrance, a telephone begins to ring. 'Hey up,' the older man says. 'Duty calls.' He heaves himself up off the bench, picks up the bag. 'Take care, love.'

'And you. Thank you.'

I watch them going back inside. Whatever else Fan might have packed in the bag, it feels like my heart's gone with it.

Somewhere, just off the chaos that is Gold Beach, an auxiliary field hospital is taking stock. Getting ready. Counting scalpels, bandages, phials of morphine. Personnel. For the last few days, the private hells of seasickness and anticipation have cut a swathe through their ranks, isolated so many of them in solitary misery. Now, in the thick of it, and once more gathered together, they discover they are a man short. No one can remember the last time they saw their missing surgeon. No one knows if he might have fallen to enemy fire out there in the sea, or on the sand. Or even if he embarked at all.

Though it's not the most direct route to Romsey, I can't resist going back through Nursling and Lee, past the site of the car fire. It's a few minutes after seven when I reach the scene, to find the vehicle's already been towed away, leaving behind clumps of dark, oily-looking ashes and other debris scattered across a wide expanse of scorched earth and withered vegetation. A rope cordons off the scene, and a mopey-looking police constable is standing on the public side of the rope, a bicycle lying on the ground beside him.

I pull up, wondering if he's had some kind of accident, fallen off his bike, perhaps. But before I can ask, he looks over, eyes me sourly. 'Mrs Lester,' he says. 'Suppose you've come to catch me napping?'

Puzzled by the accusation in his tone, I stop the engine, get off the Cyc-Auto. He's new to Romsey, and though I haven't had any face-to-face dealings with him before this, I've seen him once or twice when I've been on an errand to the police station. While it's obvious he knows who I am, I've no idea why he'd suppose I'd want, or even have the authority, to check up on him. Except now, of course, he's made me think I should be doing just that. 'Constable . . . Summers, isn't it?'

'That's right.'

'Have you been here all night?'

'No,' he says sullenly. 'I'm on a six to two today. Sergeant sent me to sift through the ashes.' He gestures across the site to where a motley assortment of equipment is stacked. I make out a couple of buckets and brushes, a spade and what looks like an old garden sieve.

'I see.' It was one of the jobs on Bram's list. One that needs to be done with great care if we're going to pick up any clues to the identity of victim or killer. 'Did Sergeant Tilling send you on your own?'

He shrugs. 'He said he'd be along later.'

I know Tilling's short-handed, but I've no confidence this copper's the right man for the job. An hour or more into his shift, and he's still just standing and looking? No wonder he had a guilty conscience. 'Better get going, then,' I say. 'You've got a lot to do.'

'Don't see the point. Bloke was burned to a crisp, wasn't he? Nothing left but a load of bloody ashes.'

I swear myself, use language unbecoming to a lady and all that. But his insolence ... his *indolence* makes me see red. 'It's not your job to see the point,' I say tartly. 'Just get on with it.'

He kicks at the ground, sends a clod of charcoal flying. 'None of your business,' he says.

'You've just made it my business, kicking the ashes about like that. For all you know, you've just destroyed vital evidence.'

'I suppose you'll go and report me now.'

'I suppose I won't have to,' I say, nodding towards an approaching car. 'Looks like Sergeant Tilling's just arrived.'

The car halts, and the sergeant and a smart young auxiliary policewoman who often acts as his driver climb out. Beside me, PC Summers groans, but he doesn't seem to have the initiative even to pretend to be busy.

'Mrs Lester,' Sergeant Tilling says, 'I hope you're not obstructing my officer in the performance of his duties?'

What is it with these policemen that every greeting comes as an accusation? Even though Tilling's tone is jocular, it grates on my nerves, and I can't help feeling he's not entirely joking. I'm tempted to spoil his morning – and ruin more than that for the police constable – by telling him what's been going on. But there are more ways than one to get what you want, so I smile, say, 'Not guilty, Sergeant Tilling. Summers and I were just talking about preserving evidence, weren't we, Constable? How careful he'll have to be in case he finds something that will need to be presented in court.'

'That's right, sir,' Summers confirms quickly.

'With reference to that,' I go on, ignoring the interruption, 'don't you think you should have two officers here while the job's being done? We wouldn't want anyone to cast doubt on what's found – or not.'

Tilling frowns. 'I'm not sure what you're getting at, Mrs Lester.'

'It's about preserving the chain of evidence, isn't it? You'd know better than me. If you leave one man alone to do the job, someone could say he'd deliberately lost something. Or planted it, of course.'

An angry flush colours Tilling's face. Or perhaps it's embarrassment, because when he speaks, his tone is conciliatory. 'Hmm. See what you mean.' He surveys the site gloomily, in much the same way I'd caught Summers doing earlier. 'You don't really think we'll find anything, though, do you?'

'Who knows? Mr Nash thought it was important.'

'Mr Nash. Yes . . . Have you heard how he is this morning?'

I shake my head. 'I know they had to operate last night.'

Tilling sighs. 'Right, well. Shaw, you'd better help Summers here. Grid up the site, do it systematically. Log any remains, any artefacts with the position you find them. And be careful.'

Policewoman Shaw shoots Tilling and me a glance that suggests she's less than pleased with the prospect. Summers doesn't seem much more popular with her either, judging by the way she hunches away from him as they move off. Skirting around the burned ground, they start to pick over the pile of equipment in a way that suggests deepest reluctance.

'My God,' Tilling says. 'Would you look at that? Excuse me, Mrs Lester. I'd better give them a hand. Get 'em started, or they'll be here all day.'

I say goodbye, get back on the Cyc-Auto. Hope he doesn't see my smile of satisfaction as I ride off. With three of them working, there's a real chance they might actually uncover whatever evidence there is to be found before weather and animals, even passers-by, contaminate the scene any further.

The dreams are different now. He's out of the tunnels, under a sullen sky, a failing light. But there's still the same heat, a humid, sticky oppression. He should get on: there's work to be done, yet his limbs are mired in a clinging heaviness that won't let him move.

This place he's reached feels like somewhere he almost remembers. Was it yesterday? There's rain now, like France, but surely he's not gone back as far as all that?

Around him now, there are hazy groups of men, dotted fires. The air's full of the scent of crushed grass, diesel fuel. The steady drumbeat of sound from before is eclipsed by the intolerable noise of engines revving, a cacophony of voices clamouring for his attention.

'Mr Nash, Mr Nash.'

There's a man's voice, shouting. A woman crying. What do they want? Can't they see he's not well?

A sudden sunburst flares in his face, a dazzle that hurts his eye, his brain. 'Look at the light, Mr Nash.'

His own voice. 'No.' Or is it 'Jo'?

He lashes out. A scream, a shout. 'Bloody bastard you—'

A grapple of hands holds him back, holds him down. He can't move, can't get away. Arms tremor with effort, legs cramp, convulse. He can't see, can't hear.

He's falling down into pitch and heat. No end to the drop.

'No! I didn't mean—'

His own voice again, jagged, tearing out of his throat as he falls.

'No.'

6

Tuesday, morning

B Y THE TIME I REACH the office, Aggie Haward is already at work. She tells me she's contacted everyone on Bram's list, so the jobs should all be in hand. She's so scandalised when I tell her about the scene in the lane that I can't help but laugh.

'It's no laughing matter,' she says reproachfully. 'Really, Mrs Lester, at a time like this . . .'

'I'm sorry, Aggie. I know. I promise, I was every bit as upset as you they hadn't started the work before. But now Sergeant Tilling is there, I'm sure it will get done properly.'

She sniffs. 'All right. I'm sorry too.'

'Look, I know we haven't always seen eye to eye, and I know . . . well, there are reasons you might wish I'd never shown up in Romsey at all, but until Bram . . . Mr Nash is better, we're going to have to work together, present a united front, because otherwise people will start thinking they've got to take the investigation into this death away from the office. From him. And he'd hate that, wouldn't he? If we can show them we can carry out the work as if he were here, get everything ready for him when he's better, they might just leave us to get on with it.'

'Well, I should think so, too.' She looks indignant at the very idea Bram's function might be usurped. 'But you've got a point.'

'Truce?'

'Whatever it takes,' she says. 'But you'll be the one who has to convince them. I've never wanted anything to do with his work as coroner.'

'That's all right,' I say. 'I can handle that side of it. And you, well, you're the respectable face of the office, aren't you? With you as our figurehead, no one's going to doubt our capabilities.'

'Huh.' She sniffs again, but there's a gleam of amusement in her eyes. 'Reckon you'll catch more flies with sugar than vinegar, do you?'

Despite everything, I can't help grinning with relief. If she's going to take that view, we'll be all right. 'Nothing's ever all sweetness and light,' I say. 'But I think we can do it, don't you?'

She nods. 'We can but try.'

'What about Mr Simmons? Will he back us?'

'When I spoke to him yesterday, he told me he'd be in by nine. You can put it to him then.'

'Have we got a map? A big one, so I can work out where things are. I'm not all that familiar with Lee.'

She goes to the filing cabinet, rummages in the bottom drawer. Produces an Ordnance Survey six inch to the mile. 'Best I can do.'

I open it up. It's dated 1911. 'Haven't we got anything more recent?'

'That's it,' she says. 'There was supposed to be a new edition just before the war, but they didn't bring it out in case it helped the Germans bomb us.'

'Fair enough.' I spread the map open. 'Anyway, I don't suppose it's changed much down this way.' I trace the line of Lee Lane along to the spot the car was found. 'Look, this is the place. Not far from where this little lane crosses.'

'That's Spaniard's Lane,' Aggie says, tapping the map with her finger. 'It's not a public right of way. All round here, it's Broadlands estate. The park is pretty much fenced off, one way or another, but these fields below, it's all still their land. Used to be big notices up about trespassers when I was a girl.'

'You know it?'

'Not to say know, exactly. But my father worked at the sawmill on the farm. It used to be a great treat to go and see him at work, I loved the smell of the cut timber.' She traces a reminiscent finger across to the river. 'There's a little island here that always fascinated me. Straight out of *The Water-Babies*. I'd sit for hours, trying to spot a water fairy.'

Aggie and fairies? I'd never have guessed it of her. 'Did you ever see one?'

She grins. 'No. No matter how many times I tiptoed along the path looking for them. Now then, to business . . .'

Somehow, the revelation has made us more companionable, and we settle to work together as if we've been doing it forever. We divide up the tasks she'll do from the stuff I'll have to deal with myself. It'll be mostly telephone calls and holding the fort here at the office for her, while I'll be out and about.

Despite the continuing anxiety about Bram that murmurs on in my mind under everything else, my restless night has at least given me time to think through what has to be done. It's just a question of running through it with Aggie, hoping she'll pick up on anything I've forgotten despite her protestations about not understanding Bram's work as coroner.

The first priority is to find out who's been asked to do the post-mortem examination, check whether it's been completed. Aggie offers to do that, and to make an appointment for me to speak to whomever I need to about the findings: any clues to the victim's identity, the cause of death.

'But surely,' Aggie says, 'they must have died in the fire?'

'I hope not.' I shudder. 'Think about it, why would . . . how *could* anyone just sit there while the flames . . . ?'

'I hadn't thought.' But it's clear from the way the colour leaves her face, that she has now. She swallows, writes something on her pad in her neat indecipherable shorthand. 'Horrible,' she says, half under her breath. And then again, louder, 'Horrible. I don't know how Mr Nash can . . .' She looks at me, a hard stare that might still be hostility or might, perhaps, be concern. 'How you can. Or . . . well, I suppose you can?'

'Of course.' A smile doesn't seem entirely appropriate, but I don't know how else to reassure her. No need to tell her how I'd tossed and turned last night, thoughts of Bram and the day ahead competing with images of that blackened body in the flames.

I'll need to speak to the fire officer again, see if White has come up with any further thoughts about the way the fire was started. Catch up with Tilling, see if he's had any luck finding out who the car belonged to. Once we know that, someone will have to follow it up. I give myself a mental kick. If I hadn't stranded the sergeant out at the site of the fire, he could have done that, but now I'll have to wait. Maybe that's not such a bad thing after all. With any luck, they may get some evidence out of the ashes.

I'm trying to think what else we need to do today when old Mr Simmons arrives. Silver-haired – what there is of it – and slightly built, he walks with a stick since his stroke three years ago. On the advice of his doctor, and the insistence of his wife, he'd taken semi-retirement then, only coming into the office when one of his long-standing clients wants to see him. Bram's illness is going to be hard on him.

'Morning, Aggie, my dear,' he says. 'And you, too, Mrs Lester. Good news, hey? At last.'

I suppose I must look as puzzled as Aggie. Good news? With Bram lying ill in hospital?

Simmons tuts. 'I thought you were looking at the map.' He peers at it. 'Oh, it's not France. Haven't you been listening to the news this morning? The eight o'clock bulletin said our paratroopers went in overnight. Looks as if the big day has finally come.'

It *is* good news. Of course it is. We've waited long enough for it, hoped for it. Guessed it would come soon. But for me, most of that's been swallowed up by my fear for Bram.

'I've been out since early on,' I excuse myself. 'I went down to the hospital to see if I could get any information about Mr Nash.' I catch Aggie's sharp look. I hadn't got round to telling her about that part of my trip.

'Yes, of course,' Simmons says. 'How is he this morning?'

I shake my head. 'I don't know. I couldn't get in. But . . . I gather he had some kind of operation yesterday evening.'

'Hmm.' He looks grave. 'That's all you know?'

'It's the rules,' I say. 'No one will tell me anything officially. They won't speak to me. It has to be his next of kin. So we're stuck unless you can pull some strings?'

'Well, now.' There's a gleam of something almost mischievous in his eyes as he nods his head. 'I think something might be possible. You and I need a little talk, Mrs Lester. In private. We'll just pop through to my office and . . . Aggie, my dear, give us ten minutes or so, will you, and then perhaps you'd be kind enough to fetch Mrs Lester and me a cup of your excellent coffee? One for yourself, too, and bring your notebook, because we'll want your opinion on what our next steps should be.'

Mystified, I follow him through to his ground-floor office. Once upon a time, before the house was converted to offices, his was the dining room. With its dark panelling and crimson wallpaper, it must have seemed the height of fashion. A grand place to be on a winter's evening, with a fire burning in

65

the fancy marble hearth and candles in the sconces, dozens more glittering in the chandelier. But these days, even in daylight, it's all wrong. The windows, with their faded velvet drapes, let in very little light since they look out over the alleyway that runs in front of the office, and opaque glass has been fitted to keep out curious glances. Even in the middle of a summer's day like today, Mr Simmons has to put the electric lights on as we enter. The wartime bulbs cast a sickly, economy pall that's depressing, but he doesn't seem to notice at all.

'Take a seat, Mrs Lester,' he says. 'I just need to find . . .' He props his stick against his desk, a vast affair of oak as dark as the panelling, turns to the equally large armoire he uses to store his papers. 'Now, where did I . . . ?'

I sit, try to curb my impatience. I don't offer to help find whatever he's looking for, because although he may put on a show of doddery incompetence, his mind is as sharp as a razor. For all his kindly manner, he's an old-fashioned lawyer, a stickler for protocol.

I can't work it out. Why would he want to talk to me and so pointedly leave Aggie out? I quell the urge to fidget. No good to try and hurry him, prompt him. No doubt it's all in the rules. More bloody rules. I hate the feeling of being trapped by bureaucracy, smothered in red tape, when all I want to do is help Bram.

'Here we are.' At last he turns, a thin folder in his hand. He flaps it down onto his desk, sits with a little grunt of effort. 'So, no doubt you're wondering what all this is about?'

Understatement of the day. 'I am.'

He pats the folder, gazes across at me and smiles. His manner is so like a dear old uncle I half expect him to ask if I'd like a sweetie. 'And you've no idea what I have here?'

I swallow down my irritation. Why can't he just get on with it, especially since he's already set a time limit on our meeting? It's as if he's playing with me, though I don't know why he should want to. 'Something to do with Mr Nash's affairs?'

He nods approval as if I've produced the solution to a universal mystery. 'That's right. But you see, what I'm wondering is whether you know more about them than you seem to do?'

'Me? No. Why would I?'

'You're not a fool, my dear, and neither am I. You and my colleague are . . . close.'

This again. I feel like St Peter, forced to keep denying my true allegiance. 'Were,' I say quickly. 'We were. But not since my husband came back.'

'Quite. A tricky situation. Forgive me, my dear, I don't like to pry but . . . a little bird told me there was something of an altercation in the office on Friday between you and Mr Lester?'

Both Mr Simmons and Bram had been out of the office when Richard had breezed in, pleased as Punch with himself. And thankfully, they'd still been absent when he'd slammed out again twenty minutes later, mad as the Crocodile. I suppose Aggie must have told Mr Simmons about it. I just hope she didn't tell Bram as well. 'Yes. I'm sorry. He was trying to persuade me to go back to him. Playing the hero card again.'

The old lawyer raises his eyebrows at me. 'The hero card?'

'Dashing off to Dunkirk in 1940. Volunteering to go with the troops this time. It's all very patriotic, but it doesn't stop him being a rotten husband.'

'There's no prospect of divorce?'

I shake my head. 'Richard won't contemplate it. It's just dog in the manger because the marriage is over. He knows I'll never go back to him.'

'Hmm,' Simmons says. 'Things may change, perhaps? When the war is over?'

I shrug, look away from his keen gaze.

There's a pause which the old solicitor obviously expects me to fill. Except I've nothing to say. He sighs. 'Well, my dear, we must get on, or the estimable Aggie will be upon us before I've said what I have to.' To my relief, his tone is brisk now, all business. He opens the folder, takes out a sheet of paper. 'My colleague ... I should tell you that regardless of your current situation, it would appear Mr Nash holds you personally in very high regard.'

Even if it's true, there's still nothing I can say.

He sighs again, passes the paper over. 'Read that.'

To whom it may concern:

In the event of my impairment, incapacity or death, I appoint Mrs Josephine Lester, née Fox, to act for me as my de facto next of kin.

[signed] A Nash

[witnessed] CW Simmons

I read the single sentence twice, a third time. The words blur. I know what it says, but somehow, I can't work out what it means. I look up at Simmons.

'Me?'

He nods. 'He did it last year, after that business with George Hine. You remember the problems it caused because the man didn't have a next of kin on record.'

After Hine? I hadn't even noticed the date on the document till now. February 1943. But that means . . .

My brain seems to be running slow, thoughts struggling to keep up with my racing emotions. I do remember, of course I do, how difficult it had been for Bram to resolve George Hine's affairs because he'd had no living next of kin. Though it hurts to think of it, I can see why Bram might have reviewed his own situation in the light of that, decided to put his house in order. But what I don't get is, why choose me? Why then? By February 1943 Richard had come back, and Bram and I . . .

When we knew . . .

When I thought I knew it was all over between us.

7

Tuesday, morning

WHATEVER I MIGHT HAVE SAID to Simmons or he to me is abruptly cut off by the door bursting open. Our typist, Cissie, rushes in breathlessly. 'Mr Simmons, Mr Simmons, they've confirmed it,' she calls.

Simmons frowns. 'What the dickens . . . ?'

'Eisenhower's just been on the wireless. Fred was listening, he's had it on ever since the early broadcast this morning. It's really started! The invasion of France!' She's laughing and crying together. 'It's really happening.'

Aggie appears in the doorway, her face flushed with emotion. 'I'm so sorry, sir.' She puts a hand on Cissie's arm, tries to draw her away. 'Come on now, do. Mr Simmons is trying to have a private talk with Mrs Lester.'

Cissie shrugs her off. 'But it's important, really important. Mr Simmons?'

He smiles. 'Yes, my dear, it is. But—'

'It's OK,' I cut in. 'Isn't it? We were pretty much finished, weren't we?'

'I suppose.' He scans the desktop. There's only the folder on it now, because while he was looking at Cissie, I've palmed the letter, folded it up and slipped it into my pocket. He cocks his head enquiringly in my direction. 'Well, I suppose if you want to leave it like that?'

I nod. 'I think I've got all I need for now.'

His lips twitch. 'I see. Well, you can come back to me if you have any further questions. So, Aggie, let's have that coffee. Cissie, if you'd just nip down to Fred, tell him to keep listening. Update us on any news.'

As the two women withdraw, he smiles. 'Quick of you, my dear,' he says. 'Just as well I've got a copy for the files.'

'Um . . .' I reach into my pocket. 'You can have this one back. I just didn't want—'

'You'll need to keep it if you're to act for him. No doubt the hospital will insist on seeing it before they discuss his condition with you.'

'You won't object if I go back as soon as we've finished here?'

'It must be your first task. The very first,' he says soberly. 'We all want to know how poor Mr Nash is getting along.'

'It was silly of me to try and hide it,' I say. 'I'll have to tell Aggie.'

'Tell me what?'

I jump. Laden though she is with a tray of coffee cups, spoons neatly in each saucer, not a rattle has betrayed Aggie's arrival. 'Mr Nash wrote a . . . thing. Last year. Making me his next of kin.'

She sniffs. 'A "thing"? Really, Mrs Lester. Haven't you learned more than that working here all this time? I presume you mean a declaration of intent?'

I hunch defensively, expecting a blast of disapproval. 'I suppose.'

Instead, she just nods, hands me a cup. 'Good,' she says. 'That should make the situation easier to deal with.'

Mr Simmons clears his throat. 'Now, ladies, if we could just turn our minds to the business in hand?'

Firm, deceptively gentle, he steers our discussion away from personal issues and back to the intricacies of running a busy solicitors' practice when the main player is out of commission. He listens while I tell him what Aggie and I have already discussed about the investigations into the burned body, gives his approval.

'I'll back you,' he says, 'if you need backing. But I have every confidence in your ability. Just let me know if there's anything you want me to do.'

Then it's Aggie's turn. 'You and I must go through Mr Nash's appointments,' he says. 'Postpone those we can. Rearrange anything that's vital, of course. I'll put in a few more hours in the office. My wife will be glad to get me out from under her feet, no doubt.' He gives Aggie the twinkly uncle smile he used on me. 'I'm afraid this is going to give you a great deal more work, my dear. But I know we can always rely on you, our mainstay and prop. Can't possibly manage without you in challenging times like these.'

Aggie straightens her shoulders; agrees she'll do whatever she can. I think of what she said to me about catching flies with sugar and give Simmons top marks. He's a real old smoothie, must have been lethal in his youth.

I'm impatient to get going, but propriety keeps me tethered another ten minutes, sipping politely at cooling coffee I no longer want while Mr Simmons settles the finer details of our plan for the week ahead.

He surfaces, reluctant. Turns once again from the beckoning dark. Still, there's the knowledge he has to go on, something he needs to do, to find before he can rest.

Back through the flames that threaten to engulf him.

And there it is. The thing he's been searching for. A blackened outline of machinery, a twisted, organic shape. Dear God, it's a body. A man.

Burned beyond recognition, yet he's not dead. How can he be dead when he opens his eyes, piercing and accusatory? Speaks from a tongueless mouth.

'Find out, you have to find out who did this.'

Bony arms reach out, hands without fingers. 'Your job is to find out.'

Out in town, the buzz I'd noticed in Southampton has spread to the streets of Romsey. Everywhere there are people talking, bright smiles or concerned frowns on their faces. I go with the frowns, myself. There's still so far to go, so many soldiers, sailors and airmen who'll die, so many civilians in France who'll lose their homes and maybe their lives. But I can't deny the sense of hope, the feeling that Cissie evoked with her interruption. It *has* started, and if today isn't the end of the war, perhaps it will be the beginning of the end.

Though I'm keen to get to the hospital and find out how Bram is, I choose to go back down the lane through Lee. I tell myself it's purely professional interest to see how the police are getting on with the search at the site of the fire, but there's a kind of ghoulish curiosity too. After the ferocity of the fire, what can possibly remain of the victim and any possessions they might have had with them?

Tilling's car is still parked up on the verge clear of the scene, and it's been joined by another which I recognise as Chief Fire Officer White's. I park the Cyc-Auto and make my way to where the two of them are standing, heads together as they inspect something Tilling is holding in the palm of his hand. Across the burned ground, which has been swept clear of debris, PCs Summers and Shaw are packing up their equipment. Though Summers has streaks of soot on his face while Shaw's white shirt collar is no longer immaculate, at least they seem to be working together now.

'Mrs Lester,' Tilling greets me as I approach, closing his hand so I can't see what he's holding. 'Wasn't expecting you to come back so soon.'

'I'm on my way to the hospital again,' I say. 'To find out how Mr Nash is.'

'I thought that's where you'd been earlier?'

I shrug. 'I couldn't talk to anyone then.'

'Ah?' There's curiosity in the monosyllable, but I'm not going to satisfy it. If word gets round that Bram has made me his next of kin, it'll set the gossips buzzing again. Anyway, I've got questions of my own.

'Looks as if you've finished here already,' I say. 'Have you found anything that might help us identify the body?' Though I address the question to Tilling, the way the two men had their heads together when I approached suggests White will be equally in the know.

'A few bones,' the police sergeant says, pushing a cardboard box on the ground towards me with his foot. Inside, I can see a scatter of what looks like charred twigs of varying thicknesses. 'I'll get them sent off to the pathologist straightaway. And these.'

He picks something from his half-closed palm, holds out a flattish small disc of metal, blackened and blurred by the heat. 'It's what's left of a button,' he says. 'Military, by the look of it. We'll get it cleaned up, see what's what. If we can identify the insignia, that'll narrow the field a bit.'

I peer at the markings, but I can't make anything of them. 'I suppose it might,' I say doubtfully. 'Where did you find it?'

'Over there.' He points to a place that would, as far as I can remember, be close to where the passenger side of the car had been. 'Buried deep in the ash, it was. Lucky to find it at all.'

My doubts increase. 'If it was deep,' I say, 'it might have been there *before* the fire. Think of all the soldiers bivvied round here. It could have been lost any time.'

75

He frowns. 'All right,' he says. 'I take your point. What about this, then? Found it right under what was left of the driver's seat. Just where the body was.'

This time, he opens his hand fully. His palm is grimy with ash, but the circle of gold he displays is gleaming, unmarked by fire. I pick it out of his hand, turn it in my fingers. It's small, and from the shape it's not a wedding ring. A man's signet ring, too chunky for most women to wear.

Heavy, good quality gold, its surface gleam a mark of much wearing. A prized possession, not something to lose and walk away from carelessly. Almost certainly, only there since the fire. Something that belonged to the body in the car? Or could it be from the person who put him there?

I twist the engraved surface to catch the light, feel my heart give a double-bump of shock. Of recognition.

'Mrs Lester?' Tilling frowns at me again. 'You all right?'

'What? Yes. Of course.' I drop the ring into his hand as gratefully as if it's still hot. 'Here, you'd better have it back. Keep it safe.'

He inspects it a moment, almost as if he's suspicious I might have practised some kind of sleight of hand. Then he slips it into his pocket for safe keeping. Not the right way to treat evidence, but I'm not in the mood to argue the toss with him about it.

'For a minute there,' Tilling says, 'you went awfully pale. Are you sure there's nothing wrong?'

I shake my head, try to laugh it off. 'I'm all right. Put it down to an early start. Excitement over the news, anxiety about Mr Nash. Saying which, I need to get on. You'll let me know when you track down the car's owner?'

'Of course. And you'll keep us updated about Mr Nash?'

Easy to agree, to get back on the bike and ride off. Easy to wave, pretend I haven't a care in the world, especially if they can't see my face. Not at all easy to get my thoughts in order.

Impossible, in fact.

Because the ring is Richard's. I'm almost sure of it. I recognised the half-erased crest. An eagle, he'd always insisted on calling it, though once upon a time I'd teased him that it looked more like a chicken.

Either way, now it's tucked away in Tilling's pocket. Out of sight, but it's far from being out of my mind.

I should have told him, but . . .

Not yet. Not before I've thought it through. What earthly reason would Richard have had for being there? The memory of the burned body flashes before my eyes. My stomach revolts, and it's all I can do to stop the bike before I begin to vomit. The question is . . .

. . . is Richard dead or alive?

Is my husband the victim, or the killer?

8

Tuesday, midday

I'M PRETTY GOOD AT PIGEONHOLING my thinking. I've got used to putting personal issues aside for work, keeping ordinary life going despite news from the war. And now, though it's almost the hardest thing I've ever done, I make myself disregard the sickening fear in my belly, stop thinking about the evidence that puts Richard at the site of the fire. I can't afford to be distracted from what I have to do now: toughen up, deal with the authorities at the hospital.

They take some dealing with. While Miss Scott, the almoner, does what she can to help, everyone else I come up against seems hell-bent on denying my right to visit despite the document I've brought. By the time they finally concede its validity and I'm registered as Bram's next of kin, the letter and I are both in a sorry state, dog-eared and limp. I just wish I'd had the sense to lie to them in the first place, tell them I was Bram's wife, his sister, his cousin. Anything, to break through the officialese.

Eventually, though, I'm permitted to go up to the ward where Bram's being treated. I've been told I wouldn't normally be allowed to see him out of visiting hours, even as next of kin. It's only because he's on the 'Seriously Ill List' that I have the dubious privilege of out-of-hours access.

'Five minutes,' the ward sister says. 'That's all I can allow. Don't expect him to recognise you. He may not even be aware you're there. He's a very sick man.'

If she thinks I'll scuttle away meekly before I know the truth about what's wrong with Bram, what they're doing to get him better, she's got another think coming. But right now, I won't rock the boat, risk getting thrown out. The most important thing is to see him, know he's being taken care of. Touch him, even if he doesn't know I'm there, speak to him even if he can't hear.

The ward has a row of beds on either side of a wide central area, a high ceiling that gives the place a spacious feel. But there's still the all-pervasive smell of every hospital I've ever been in: disinfectant and floor polish, old food, stale sweat and fresh urine. And under it all, something less definable. Pain and infection, despair.

The sister leads me through to a bed that's close to the nurses' central desk, screened by pale green curtains held in heavy wooden frames. With a facility that speaks of years of practice, she levers one of the screens aside to let me go in.

Bram's lying almost flat in the bed, one thin pillow under his head. He's still as stone, and almost the same grey-white colour. Bandages wind round his head, cover the scarred side of his face. A bottle of clear fluid hangs from a stand at his bedside, drips slowly through a glass tube which connects to a snaking line of rubber tubing that vanishes somewhere under another bandage round his left arm. Next to him, the nurse who's monitoring his condition looks up as the sister and I enter.

'Observations?' the sister demands.

'No change.' The nurse speaks quietly, her eyes as fixed on Bram as mine are. But she moves aside as I approach, lets me get close enough to touch his free hand. There's a graze on his knuckles, and I run my fingers gently over the roughened skin.

I'm expecting him to be cool, even cold, but he's not. His flesh is hot, a dry heat that belies the grey pallor of his skin. After the first shock of it, my instinctive withdrawal, I reach out again, enfold his unresisting fingers between my two hands.

'Bram? Bram, it's me, Jo.' Almost without thinking, I chafe his hand in mine, hoping for some kind of response. But there's nothing: he's withdrawn to somewhere far beyond my reach, utterly remote. A crusader on a desert tomb, burning with midday heat.

'Is he sedated?' I ask the sister. 'Why is he so hot?'

She shakes her head. 'Not here,' she says. 'Not where the patient may hear.'

'He might be able to hear me?' A tiny flicker of hope. 'I thought you said he wouldn't know.'

The nurse exchanges glances with the sister, who nods. Unspoken permission has been given.

'He might,' the nurse says. 'Sometimes he does seem to respond.'

It's all I need. Regardless of the onlookers, regardless of his impassive face, the lax fingers in mine, I stoop down by the bed, bring my face level with his. Lift his hand close to my lips.

'Bram,' I say, 'it's going to be all right. *You're* going to be all right. Aggie's keeping the office going, and Mr Simmons is covering for you. I'm . . .' I falter a moment, thinking of the ring, the implications of it. 'The body in the car? I'm going to find out who it is. I've got some new evidence already.'

The sister tuts. 'That's enough,' she says. 'The last thing he needs is to be worried with business.'

You don't know him, I think. It's his first priority, always. If he's aware of anything, he'll be worried *not* to know. But there's something else, something more I have to say. Whether he can hear me or not, I need to say the words.

'Bram.' I press my lips to the back of his hand, where the blue veins lie corded under his skin. There's a moment so brief I can't be sure it isn't imagination when his thumb seems to twitch in response. A reflex perhaps, because it doesn't happen again when I repeat the kiss, say the words. Whisper them almost, a kind of Braille against his flesh. 'I love you, Bram. Don't you dare bloody die.'

In his dream, he can't move. Can't evade the flames, the nightmare shapes, the dead man. It's his job to bring justice, but what can he do?

Sleep. The urge to sleep is overwhelming. To escape from the dreams, the heat, the thrum of pain. But in some small corner of his mind he's aware he is sleeping, something like sleeping.

If he lets himself drift down into the merciful dark, there's a risk he'll never get back. Right now, he can't seem to care if he doesn't.

A garble of voices.

He's heard them before, these women who mean well, who tend his body, try to call him back. Once or twice, he's opened his eyes to pale lavender cotton and starch as they lift him, turn him, smile as pain jolts through his head.

It's all too much effort. What does it matter?

Bram.

The voice he's been waiting for. The touch. All his strength goes in the effort to respond. To turn his hand, to touch as he is touched . . .

. . . love you, Bram.

Words he feels through his skin, in his overheated flesh. It's enough.

Mustn't let himself drift, sleep, slip into the dark. Not now. Not if she . . .

'Right,' I say to the sister as she escorts me away from Bram's bedside. '*Now* tell me. I'm not leaving until I know what's wrong with Mr Nash. What you're doing to help him.'

She sighs. 'I suppose you'd better come to the office.'

It's a tidy space, as I would have expected, but not a generous one. Once the sister shuts the door, we're crammed together in a room that's hardly more than a cupboard. She takes her place at the desk, indicates a chair every bit as uncomfortable-looking as the one Aggie keeps to deter visitors, tells me to sit down. 'What do you want to know?' she says abruptly.

'Everything,' I say. 'What's made him ill, what you're doing to help him. Why he's unconscious and so hot.'

'Forgive me, but I don't quite understand . . . your relationship with Mr Nash?'

'It's none of your business,' I say. 'You've seen the letter. He's given me the right to ask.'

'Hmm. But have you got the courage to hear the answers?'

I blink at the punch of it. 'He's not going to die,' I say fiercely.

'Not if we can help it,' she agrees. 'But . . .' She stands, selects a small glass jar from a collection of similar jars on a shelf above her desk. As she sets it down, pushes it towards me, something inside rattles.

I pick it up. An irregular-shaped, brownish spike of what might be metal, about the size of my thumbnail, slides inside the jar. 'What is it?'

'Shrapnel from the last war. The surgeon took it from the wound on Mr Nash's face. It had begun to work its way to the surface, through the old scarring. It's not an uncommon occurrence.'

Hastily, I put the jar back on the desk, resist the urge to rub my fingers against my skirt. 'That's what caused the bleeding?'

She nods. 'Has he been complaining of pain?'

83

'Only a headache. But he's had those for years.'

'Hardly surprising, in the circumstances.'

'Right. But I don't understand. If they got that . . . thing out, why is he still so ill?'

'Are you sure you want to know all this?'

Impatience makes me rude. 'Don't be stupid, of course I do.'

I see her blink at the careless insult. 'There are two factors,' she says stiffly. 'The first is infection. While we are treating that with what we have available, as you observed, Mr Nash's condition has not improved as much as we would like. His temperature is still extremely high.'

'Which means the infection isn't under control.'

'It seems not.' She's guarded.

'Isn't there a new drug? Penicillin? They say it works miracles.'

'So I believe, though I haven't personally seen it used. The problem is, of course, the current situation with the troops.'

'D-Day? What the hell's that got to do with it?'

'The government has ruled that all stocks of vital drugs are to be reserved for the armed forces. You'll understand they have to be the priority.'

A priority, I think. But not the only priority. 'Would it help Mr Nash, do you think?'

'Mrs Lester, I'm not a doctor. I couldn't possibly speculate.'

'But you think it would? It could?' If she says yes, I don't care what I have to do. Plead with the doctors, go to the black market, beg Churchill himself.

She shrugs. 'Perhaps.'

It's all I can do to contain my exasperation. Is that the best answer she can give? What I need is a doctor, someone like Richard . . . The irony is not lost on me, though whether he'd help if he knew it was for Bram, I don't know.

Could I even find him? He might already be in France. And I have to face it, he might be dead. A pang goes through me. But worst of all, somehow, is thinking he might be alive, and a killer.

I can't sort out the chaos of my thoughts, and I miss most of what the sister's saying next. Something about the second factor, the surgery Bram's had. I'm jolted back to reality when she says a name I recognise, though I've no idea what the context is.

'. . . if Mr Corby-Clifford . . .'

'What? *Alec* Corby-Clifford?'

She frowns, perhaps at the familiarity of my using his given name. Or perhaps because she realises I haven't been listening. 'You know our consultant surgeon?'

Another jolt. But this time I keep my head. 'He's an old friend of my husband's. You were saying if he . . . ?'

'I was saying,' she continues with heavy patience, 'that it's a pity Mr Corby-Clifford wasn't the one to carry out the surgery. While our registrar is perfectly competent, our emeritus consultant is . . .' a flush spreads across her cheekbones, high spots of colour that tell a story of their own '. . . quite extraordinary. Now he *is* a miracle-worker if you like. It was a heavy blow to us when he volunteered to go with the invasion forces, though we've been fortunate enough to have the benefit of his services in the interim. But then we heard yesterday he'd been injured here in England. An awful thing to happen.'

'He had his arm in a sling when I saw him yesterday,' I say absently. My mind's already busy working out how I can contact Alec, make him listen to me. What I can do to persuade him to help. 'I didn't realise it was so recent. What happened, do you know?'

'It's none of your business,' she says, returning my earlier comment with relish.

'But—'

'I'm a busy woman, Mrs Lester. You must excuse me. The doctors are due to make their rounds at any moment.'

'Will Alec be with them? Could I speak to him, perhaps?'

She sighs. 'Weren't you listening? Mr Corby-Clifford hasn't been dealing with routine matters for several weeks. Only special consultations. Added to which, he's now injured. So no, I don't anticipate he'll attend today. Now, if you'll excuse me, I must ask you to leave.'

I consider waiting, insisting on speaking to Bram's doctors. But it seems unlikely I'll learn anything more than the sister has already told me. So I go. The only thing reconciling me to leaving Bram is the thought that I might be able to help him by getting in touch with Alec.

It turns out that it's not as easy as all that. My first thought is that he'd said he would be having daily dressings for his injury, so there's an off-chance I might catch him downstairs, where we met yesterday. It's a bit of a stretch, but it is around the same time of day, so it's worth a try. But there's no sign of him, and though I hang around for a few minutes, painfully conscious of time passing, I know better than to ask anyone for information about him. They're bound to quote confidentiality at me, and I've had my fill of that nonsense already today.

The next thing to try is a call to the White Horse. Alec had said yesterday he'd be staying there for the time being. I don't fancy being overheard by his colleagues while I try to persuade him to break government regulations, so I ignore the phone booth in the waiting hall, go out to the telephone box in the street. Thankfully, I've got plenty of pennies, but the telephone directory is missing so I have to get the operator to put me through.

'Reception. May I help you?'

'I'm trying to contact a guest at your hotel,' I say. 'A Mr Corby-Clifford. It's important.'

'I'm sorry, madam, I'm afraid he's not here at the moment.'

'But he is a guest of yours?' I persist.

'He is,' the woman admits with a degree of reluctance.

'Do you know when he'll be back?'

'I'm afraid I couldn't say.' She's impeccably polite, but there's a steely quality in her voice which tells me even if she did know, she wouldn't say. 'I could take a message for him if you like?'

'Yes. Tell him . . . ask him to get in touch with Mrs Lester at Nash, Simmons and Bing, please. It's urgent I speak to him.'

'I'll let him know as soon as he comes in.'

'Thank you.' I don't feel very grateful, but it's not her fault.

'Goodbye, madam.'

'Goodb—' but she's gone.

I stand with the receiver in my hand, listening to the disconnect. Now what shall I do? The only thing is to get on with the job Bram pays me for. I clear the phone line, insert my pennies, and dial again.

Aggie answers at the first ring. I tell her what little I know about Bram, try to sound positive. I'm not fooling either of us: I can hear the disappointment in her voice that it's not better news as clearly as if I were with her and could see it on her face. But she's a trouper, and she doesn't say any of the things that must be going round in her head the way they are in mine, like *What are we going to do? How will we manage?* and *What if he doesn't . . . ?* Instead, she tells me what she's managed to find out this morning. As disappointing in its own way is the news that the specialist pathologist has been called away and won't be able to do the post-mortem tomorrow after all. I suppose there's a kind of relief because it means I won't have to own up about the ring just yet. But there's horror too. It'll be at least another forty-eight hours before I'll know the truth.

'Mrs Lester?' Her voice calls me back from the brink. 'Are you still there?'

'Sorry, Aggie, yes.'

'Sergeant Tilling says they've found out who owned the car.'

'They have?'

'It's a retired army colonel by the name of Beech. He lives in Coldharbour Lane.'

'That's not far from where the car was found, is it?'

'Just over a mile, the sergeant said. He told me to tell you he'll be seeing the colonel at two thirty, and to ask you to join him if I heard from you in time.'

I look at my watch. It's five to two now. 'It'll be a bit of a rush, but I should make it. What's the address?'

'The house is called Lee Water Cottage,' she says. 'It's on the corner of Coldharbour and Lee Lane. A pretty thatched place if I remember rightly.'

I've got a vague memory of seeing it on my journey this morning. Or at least, seeing somewhere that might answer the description. But there's no time to waste debating it. 'OK. I'd better get on. Thanks, Aggie.'

'I'll let Sergeant Tilling know you'll be there, shall I?'

'Tell him I'll try.'

He's been struggling for what feels like hours, trying to free himself from the cloying dark. He must see her, speak to her. But when he finally shrugs off the last tendrils of dream holding him back and opens his eyes to the real world, he's confused. The light is dim, suffused with green as if he's in some mossy forest cave. He tries to turn his head, but his muscles won't obey his mind's instructions. By squinting ferociously sideways, an effort that makes him feel sick, he can make out the pleated material that screens him from the world and remembers. He's in hospital.

Sounds from outside confirm it. A muted hustle and bustle, the squeak of rubber soles on a polished floor. There's the smell of bleach and mutton stew and he groans as the nausea rolls over him in a wave.

'Mr Nash,' a voice says. 'Are you awake?'

He tries for words, but his mouth is dry and only an inarticulate sound comes out.

A blurred face arrives in his vision. A young face, brow wrinkled with worry, surmounted by a halo of white. A nurse. 'It's all right, Mr Nash,' she says. 'Just rest.'

She pats his hand. The gesture reminds him why it was so urgent to wake, and he makes another effort to speak. 'Jo?' he tries to say, though it seems as if the nurse thinks he's said 'You?'

'I'm Nurse Baker,' she says. 'I've been looking after you today.'

'Jo?' One final effort to make himself understood.

'Oh yes,' the nurse agrees. 'Your friend was here a few minutes ago. I'm afraid she's gone now though.'

It's too much. Frustrated, exhausted, he closes his eye. Ages later, or perhaps it's only a few minutes, he hears voices close by.

'Yes, Sister,' the girl who's nursing him says. 'He was awake. Yes, definitely awake. He tried to speak.'

'. . . did he say?' The sister's voice is further away, more muted. 'Was he coherent?'

'Just his friend's name, I think. I wasn't sure . . . should I have called her back?'

'Absolutely not. He needs rest, not visitors. I'll tell her if she calls.'

He'd shout if he could, tell the woman he needs this particular visitor more than rest. But he's dumb, his throat dry as dust. The thought that Jo has been there, that he's woken too late, is a torment. Heat is burning him up again, but before the darkness claims him once more, a drop of moisture rises to his eye, spills over. Helpless, he feels it track down his face. He can't even lift his hand to wipe it away.

9

Tuesday, afternoon

I TRY MY BEST, BUT THERE'S more traffic on the roads around Southampton now, and the trip I managed in less than half an hour this morning takes twice that this afternoon. I know I must be late, because Tilling's unmarked police car is standing at the gate, with the ubiquitous WPC Shaw waiting behind the wheel. I give her a wave as I pass, hurry up the path to the front door.

I've never been all that keen on thatched cottages: they make me think of spiders and birds' nests infested with mites rather than old-world charm. But it has to be said, Aggie was right. Colonel Beech's cottage is very pretty with its black and white beamed walls and a neat thatch of straw gleaming in the watery sunlight. It's even got roses round the door. Tiny apricot-yellow blooms drop petals into my hair as I wait for my knock to be answered, give off a heady fragrance that's almost like incense.

I'm surprised when it's a man who answers the door. I suppose I'd expected a wife or housekeeper, but this is a whip-thin wisp of a man who looks as if he might once have been a jockey.

His face is deeply lined, tanned to the hard colour of teak, and the shapeless old cap which is pulled down low over bright blue eyes is the same faded tweed as the ancient jacket he wears.

'What do you want?' he says. His tone is acerbic. 'We don't buy at the door.'

'I'm not selling,' I answer, equally crisply. 'I'm Mrs Lester, from the coroner's office. I'm here to see Colonel Beech. Sergeant Tilling asked me to come.'

'You're a bit late, then, aren't you? He's been here twenty minutes already.'

'Yes.' I'm not going to apologise, though if it turns out this is Colonel Beech himself, I'm going to look very silly, as well as rude. 'And you are . . . ?'

'The colonel's batman,' the little man says. 'Capstaff's the name.'

'Right. Well, you'd better let me in, then, hadn't you? Otherwise I'll be even later.'

'Tuh.' He steps aside, ushers me into a long, narrow hallway with closed doors on either side. As soon as he shuts the front door, the corridor's plunged into gloom, and I'm left hesitating in the near-dark.

'Straight down to the end,' Capstaff mutters behind me, and I fumble my way along the hallway, stumbling over the edge of an unseen rug here, just managing to avoid a looming grandfather clock there.

Beyond the tick of the clock, there's the shape of a door, outlined by faint shreds of light. I put my hand out, find and lift the latch.

The door opens on what seems like a blaze of daylight after the Stygian corridor. For a moment, I can't make out any details, but when my eyes adjust, I see I'm in a low-ceilinged parlour cluttered with an assortment of armchairs and sofas, small, polished tables and display cases. While there's hardly room to move, everything is glossily clean, not a speck of dust in sight.

Tilling is perched on a squashy wing chair, while opposite him, in the chair's near-match, sits an enormous man with an inflamed, shiny pink face. There's not a single hair anywhere on his head: he's bald as a toad, no sign of stubble or eyebrows. It doesn't even look as if he's got eyelashes.

'Ah, Mrs Lester,' Tilling greets me. 'Glad you could make it. This is Colonel Beech.'

'Meetcha,' the hairless man wheezes. 'Siddown.'

The moment when I might have apologised for my lateness seems to have passed, so I take a seat in a harmless-looking Windsor chair between the two men.

'Capstaff.' The colonel speaks again, breathless as if he's been running. 'Gin for the lady.'

'Colonel—'

'Thank you, no,' I break in quickly. 'I'm fine.'

'Please yourself.' He screws up his face. 'Get on, Sergeant. Infernal waste of time.'

'You say neither you nor your batman, Mr Capstaff, had noticed your car was missing from the garage?'

'No call to look. Not going anywhere.'

94

Tilling turns to the batman. 'You'd confirm that, Mr Capstaff?'

'Like the colonel says. We haven't used it for weeks. Can't get the fuel, for one thing.'

'Had it been immobilised as per regulations? The rotor arm removed, for instance?'

Capstaff looks uncomfortable. 'I can't actually speak as to that. I suppose if it had been . . .'

'Yes?' Tilling is dogged.

'I suppose it'll be in the workshop somewhere.'

'Perhaps we could take a look?'

Before his batman can reply, the colonel shuffles forward in his chair. 'Have to wait. Need the bog. Capstaff!'

The slight little man heaves his master from his chair with an adeptness that speaks of much practice. They totter urgently together towards a door at the far side of the room which opens into the back garden. A definite strike against all the charm of the cottage, I think. If it were me, I'd swap every bit of it for indoor plumbing.

Tilling sighs with exasperation. 'You can see what it's like, Mrs Lester. I swear the old buffer's doing it deliberately. He and that man of his are like a double act. Ask one of them a question and the other butts in.'

'He's saying he didn't know the car was gone?'

Tilling nods. 'That's right. I don't believe a word of it, though. Look at this place. It's a right old clutter but everything's shipshape. Even if the colonel hadn't noticed the car was missing, I bet that man of his would have done.'

'He wasn't surprised?'

'Couldn't tell,' Tilling says gloomily. 'Didn't seem bothered, but what with the breathlessness and that manner of his, he could have been laughing for all I know. Claims he's having an asthma attack, but I reckon it's down to fat.'

'What did he say when you told him about the body?'

'Nix to that. I haven't told him. Didn't want to risk it if he's really ill. Shock might do him in.'

'Did you notice his face?' I say. 'Do you think that colour's natural? I couldn't help thinking ... it almost looked as if he'd been too close to a fire, scorched off his eyebrows.'

Tilling looks startled. 'Never crossed my mind. Put the colour down to blood pressure. But now you come to say it ... Good Lord, what if ... ?'

A loud tapping rattles at the window. My first thought is that it's Capstaff, trying to alert us to some problem with the old man, but then I see it's WPC Shaw. She's signalling urgently to Tilling and he motions her towards the open door.

'What is it?' he says when she appears in the doorway. 'Better be important.'

'It is, sir.' She glances uneasily at me. 'Could you ... ? I don't like to ...'

Sighing, he gets up, goes over to her. A muttered conversation follows, and though I don't catch what's being said, the look on Tilling's face tells me a lot. His expression goes from weary exasperation to puzzlement and annoyance, finishes up with what looks like suppressed excitement.

There's a trace of that too in his voice when he comes back towards me.

'I'll have to go,' he says. 'Message just came in over the transceiver. There's been a bit of a to-do. A break-in. Important, but I can't . . .' He pulls himself together with an effort I can see. 'You'll have to make my excuses to the colonel when he comes back. See if you can get anything useful out of him or that man of his.'

'Do I tell them about the body?'

'Better keep schtum for the moment. If they don't know . . .'

'Or don't know we know?'

Tilling grins, taps his nose. 'Got it. I'll be back at the station later. Give me a call if you come up with anything useful.'

It's beginning to feel like a farce, I think, as I watch Tilling disappear out of the door, see him and WPC Shaw scurry past the window. Now all I have to do is wait for the reappearance of the villain. But it's not right to think like that, I've no evidence Colonel Beech or his batman have done anything wrong. Even if they are lying about noticing the car was missing, it doesn't mean they're criminals.

The wait for them to come back seems interminable. Fidgety with impatience, I get up. I'd pace, but there's no room, so I prowl around, dodging the furniture as best I can and thinking they've definitely missed their cue for a timely entrance. Perhaps they're hoping Tilling and I will both have given up and gone by the time they get back.

The display cases are full of bits and pieces which I suppose must have some kind of military significance. I recognise medals and badges, buttons and bullets, but the majority of objects are beyond me to identify. The overall impression is sad and slightly sinister, as if time has stood still since the Armistice. I turn away, thread across the room to where an array of photographs stands on a low table, each lined up with such precision I daren't touch them in case I shift them out of place. I tell myself it's my duty as an investigator rather than vulgar curiosity that drives me to inspect them. I stoop down, survey them one by one.

Most show the colonel as a much younger, much thinner man. In all of them he's in uniform, pictured with an assortment of other soldiers and dignitaries. Impressive, maybe, to recognise Field Marshal Allenby or Baron Mount Temple among the faces, but all very impersonal. And as far as my curiosity about his hairless state goes, I'm no wiser. In every picture Colonel Beech's face is as smooth as if he's been freshly shaved, and his headgear, pulled low over his eyes, conceals his eyebrows as well as his head. For all I can tell, he might have been blamelessly devoid of hair all his life.

Among all the military personnel, one picture stands out. It's a studio portrait of a girl – a young woman – the kind that's popular to mark a special occasion. A twenty-first birthday or an engagement. While the sepia tone suggests it's old, the young woman's pose and clothes, even her sturdy body shape, are much more modern. She's looking directly out of the picture, a confiding smile on her lips that seems to suggest she thinks the world is her friend. Her hair is flaxen pale: if she's the colonel's daughter and gets her colouring from him, I can imagine an army haircut would have made him seem as good as bald all his life. But there's no time to check it out. There's the sound of erratic footsteps, the puff and blow of the colonel's breath and Capstaff's sotto voce grumbling as they make their way back into the room. I've just time to distance myself from the photographs, pretend interest in the nearest cabinet of militaria before they're back inside.

Capstaff eases the colonel back down in his chair. My eyes are drawn to a dark spot of damp high up on the old man's trousers, and I catch the whiff of urine floating up as he settles into his seat. A kind of alibi for this afternoon. His exit hadn't just been engineered to avoid answering Tilling's questions.

In response to his master's impatient gesture, Capstaff blurts out, 'What's happened to the copper, then?'

'Sergeant Tilling was called away,' I say. 'He asked me to give you his apologies, Colonel Beech.'

'Damn bad manners,' he puffs. Rattles the empty glass on the table beside him. 'Top up, Capstaff.' Then, with a glare at me, 'What're you waiting for?'

'I'd like to ask you a few more questions if you don't mind.'

'Say I do?'

I shrug. I'm beginning to get the measure of this old man. 'Then Sergeant Tilling will send someone else. He won't give up.'

He takes a noisy slurp from the freshly filled glass. 'No choice then.'

I take it for assent. 'Your face looks very sore, Colonel. Have you had an accident?'

'Thundering cheek,' he says. 'What's it to you if I have?'

'Think about it,' I say coolly. 'Sergeant Tilling's told you your car was set on fire. To me, it looks as if you might have been standing too close to a flame not so long ago. And perhaps your breathlessness comes from smoke inhalation.'

He blinks at me, and I see he does have lashes, very sparse and pale. 'You're damn high and mighty for a flunkey.'

'I've been called a lot worse in my life, Colonel. You won't distract me like that.'

'Tell her, Capstaff.'

The little man glowers. 'The colonel was having a bonfire yesterday. Stuff was wet, so he put some paraffin on it. Went up in his face.'

'Is that right? It looks painful, Colonel. Did you call a doctor?'

'Damn doctors. Capstaff takes care of me.'

'You've no comment to make about your car?'

'Nothing at all.'

'Nor when you saw it last?'

'None.' He leans his head against the back of the chair. 'I'm done in. Send someone else if you like, but I'm tired now.'

It's the longest speech he's managed, and if he wasn't struggling before, he does truly seem to be exhausted now.

'All right. I'll let Sergeant Tilling know what you've said. Perhaps Capstaff can show me the workshop? And I'd like to see where you had this bonfire of yours.'

'Any damn thing,' he says. 'Just get out.'

It doesn't take long for Capstaff, monosyllabic with resentment, to show me an irregular area of burned ground out in the back garden. A few odds and ends of sticks and ashes make it horribly reminiscent of the site of the car fire, but there's no way to know if the fire was lit yesterday or last week. Nor to tell what might have been burned, beyond garden rubbish. If he had evidence to get rid of, it's gone.

'The garage and workshop?'

For a moment, I think he'll refuse, but muttering something I'm glad I don't hear, he leads me down the garden to a brown brick building with a curved, corrugated iron roof. The double wooden doors at the front of the garage are shut tight, but he lets me in through a side door. Inside, there's empty space at the front, shelves and a bench at the far end. A patch of oil glistens on the dry earth floor where the car must have stood, makes me think the vehicle can't have been missing for very long. I move across to the doors, push gently. I'm expecting resistance, but they swing soundlessly open on well-oiled hinges.

'See,' Capstaff says, with a sly kind of satisfaction. 'Anyone could have got in. We'd never have heard a thing.'

'You don't keep the doors locked?'

'Nah,' he scoffs. 'Nobody locks their door round here.'

It's true enough, I know. It's almost unheard of, even in town.

'You weren't worried with all the soldiers about?'

'We weren't.' He shrugs. 'Turns out we got it wrong, though, dunnit? Suppose it must have been some of the boys out on a spree. Can't hardly blame them, seeing what they must be going through now.'

He's right about that, I think, but it doesn't explain Richard's ring. 'Perhaps,' I say, careful to make sure my tone doesn't suggest commitment to the theory. 'What about this rotor arm?'

He scuffs his foot against the ground, raises a tiny cloud of dust. 'Well, that's a bit awkward. I usually take it out, but I hadn't done it after the last time we went out.'

'Sergeant Tilling won't be happy to hear that.'

'The colonel, he's one for making up his mind all of a sudden. Takes a whim to go out somewhere, we have to just get up and go.'

'And when was this last time? Do you remember?'

'Tuesday a fortnight ago,' he says promptly. So much for not being able to remember when they'd last seen it. I can't help wondering what's behind his sudden spirit of co-operation. 'I took the colonel into town. Wanted to buy a pair of boots. And then after, he went to see his daughter, Alice.'

The girl in the picture? There's a sick feeling in my stomach as an awful possibility occurs to me. White thought the body in the car was male but . . . 'Alice? Does she live locally?'

'Latimer Street,' he says.

'Would she . . . ?' My voice hitches unexpectedly and Capstaff darts an enquiring look my way. I clear my throat. 'Could she have borrowed Colonel Beech's car, do you think?'

'Nah.' He grins. 'Keep death off the roads. Poor cow can't drive, can she? Tried to teach her myself, but she had no idea. Couldn't tell left from right.'

If he's expecting me to laugh, I don't. The uneasy feeling persists. That picture . . . she's exactly Richard's type. I can't ask, but by the way he's looking at me, my hesitation has made him curious. A moment more and he'll be interrogating me.

'She'd confirm this visit, would she?' I try for an official tone, manage to sound offhand instead.

He shrugs again. 'Why wouldn't she?'

I can't tell him that. 'And where exactly in Latimer Street does she live?'

'D'you know, I can't tell you the number.' He's pleased with himself, almost gloating at this attempt to block me. The co-operation's obviously over.

'So give me a clue,' I say impatiently.

'At the end, near the pub. Red door.'

'Right.'

'If that's all, I need to get back to the colonel.'

My turn to shrug. 'Sergeant Tilling may want to speak to you again,' I say. 'He'll let you know.'

10

Tuesday, afternoon

ONCE, AN AGE AGO, WHEN I still had hopes my marriage might last, Richard had given me perfume for Christmas. It came in a fancy bottle, no doubt at an equally fancy price. I can't remember the name of it now, but I remember the scent, heavy on sandalwood. Blatantly sensuous and bought, I suspected, more for my husband's gratification than my own. Not a fragrance for daytime, for a casual dab behind the ears on a Monday morning. The sort of thing that's for special occasions only. I kept it for when I felt confident enough to carry it off, but afterwards, the smell would linger on my skin for days: disturbingly imprinted on my flesh. I'd be doing something quite ordinary, and I'd suddenly catch a flash of it, heady and unmistakable. At first, it would make me smile, remembering. But in the end, I had to stop using it. I didn't have the resources to deal with how it made me feel.

Now, the smell of smoke is like that. Since that first sickening whiff yesterday morning, it keeps coming back. Not only when I've passed by the place in the lane where the car burned, not even when I stood in the colonel's back garden by the spot where he had his bonfire. It was there just the same back in the office, underlying the scent of coffee, and at the hospital, stronger than disinfectant. It drifted through the jumble of my dreams when I slept, woke with me despite all I could do with soap and shampoo, fresh clothes down to my skin. Even on the bike with the wind blowing in my face, I can smell it deep in my nose, taste it at the back of my throat.

Urgent as it is to contact Tilling, and to satisfy myself that Alice Beech is safe, for me it's even more urgent to find Alec Corby-Clifford. Bram needs the penicillin, and Alec's the best chance I have of getting it for him. So as soon as I get back to Romsey, I go straight to the White Horse to see if he's there. But the woman at the reception desk tells me he's not returned yet. She shows me the folded slip of paper with my message is still waiting, tucked away in the pigeonhole where his room key hangs. All I gain from the visit is knowing which number room he's in.

Tilling's not back at the police station either. That only leaves one item on my list: and it's the last thing I want to do. But there's no choice. I'll have to go and see Alice Beech. It should be simple enough, but the whole affair is fraught with pitfalls. The best outcome would be to find her at home, with no knowledge of what's happened to her father's car, and no connection to my husband. But the uneasy feeling in my gut persists, and I'm far from optimistic that all three conditions will be met.

I leave the Cyc-Auto in the passageway beside the office, and make my way to Latimer Street on foot. I tell myself that as long as the girl is safe and well, the rest doesn't matter. Except I'm fooling myself. If it turns out she is ... that she *has* been involved with Richard, then it means all the fuss on Friday was just him playing another of his mind games.

The house at the very end of the terrace has a cherry-red door, the only one of that colour in the row. It must be the one Capstaff meant. It looks well kept, with sparkling white lace curtains at the window, a trough of geraniums on the window ledge next to the door. The flowers are a perfect match for the paintwork, but the strong, green-and-pepper smell adds to my queasiness, as does the surprisingly macabre knocker, shaped like a bony hand which seems to reach out through the door towards me. To use it, I have to take the metal fingers in mine as if they're a child's or a lover's, bash them down against the stop. I grit my teeth and do it.

There's a long silence. I'm beginning to think there can't be anyone home when I notice a twitch of the net curtains. Someone's definitely there. But for the movement, I probably wouldn't have noticed the dark shape behind the window embrasure. I've no idea how long they've been standing there, watching me. I hesitate. If it is Alice Beech and she's OK, I don't need to get involved. Tilling can send one of his police officers to talk to her about her father's car.

Even though there's a sense of hostility radiating from the motionless watcher – or perhaps because of it – I can't just turn and walk away. It'd be rank cowardice. Instead, I nod towards the figure, force my face into a kind of smile. Two can play this waiting game.

Minutes pass. It feels like minutes, anyway. I have to step aside momentarily for a woman with a squalling baby in a pram, and when I move back the shadowy figure has disappeared. But my blood's up now and I brave the uncanny hand, knock again. 'Miss Beech,' I call. 'I'm not going away. You'll have to open the door.'

More silence. 'Miss Beech.'

The door opens abruptly. A tall young woman confronts me. Her hair is white blonde, her eyes the light blue of aquamarines. On a better day, I think, she'd be pretty, but today she's either got a terrible cold or she's been crying. Her eyes are bloodshot and puffy, and her nose is a pink beacon. She must be about twenty-five, and the knot in my gut twists tighter. Her photograph hadn't lied. She's precisely the kind of girl Richard likes to dally with, my opposite in almost every respect.

'What do you want?' she snaps.

'Miss Beech, my name's—'

'I know who you are.' Tears fill her eyes, and she mops at them with a scrap of lacy handkerchief. 'Chief . . . *she-dog* in the manger.'

'Whoa, don't pull your punches,' I say. 'Speak your mind, why don't you?'

'Well, you are, aren't you? A real . . .' she drops her voice to a whisper '. . . bitch.'

'Now we've got that straight, perhaps you'd like to invite me in? Unless you really want to argue on the doorstep.'

There's a moment when I think she'll slam the door in my face, but she hesitates. 'I've nothing to say.'

I raise my eyebrows. 'Seems like quite the opposite.'

Across the way, a woman in tweeds and a hat that's bristling with so many feathers and bits of birds' wings I wouldn't be surprised if it took off and flew away, pauses to stare across at us. I nod, smile sweetly at her. She raises her hand in greeting, steps off the kerb to come towards us.

'What do you think you're doing?' Alice Beech grabs my arm, pulling me inside the house and slamming the door behind me.

I find myself in a small living room, where every piece of furniture seems scaled down to fit the available space. Two narrow armchairs face an unlit hearth, a drop-leaf table and two chairs stand against the opposite wall. A single shelf above the table holds books and a pair of china dogs. In the far corner, a candlestick telephone flanks a potted fern on a stand.

'That was Miss Butler,' my reluctant hostess hisses. 'She's the biggest gossip in town.'

'Yes, I know.'

'You . . .'

'Bitch,' I say, rubbing my arm where she grabbed me. 'I am. You're right. But I thought you'd rather invite me in than have her see you crying.'

'What do you care?'

'Look, what is this all about?' I say, though I'm pretty sure I know. 'Why are you so angry with me when we've never even met till now?'

She shakes her head, plumps down on the arm of the nearest chair.

'It's Richard, isn't it?'

'Why won't you divorce him?' she bursts out. 'Everyone knows you're sweet on Mr Nash.'

'Me, divorce Richard? My dear, I'd do it in a heartbeat.'

'You're saying he's the one . . . ?'

'Afraid so.'

'I don't believe you.' But it's clear from her tone that she might. This is misery, not defiance.

My irritation vanishes as she mops her eyes again. There's heartbreak in store for her, whatever happens now. Whatever I find out. 'I think we'd better make ourselves comfortable, don't you? This is going to take a little while.'

'Comfortable?' Now she's crying in earnest. 'How can you be so unkind?'

'That wasn't my intention,' I say. 'I know I wasn't very nice just now but . . . Can't we start again?'

She blows her nose. 'Oh, sit down, why don't you? I suppose at least you might be able to tell me where he is.'

'Do you want a cup of tea or something before we start?'

'Just some water.' She hiccups, mops her eyes. 'If you would . . . The kitchen's through that door there.'

I hardly need telling. The door she's indicated is right beside me. It leads straight into another tiny room with an elderly gas cooker and stone sink with a single cold tap. The only other piece of furniture is a standing cupboard painted pale green. Taking it as slowly as I can to give her time to pull herself together, I find two glasses behind one of the cupboard's zinc mesh doors, let the water run icy cold before filling them.

When I get back to the living room, she does seem calmer. She's moved to sit properly in the chair, and though she's staring hopelessly into the cold hearth when I go in, she looks up and gives me a tentative smile as I hand her the water.

'Thank you,' she says. 'I'm sorry.'

'Me too.' I take the chair facing her, sip from my glass. 'Why don't you tell me about it from the beginning? From when you met Richard.'

'We met at a dance in the spring. He was so charming, so handsome, so ... sweet to me. I fell in love with him straightaway.' She looks at me with a trace of her earlier defiance. 'You probably hate me, but I didn't know he was married.'

'I'm sure you didn't. And I don't hate you. I'm just sorry—'

'You don't need to be sorry for me,' she says quickly. 'He loves me, he said so.'

It's years since I've had to deal with one of Richard's distressed girlfriends, though one way or another, it seems it's likely to be the last. 'Of course he did.'

'He said it was you. That you wouldn't let him go.'

'Miss Beech ... or can I call you Alice?'

She shrugs. 'I suppose.'

'Did he tell you *why* our marriage broke down?'

'He said it was because he'd been a prisoner of war and you'd come here and—'

'And?' If I wasn't intentionally being cruel before, I know I am now. But the only chance to make her understand how ridiculous it is for her to suppose I'd stand in the way of Richard's freedom is to get her to see it for herself.

'He said you had a fling with Mr Nash.' She shudders. 'He said, after he escaped and came to find you, you wouldn't go back to him even though he begged you.'

'Does that make sense to you?' *Surely* she must see it . . .

'No.' She's eager now. '*Why* wouldn't you? I mean, Richard's so . . . and Mr Nash, he's kind but . . .'

I take a deep breath. I mustn't lose my temper with her. But I can't lie and tell her it was nothing to do with Bram. I skirt round that part, tell her the truth, if not all of it. 'Richard and I split up before the war. We hadn't lived together for years before he got captured at Dunkirk. And it was months after that before I came back to Romsey looking for my father.'

'So why . . . ?' She's being very dense.

'Why what? Why wouldn't I agree to a divorce? I told you, I would. I'd do it tomorrow if I could. I'd have done it any time in the last six years. No, more than that. Seven.'

'I don't understand.'

'Look, I'm sorry, but you're not the first. Before you, there was Amy, and Sophie, and Carol. That's just the ones I know about. I don't know what he feels now.' It's true, I don't. If he had feelings for this girl, what was all that fuss about on Friday? 'All I know is he's always refused to agree to a divorce. I'm a good excuse, you see. If he can say he's married, he doesn't have to commit himself to someone else.'

'That's not true.' Her faces flushes scarlet.

'It is. Don't you see? The truth hurts me as much as it does you.'

She squeezes her eyes shut. The flush has faded. 'What a fool I've been.'

What can I say? She has, but no worse than me. I'd been every bit as stupid for years, thinking if I just hung on, he'd change his ways.

'Alice, I know how it feels. How amiable he can be . . .'

'Did you know about us?' she says, opening her eyes. 'Is that why you came?'

It's the perfect opening, but part of me doesn't want to take it. Sooner or later, I'll have to tell her about the body. 'No. I came to ask you about your father's car.'

'My father's car?' she echoes. Another wave of colour suffuses her face. 'What do you know about that?'

'Not as much as you do, obviously. But I'm guessing' – my guts twist viciously again – 'that Richard comes into the story somewhere.'

'And Mr Nash,' she says. 'They're both in it.'

11

Two days earlier
Sunday 4ᵗʰ June 1944

*T*HEY'VE HAD SUCH A LOVELY *day. Bittersweet, because it will be the last for who knows how long, though it affirms what Alice has known from the first moment she met this man. He'd asked her to dance, swept her away on a tide of music and tender embraces that made her feel like a princess. So handsome, so distinguished. A man of the world, a surgeon dedicated enough to go back to France with the invasion forces despite his terrible experiences after Dunkirk. He's her hero, her soulmate, her perfect gentle knight. It had been such a blow to learn he was married, but he's promised her that it's all over now. If only she'll trust him, he'll marry her as soon as he's able. The moment he can persuade his nuisance of a wife to let him go.*

When he'd told her he'd be leaving so soon, she'd cried. He'd held her in his arms, promised her one special day together, though it meant he'd have to break the rules; take unofficial leave from his unit.

It made it all the more exciting, somehow. The way they'd got round all the obstacles keeping them apart. The moment this morning when they crept into Daddy's garage to borrow the car, pushed it out into the lane at the crack of dawn, careful not to start the engine where they might wake Daddy or Capstaff. The drive out into the countryside had been glorious, though the weather was anything but. She hadn't cared, even though the mizzling rain cut their view to a few yards, made her hair go frizzy in the damp. None of it mattered, only the road ahead. Choosing their way at random, no plans except to please themselves. Then finding the perfect little pub where they'd lingered over a pie and a pint: not her usual choice but today, food of the gods couldn't have tasted any better.

She'd made up her mind long before he asked. Not the first time he'd tried to persuade her, but today he's almost shy, as if he's resigned to the answer no. But she can't send her true love off to war without ever having been his lover. He's so . . . joyous, *when she says yes, though she doesn't know how it can be managed. Too wet for an outdoor tryst, and the back seat of the car seems irredeemably sordid. She's on the point of suggesting they go back to her house, but somehow, he's talked the pub's landlord into lending them a room for a few hours. It's all part of the magic to find the bed in the little room under the eaves has a fairy-tale mattress of goose down, soft as a cloud.*

She won't be half-hearted. She's not going to hold anything back, regret anything. This is going to be her wedding night and honeymoon all in one, even if it can only span a few short daylight hours. He's so gentle, so kind, so experienced. He woos

her with poetry, John Donne's erotic lines: Licence my rov-
ing hands and let them go, Before, behind, between, above,
below. *And she does, she lets those skilful surgeon's hands go
where they will, touch her everywhere, though it's her heart
he touches most when he cries out in wordless triumph at the
moment of climax. It's her own inexperience, no fault of his if
she doesn't quite reach the same ecstasy.*

*Too soon, it's over. He has to be at the docks by midnight,
no time to linger. One last glance behind her as they set off
back to Romsey, a jolt of private fun as she notices the pub's
sign. Traveller's Joy.*

*But all too soon, it starts to go wrong. She's feeling chilly,
somehow lonely, but he's distracted, focused on finding their
way back through the lanes to Romsey. They're still miles out
when the car seems to hiccup. He swears angrily under his
breath. They're almost out of petrol. She hunches in her seat,
feeling as if it's her fault that her father hasn't kept the tank
full. Nothing for it but to go on: there's no chance of buying
fuel this time on a Sunday night.*

*She sits quietly as he nurses the car along. It seems as if
they're crawling, but her hopes rise as they turn into Lee Lane
at last. Surely they'll make it now? It's almost nine, and the
light is fading, though it's far from dark. She can't help seeing
how empty the lane and lay-bys are, with the soldiers all gone.
But she doesn't dare comment, not when he's so worried about
getting back in time.*

*With one last splutter and wheeze, the car's engine coughs
into silence. He manages to get the dying vehicle onto the*

grass verge before it finally seizes, refusing to go any further. He hammers his hands on the steering wheel in frustration, swears audibly this time.

'Bloody thing. Just when I need to get on. How far are we from your father's place?'

She looks around, trying to pick out a landmark. 'A mile,' she ventures. 'Perhaps a little bit less.'

'Damn.'

She lays her hand on his. 'We can make it in no time, Richard. Don't let it spoil our lovely day.'

He shakes her hand off, slams out of the car. 'Too late,' he says. 'It's over.'

The words have a resonance that makes her shiver. They sound so final. She follows him out of the car. 'If we walk back to Daddy's, there's bound to be a can of petrol in the garage.'

'Now she tells me,' he says, exasperated.

'We can bring it back here all right. I'm sure Capstaff won't mind running you down to the docks.'

'Right,' he says, heavily sarcastic. 'Just the little detail of having taken the car in the first place.'

She smiles in relief. 'Daddy won't mind. He'll be so pleased when we tell him we're going to be married as soon as we can.'

He goggles at her disconcertingly. 'Whatever makes you think that?' he says.

'Oh, but you ... after this afternoon, I thought ...'

He grins. 'You're not that naive, surely?'

Tears prickle her eyes. She can't help it. After all the emotions of the day, it's too much. 'Richard ...'

'Don't turn on the waterworks,' he says dismissively. 'I haven't got time for it.'

'Or for me?' Her temper is rising, and with it her voice.

'Ah, don't make so much of it,' he says, turning on his heels as he surveys the landscape. 'Now, Broadlands camp must be over that way, I think. If I get a move on, I might still be in time for a lift.'

'The car,' she says. 'You're going to abandon it?'

'You can get Capstaff to fetch it in the morning.'

'What will I say to him?'

'You'll think of something.'

'And me?' It comes out shrill, almost a shout.

'Shh,' he tries to quiet her. 'There's somebody coming.'

'What do I care?'

'Come on,' he cajoles. 'You know I've got to get back. You said yourself, it's not far to your father's house.'

'You'd let me walk there on my own? At this time of night?'

'Why not? The men have all embarked. You'll be safe enough. Besides, it won't be dark for another half-hour at least.'

'You pig,' she yells, then bursts into noisy tears. 'You utter pig.'

Footsteps coming closer. She scrubs hurriedly at her face, looks up to see who the newcomer is. Mr Nash, the solicitor who acted for her when she bought the house in Latimer Street.

'Miss Beech?' he says. 'Is this man upsetting you?'

She doesn't have a chance to answer before Richard speaks.

'Nash,' he says with venom. 'It just had to be you.'

'What's going on?'

'None of your business. We ran out of petrol, that's all.'

'Miss Beech seems very distressed.'

'I'm leaving tonight, that's all.'

'Leaving her in the lurch,' Nash says. 'By what I heard.'

'If you're worried, why don't you escort her home? You're good at taking my leftovers.'

12

Tuesday, evening

'H E HIT HIM,' ALICE BEECH says. 'Mr Nash, I mean.
He hit Richard. Knocked him down.'

I suppress the twitch of a smile. 'I'm not surprised. What happened then?'

She shrugs. 'Mr Nash walked me home. All the way back
here. And he didn't let on he had a headache till we got back,
poor man. I felt so guilty, but I didn't want to go to Daddy's
even though it was nearer, not while I was so upset.'

'And Richard?'

'Mr Nash pointed out the quickest way to Broadlands.
Richard thought he'd get a lift down to the docks from there.
It was getting late, and he was upset and worried. He didn't
mean what he said, I'm sure he didn't.'

From what I know of Richard, that's true enough. But
probably not quite in the way she means it. 'Have you heard
from him?'

'No. But I wouldn't, would I? He was leaving at midnight.
He'll write to me; I know he will.'

119

'Did you tell your father about the car? Or Capstaff?'

She shakes her head. 'I was too upset. I didn't want to talk to anyone. It wasn't going to come to harm, was it? Nobody was going to steal it when it was out of petrol. Beastly thing spoiled our day completely.'

'You haven't been in touch with your father at all?'

'I told you. I was too miserable to want to speak to anyone. You're the first person I've seen in two days.'

'Right.' What am I going to tell her? How much dare I say?

'What is it?' She looks at me with dawning apprehension. 'Why are you here, after all? Oh, goodness. You're Mr Nash's assistant. Has something happened to Daddy?'

'It's not your father,' I say. 'When I saw him earlier, he was fine.' No need to sidetrack her with the business of Colonel Beech's asthma.

'You saw him? You didn't come here because of Richard and me?'

'No.' I shake my head. I can see her thinking it through. Perhaps wishing she hadn't told me so much.

'So what's all this about? Just because we left the car . . . ?'

'It wasn't stolen, Alice. Someone set it alight about three o'clock on Monday morning.'

'Oh my . . .' Her shock is genuine, I'd go bail on it. 'Daddy must be very cross.'

'He didn't seem to be. In fact, he claimed he didn't even know it had gone from the garage. But perhaps that was because he'd guessed you'd taken it?'

'I don't see why he would.'

'You've never done it before?'

'No. I don't drive. It was only . . .'

'Go on.'

'It was only because it was the last chance. Before Richard . . . before he had to go.'

'Does your father know about your relationship with Richard?'

'N-no.' Colour rises in her face again.

'He wouldn't approve?'

'It would've been all right if you'd just agreed to a divorce.' It's almost a wail, but I really don't want to go back over all that again.

'It was a secret, then? You and Richard? Was it because you were afraid I'd hear about it?'

The flush deepens. 'I wasn't afraid,' she says indignantly. 'But he . . . he said it wouldn't be wise to let you find out.'

I bet he did. His cover story would have been blown straightaway if I'd known.

'Capstaff saw us,' she says in a rush. 'He met us out on a walk one day. And old Mr Fox knew, of course, because Richard was staying with him.'

For a moment, I can't take it in. Though I knew Richard had been back in the area since the spring, his surgical skills commandeered by the army, I'd kept out of his way as much as I could. Assumed he'd been posted to some military camp nearby. But to discover he's been staying with my grandfather, like he did last year when he got out of Germany, hits me like a bombshell.

No chance Grandfather has been playing host to my estranged husband out of kindness, or family feeling. It's mischief, not so pure but very simple. He's held a grudge against me since before I was born, because of my illegitimacy. My mother named me after him, but it hadn't softened that hard heart of his. He'd turned her out onto the street as soon as I was born, forbidden her ever to go back. He'd kept me, an everlasting thorn in his flesh, because my grandmother insisted. But when Granny died, he'd turned me out too. The day after her funeral, two weeks short of my fourteenth birthday, I'd found myself on Romsey railway station with a third-class ticket to London and five shillings in my pocket to tide me over until I could contact the mother I couldn't remember.

Like some old Victorian paterfamilias, he'd told me never to darken his door again, and I'd vowed I never would. But three years ago, things had changed. I'd come looking for my father and stayed. Grandfather had made no secret about how much he hated the situation, and me.

He'd spare no efforts to do me a bad turn. He's the last person, the very last I'd have wanted to know about the relationship between Richard and the girl. If the body turns out to be my husband's, I'll be first suspect as far as he's concerned. And Capstaff, too. There's another man who's decidedly not my friend.

It's after six by the time I leave Alice Beech's little house. Though we'd gone on talking for a while after she'd dropped her revelation about my grandfather, I hadn't learned much more about the events of Sunday evening. She'd answered a few of the questions on my list: the last time she'd seen Richard had been around nine fifteen, when she and Bram started to walk back to Romsey. They'd arrived at her door as the abbey clock was striking ten. She'd also confirmed they'd left the car where it had been found in Lee Lane. Though it seems a bit far-fetched, I suppose it doesn't entirely rule out the possibility it could have fuelled up and moved at some point between then and three in the morning, brought back to the lane before being set alight. Richard might have been too late for a lift and decided to fetch some petrol, driven himself down to the docks. In which case, who'd brought the car back, and why?

The fire officer had said it was possible the blaze had started by accident as someone was filling it with fuel. If it had, wouldn't the person just have run away? Why get back in the car, sit and wait for the flames to engulf them? Unless it was an intentional act. Even then, why would anyone choose to kill themselves in such a horrible way?

If it wasn't an accident or suicide, then it had to be murder. There'd been a case years ago, when a man had tried to escape a tangle of personal problems by faking his death in a car fire. He'd picked up a hitchhiker, knocked him unconscious, then set the car on fire, leaving the hitchhiker to burn to death. It had been in all the papers, and though the killer was soon arrested, the body was never identified. Richard had always been an avid follower of sensational cases, and I remember how he'd gloated over the details, reading bits out of the paper every morning at breakfast. Could it possibly have given him the idea to disentangle himself from Alice the same way? But it's so far-fetched. I can't believe he'd want to do away with himself, even by proxy.

The simple fact is, if it's murder, at least two people must have been in the lane at 3 a.m. And if one had been Richard, what was he doing there? He should have embarked at midnight, been sitting seasick on some vessel down on Southampton Water, waiting for the off.

Perhaps it was nothing to do with him at all. Despite our differences, I can't help hoping he's safely away from it all in France, completely blameless about Sunday night's events. But how I'm going to find out if he is with his unit, I don't know. With all the chaos and secrecy of the invasion it's not going to be easy.

The office is closed and dark when I arrive back to pick up the Cyc-Auto. Aggie must have gone home. No need to go trekking after her, disturbing her evening. What I've learned from Colonel Beech and his daughter can wait till tomorrow, and I've no more news about Bram since I spoke to her earlier.

Fan ... A pang of guilt goes through me. I should have got in touch with her earlier, told her what happened when I'd seen Bram. But I'd been in such a rush to get back from the hospital, I'd forgotten all about her. She deserves better. Much as I want to get home, I stop the bike at Basswood House, knock on the door.

Seems like I'm fated to wait on this doorstep. I suppose Fan might be out? I dither. Knock again, or go? Just as I've

made up my mind to leave, the door opens. Fan, looking flustered, stands in the doorway.

'Mrs Lester.' A hand flies to her throat.

'It's not bad news,' I reassure her hastily. 'I just wanted to
tell you I managed to see Mr Nash this morning.'

'Oh.' Her hand drops, but she still looks flustered. 'Was
he . . . is he all right?'

'Well . . .' I hesitate, glance into the street behind me.
Standing on the doorstep doesn't seem like a good place to
be discussing the details of Bram's condition.

'Mother?' a voice calls from within. 'Your dinner's getting
cold.'

'It's Billy,' she says apologetically. 'We were just sitting
down to our meal. I can't really talk now.'

I've come across her son a lot in the course of my work.
He's the mortuary assistant at Romsey Hospital. Very neat
and precise, an asset in his work. But everything has to be
done by the book and I know from experience any hitch in
his routine makes him terribly upset.

'Not to worry,' I say. 'Mr Nash, he's – in good hands.'

'Mother!'

Poor woman, she looks completely torn.

'Go on,' I say. 'I'm sorry to have disturbed you. Give my
apologies to Billy.'

'Thank you.' She nods, shuts the door firmly in my face.

I stand where I am for a moment, try not to feel rebuffed.
I know it's because I'm tired, but it feels like the last
straw after everything that's happened today. I gather my

thoughts, what's left of my energy. Trail down the steps to my bike.

It's less than a hundred yards to the police station. I'll have to pass the door on my way back to my lodgings with Dot. I should stop, go in, try and see Sergeant Tilling. Report what I've found out from Colonel Beech and his daughter. But I can't face it. I engage the bike's little motor, hop on. Turn my face resolutely to Tadburn Road and thoughts of supper, a hot bath and bed.

13

The night of Tuesday 6th June 1944

I'M DEAD ASLEEP WHEN A noise wakes me. I'd gone to bed before it was properly dark, but my room is bright with moonlight now. As usual, I'd opened the blackout curtains and left the window ajar before I'd gone to sleep, so now I don't need the luminous paint on the hands of my alarm clock to show me the time. The dial is almost as clear as day. Just after 2 a.m. For a moment I can't work out what's woken me, then I hear it again. A rattle of small stones against my windowpane. And my name, an urgent sibilance on the air.

'Mrs Lester. Jo.'

It's Alf, Dot's young nephew who works at Wills' nursery, stoking the boilers. He's got a problem with his feet which means he's not fit for military service, but it doesn't stop him being the best poacher for miles around. He calls it foraging, and only ever takes enough to feed those of us eating at Dot's table, but that wouldn't cut much ice if he ever got caught. Gamekeepers for miles around would love to put a stop to his night-time activities. My first thought is that he's in some kind of trouble, so I slide out of bed, pad across to the window just as another shower of gravel hits the glass. I jerk back instinctively, curse under my breath.

I push the window further up, lean out. 'What the hell? You frightened me.'

'Sorry.' His voice is low, carrying on the night air less obtrusively than a whisper might do. Confirming my guess, he's fully dressed in his night-work gear: dung-brown trousers and a dull, dark green jacket, a dirty old tweed cap pulled low on his head. 'I need you to come with me.'

'What? At this time of night?'

'I found something you need to see,' he says. 'Down by Spaniard's Lane.'

Spaniard's Lane? Aggie had pointed it out to me. It's very close to where the car was found, but I'm tired, longing to get back to bed. 'Can't it wait till morning?'

'No.' He's emphatic. 'You've got to come. It's important.'

'All right. Give me a couple of minutes.'

Old trousers, I think, if we're off to the woods. A dark jumper's next, the least visible item of clothing in my wardrobe. And since it seems this is a clandestine outing, better cover the telltale ginger of my hair with a scarf.

It doesn't take me more than five minutes to get downstairs, but Alf's practically dancing with impatience by the time I let myself quietly out through the back door, shoes in hand. I stand on the doorstep to slip them on.

'Right. What's all this about?'

'Blood,' he says. 'A whole lot of it.'

Without giving me a chance to ask questions, he's off. Out through the back gate, darting across to the hedgerow that skirts the open ground beyond the glasshouses at Wills' nursery. Following the field boundaries, we zigzag south and west, heading more or less towards Lee.

'Have to keep out of sight,' he cautions. 'Don't want everyone knowing our business.'

Despite the built-up boots he wears, he's sure-footed and fast. No one watching us tonight would suspect he's got a problem walking. I'm the one stumbling along, tripping over roots and running into bramble whips. If it weren't for the moonlight, I'd have fallen flat on my face a dozen times in the first hundred yards.

After ten minutes or so, he turns sharp right at another field boundary, crosses directly towards the railway line to Southampton. There's a straggle of bigger trees here, and he slackens pace enough for me to catch him up. He'd be off as soon as I reach him, but I grab his sleeve.

'Hang on,' I say. 'I need to get my breath back.'

He grins. 'Just as well Dot doesn't rely on you for supper. It's like having a herd of elephants trundling along behind me.'

'Cheek.' But he's probably right. Any self-respecting bird or rabbit must be long gone, the way I've been blundering about. 'Don't forget, I'm not used to these nocturnal ramblings.'

'Good practice for you, then,' he says. 'Got your second wind?'

'More or less.'

'Right. We can stay along by the railway till we get past the bridge by Ashfield. Keep as quiet as you can, mind. There's a bloke on watch at the lodge.'

He turns, slips off through the trees like a ghost. I follow in my tentative way, trying to be less elephantine. There are signs everywhere of the soldiers who've been camped in the lanes and fields, and though they're gone now, I wonder how Alf managed to keep finding food all these months with so many eyes around. And no doubt, every bit as eager bellies to be filled.

It's easier going along by the railway track, or else I've found my stride. Except for a kind of low-level dread about what's awaiting us, I'd almost be able to enjoy the walk. It's a pity we couldn't have cut straight to the railway line at the back of Wills' in the first place. But he'd been so keen we shouldn't be seen. Poacher's caution, or something more? The dread ramps up a notch. Blood, Alf said. A lot of it. And close by the place where the car – and the body – burned.

We get past the lodge without incident, though as we're about to emerge from beneath the road bridge a few yards further on, Alf suddenly gestures a halt. I quiet my breathing, hear the sound of a vehicle approaching on the road. We wait in the shadows till it's past, then go on again till we reach a place where Lee Lane and the railway line are running close together in a thicket of trees.

There's a fence along the track, metal posts and five horizontal strands of wire. 'Need to get out to the lane,' Alf says, slipping between the strands, pausing till I'm safely through.

We check the line is clear, then we're over, feet shuffling on the sleepers for quietness' sake. Another fence to manoeuvre through, a water-filled ditch to negotiate and we're clear onto the metalled surface of Lee Lane.

'Not far now,' he mutters. 'But we've got to be quick along here.' True to his word, he sets a cracking pace down the road. I try to keep up, but the moonlight pouring through the trees casts shadows so definite and densely black across the road that once or twice I'm fooled into thinking there must be some kind of trench or pothole in front of me. I get a queasy kind of vertigo, find myself hesitating about where to put my feet down in case the solid ground is not solid after all.

When I force myself to look up and just walk, Alf's vanished. A flick of panic brushes over my skin. Where has he got to? I'm looking in quite the wrong direction when a jerky movement like the stop-start motion of an old silent movie catches at the edge of my vision. A shadowy shape signals from beneath the trees on the Broadlands side of the lane.

'This way,' Alf calls.

I scramble after him, find myself in a kind of corridor between lines of ancient trees. It's darker in here but splashes of moonlight do still reach into the gloom, patterning the ground with the same disquieting jigsaw of black and silver.

'Go careful now,' Alf says close to my ear. 'It's just up ahead.'

But I don't need Alf's whisper to tell me we've arrived. The butcher's shop stink of blood that I remember from the Blitz the autumn I was living in London with my dying mother fills my nostrils, blots out the clean forest scent of leaves and earth. Nauseated, I pull up short.

All through the tunnel of trees, we've been walking on a thick carpet of leaf litter. But a few feet away from where we're standing now, there's a patch of exposed earth. Heaps of leaves are scattered about, clotted and spattered with something darker than shadow that glistens in the moonlight. An irregular oval of the same inky black shows on the bare ground. Blood. A pool of it. The earth has soaked most of it up, but I can see what's left is sticky with maggots already.

So *much* blood . . .

I'm not squeamish, but the thought makes me feel dizzy. I can see why Alf wanted to show me. It's a killing field, but for what?

Alf goes to move forward, but I grab his arm. 'Don't go any further,' I say. 'Whatever's gone on here, Sergeant Tilling needs to know. We mustn't muck up the evidence.'

He shuffles his feet.

Even in this chancy light, I can see he's uneasy. 'What happened?' I ask. 'How did you find the place?'

'I was on my way home when I got wind of it. The smell, like now. Thought it might be a dead deer, but when I got here and saw all that blood . . . Fair turned me up.'

'I'm not surprised. But it's important, Alf. Did you go closer than this?'

'Yeah.' He sounds disgusted with himself. 'Stupid, a beginner's mistake. I thought . . . well, I wanted to see what was what.'

'You cleared the leaves off?'

'Some of it was done already or I'd never have known . . .'

My heart sinks. It's going to be the devil, finding a way to tell Sergeant Tilling about this without getting Alf in trouble. They're bound to find traces of his earlier visit, those distinctive footprints of his. If we're not careful, he'll be suspect for more than simply finding the place.

'It wasn't an animal that did this, was it?'

'Nah. Proper spooked me when I realised. Whatever bled like that never walked away.'

I know, really, what the answer must be, but I'm not sure if he does. The body in the car's supposed to be a secret, but though it may have been possible to keep the information from an old man isolated by ill health and a woman who's been brooding at home for two days, I wouldn't bet against Alf having heard about it.

'There weren't any other signs around?'

'Signs of what?' he bursts out, exasperated. 'A body, you mean? Not far to look for one of those. There was a body in that bloody car and we both know it.'

'You're not supposed to. No one is outside official channels.'

'You think that fire crew and a lot of stupid coppers all kept their mouths shut? In Romsey? What did you do, come down in the last shower?'

It feels like it sometimes, I think. God, why does Bram have to be sick? He'd know what to do.

'We'll have to report it. It could be a coincidence but . . . I can't believe two people have died violent deaths round here in less than two days. And there's only one body we know of.'

'Yeah.' He shrugs. 'I'll be for it, then. They'll have me for poaching if nothing else.'

'Not if I can help it.' But there aren't really many options. Sergeant Tilling's never going to believe I could have found the place on my own. I could trample about, I suppose, take the blame for any disturbance of the site, but Bram's trained me too well. I can't bring myself to falsify evidence. My conscience pricks. Except that's exactly what I'm doing by not telling the sergeant what I know about the ring.

'What are we going to do, then?' Alf's voice breaks my train of thought.

'Which way were you going when you found the place?' I ask him.

He points. 'I was coming from the top of the park. On my way home.'

'Through the trees, like now?'

'Not right in. Along by the edge.' He grins. 'Best place for snares.'

'I don't want to know. You smelled the smell, thought it was a deer?'

'That's right.'

'You hadn't caught anything, then?'

Another grin. 'I never said that. I'd got your supper all right. Dropped off a couple of rabbits in the scullery before I woke you. But I bet you wouldn't have said no to a nice bit of venison if I could have got it.'

I might, I think, if I'd known it had come from a stink like this. I hunker down, look low along the ground past the bare patch of earth. 'You didn't go out onto Spaniard's Lane?'

'Not me. I skedaddled back up the way I'd come.'

'Scoot down here beside me. No, not too close. Look, over on the far side. Can you see those marks in the leaves? It could be where something's been dragged.'

'Or someone?' He bounces up. 'Better have a dekko.'

'Better not. Leave that for Tilling.' I stand up too. 'But I don't think it would do any harm if we went round and had a look along the lane. We might be able to spot something there. And I'd like to see how far it is to where the car was found.'

'Wouldn't be more than a quarter of a mile if you went across the field,' he says.

'Show me.'

It's a matter of retracing our footsteps a little way before scrambling down the bank into Lee Lane. I'm hesitant at first, because it looks as if this is a trodden path, but Alf assures me it's a fox trail, not a human one. He chuckles, points out a clump of coarse red hair caught on a rough edge of bark. 'Your namesake,' he says. 'Wouldn't you just know it.'

Back at the corner, we turn into Spaniard's Lane. We go carefully, searching along the treeline for signs that someone's come this way. So many possible places, but it's hard to be sure. The moon's sinking low in the sky, and I'm too tired – or too thick-headed – to know what I'm looking at anymore. It all seems vaguely menacing, equally unfathomable. I give up. If there's anything to be found, it'll be Alf who does it.

Turning, I stare across at the wheat field on the other side of the lane. A light breeze ripples through the crop, carries the scent of ashes with it. Not my imagination this time, I think, but the proximity of that burned patch of ground. I close my eyes, glad to be free of the fleshy stench of blood.

In daylight, I'd probably be able to pick out the site where the car was found easily enough, but in the dwindling light the monochrome landscape offers no landmarks. The far hedgerow is one indistinguishable outline of black beyond the pale gleam of wheat. A quarter of a mile, Alf said. I try to picture it. A tall man – Richard is tall – carrying a burden. Or being carried . . . Over a shoulder, like a fireman? Slung like a sack across a back or being dragged along the ground. Like now, the moon would have been almost set. Would he have risked the road, or cut across the field?

If it wasn't Richard, who? Who knew about the car standing abandoned in the lane? And why? Why would Richard kill, or be killed?

14

Wednesday 7ᵗʰ June 1944, early morning

I T WAS AFTER THREE BEFORE Alf and I got back to Tadburn Road. I'd snatched a couple of hours' fitful sleep, but by six I'm wide awake again. Restless rather than rested, but I know I can't put off reporting to Sergeant Tilling any longer. I have to let him know what we've found, as well as sharing what I learned from the colonel and his daughter.

Maybe that will distract him, save him from looking too closely at Alf. One thing that might make Tilling believe the discovery could have been mine is that I did find a place where it looked as if someone had broken out onto Spaniard's Lane. And though it was almost dark by then, there had been signs that someone had pushed into the wheat field there too. Alf and I had left both places strictly alone for Tilling's men to investigate. But it would be just our luck if he sent Summers to do it.

In the mirror, combing my hair after a tepid bath that's shocked me fully awake, I think I look twenty years older: a tired sixty-something instead of forty-three. But perhaps that won't do me any harm with Tilling either. He might feel sorry for me.

The thought makes me squirm, and though I'm not much of a one for makeup, I still have the cosmetics I used when I was posing as Joy Rennard last year. Nothing's going to hide the dark bags under my eyes, but mascara at least takes away the bald look of my naked lashes. I'm out of rouge, but a dab of lipstick rubbed into my cheeks lifts my pallor, a bit more on my mouth makes me seem ready to face the day.

At the police station, it's PC Summers who's behind the desk. His smirk as he looks me up and down makes me think I've not been as successful as I'd hoped in disguising my tiredness.

'Mrs Lester. What can I do for you?'

'I need to speak to Sergeant Tilling.'

He raises his eyebrows so high his forehead crinkles like a bloodhound's. 'He's not in yet,' he says in a tone that suggests he thinks I'm an imbecile for imagining his superior officer might be on duty so early. 'Do you want to leave a message?'

If he takes it, I think, there's no knowing how he might garble it. 'Ask him to ring me. As soon as he can, please. I've got some information for him. It's important.'

'All right,' he says. There's such a long pause before he adds 'madam', that I know he's another recruit to the ranks of my non-admirers.

Since yesterday's brief awakening, Bram Nash has surfaced from his heated, semi-conscious state several times more.

Though there's been no further hint of Jo, not even in dreams, there's the unfailing presence of the nurses each time he wakes. Their faces change: in the green aquarium light of day that filters through the screens round his bed there's the one called Baker; a different woman, older, wearier, in the blue facsimile of moonlight at midnight. And whenever he wakes, somewhere there's the pervasive sound of trolleys passing and repassing his bed. He's come to recognise the heavy rubber wheels and whispered voices as a new patient is admitted. Had his first sips of tea dispensed from a trolley rattling with teacups; suffered through dressings performed like a silent cadenza for solo nurse and forceps.

This morning, he's almost sorry to wake when he realises how wretched he feels. There's a sickly cotton-wool heat in his head and behind the socket of his eye, and every muscle in his body aches as if he's been shovelling coal all night. He lies waiting in the half-light for the first trolley of the day, the soprano chatter of thermometers in a jar. He doesn't protest at the bite of spirit in his mouth as the nurse slips the cold bulb under his tongue, or feel surprised when she tells him chidingly, as if it's his fault, that his temperature is 105 degrees and rising, just when it should be at its lowest.

There's nothing he can do, no message he can send. Only a sense of regret as the heat begins to swallow him up once more, as he feels his thoughts twist like vapour from a stove. If only he could feel rain on his skin, or a cool breeze. A friendly touch.

Oh, Jo.

*

I begin to feel as if I'm on a treadmill, retracing the same steps over and over again, getting nowhere. No luck contacting Tilling. The same at the White Horse. Alec isn't there. I can't believe it. What am I going to do? I *must* get that penicillin for Bram.

'He did leave a message for you,' the receptionist tells me, 'if you're Mrs Lester?'

'Yes,' I snap, trying to curb my impatience as, with what feels like glacial slowness, she retrieves an envelope from somewhere under the desk, passes it across to me.

I rip it open. *Lunch with me*, the note inside says. It's not so much an invitation, I catch myself thinking, as an instruction. *Twelve thirty, table for two, dining room here.*

The words sprawl across the sheet of paper. Not hesitant, despite the injury to his hand, but confident, flamboyant. So typical of the Alec I remember of old. I crumple the paper up, dump it into the wastepaper basket next to the desk. I'm torn between irritation at his high-handedness, frustration with having to wait another four hours.

'Is everything all right, Mrs Lester?' the receptionist asks me.

I take a deep breath. 'Yes, thank you. I'm sorry if I was rude.'

She blinks in surprise. It's obvious she's more used to rudeness than apologies, and I find myself being extra polite in response.

'If he does come back before lunch, perhaps you wouldn't mind telling him I'll meet him as he suggests?'

'Of course.' A smile. *This time, perhaps, I've made a friend rather than an enemy.*

Although it's still early, Aggie's waiting when I get back to the office. 'Have you heard?' she says, the minute I step inside the door.

'Heard what? Something about the war?'

'No.' She's scornful. 'Have you heard how Mr Nash is this morning?'

'I haven't had a chance yet. You know there isn't a telephone at Dot's. And I thought I'd better go into the police station on my way to work, speak to Sergeant Tilling about what I found out yesterday. But it was a complete waste of time because he wasn't there.'

Aggie pushes the telephone across the desk towards me. 'So ring now, for goodness' sake. It's no use me trying.'

My call's answered straightaway, and I recognise the voice of the friendly porter from yesterday. 'I'll put you through, love,' he says, 'though I shouldn't, not really. It's ward cleaning this morning.'

I suppose ward cleaning – whatever that implies – is the reason it's not the haughty sister who answers, but a nurse who sounds almost jolly when I ask her about Bram.

'Oh, Mrs Lester. Good news. He had some lucid spells yesterday. Funnily enough, he woke up just after you left. Asked for you.'

Funny? I'm almost speechless for a moment. 'Why didn't you call me back?'

'Sister said not to bother you.'

141

I breathe down my frustration. 'What about today? Could I come in now?'

'I'm sorry, there's no visiting till after three today,' she says, still chirpy.

'But he's all right? I will be able to see him then?'

'W-ell.' There's the first tiny crack of doubt in her voice. 'You probably should know Mr Nash's temperature started to go up again this morning.'

How long can he go on like this? These spiking temperatures must be sapping his strength, making him weaker every time. But I daren't ask. I don't want to hear her agree in that careless way of hers, as if it couldn't matter less. 'I'll be in later,' I say instead. 'Please, make sure he knows I'll be coming.'

'Okey-dokey,' she says brightly, 'Cheerio.'

I find myself wishing that I'd reached the sister after all. She might be stuffy, but at least she seems to take a sober view of her responsibilities.

'Well?' Aggie says as I'm hanging up the receiver.

'Improving,' I say, knowing I'm being every bit as false as the girl I've just talked to. 'He's been talking to the nurses.'

Aggie smiles with such relief it's worth the weight on my conscience. If something happens now ... But I won't let myself believe it might. All I have to do is persuade Alec to prescribe this blessed penicillin.

'Right,' I say. 'We need to catch up. There's someone I have to see at lunchtime, then I'll go down to Southampton to visit Mr Nash. So we'd better try and get as much as we can sorted out this morning.'

'Very good, Mrs Lester,' Aggie says. 'Now, sit down. I've got a number of messages for you.'

I sit gingerly, wishing as much that I could get her to call me Jo as that she'd allow her visitors a more comfortable chair.

'First things first,' she says as she fetches out her notebook, flaps it open. 'On my own behalf, I think we need to keep a record of what we say and do with regard to this investigation. Mr Nash is bound to want to review the case when he's better. I propose to take shorthand notes as we go along, type them up later. Are you agreeable?'

'It seems a bit formal but you're right, we should.' I'll just have to be careful what I tell her.

She makes a notation on the next blank page in her book.

'Date it,' I say, suddenly urgent. It may protect her later if she can show I didn't tell her everything I know. 'Put the time in as well.'

The spidery eyebrows lift, but she glances at her watch, scribbles something at the top of the page. 'Now, let me give you the messages I have for you. Unless you'd rather speak first?'

'No. I'm hoping you'll have heard what's happening about this post-mortem.'

She turns a couple of pages back in her book. 'The expert pathologist will come down from London first thing tomorrow. The examination is booked for 10 a.m. Sergeant Tilling said to tell you he'll be sending a man to observe, but you can go along too if you want.'

I feel myself go pale.

'Are you all right, Mrs Lester?' The second time I've been asked a version of that question this morning. But she's entitled to wonder, since I promised her at the start, I wouldn't be upset by the things I'd have to see. Now I have to make good on it.

'I'm fine, Aggie. I can't say I'm actually looking forward to it, but I'll get there if I can. It's at the mortuary in Southampton, isn't it?'

'That's correct. The hospital where Mr Nash is. Perhaps you'll be able to go and see him afterwards?'

'I'll certainly try. You said you had other messages?'

'Yes. Officer White rang to say the examination of the car revealed no mechanical defects that might have caused the car to burn spontaneously.'

'Did he say whether there had been petrol in the tank?'

She runs her finger down the page of shorthand hieroglyphs. 'I don't believe so. I don't have information on that point here.'

'Could you ring him back later? Ask him whether he thinks the fire started in the tank, or from petrol splashed around outside. I'd like to know how much fuel he thinks it would take to cause a blaze like that, and whether it would have been more volatile if the tank was empty.'

'Surely if it was empty, it wouldn't have burned so well?'

'I don't know. I wondered whether, if the tank had been full of fumes, it would have been easier to set alight.'

'I'll ask.' She turns to the page she's been using to record our conversation, writes something in a separate column.

'The thing is,' I say slowly, conscious that once I've admitted what Alice Beech told me, there'll be no going back. 'Someone said the reason the car was left in Lee Lane was because it had run out of fuel.'

'Someone?'

I'm gearing myself up to answer when the telephone rings. A brief reprieve for me as Aggie answers. I take the opportunity to get up from my uncomfortable perch and wander across to the window. Like the ones in Mr Simmons's office, it looks out over the alleyway in front. Unlike those, though, Aggie's has never been part of a grand room. No velvet curtains or opaque glass here, only nets that Aggie takes home to wash. But no matter how often she does it, or Fred, the caretaker, cleans the glass, the view always seems dusty and dull. Across the alley, there's a plain brick wall, a faded red door. A pigeon pecks at the moss on a low tiled roof.

Behind me, the sound of the telephone receiver being replaced. I turn, but stay where I am.

'Now then,' Aggie says. 'What's all this about the car?'

'Finish what you were saying first, Aggie. Better if I tell you my story all in one go.'

'Very well. Sergeant Tilling gave me two other messages to pass on. First, they didn't find anything at the site other than the items he showed you yesterday. A ring and ...' she checks her shorthand notes carefully '... a button.'

'OK.'

'He said the button's military, but too degraded by heat to identify. He thinks the ring should be more helpful. He's

145

going to get it photographed, have some posters made to put up around town. He's hoping someone will recognise it.'

Alice surely will. Once the posters go up, it'll only be a matter of time before she, or even my grandfather, identifies the ring. Then I'm sunk. I didn't want to tell Tilling yet, not before the post-mortem. Before I know for sure.

'Did he say when the posters will be ready?'

'A couple of days. Certainly by the weekend.'

A small reprieve. 'You said there was another message from Sergeant Tilling?'

'That's right. He said to tell you they've sent the small bones they retrieved to the mortuary for the pathologist tomorrow. And the site's been cleared as having no more evidential value.'

'Mm.' The thought of the bones makes me uneasy.

'Are you sure you're all right?'

Third time lucky, or time for a third denial? My chest's so tight, I have to make a conscious effort to breathe.

'Before I start on my news,' I say, 'would you mind if I asked you ... This Colonel Beech and his daughter, Alice. What's the word about them in Romsey?'

She bridles, as I was afraid she might. 'I hope you're not implying I'm a gossip?'

'No. But Mr Nash always says you're a fount of knowledge about Romsey people and Romsey ways.'

'Hmm.'

'I told you yesterday, I can't do this without you, Aggie. You've been in Romsey all your life, you know what's going on. I was away for so many years I still feel like a stranger most of the time. I'd never even heard of either of these people till yesterday.'

She sighs. 'The colonel's always been well thought of. Regular army, served his time with distinction. He was widowed when his daughter was only a couple of years old. He and that man of his, Capstaff, brought her up between them. He's said to dote on the girl, but she doesn't live with him anymore. Word was she was tired of him watching her every move, wanted to get out from under his thumb. She's got a nice little place in Latimer Street now.'

'Yes.'

'You know already?' she says sharply.

'Part of my story. Please, go on.'

'I don't know much more than that about her. Keeps herself to herself. Tall girl, blonde. Quite pretty.'

'Boyfriends?' I keep my voice light.

'Nothing till lately. But I believe there's been some talk about her being seen with a man in uniform. All these soldiers about, it's hardly surprising.'

I turn back to the window, unable to face her. My voice comes out muffled against the glass. 'She tells me it's my husband who's been courting her.'

'What?' Aggie explodes. 'What was all that nonsense on Friday about, then? All that bluster, trying to get you to go back to him?'

*

147

Friday 2nd June 1944, mid-afternoon

It's peaceful this afternoon, right at the tag end of the week. Bram and Mr Simmons are out seeing clients, and Cissie's gone home. It's just Aggie and me in the office, waiting for five o'clock.

From my corner in the corridor, I can hear the murmur of music that means Fred's retreated to the basement for his tea break. Any chance he gets, he's down there, glued to the wireless set, waiting for the latest news about the war. I take a sip of my own cup of tea, return to the report I'm typing about some bones that were found on a farm at Halterworth. An archaeologist from the university has inspected them, ruled them human, but ancient. Not within the coroner's remit, but Bram likes everything properly recorded. I'm just trying to puzzle out the archaeologist's handwriting – whether he's written 'conclusively' or 'confusingly' – when I hear the office door rattle open.

At first, I don't take any notice. I'm dimly aware of hearing Aggie speak, though I can't make out what she says. The standard, 'Can I help you?' I suppose. But the male response sets all my senses on alert. I can't mistake that voice. It's Richard. What the hell does he want?

Though I've been aware that he's been in the area for a while, attached to one of the RAMC training units waiting to go overseas, I've managed to keep out of his way most of the time. I'm just trying to make up my mind whether I should slip down to the basement, escape through the backyard, when I hear the tap of Aggie's shoes as she comes to find me.

'I'm sorry, Mrs Lester,' she says. 'It's your husband. He says it's urgent that he sees you.'

Feeling as if I've swallowed a lump of lead, I nod. 'All right. Tell him I'll come as soon as I've finished this.'

She raises her eyebrows. She knows as well as I do that the report isn't urgent. 'I'll put him in the small waiting room, shall I?'

'Perfect.' It's a cold, grim little room we hardly ever use, but it seems ideal for the situation. The more uncomfortable he feels, the sooner he'll leave.

She patters away, and I return to the report. I take my time, but there's only one paragraph left to do, and all too soon I've finished. I type the last sentence, pull the paper out of the type-writer. Separate top copy and carbon, square them up neatly on my desk. A trip to the lavatory makes one final delay. I tidy my hair, pinch some colour into my cheeks. I don't want Richard to see how anxious his visit makes me feel.

If I'd hoped he might get tired of waiting and leave, I've miscalculated. All I've done is annoy him. He springs to his feet as I go in, reaches out to slam the door shut behind me. I retreat as far as the confines of the room will let me.

I have to admit, he's looking good, my estranged husband. He wears his uniform with an air of ease that surprises me. His short-term attachment to the army has obviously suited him. But as soon as he opens his mouth, I know nothing has really changed.

'Didn't that woman tell you it was urgent?' he snaps.

'And a good afternoon to you, too, Richard.'

He snorts impatiently. 'I've no time for your games.'

I sidle round as he moves closer, manage to reach for the door and open it again. 'What games?' I say. 'If you come barging in when I'm working, you have to expect to wait. I'm busy too.' A barefaced lie, but I know him of old. I daren't give him the slightest hint of a weakness he can exploit.

'All right, all right. We need to talk, Josephine.' I can almost feel the effort he's making to sound more reasonable. He casts a reproachful glance at the open door, the austere waiting-room furniture. 'Can't we at least sit down?'

'Sit if you'd like to,' I say, unconvinced. 'I'd rather stand.'

'You don't seem to realise I'm taking a chance even being here. The camps have been locked down for a week. We're supposed to be leaving on Sun—' He breaks off, a look of horror on his face.

'I'll pretend I didn't hear you say that.'

'It's your fault for winding me up. You make everything so damned difficult.'

'What do you want, Richard?' I look pointedly at my watch. 'Say what you've got to say. Let's just get it over with.'

'Come back to me, Josephine. I want you to come back.' For all the emotion in his tone, he might as well be laying claim to a lost dog or a piece of left luggage.

'Why? You don't love me. You don't even like me.'

'You're my wife.' No attempt to deny what I've said. 'You belong with me.'

'To you, you mean? That I don't.'

Angry spots of colour bloom in his cheeks. 'You're my wife,' he repeats. 'This ridiculous situation has gone on long enough.'

'I couldn't agree more. Let it go, Richard. Let me go. Give us both our freedom. You'd be far better off with someone like Amy or Carol, you remember them?'

'Never let it go, do you? If it comes to that, you're no saint. I suppose you're still screwing around with the boss?'

I feel sick. It must show in my face because he grins.

'Oh ho, don't tell me there's trouble in paradise. Gone off you, has he? Bet that doesn't suit you.'

'None of your business.' My voice comes out in a strangulated croak.

'Exactly my business.' He laughs. 'Ah, well, that throws a whole new light on things. Reckon all I'll have to do is wait. You'll soon come crawling back if you're not getting any. Always were like a bitch on heat.'

He's right in my face, so close I can feel the heat off his skin. With all the strength I can muster, I push him away. 'I'd rather die,' I say. 'I wouldn't want you if you were the last man on earth.' Not very original, but in the moment, I couldn't mean it more.

He stumbles away from me, rapping his elbow on the door jamb. He swears unrepeatably, reels away into the corridor. He pushes past Aggie, standing in the doorway to her room, pauses with his hand on the front door handle. 'You always were a cold-hearted bitch,' he shouts, making a performance of it. 'You and that freak-faced lawyer, you deserve each other. I suppose you hope I won't come back from France this time? Well, let me tell you, I'm going to do my best to disappoint you.'

*

'Are you sure Miss Beech wasn't having you on?' Aggie says. 'I mean, why would he—?'

'Want me back?'

'I didn't mean . . .'

I take pity on her. 'It doesn't make sense,' I say. 'But he's always played it like that. Right from when we were first together.' I hunch my shoulders, let them drop. Not a shrug, more an expression of how helpless I feel. No need to tell her my whole history. 'He likes to have two strings to his bow. I keep his girlfriends at bay, they . . . I was always supposed to ignore them. Pretend to be the dutiful wife.'

'Doesn't know you very well, then,' she says tartly. 'Just as well he's off to France.'

I turn towards her again, move back to the chair beside her desk. 'Y-es.' If he has gone, of course. 'Did you . . . does Mr Nash know about Richard's visit?'

She prims her lips up into a tight little knot, and I think I've gone too far this time. She's bound to refuse to answer. For a moment, her fingernail digs at the edge of her short-hand notebook, raises a fibrous fluff from the soft, wartime paper. Then she looks me defiantly in the eye. 'Yes, I told him. I thought he should know.'

'And?'

'What do you think? He wasn't very happy about it. In fact, I'd go so far as to say—'

'Don't,' I cut in. 'Don't tell me any more. Not yet.' Because the last thing I want is for her to say Bram was angry, to have my nose rubbed in the fact he had a motive for wishing Richard harm.

'All right,' she says, but I can see that she's offended. Poor woman, first I force her to speak, then I cut her off. I'd be offended too. But perhaps, when I'm finished, she'll understand. See the danger for herself.

A glance at my watch. It's still only just after 9 a.m. It feels as if it should be much later.

'It's all right,' Aggie says. 'No clients this morning, so Mr Simmons has gone fishing. And it's Cissie's day off.'

So I settle in, recount my visits to Colonel Beech and his daughter in as much detail as I can remember. All of it, including Alice's story about Sunday evening. Right up to the moment Bram hit Richard, and escorted Alice home.

'Oh my God.' The busy pencil stills, and she looks up at me, a reflection of my own anxiety in her face. 'You don't think . . . ?'

'What?' It's wickedly unfair of me, but my temper snaps. 'That Mr Nash went back later and killed my husband? Dumped the body in the car and set it on fire?'

'No,' she retorts, rising from her chair. Though her eyes are brimming with tears, she stares defiantly down at me. 'How dare you? That's a monstrous thing to say.'

'Yes. But once Alice's story gets out, other people will say it too.'

'What are we going to do?' Her expression changes, and I can almost see her working it out as she subsides back in her chair. 'You're saying . . . does that mean you think . . . the body . . . it's your husband?'

15

Wednesday, morning

BEFORE TODAY, I'D NEVER HAVE guessed Aggie Haward would turn out to be such a good listener. Or such a good friend, either. As I confide in her, words pouring out as I tell her about the ring, my anxieties for Richard and Bram, she doesn't interrupt me once. I even tell her about the night-time excursion with Alf. And though I expected it, there's no censure in her face whatever she thinks of my story.

When I finish, I'm exhausted and yet lighter, too. I've been magnifying everything in my head, letting my imagination get the better of me. Richard doesn't have to be dead in the Southampton morgue, or on the run as a killer. He might just have lost the ring in the scuffle, gone off without noticing.

And Bram? He's no killer. I'd stake my life on that. Besides, Alice said they'd seen Richard go off towards Broadlands before Bram had walked her back to Romsey, and he'd told her then he'd got a headache. That's alibi enough for me, I know he couldn't have been in the lane at 3 a.m. But will

Sergeant Tilling believe it? He and Bram haven't always seen eye to eye. Last year the sergeant even suspected him of being involved in George Hine's death. If only Bram hadn't been ill. If he'd been on shift with the ARP on Sunday as he'd been meant to be, he'd have had a perfect alibi.

'What are we going to do, Aggie?' I say at last.

'I'm going to make us both a nice cup of tea,' she says decisively. 'I think we deserve it, don't you?'

While she's gone, I close my eyes, listen to the homely sounds coming from the kitchen as she makes the tea. Water running as she fills the kettle. The pop of the match as she lights the gas ring. A cupboard door opening, the clatter of teacups in their saucers. Aggie would never countenance using mugs. She's always so proper.

The doubts creep back. She *is* a gossip, whatever I might have said to her face. Am I going to find the juicer parts of the story are all around town by closing time? Though I know she'd never pass on anything she learned about a client, her life has little enough excitement in it. A single woman, her time's divided between work and looking after her ageing parents. Small blame to her if she gets second-hand pleasure from speculating about other people's affairs. A wave of self-loathing sweeps over me. What I do for a job isn't that much different. Poking into other people's lives, making judgements, passing on what I learn.

Perhaps that's it? Perhaps I'm hoping she'll do what I'm too spineless to do myself. Go straight off to Sergeant Tilling and report all the sordid details. As a good citizen, of course she should. I ought to have made sure to have done it myself by now.

I open my eyes, reach for the telephone. I'd expected to hear from Sergeant Tilling by now, but I wouldn't be surprised if Summers has forgotten to pass my message on. No use making excuses, it's my responsibility. I can't put it off any longer. I'm dialling the police station's number when I hear the soft whistle as the kettle comes to the boil. My mouth's dry with nerves and I think longingly of the promised cup of tea. But if Sergeant Tilling wants me to go straight round and make a statement, I will.

It's all wasted heroics, though. When I get through, it's PC Summers who answers the telephone again. His tone lets me know he's offended I'm checking up on him. He tells me the sergeant's gone off to report to the chief constable about yesterday's burglary.

'I gave him your message, madam,' he says stiffly. 'No doubt he'll be in touch when he gets back this afternoon.'

She's coming. Through the heat-haze mirage of his rising temperature, he holds on to that one fact. He has to see her, to tell her . . . Frustration beats deep in his brain as the thoughts skip away. What is it? It's something important, something about his dreams. A burned man crying to him for justice.

Or perhaps . . . perhaps it's what she can tell him? What news she may have. Surely she'll know.

How long has it been? Minutes, days? Half a lifetime?

*The pain in his face blurs time with the past, after Passchen-
daele. The anguish of waking in France, knowing he wouldn't
die, the long attrition of weeks and months under the surgeons'
care in Sidcup. It's all diamond-sharp in his mind compared to
these fever dreams now.*

*All he can hold on to is knowing there's something he has to
do. Even if he can't remember exactly what it is.*

The vapours rise.

Something he has to say. Hold on, dear God, hold on.

She's coming.

The dining room of the White Horse in Romsey's Market
Place is in the oldest part of the hotel. The receptionist – who's
beginning to seem like an old friend now – directs me through
dimly lit corridors to a glazed door. Beyond, the room is long
on dark wood beams and oak panelling, short on available
light.

I know I'm a few minutes early, but my heart sinks when
the restaurant manager tells me Mr Corby-Clifford hasn't
arrived yet. I can't help wondering if he'll turn up at all. So
far, the omens aren't good. But I let a waiter show me to a
table at the back of the room, take small comfort from the
reserved notice on it, the courtesy with which the man settles
me into my seat.

'May I get you a drink while you wait, madam?' he says.

After so little sleep I'm aware that alcohol isn't really what
I need. I've got to keep my wits about me if I'm to make my
case with Alec. But he's not here, and a little Dutch courage

wouldn't go amiss while I wait. A compromise. Not the gin and tonic I'd prefer, but a sherry. It seems fittingly genteel for a place like this.

Edgy with nerves, I try to seem calm. Sit without fidgeting, refrain from drumming my fingers on the table or chewing my nails. It brings back all the times Richard would keep me hanging around in some hotel dining room or restaurant, excusing himself by claiming a patient had suddenly been taken ill, or an operation had gone on longer than expected. At the beginning, I'd believed him when perhaps I shouldn't have. By the end, equally unfairly, I hadn't trusted a word he said.

There's a nice old longcase clock ticking away the seconds across the room from me. I avoid looking at it, seeing the minutes slip by. Try not to listen to the slow beat of the pendulum, the click of the hand inching round to twelve thirty, the time Alec had set for our meeting. If I'd arrived too early, now he is definitely running late.

The waiter brings my drink and I sip carefully, trying to eke it out. It's good to have something to occupy my hands. The sweet buzz of alcohol warms my mouth and throat. Gradually, my nerves begin to ease.

How long shall I wait for him? The dining room's half empty, so I don't feel guilty taking a table that's wanted for someone else. But I'm aware of curious glances, the waiter's sympathy. He obviously thinks I've been stood up.

I tell myself if Alec doesn't come soon, I'll leave. But really, I know I won't. I'll wait as long as I have to, do whatever it takes, because this isn't a matter of my pride. It's Bram's life. I have to get that penicillin for him, and I have to get it soon. Alec's my best chance – perhaps my only chance – of doing it.

My throat tightens. I've tried not to think what happens if Alec can't help. If he won't . . . I can't let that happen. I *have* to persuade him.

A discreet cough at my elbow. The waiter. 'A message for you, madam,' he says. 'Mr Corby-Clifford sends his apologies; he's been unavoidably delayed. But he should be with you by one o'clock.'

'Thank you.'

He seems almost as relieved as I am. 'May I bring you another drink?'

A look at the clock seems justified now. Twenty minutes to wait even if he turns up on time. I think longingly once more of a double gin, settle for another sherry.

While I try to seem calm, my skin crawls with impatience. At least Aggie doesn't expect me back in the office this afternoon. I get out my notebook to distract myself from the clock, look at the notes I made this morning after she and I had talked. There's a compensatory warmth that runs through me that's nothing to do with the sherry. I never thought I'd see the day when she and I would be friends, but it seems we are. Or if friends is too strong a term, then we're allies at least: united in the face of danger, determined to protect Bram as best we can. It may not last, but it's good for the moment not to feel so alone.

Another glance at the clock. Five to the hour. Behind the overwhelming anxiety about whether Alec will turn up, a whole host of other worries jostle for attention in my brain. I've got to get in touch with Sergeant Tilling. The longer it is before he sends someone to investigate the site Alf and I found, the more chance vital evidence will be lost. All that blood . . . it has to be connected somehow. It can't have got there innocently. Though Aggie promised she'd keep trying to contact the sergeant about it, it's my responsibility. Mine, too, to tell him what I learned from Colonel Beech and his daughter.

And that's another level of worry. Alice's story, on its own, can't really do Bram any harm. But if I tell Tilling about the ring, how it links Richard to the car fire, he's bound to think the fight in the lane on Sunday evening throws suspicion on Bram.

So I won't tell him, not about the ring. Not yet, anyway. Not until I have to.

The clock strikes one, and there's a flurry at the dining room entrance. Wonder of wonders, it's Alec. His suit is navy pin-stripe, tailored to make the most of his shoulders. His shirt is impeccably white, and his grey and blue, discreetly patterned tie has the expensive gleam of silk. He's dressed to impress, I think, though I doubt it's for me. I'd have been more pleased if he'd taken the trouble to arrive on time. He's no longer wearing the sling, but his right hand is still heavily bandaged.

I see him palm something to the waiter before he comes striding over in an exuberant gust of Aqua di Parma and apology. 'Josephine, my dear,' he booms. 'I'm so very sorry to have kept you waiting. Are you dreadfully angry with me?'

Every head turns our way for a moment, and I wince, exasperated by the way he's drawing attention to us both. 'Not at all. Sit down, Alec, you're making the place look untidy.'

He grins. 'Dear girl, do you ever take anything seriously?'

'Of course.' You're about to find out just how seriously I do take some things, I think.

'I don't know about you,' he says. 'But I'm famished. Now, where's that waiter with the menu?'

He lifts his left hand, clicks his fingers to attract attention. Another wince. I hate imperious gestures like that. But today's not a day to be critical, not when I need Alec on my side so desperately. With a change of mental gear that somehow makes me think of my poor Cyc-Auto on a potholed road, I set out to make myself pleasant.

The three-course, five-shilling lunch menu is a far cry from my usual beetroot or cheese sandwich eaten at my desk, or if it's sunny, out on a bench by the cricket ground, a bit of Dot's sponge cake for afters. Here, there's a choice that almost seems extravagant, despite the regulation government notice at the top of the paper. *By Order of the Ministry of Food not more than Three Courses may be served at a meal, nor may any person have at a meal more than one main dish containing meat, fish, eggs, or cheese.*

With much muttering and frowning, Alec picks his way through the menu. More embarrassment for me as he ignores the choices that have been set for lunch and insists on ordering à la carte: asparagus vinaigrette and game pie, a rhubarb fool. Flustered, I choose soup and fish, decline a dessert.

'You want to live a little,' he says with a wink. 'At least share a bottle of wine with me.'

I weigh it up. If I accept, perhaps he'll drink himself into a compliant frame of mind. But I've had enough with the two sherries if I'm to stay clear-headed. I refuse, make the excuse I've got to work this afternoon. He shrugs, orders a whisky and soda.

As we sit waiting for our first course to be delivered, he gets out a cigarette case, offers me one. 'I've given up,' I say, thinking guiltily about my chain-smoking reaction to Bram's collapse.

'You won't mind if I do?'

Actually, I do, but I shake my head. All part of keeping things pleasant.

'Now then,' he says, 'what's all the mystery about you and my old friend Richard? What's the state of play between you?'

There's something about the way he's looking at me, a kind of knowingness that seems like a test. As if he's already aware of the answer. The question is, why is he asking? To poke at what he thinks may be a sore spot, or just for the plain mischief of it?

'We're separated. You must know that. You were with him at Dunkirk. We'd been living apart for two years by then.'

The waiter arrives with his asparagus, my soup. It provides Alec with a nice distraction but I'm not going to let it go.

As soon as the waiter's safely out of earshot, I prompt him. 'Well?'

He grins. 'Guilty as charged, Josephine dear. I can tell your work has sharpened your detective instincts.'

'Detective instincts be damned.' I refuse to be distracted. 'I'm surprised you haven't seen him around Romsey. He's been here since the spring, waiting to go overseas with the troops. A medic, like you.'

'Surgeon, please.' He tuts disapproval of my careless terminology. 'This asparagus is woody.'

'You haven't seen him?'

'I didn't even know he was out of Germany.'

'He escaped,' I say. 'November 1942. They had him working at a private hospital for German officers in Dijon. He'd been co-operating, and they'd come to trust him. His guards got sloppy and one day he took his chance and slipped away. Got himself back to England through Vichy France just before it was occupied.'

'Jammy bugger always did fall on his feet.'

'What about you? They must have interned you, too.'

'Oh, you know what they say. Can't keep a good man down.' He pushes his plate away and lights up another cigarette. 'Now, where's that waiter? I hope the game pie is better than that miserable vegetable.'

This time, I take the hint and let myself be diverted. Though I'm surprised he's not as full of himself about his time as a prisoner of war as he is about everything else, I don't blame him for not wanting to share his experiences. From what I'd gathered from Richard, they'd had a horrible time after Dunkirk. They'd gone haring off as civilians, full of bravado, in a yacht that was far too slow to be of much use to get our troops off the beaches. When they'd capsized and been captured, there'd been a real danger for a while that they'd be shot as spies.

Our main course arrives. Alec's choice looks appetising with its pile of latticed game chips on the side, while my fish is less so. It's come whole: head, fins, backbone and all. I'm wishing I'd ordered something – anything – else when he speaks again.

'Now, what's all the urgency about? The girl on the desk says you've been haunting the place wanting to see me. Surely it's not all for the sake of my blue eyes?'

'No.' I abandon the fish, put down my knife and fork. No use beating around the bush. 'I want a favour, Alec. A big one.'

'Oh?'

'When we met at the hospital on Monday, I told you I was there with my employer. The coroner, Mr Nash.'

'I remember.'

'It turned out he had a problem with an old war injury. His face . . . well, his eye. Where his eye was. Apparently, a piece of shrapnel moved, worked its way to the surface. They operated, got it out, but the sister said it was a shame you hadn't been available to do the surgery.'

He tilts his head, crunches a game chip. 'That'd be Sister Fraser, I expect. She's a great fan of mine.'

'She was full of praise for you,' I say, trying not to let my impatience with his vanity show. 'But the thing is, on top of everything else, he's got an infection now. He's really unwell. Most of the time he's not even conscious. The sister said – well, I asked her – if this new drug, penicillin, would help him. She wouldn't commit herself, but it seemed as if she thought it might.'

'Hmm. Tricky.' Another game chip meets its fate between strong white teeth. 'Penicillin is supposed to be reserved for the troops.'

'So she said.' But his use of the word 'supposed' gives me a glimmer of hope.

'He's not my patient.' Alec lifts his bandaged hand as a kind of demonstration. Or perhaps it's an excuse. 'And as you must know, it's considered poor form to go horning in on another fellow's clientele.'

'Oh, but . . . surely, sometimes you're asked for a second opinion?'

'If there's neurological damage.'

'That was the implication.' The glimmer's grown a little stronger, a little brighter.

'You're asking me to see him? With a view to prescribing penicillin?'

'If that's what he needs. Whatever he needs to get better. I'll pay for the consultation, of course.'

He raises his eyebrows at me, forks up a stray piece of pie. 'Not such a big favour, then?'

'Alec, it's important to me. He's important. If you can help him, I'll owe you more than money.'

Another of those roguish grins. 'I'll hold you to that, my lovely. Are you going to eat that fish?'

'Sorry, no. I can't face it.'

'It does look grim. Let's see what we can do.'

'Please, Alec, no.'

But he ignores my protest. When the waiter comes over, Alec is at his haughtiest, commanding him to take away my meal and bring me something else.

'I really don't want ...'

They both ignore me. The waiter suggests I might like cheese and biscuits 'while sir has his pudding', to which Alec gracefully – if condescendingly – agrees. So much for only one course containing meat, fish or cheese.

I don't like the way Alec's overruled me, but there's nothing to do but bite back my resentment and smile if I want him to go and see Bram. I'm desperate to ask when he'll do it, but he steers the conversation away, starts to reminisce about the past. People we'd known, parties we'd been to back in the day.

The longcase clock is striking two when Alec's rhubarb fool and my plate of cheese and biscuits arrive. Restrictions have limited the serving to a small piece of cheddar and two cream crackers, but someone's added a stick of celery and a tiny bunch of grapes, a vivid little heap of watercress to garnish the plate. Alec looks sideways at the offering, and I jump in quickly before he can complain, thank the waiter effusively. I don't care about the food, or what happened at that party in 1930. I don't want to think about a time when I was stupid in love with Richard, before I'd realised what kind of man he was. I'm on fire to get going, to get Alec going. To see Bram.

At last Alec sets down his spoon. 'Coffee?'

'No.' It comes out sharper than I meant. Enough so a woman sitting nearby glances across curiously. Not that Alec seems bothered. If anything, he's amused.

'Tea, then, perhaps? I can recommend the lapsang souchong.' There's that half-smile again, almost sly, and I'm uneasily aware he's doing it deliberately, goading me to challenge him.

I take a deep breath, moderate my voice. 'No. Thank you. I just want . . . I need . . . Won't you come to Southampton with me this afternoon? Every minute could make the difference.'

He leans back in his chair, laughing. 'I wondered how long it would take you. Of course I'll come. Just let me get a couple of things from my room and we'll go. You'll stretch to a taxi?'

I'd promise him Cinderella's coach if it would get him moving more quickly. But it seems he's finished teasing me because he heads off to his room straightaway. All that's left for me to do is get the receptionist to telephone for a taxi.

Bram's favourite taxi driver, old Mr Mercer, turns up in response to the call before Alec comes back down. I stand talking to him outside in Market Place, trying not to show my impatience.

'Sorry to hear your boss is poorly, duck,' he says. 'A proper gentleman, he is. Dun't seem fair now, does it?'

'No. But I'm hopeful. The man I'm waiting for is a doctor. A specialist. I think he'll be able to help Mr Nash.'

'Righty-ho. Now then, what's all this about that car got set alight? I'm hearing things about a body.'

Not just Alf who'd picked up rumours, then. He'd been right, the gossip is out there already. It puts everything to do with the investigation under pressure. Only a matter of time before Alice Beech hears, then the game will be up as far as I'm concerned.

'I'm afraid I can't say, Mr Mercer. It's all hush-hush at the moment.'

'Ah, ne'er mind. Here's your bloke, I reckon.'

I turn, see Alec standing in the doorway. He's got his doctor's bag in his hand, and he looks every bit the consultant in his natty suiting. 'That's him.'

'It's the Royal South Hants you're wanting?'

'Yes, please.'

'I can wait for you if you like,' the old man says as he opens the door for me. 'I've got nothing else on this afternoon.'

'That's kind of you, but I don't know how long we'll be. And I'm sorry, but I'll have to ask you to put the fare on the office account. I'll make sure it gets paid straightaway.'

'That's all right, duck. I can trust you, I reckon.'

Alec gets in next to me in a fresh gust of cologne and toothpaste. 'Is this old rattletrap the best Romsey can offer? Doesn't look as if it'll make it to Southampton.'

He makes no attempt to keep his voice down, even though there's no screen between us and Mr Mercer in the driver's seat.

'Shh,' I caution him. 'Mr Mercer never lets us down.'

Alec laughs. 'If you say so.' He nods towards the ashtray which is empty but shows signs of use. 'I guess he won't mind if I smoke.'

'That's all right, sir,' Mr Mercer says in a tone I've never heard him use before. 'So long as the lady dun't object.'

On the way, Alec asks me a lot of questions about Bram's injuries, most of which I can't answer. Only that I knew he'd been in hospital for a long time, had a number of operations before they'd finally decided they couldn't do any more for him, issued him with a mask to cover the loss of bone and flesh, and his eye.

'You've seen the scars?' Alec says as Mercer draws up outside the hospital entrance. There it is again, that sly goading tone in his voice, his glance. I meet his eyes steadily.

'Oh yes,' I say, answering the question he hasn't voiced. 'I've seen them.'

'Good to know where we stand,' he says as he gets out of the car. 'Richard know?'

'Guesses. Does it matter? To you, I mean? Does it change whether you'll help Mr Nash?'

A huge grin, all the mischief out in the open. 'What do you take me for? Don't care who you've been fucking, my dear. Only wish it were me.'

My face is scarlet. I'm sure Mr Mercer must have heard. But there's no chance for me to answer because we're at the main door and there's Cess the porter touching his forelock to Alec and winking at me, holding the door wide. Alec sweeps in as if he's royalty, leaving me two steps behind in his train, feeling like some bedraggled and bewildered courtier.

*

Nash wakes to find himself besieged. Surrounded – as far as he can tell within the limits of his curtailed vision – by a ring of faces. It takes a moment for him to remember where he is, and why, and when. He's in hospital, a problem with his old wound. He blinks the faces into better focus. Some, he recognises. Nurses, young men in short white coats. Medical students, junior doctors. There's Curtis, the surgeon who operated on him. Usually, he's the most senior in the group, but today there's someone new, a tall man in the pinstriped suit of a consultant. A very English kind of face, sharp-featured, blond hair beginning to turn grey at the temples.

Nash frowns. What's going on? Some new crisis in his treatment? He tries to speak, but his mouth is dry, and he croaks like a frog. Licks his lips, tries again. 'Who?'

'Name's Corby-Clifford. Consultant surgeon with a special interest in brain injury. I've been asked to take a look at you. I'd shake your hand but . . .' The tall man lifts his right hand, displays a bandage.

Nash wants to acknowledge the man; show him he's understood. That it's purely mechanics stopping him speaking, not a failure of his brain. With what feels like a huge effort, he raises his head. Out of the corner of his eye he can see there's a spouted cup standing on the locker beside him. 'Drink?'

The surgeon is closest, but he doesn't make a move. 'Sister, water for the man,' Corby-Clifford says.

'Nurse.' The sister speaks sharply. 'Give Mr Nash a sip of water.'

It would almost be funny, Nash thinks, if it weren't so ridiculous. The way the nurse has to edge past her seniors to reach him, to bring the cup to his lips. The liquid's tepid, stale-tasting, but it's welcome enough. Another quick mouthful before the cup's withdrawn and the nurse, red-faced with embarrassment, returns to her place.

'Now.' Corby-Clifford is brusque, addressing his words not to Nash but to the watching group of medicos. 'The first question is to determine whether the surgery Mr Curtis performed on Monday night was sufficient to remove the accessible foreign matter from the old wound. Brown, have you looked at the patient's post-operative X-rays?'

'Yes, sir.'

Nash can't see the man who's spoken, but he can hear the nervousness in his voice. A student, perhaps?

'Your conclusion?'

'Ah . . . they seemed all right.'

'All right? That may be good enough for the unfortunate patient, Brown, but I expect more clinical precision. Try again.'

'Ah . . . the surgical field was clear of extraneous material and bone fragments, sir.'

'So, your view of these troublesome pyrexias Sister has told us about. What do you make of those?'

'Wound infection, sir.'

'Or?' Corby-Clifford prompts irritably.

'Ah . . .'

'Idiot. Ford, what about you? Differential diagnosis?'

'Periostitis, septic meningitis, septicaemia.'

'Better. Though not necessarily for Mr Nash, eh? What do you suggest we do for him?'

The discussion washes over Nash. He's not unfamiliar with the way some doctors treat their patients as if they're deaf, dumb and blind, oblivious as a piece of meat. It's best not to listen. Except he can't escape: Corby-Clifford throws the bedclothes back, tests his reflexes. A tap of the tendon hammer on each knee, a scrape of a thumbnail on the sole of each foot.

'Good. Grip my hand.'

It's almost a surprise to be addressed as a sentient being. He does his best to comply, but the intravenous apparatus in his arm hampers the demonstration.

'Hmm.'

A blast of light in his eye that blots out everything but the consultant's own grey eye, monstrously magnified, peering into his.

The light is withdrawn. 'Right. We'll have that dressing down, Sister.'

A fuss he hears rather than sees, his vision blurred with sparkling after-images. The rattle of another infernal trolley, a sound he's come to dread. Apprehension knots in his belly.

Hands lift his head, and there's a seasick shift as the bandage is unrolled. He's beginning to wish he hadn't had so much water after all. The air feels cool on his exposed skin, but there's an overwhelming sense of vulnerability too. He closes his eye, steels himself for what comes next.

He already knows the sister believes in the doctrine of the short, sharp tug to lift the inner dressing where it is stuck to the wound. No gentle unpicking for her. He's braced for the tearing sensation, the burn and ooze that follows.

'Gloves please, Sister.'

A pause. The smell of rubber, the press of ungentle fingers against the damaged architecture of his face.

'Hmm. What do we see, Brown?'

A shift of the air around him, the sense of other eyes staring.

'Redness, sir.' The nervous boy's voice. 'I mean, erythema. And swelling. And, ah, bloody exudate at the lower border of the wound.'

'Yes. We'll have this lower stitch out, Sister. Scissors.'

A tug, a sharp pop Nash both hears and feels. The oozing sensation again.

'Swab. And the fine probe. Yes. You'd better hold his head.'

Hands, chilly, place themselves firmly on either side of his face. At once, an obscene invasion of his flesh begins. A pain that intensifies, goes on much too long, that seems to drill through the orbit of his vanished eye and into the substance of his brain. Try as he might, he can't suppress one inarticulate sound of denial.

'Sorry, old man.' Corby-Clifford's voice comes faintly through the haze of pain. 'Bit clumsy with this hand of mine.'

A final jab of agony, a rush of something hot on his cheek.

'There we are.' Corby-Clifford again. Nash registers the satisfaction in the surgeon's voice. 'A nasty little pocket of pus forming in the deficit behind the orbit. Not your fault, Curtis, a nice neat surgical procedure. But he'll be better with that draining. And I think . . .'

Nash holds on to consciousness. Dimly tracks the snap of rubber gloves, the shuffle of feet as people move around him.

'Clean him up, Sister. Irrigate the wound, then some of our magic powder applied directly. Follow up with six-hourly intramuscular injections.'

'Penicillin?' the sister says.

'That's it. I've got the stuff in my bag. Issued ready for the off, but since I'm still here, why not? I'll write the prescription.'

A scraping sound as a screen is pushed aside. More shuffling feet, and one assured tread. With one last effort, Nash opens his eye.

'Thank . . .'

Corby-Clifford looks back at him. Grins. 'Don't thank me, old man. Wouldn't even have heard of you if it hadn't been for Mrs Lester.'

16

Wednesday, afternoon

I DON'T KNOW THAT I'VE EVER felt worse in my life. Sitting in the ward corridor, having insisted on waiting despite the sister's disapproval. Knowing full well she'd have thrown me out if it hadn't been for Alec, her little god of the ward rounds, who'd brought me there himself.

Waiting anxiously for him, to find out what he can do for Bram. Waiting to see Bram for myself, hoping he might be conscious this time and know I'm there.

Waiting while endless protocols are observed: the business of consultation between colleagues, the stately gathering together of medics and hangers-on. And at last, with his proper train of followers, Alec making his way to the screened-off bed.

Wondering if I've done the right thing to involve him, as I listen to the casual cruelty of his comments as he examines Bram. Hating it more every moment, hating him more. Hating him most, hearing that one muffled cry of pain.

And in the end, my vigil is all to no purpose. They won't let me see Bram after all. He's exhausted, the sister explains.

Mr Corby-Clifford has prescribed sedation: absolute rest for twenty-four hours.

'Tomorrow, then,' I say to her. 'I'll be back tomorrow. Please make sure he knows.'

She nods, and I catch – or perhaps I imagine – a surprising look of sympathy in her eyes. What Alec feels, I don't know. I can't bear to look him in the face when he detaches himself from the group of doctors and comes striding down the corridor towards the sister and me.

'Josephine, my dear, you'll forgive me if I abandon you? There's another patient Curtis has asked me to consult upon.'

A surge of relief goes through me. The last thing I want is to be cheek by jowl with him in a taxi, obliged to be pleasant to him. Not after what I've heard. I don't think I'll ever forget it.

'That's all right.' My lips feel frozen as I force the words out. 'Thank you.'

'Hey, hey, what's all this?' Regardless of the sister standing by, his colleagues waiting, he puts a hand under my chin, compels me to look up at him. 'He's going to be fine,' he says. 'He's as tough as old boots. Trust me, I'll keep an eye on him.'

God, what have I done, committing Bram to this man's care? I used to think Richard was ruthless, that clinical detachment was the mark of a good surgeon. By that measure, Alec must be exemplary.

'Josephine?'

'Yes. All right, yes.' I step back, out of his hold, but not before he leans forward, kisses my cheek.

'I'll catch up with you later, my dear. Keep you in the picture.'

'Yes.'

A grin, a wink. 'Present you with my bill.'

I can't get away quickly enough. I scurry, just decorum's side of outright running, along corridors that seem endless, clatter my way down the wide staircase that leads to the main entrance.

Outside, in the fresh air, I realise I'm trembling, shaking with emotion. Anger and frustration, fear for Bram. And yet, and yet . . . what have I got to complain about? Alec's done what I asked. Seen Bram, prescribed the wonder drug.

Tough as old boots . . . I hope he is. But I know I'm not, not right now. It's all too much.

'Mrs Lester? Over here.' It's Mr Mercer, despite what I said about not waiting. I want to hug the old man and his car. An afternoon of absolutes. Of kindness, and its polar opposite.

'Ready to go home, duck? You look all in,' he says.

'Pretty much. Thank you for waiting.'

'What about that bloke, is he coming?'

'Not this time.'

'No loss there. Why don't you hop in next to me? It's a much better ride in the front of my old rattletrap.'

'Mr Mercer . . .'

'Just me teasing,' he says. 'Take no notice. 'Tis an old banger, but it does the job.'

I settle myself in the broken-down embrace of the worn leather bucket seat, close my eyes. Next thing I know, Mr Mercer is slowing the car to snail's pace. A bleary glance round shows me we're not back in Romsey yet. Instead, I recognise the all-too-familiar trees and hedgerows as part of the landscape of Lee Lane.

Confused, I straighten up in my seat, wipe a line of drool from my chin. 'What?'

'Police,' the old man says.

'What?' I repeat as I peer through the windscreen. We must just have passed the site where the burned-out car was found, because the little crossroads of Spaniard's Lane is dead ahead. Sergeant Tilling's car is drawn up on the verge, with Tilling and an even more familiar figure standing alongside. Alf. I can't see his face, but the way he's standing, hands in pockets, head on one side suggests defiance. And even from this distance, I can tell why. Tilling looks as mad as a hornet, scarlet in the face and waving his hands in the air.

'Sorry, Mr Mercer,' I say. 'You'd better let me out here. No need to wait this time.'

As I climb out of the car, Tilling's voice carries across to me.

'. . . want to be careful, my lad. I'll have you for wasting police time.' He looks up at my approach, and his expression settles into a grim kind of satisfaction. 'Look at that. Right on cue. Here's your co-conspirator.'

I'm only a couple of yards short of Tilling when Mr Mercer draws up beside me, engine running. 'You sure you're all right?' he says. 'I can wait.'

'Oh, no,' Tilling says. 'You can't. On your way, Mercer. I want a word or two with Mrs Lester.'

Alf fidgets, looks over at me as if he's going to say something. Tilling cuts in, 'And you, my lad, stay where you are. And keep your mouth shut till I ask you to speak.'

We wait in an awkward silence while the taxi moves off towards Romsey. In the pause, I can hear voices and the crackle of movement in the undergrowth just beyond, where Alf and I found the blood. I've no idea why the sergeant should be so angry, but at least the wait means he's got a chance to calm down a bit.

'Now then,' he says, just at the same moment I speak.

'What's all this about, Sergeant?'

'Miss Haward gave me your message.' He may be calmer, but his tone is biting. 'About this suspicious site. Didn't take a genius to guess if you'd found anything hereabouts this lad would be involved, so I picked him up on my way. Lucky I did because—'

'It's all gone,' Alf bursts out. 'There's nothing left.'

'I told you to keep quiet, lad.'

'But it's true. It has.'

Tilling narrows his eyes, stares at Alf. 'You stay here until Mrs Lester and I come back,' he says emphatically. 'You don't move, and you don't say anything to anyone not even if your arse catches fire. Understood?'

Alf nods.

'Right, Mrs Lester. Follow me.'

He moves off, cutting his way up through the bank of trees bordering the lane. He doesn't seem to be worried about the possibility of destroying evidence, but I follow more cautiously. I look back before I step up onto the bank myself and see Alf shrug. Guilt swells through me. Someone else I've brought hurt to today.

'Mrs Lester.' Tilling's voice comes from somewhere in front. I can't see him anymore, but I know where he must be.

One more glance at Alf, and I'm reassured to see him wink. Maybe things aren't so bad after all.

But when I catch up with Tilling at the place where Alf showed me the marks of a killing, it's bad enough. The leaves have been swept back, but instead of the bare patch of hard, discoloured earth we'd seen last night, now it looks as if someone's raked it over. The ground's been turned into a chocolatey tilth almost all across the site. Only one place is different: a shallow hole has been dug practically in the centre. PC Summers is standing next to it, leaning on a spade, and mopping his face.

I turn accusingly on Tilling. 'Did you tell him to do this? All the evidence ...'

'Hold your water,' he says. 'It was like this when we got here. All my officer has done is try and see what's been going on.'

'And?'

'Show her, Summers.'

The policeman picks up his spade, slides it under what looks like a heap of soil. As he trudges towards me, I see whatever it is has fur. Closer, and I recognise the black and white markings, clotted with dirt and old blood. A badger, and from the smell, it's been dead a good few days.

'There's your victim,' Tilling says, waving Summers away. 'Bloody wild goose chase, Mrs Lester. Like I told the lad, wasting police time. I've got a good mind to haul you in for a few hours. Teach you a lesson. Excepting it'd be more trouble than you're worth.'

'But . . .'

'No buts,' he says. 'Summers.'

'Sir?'

'Knocking off time. Now, Mrs Lester, after you.'

He practically shoos me out onto the lane in front of him. Alf's still waiting, all innocence.

'Right,' Tilling says. 'This is how it's going to be. Mrs Lester, I'll see you tomorrow at the hospital for the post-mortem. Ten o'clock, and don't be late.'

I open my mouth to speak, but he holds up a hand, palm towards me. Like directing the traffic, I think inconsequentially. *Stop.*

'Anything you want to say to me can wait till then. I was out at the site of this burglary half the night and I'm fit to drop. I'm heading off home, and I strongly suggest you do the same. Take that lad with you. And you, Alf Smith, if I hear so much as another whisper about you being out and about after midnight round here this week, you'll be up before the magistrates on suspicion. Get it?'

Alf nods. 'Yes, Sergeant.'

'Right. Summers, don't get in the car with all that mud on your boots. Clean 'em off, man, do.'

As he turns away, Alf calls out, 'What about a lift back to town, Sergeant? You sent Mrs Lester's taxi away.'

'If I put you in the back of that car, lad, there'll be a charge at the end of it. And I don't mean a fare either.' He sighs. 'But I suppose it's only fair I offer you a lift, Mrs Lester.'

Though I feel ready to drop, I shake my head. 'I'll go with Alf.'

'Right. Don't say I didn't offer.'

And don't say I didn't try to speak when I finally manage to tell you what Alice Beech said, I think, as I watch him climb heavily into the passenger seat of the police car, which drives off in a cloud of oily exhaust. Or about the ring, either. Even if I hadn't meant to tell him about it, his impatience has given me a respite. He won't be able to blame me for not telling him today when he does find out.

'You OK, Jo?' Alf says as we set off. 'You look a bit . . . pale.'

'Mm. Quickest way home, yeah?'

'All the short cuts.' He grins. 'Since it idn't midnight yet.'

'Another couple of nights and we'll be past full moon.'

He laughs. 'Don't you worry, I've got a trick or two up my sleeve. Talking of tricks . . . ?'

I feel like I'm walking the way it happens in a dream: feet moving but getting nowhere. 'Yeah?'

'What do you think happened back there?'

'Only one thing to think, isn't there? After we left last night . . . this morning . . . when it got dark, someone came along and raked the ground over to hide the blood.'

'And bury poor old Brock.'

'Yeah. We'd have known if that badger had been there last night, wouldn't we? I mean, that was a different kind of smell altogether.'

'Too right. Anyway, it'd take more'n one badger to make all that blood.' He stops short, so I almost run into the back of him. 'Better have a look at this.'

'What?'

'Dunno what to make of it myself.' He pulls something out of his pocket, holds it out on the flat of his hand. 'Never seen anything like it in my life.'

But I have, dozens of times. A narrow strip of stainless steel with rounded edges about five inches long. There are knurled surface markings and a blunt point at one end.

'Looks like a handle,' Alf says, tracing his fingers over the point.

'It is.' A Bard-Parker scalpel handle number 3, to be precise. 'Where did you find it, Alf?'

'Saw it when that copper swept the leaves off. Blind as a bat, that one. Never had a clue.'

'You didn't tell him?'

A shrug. 'Didn't give me a chance, did he? Going on like I'm some kind of idiot, having a fit of the vapours over a dead badger. I've been in these woods half my life. I can read the ground better'n he can.'

'Look, trust me with it, will you? You don't need any more trouble from Sergeant Tilling. I'll say I found it.'

He turns his hand over, drops the handle into my palm. 'You reckon it's a clue?'

'Oh, yes.' A very specific one. Richard was here. Though there's no blade here, a scalpel's sharp enough to spill any amount of blood.

'Gonna let me in on it?'

I shake my head. 'No, not right now. Sorry, Alf.' I'm seized with a sudden fit of yawning that makes me feel like my jaw will dislocate.

'Blimey. Better get you home, Doc.'

It takes me a moment to realise he's not suddenly become clairvoyant. His addiction to cartoons, especially Bugs Bunny, was one of the first things I'd learned about him.

'Better had. Don't want to finish up like one of the babes in the woods, sleeping under a blanket of leaves.'

If I felt I'd been walking in a dream earlier, the rest of the trip home is like a nightmare. I'm so tired I'm stumbling along with my eyes closed half the time. Just as well, then, that Alf does take the short cuts, along the smoother ground beside the railway line and across the back of the nursery. At Dot's, I fall in through the door, and though it's not much after six and bright daylight, I go straight upstairs, drop fully clothed onto my bed and sleep.

17

Thursday 8th June 1944, morning

I WAKE – AS I'D FALLEN asleep – to full daylight. I'm stiff and stale in yesterday's clothes, and my sense of time is shot. I've no idea how long I've slept except that it must be a long time, judging by the dryness of my mouth and the urgent pressure on my bladder. I hurry to the lavatory without looking at the clock. I'd forgotten to wind my watch yesterday and it's stopped at four o'clock, so that's no help either. I strip-wash and brush my teeth, feeling a growing sense of urgency. I can't hear any other sounds in the house beyond the bathroom door, and the light's too strong to be very early. If Alf's gone to work and Dot's out shopping already, it must be well after nine. And Tilling said I had to be at the hospital for the post-mortem by ten. I dart into my bedroom to dress.

Dismayed, I discover it's already too late. It's ten to ten, and the way the traffic is on the Avenue, it'll take me at least half an hour to reach the hospital on the little Cyc-Auto.

Despite Tilling's instructions, I'd never had any intention of being present for the post-mortem. The idea's too gruesome for me: standing and watching while the burned body is dissected, searched for clues of identity. Especially if . . . I shy away from completing the thought. One thing at a time. It's bad enough that Tilling's going to be annoyed with me for being late.

No time for breakfast, even if I had the appetite for it. No time to call in at the office, though I really should. I'll have to phone Aggie later. No time even to find out how Bram is. If the penicillin's begun to work, will his temperature have come down, stayed down? I can only hope. At least I should be able to call in and see him once the post-mortem's over.

I push the bike's engine to the limit as I speed down the lanes towards Southampton. No sign of police at Spaniard's Lane. My throat closes at the memory of the blood Alf and I had seen. Whatever Tilling might think, that place is connected to the body in the car. A quick exploration of my coat pocket reassures me that the scalpel handle is still there. Perhaps it'll convince him, if . . .

Forbidden territory again.

It's twenty-five past ten when I arrive at the hospital. I park the bike up on its stand next to a car I recognise as Tilling's, though there's no sign of him. No sign of my friendly porters either as I search for directions to the mortuary. Not the sort of thing a hospital wants to advertise.

Eventually a nurse, hurrying across the hallway, gabbles a string of instructions that include 'turn right at the steps' and 'round by the path lab' and dashes off. Struggling to remember what she's said, I set off.

I'm on the verge of deciding I'm hopelessly lost when I catch sight of WPC Shaw, Sergeant Tilling's driver, across a little courtyard. She's leaning on a wall next to a set of arched wooden doors, her face green. When she sees me, she straightens up.

'Is Sergeant Tilling inside?' I say.

She nods. 'Think yourself lucky you're late. If I was you—' She puts her hand to her throat, swallows hard enough for me to hear.

'What?'

'I'd find an excuse not to go in till it's over. I'm damn sure I'm not going back. Don't care what Tilling says, he can go boil his head.'

'Bad as that?'

'Worse. I won't tell if you want to do a bunk.'

'Sporting of you.'

'We girls have to stick together.'

I wince a bit at 'girls'. It's a very long time since I've felt young enough to think of myself that way. 'How long do you think they'll be?'

'God knows.'

I'm wondering if I should take the chance to go and see Bram when the doors swing open. It's Tilling, looking almost as green as WPC Shaw. There's a man with him, a short, slight figure with jug-handle ears. He's wearing a red rubber apron over white surgeon's gown and hat, red rubber boots. I hardly need the sergeant's explanation that this is the pathologist. I don't catch the man's name, though. Tilling's voice is swallowed up at the crucial moment by a sound that's half belch, half groan.

'Pardon me.'

'Jo Lester,' I say, ignoring him and holding out my hand to the pathologist. 'I'm assistant to Mr Nash. The Romsey coroner.'

The doctor briefly grasps my hand in a token handshake. I can't help noticing how clean and pink his skin is, how recently scrubbed. 'Gather he's indisposed. Tell him I'll get my report to him within the week.'

'Thank you. In the meantime, is there anything – preliminary findings, perhaps, that might help us identify the victim?'

He frowns. 'I've told the sergeant here. Male, mid-forties. Time of death between four and ten hours after his last meal. No sign of disease. Old fractures of the left clavicle and wrist, well healed.'

The breath halts in my chest as if I've been punched.

'Mean something to you?'

I shake my head. 'Go on.'

'Hmm.' He pulls a face. 'Reaction like that, more than physiological. But I've no time to be dealing with fainting women. Got to get back to London. The sergeant will tell you the rest.'

Another minimal handshake for Tilling and the pathologist hustles back through the doors.

'Bloody ridiculous,' Tilling blusters. 'Green as bloody grass, the pair of you. Dunno who looks worse.' He cocks his head towards the main hospital block. 'We'll cut along to the canteen, have a cuppa before the pair of you keel over on me.'

Another hitch to my breathing, this time with annoyance. I'm nowhere near fainting, and Tilling looks pretty green himself. I could use a cup of tea, though, especially if it gives me a chance to tell the sergeant what I know in a public place where he'll have to keep his temper.

The canteen's a basement affair, the only light coming in from a row of grimy windows near the ceiling. It's half deserted at this time in the morning. Not such a safe environment for my confession after all.

Tilling leads us over to a table furthest from the windows, deep in shadow. He fishes a two-bob bit out of his pocket, hands it to the policewoman. 'Cup of tea all round,' he says, 'and tell the woman to make sure it's good and strong.'

He watches her moving away, waits till she's out of earshot. 'Go on, then,' he says. 'What's put that sick look on your face? You never even got near the corpse today.'

There's a thin crack in the wooden tabletop that's lined with crumbs. The details of the wood grain, the arrangement of each crumb is so sharp in my mind I don't think I'll ever be able to forget them. I pick at what looks like a speck of salt with my fingernail, feel my eyes swim with water.

'The body. I think . . .' It's an effort to take in enough air to say the words. 'I'm pretty sure it's my husband.'

Tilling half rises out of his seat. 'What?' His voice is sharp. 'You're telling me—'

I flick a glance upwards, feel a trickle of wetness begin to spill down my cheek. 'My estranged husband, Richard. He's ... he was attached to the RAMC this spring. He was due to ship out with the invasion force on Sunday. I thought he'd gone. I hoped he had.'

Tilling drops back down into his chair with a thump. 'How do you know?' he says. 'The broken collarbone and wrist?'

'Yes, but ...' I jump with surprise as WPC Shaw sets a tray with three thick white hospital mugs of tea onto the table between Tilling and me.

'What's up?' she says. 'Why's Mrs Lester crying?'

'Be a good girl.' Tilling flashes her a look. 'Go and sit at another table. Mrs Lester and I need a bit more of a chat.'

She flushes, but she's not easily intimidated. 'Is that all right with you, Mrs Lester?'

'I'm fine.'

She raises her eyebrows.

'Really, I'm OK. I suppose you wouldn't have a hanky to spare?'

'Girl Guide,' she says, and hands me a creased but clean square. 'I'll be just over there if you want me.'

She picks up a mug of tarry-looking liquid and sets it down next to me. Takes another for herself and turns away.

'I know I said strong,' Tilling comments, reaching to secure the last mug. 'But this is a bit much. Hope it's got a good lot of sugar.'

The look on his face as he takes a sip tells me it hasn't. 'Go on, then,' he says. 'What makes you think it's your hubby? Lots of men break their arms.'

Despite my best intentions, I can't avoid telling him any longer. 'The ring,' I say. 'I'm pretty sure I recognised it.'

'You—' It's fierce, hotly angry. 'That was Tuesday. You never said a word.'

'I wasn't positive. And then I couldn't get hold of you.'

He grimaces. 'Have to give you that. So what's made you change your mind?'

'Lots of men *do* break their arms. But that and the ring . . . I was afraid before, didn't know whether to think he was . . . well, the victim, or . . .'

'The killer. Like that, hey? You suspected him?'

'I don't know,' I say wearily. The tears have stopped but my face feels cardboard stiff. 'Why don't you just let me say what I've got to say? You can make up your own mind.'

He takes a long swig of his tea, grimaces. 'Better make it good.'

So, for the second time, I tell the story as I learned it. What happened with Colonel Beech and Capstaff first, then my visit to Alice. I go easy on the details of her day with Richard, but he's savvy enough to work it out. To understand how important a piece of evidence it is, that Richard was there, in the lane, at 9 p.m., having fallen out with both Alice and Bram. I make as light as I can of that part, play down the two men's quarrel. Emphasise how Alice had seen Richard go dashing off to Broadlands afterwards, perfectly fit and well despite Bram's blow.

'Bugger,' he says. 'Spaniard's Lane. No wonder you thought that nipper had found something significant.'

I shrug. 'You thought it was a wild goose chase yesterday. What's made you change your mind?'

'Your story for a start.' He fumbles in his pocket, pulls out a jar that's horribly familiar. Just like the one the sister showed me with the shrapnel from Bram's wound, it rattles as he shakes it. 'And there's this. That pathologist found it.' He taps his inner arm at the elbow. 'Just here. It was stuck in the bone. Funny sort of do, but the doc said it was probably what killed him. Good big artery there, see. There would have been a lot of blood.'

The blood we'd seen. The blood he'd dismissed as insignificant, a product of our overactive imagination.

'He was ... dead when the fire started?' It's the question I've been afraid to ask all along. I've had a horror of death by fire, ever since one of the teachers at school told us about Joan of Arc.

'He was, poor chap. Pathologist said there was no sign of soot in the air passages.'

Almost light-headed with a kind of relief, I squint at the tiny, shiny triangle of metal in the jar. 'It's a bit of a scalpel blade.'

'That's right,' he says grudgingly. 'I suppose you'd know. But I'm surprised you can recognise it from that.'

'I was expecting it.' Like a poker player laying down the winning hand, I bring out a fabric-wrapped bundle from my pocket. Unwrap the handkerchief I hadn't been able to use earlier. 'Because I've got the blade handle.'

'Ssss.' He lets out his breath in a long, disgusted stream. 'Where did that come from?'

'That clearing. Under the leaves.'

'More evidence withheld,' he says with rising heat. 'I tell you, Mrs Lester, I'm seriously annoyed with you.'

He's going to be even more annoyed, I think, when he examines it. Finds it's polished perfectly clean. This morning, when I remembered it, I'd been in two minds what to do. If I passed it on to Tilling as Alf had given it to me, there was a chance there would have been fingerprints on it. Prints that might lead to a killer, though every wrongdoer these days knows to wear gloves. But I knew for certain there'd be Alf's prints, and mine. Though I could have explained mine away, I'd landed Alf in enough trouble with the sergeant already. I knew he hadn't killed anything bigger than a rabbit, but the mood Tilling had been in, he might easily have arrested the boy. Might still do it if he thought he had cause. So not for the first time in this case – and probably not for the last – I'd let personal feelings override my duty, cleaned the handle as thoroughly as I'd once cleaned Granny's silver teaspoons.

'Perhaps you should be annoyed with PC Summers, instead,' I say coolly. 'Or even yourself. I tried to tell you yesterday at Spaniard's Lane, remember? You told me to save it.'

The policeman's face hardens. 'Be off with you,' he says. 'Get out before I do something you'll regret. But I want you at the police station to make a formal statement this afternoon. Four o'clock, not a minute after. No excuses.'

I stand up. My legs feel like cotton wool, but I won't give him the satisfaction of seeing it.

'And mind,' he says, 'you go straight back home now. I'll be checking up on you, and if I find you've been grubbing around, trying to get anyone to change their story, you'll be sorry.'

I shrug.

'And that means Mr Nash too.'

'He's very sick. They won't let you see him.'

'Then I'll make sure you don't see him either,' he says. 'Not before I've had a chance to talk to him.'

'But I promised.'

'Too bad. No contact till after you've given your statement.'

Bram. Oh, God, Bram. I can't break my promise to him. I can't bear it.

As I walk away, the tears begin again. I'm conscious of curious glances from WPC Shaw, the woman serving behind the counter, a couple of nurses in a huddle drinking what smells like cocoa. The bitter chocolate scent makes me heave.

In the corridor, sick, half-blinded, I run slap into the friendly old porter from Tuesday morning.

'Hey, hey,' he says. 'If it isn't our early morning visitor. Not sad news, love, surely? We heard on the grapevine your friend's doing OK. Had the great man himself come in and give him the once-over.'

I don't know what's happened to the policewoman's handkerchief, so I have to wipe my face with fingers. 'It's just . . . I've been told I can't see him. And I promised.'

'If it was Sister Fraser, love, you'll be all right. She's off duty today, she'll never know.'

Worse and worse, knowing I could have been there with him all this time. 'It wasn't Sister. I can't explain.'

'Tell you what,' he says. 'Come along to the porters' lodge with me, have a minute or two in the quiet to sort yourself out. And if you want to write your friend a little note, perhaps, I could take it along to him. One of the nurses will read it to him if he can't manage for himself.'

In one way it's an awful idea, a very poor second to seeing him for myself. But in another, it's the nicest thing that's happened so far today.

Memo: From Commander, Auxiliary Field Ambulance
Unit Number ■■■ Arromanche, France
To Dispatch, Marshalling Area C 15
08/06/44

Re Richard Lester, Surgeon, Service number ■■■■■■

The above named has failed to report for duty with this unit as posted. Unable to ascertain movements of subject prior to/during embarkation. Query AWOL, query casualty. Request update/replacement personnel asap.

18

Thursday, afternoon and evening

WHEN NASH NEXT WAKES, EVERYTHING'S changed. No more screens round his bed, no more sweet little Nightingale sitting by, eyes anxiously fixed on him. Best of all, no more sweaty furnace heat. He's warm, ordinarily warm. His mind is clear, clearer than it's been for what seems like weeks, long before his collapse. He even remembers that now, parts of it anyway. A jolting, agonising journey, Jo's voice in his ear.

He pulls himself cautiously up in the bed, careful of the tubing inserted in his left arm. Manages to half sit against the iron head rail. He could do with more than one meagre pillow.

For the first time, he's able to take in his surroundings. He's close to one end of a long ward. Directly in front, across the ward, there's a row of empty beds: black iron frames made up with impeccable neatness. Everything but the frames is blindingly white. Linen, blankets, plump pillows he covets. A window demarcates the space between each bed: each window is open the same precise few inches.

He can't see to his left, the bandages round his head cut his always limited field of vision to zero. On his right, there are more empty beds. By counting across from where he is, he reckons he must be in the fourth bed from the ward door.

'You awake, chum?' A voice from his left. With some difficulty he turns his head towards the sound. He can only manage to see the lower part of the next-door bed, where a large pair of feet mar the otherwise flat surface of the white counterpane.

'I seem to be, yes.'

'You OK? I can call the nurse for you.'

'I'm all right,' he says, surprised to find it's the truth. 'I even think I'm hungry.'

'Cor.' A laugh. 'You must be better then.'

He struggles to turn his head further, wins another few inches: the sight of sturdy legs mounding the covers. A spear of pain pulls him up short. 'Where is everyone?' he says. Muffled through the bandages he can hear the sounds of some kind of bustling commotion, though no one has passed through his line of sight.

'There's a flap on,' his unseen companion says. 'Word is, there's a lot of our boys on their way back from the beaches. Nurses are getting the ward ready for casualties. Due to arrive this evening.'

'Beaches?'

'Course, you won't know. D-Day, chum. Invasion of France. We went in on Tuesday.'

'Oh.' Nash lets out a long sigh. 'What's the news? Not another Dunkirk?'

'Nah, we're doing good. Germans falling back on all fronts. Bound to be casualties, though, in't there?'

'Of course.' He wants to know more, struggles to think of what question to ask first. But it seems rude to go on talking without some kind of introduction. 'Sorry I can't see you,' he says. 'My name's Nash.'

'Ted Warren, that's me. Next one over from me is Mr lah-de-dah Smith call-me-Smythe. Listen to him snore.'

'Just the three of us?'

'That's right. And they're getting rid of us too, this afternoon. You woke up just in time.'

'Getting rid of us? What's all that about?'

'They're moving us on. Suit old Smythe, it will. Taking us off to some posh place near Romsey. Broadlands? They've got an annexe there to the hospital. All mod cons, they say.'

'Good grief.'

'You know it?'

'Well, not to say know. Though I do live in Romsey.'

'You'll be right at home, then.'

Nash laughs. 'I wouldn't say that, exactly.' He thinks of his home with yearning. The peace of it, the familiarity. His own things around him. He'd almost welcome Fan's fussing, even her dreadful cooking.

'I wonder . . .'

'What is it, chum?'

'I was expecting a visitor. Sister told me. After that doctor saw me.'

'Him? Bloody sadist, he is. Serve him right he's got a blighty one. Hope it bloody hurts.'

'Mm.' The energy he'd felt on first waking is ebbing away. He's grateful to note he doesn't feel dizzy or light-headed, just profoundly tired. But he is disappointed. 'I suppose they'll let our people know they're moving us?'

'I hope so. Me missus won't be pleased. Proper journey from our place out to Romsey.' There's a rustle of bed-clothes and Nash imagines Ted Warren has shrugged. 'Suppose it can't be helped. What about that little redhead of yours?'

Nash grins sleepily to himself, wonders what Jo would make of the description. He's sure she'd hate the 'little', and hotly deny the possessive, as he must himself. But maybe it won't matter if he lets it ride for now.

Tilling had told me to go home, but I can't sit at Dot's, waiting for the time to pass before I can go and make my statement. If I can't see Bram, and I mustn't talk to any possible witnesses, what am I to do?

A mirage of peace swims before my eyes. The farm, Sam. No disrespect to Dot, but that quiet spot on the Downs is home as much as anywhere. And Sam won't ask questions I can't answer. How I feel, what I'm thinking.

Not about Richard, not yet. I can't let myself do that. Lock the horror and the relief away in a box, throw away the key.

I'll go and make hay or feed the goats. Anything, rather than think.

Straight up the Avenue this time. I don't want to be anywhere near Lee Lane now. Along the main road, noting the renewed bustle of troops in the camps on the Common, the military traffic buzzing down towards the docks. Through Chandler's Ford. The big embarkation camps where the Canadians were stationed are empty, there's an almost forlorn air about the place. A glimpse of the familiar prefabricated buildings at the Hutments makes me think of my brief stay with the Andersons last year. I wonder how Anita is, and her little boy. I must make the effort to come and see them one day.

Through to Hursley: turn into Port Lane with a sense of relief. No traffic here, only birdsong, the occasional squirrel flitting across my path. Further on, the scatter of smallholdings at Oliver's Battery: cows and hens, Mr Evans turning hay in the bottom meadow. I wave, but don't stop. I'm almost desperate to get to Sam's now: to the goats and Lady and Sam's undemonstrative welcome.

Thanks to the assistance of the Cyc-Auto's little engine, I arrive at Sam's within the hour. I don't have long here if I'm to get back to Romsey in time to give my formal statement, but even if it were only ten minutes, it'd be worth it.

The first place I go – the first place I almost always go – is to visit Noah in his pen, the billy goat I'd watched being born when I was looking after the farm for Sam. The kid would never have lived if it hadn't been for me. I'd rubbed life into him, helped him take his first breath. Defended him when a neighbour had laughed and said I shouldn't have bothered. No sense in rearing a billy when Sam's business was milk. I could see the point, but I wouldn't let Noah die. I'd bottle-fed him, made such a bond with the little goat that now he follows me around like a dog if I let him. He's such a consolation today as I hug his hard neck, feel his lips nibble my hair. He knows it's no good to eat, but he always has to try.

I get almost an hour out in the field, helping Sam rake hay and stook it over the ash-branch A-frames. He's every bit as comforting as Noah, and just about as silent. But I don't mind that: better that than a lot of questions.

All too soon it's twenty-five to four. I'll have to get a move on, though for two pins I'd defy Tilling and not bother. I don't think he'd know to look for me here, but I don't want to make trouble for Sam. Anyway, sooner or later I'll have to get back to Romsey and do my job. It's probably not the best idea to annoy the sergeant by being late.

'I've got to go,' I say to Sam. 'I don't want to, but I'll see you again on Friday evening.'

He gives me a shrewd once-over. 'Ah. You take care, mind. You're looking proper peaky.'

It's a rare long speech for Sam. Even rarer is the hug he gives me, awkward against his chest. I'd stay in the comfort of it, but a minute more and I'd break down and cry, so I pull away, take off running for the farm buildings where I've left the bike.

*

Nash spends the journey to Mountbatten Annexe uncomfortably strapped to a narrow stretcher high up in the roof of a decommissioned army ambulance. Though the drip apparatus has been removed from his arm, he's fastened in so tightly he can't steady himself against the movement of the vehicle as it lurches along, veers unexpectedly round corners. It's like being in a small boat in a choppy sea: the rolling pitch and sway makes him regret his lunch. Below him, similarly confined, he hears Ted Warren, his ward companion, succumb to nausea.

Hatches on either side at the level of Nash's stretcher let in air and just enough light so he can make out the shapes of the three other men sharing the journey: Smith call-me-Smythe and two cardiac patients from Crabbe Ward, sitting pressed together on the lower bunk opposite. There's no view through the hatch from where he's lying, no way of judging their progress. It's a case of dumb endurance till the ambulance pulls up and the engine is shut off, and he guesses they've arrived.

There's the sound of footsteps on gravel, and then a sudden burst of light as the rear doors of the ambulance swing open. In a dazzle of sunshine, Nash sees nurses in starched linens, waiting to help the sitting passengers out. A medical orderly bustles by, calls in as he passes. 'Hold up, gents, your turn next,' but Nash doesn't care about the wait. Even when Warren is stretchered away, he's in no hurry to be moved. First in, last out means he gets a blessed few minutes of stillness and sweet air, some precious moments when he's actually alone.

All too soon his peace is shattered by the business of extracting him from the ambulance. As a couple of orderlies tilt his stretcher down from its high perch, he gets a flash of an imposing facade: stone pillars and statues in niches on either side of an open front door. Inside, he's carried through a lofty ceilinged hall, glimpsing a grand stairway. He loses count of the turns before he's brought into a room filled with hospital beds, feet facing in towards the centre of the room, iron bedheads incongruous against crimson walls hung with pictures of horses.

'Yours is the bed by the window, mate,' the orderly at the foot of the stretcher says, cocking his head towards the far wall. 'Reckon you could walk it? Bit of a tight spot for us to manoeuvre.'

'I can try.' The yielding canvas and tightly tucked blanket make it a struggle to free himself and sit up. No need to let the orderlies know how light-headed he feels, it's only a few steps to the bed. He swings his legs over the side, feels the odd sensation of some priceless rug beneath his bare feet. A heave, and he's standing.

'Steady now, mate.' It's all a bit of a haze, but he manages one wobbly step, and then another. His vision blurs, greys. As he reaches for a handhold, something to steady himself, there's a rush of air and a rustle of starch, and he becomes aware of a reassuring presence beside him. He feels a hand slide under his arm, an arm slip round his waist.

'What the blazes do you think you're doing?' A woman's voice, sharp and authoritative. 'This man shouldn't be on his feet. He was in a coma yesterday.'

The hand supports him for three more shaky steps to his bed, somehow applies an irresistible upward pressure that has him lying down without apparent effort on his part. The greyness ebbs.

'Now that was a silly thing to do, wasn't it, Mr Nash? It is Mr Nash, I presume?'

The nurse staring down at him, hands on hips, is stick thin. She can't be more than five feet tall, because she's eye to eye with him as he rests back on the flat pillow. How she managed to support him, get him into bed single-handed seems like some kind of conjuring trick. He must be the best part of a foot taller, and easily twice her weight. But she looks completely unruffled. Her all-white uniform and the nun-like cap which hides her hair is as perfectly neat as if it's come straight from the laundry. She looks to be in her sixties, and her skin has the soft wrinkles and sallow tint he associates with people who've spent time working in hot climates. But there's a twinkle in her dark eyes and a lilting brogue in her voice that counter the reprimand.

'Yes.' The monosyllable handily admits to both parts of the question.

'So, you'll be a good fellow and stay quiet in your bed now, won't you? Unless you want me to stick you with a sedative?'

'I'll pass. I feel enough like pincushion already.'

'Ah, yes. And aren't you the lucky one with the penicillin in you? Miracle drug it may be, but just you remember, it won't raise the dead.'

'Fair enough,' he says weakly. 'I'll be good.'

She grins at him, and he sees that, severe as she might seem, she's earned the lines on her face with much laughter.

'I'll get someone to bring you a cup of tea,' she says. 'Then it's a nap before supper. If your temperature stays down, though the dear Lord knows why it should after all these shenanigans, I might let you sit up for your meal.'

'Thank you . . . Sister?'

'Staff Nurse,' she corrects him. 'O'Shaughnessy's the name, but they mostly just call me Irish.'

'One of the movers and shakers?' he murmurs and hears her laugh.

'Aren't you the smart one?' She pats his hand. 'Perhaps we won't bother with the tea. You just sleep.'

And he does.

I get to the police station in the nick of time. WPC Shaw at the reception desk greets me with a wink, goes straight off to tell Sergeant Tilling I've arrived. But though he made the appointment himself, I'm not surprised when she comes back to tell me he's busy and I'll have to wait.

It's a game, of course, all about who's in charge. I suppose he's trying to put me on edge, hoping I'll say something I shouldn't. That I'll trip myself up, change my story, admit some kind of guilt. Except there's nothing to change. What I've already told him is the truth. Oh, I've left things out, but I haven't told any lies.

The worst thing about waiting is trying to keep the flood of thoughts at bay. Not to let myself feel, to remember. I'd welcome a battle of wits with Tilling. So I'm pleased rather than otherwise when he calls me into his office at last.

'Sit down, Mrs Lester,' he says. 'You might as well be comfortable.'

But any comfort I might have felt is shattered when he cautions me. 'You understand it's just a formality?' he says.

I understand . . . *something*, I suppose. That the gloves are off. We're no longer on the same side in this investigation, at least for now. I know I'll need to be careful, but I'm not sure where the danger lies.

'Right, tell me again,' he says. 'What you told me at the hospital.'

I pull myself together. Tell my story as I told it before, not word for word, but essentially the same. He makes occasional notes, throws in a question or two, but he seems almost bored. It unsettles me in a way that keeping me waiting didn't. If this is just a preliminary round, what knock-out punch is he holding in reserve?

'Right,' he says, when I come to a halt. 'You've had your say. Now it's my turn.'

He opens a drawer in the desk, takes out a shallow cardboard box. Sets it down on the desktop and opens the lid. Inside, there's the ring that they found in the ashes of the car, and the scalpel handle I gave him. He prods the ring with a finger, rolling it over on the cardboard. If it's a ploy to draw my attention, there's no need. I can't take my eyes off it.

All this time, there's been a tiny glimmer of hope beneath my belief that Richard was part of this mystery: either victim or killer. A chance that I might have made a mistake, and the ring would turn out not to be his after all. But that hope dies the moment I see the ring again. I don't have to touch it, though my fingers ache to snatch it away. To hide it. Hide *from* it, and the truth.

'I've spoken to Miss Haward,' Tilling says. 'She was very helpful. Came up with a few details you didn't think fit to mention. Starting with the fact you had a big row with your husband, Mr Richard Lester, the probable victim of this crime, not much more than forty-eight hours before he was killed.'

If he thinks that'll upset me, he's way off the mark. I'd expected Aggie to tell him about it, told her this morning not to hold back. 'It wasn't that big.'

'That's not the impression Miss Haward gave me.'

'She lives a quiet life, Sergeant. My husband and I . . . nothing was said on Friday that hadn't been said a hundred times before.'

'He wanted you to go back to him and you refused.'

'As I've done dozens of times before.'

He gives the ring one final poke. Picks up the scalpel handle. 'You say you found this yesterday? In that same clearing where you told me you and Alf Smith discovered all the blood?'

'Yes. And yes.'

'I didn't see you pick it up.'

I shrug.

'And there are no fingerprints on it, Mrs Lester. None at all. Why do you think that would be?'

'How would I know?'

'Now that's just the question I'm asking myself. If Mrs Lester is innocent, I'm saying, and she found this here handle by chance, why didn't she tell me about it there and then? And why aren't there any fingerprints on it? Not even hers. That's a bit of a puzzle, now, isn't it, Mrs Lester?'

'I've worked with the coroner long enough to know how to treat physical evidence. I used my handkerchief to pick the handle up. Perhaps the marks got rubbed off.' I console myself with the thought that none of it is actually a lie.

'Ah, yes, all your experience of murder investigation. Stands you in good stead to know what to do.'

I have the uncomfortable feeling he's playing the same double-tongued game as me. But I can't acknowledge it. The only thing to do is shrug as if I've no idea what he's talking about.

'Funny, isn't it, how close to home it keeps coming, Mrs Lester?'

The way he keeps repeating my name grates on my nerves. 'I don't know what I'm supposed to say to that.'

'You can start by telling me where you were on Sunday night,' he snaps.

It hits me with all the force of an express train. Squashes me flat as a penny on the line. What an idiot I've been, my thoughts so preoccupied with protecting Bram from suspicion, keeping Alf out of trouble, that it hasn't occurred to me to worry about my own position. But it's the first thing anyone thinks when murder is done. A wife's dead? Suspect the husband. A husband? Must be the wife. Estranged as Richard and I were, how much more of a motive must that seem?

'You think . . . my God, you're asking me for an alibi?'

'I'm asking you to tell me where you were on Sunday night.'

'I was at Oliver's Battery. Sam Partridge's goat farm. I went over on Friday afternoon, not long after the argument. I'll admit, I was upset. I wanted to get away. I was there all weekend, didn't come back till early Monday morning. If you've spoken to Alice Beech, you'll know Richard was most definitely alive and kicking on Sunday.'

'Witnesses?'

'To what?'

'That you were at the farm. That you didn't get on that nippy little bike of yours and pop back to see your husband. Perhaps you'd found out about his affair with Miss Beech and wanted to confront him with it. Perhaps you lost your temper and stabbed him. Provocation, an accident? A jury would understand that.'

'Right. And they'd accept that after I'd killed him, I'd put his body in a car and set it alight in the middle of the night. Just as a little joke, perhaps?'

His focus narrows. I'm walking a perilous line by goading him. 'It's a theory.'

'It's ridiculous, and you know it. If I'd had anything to do with Richard's death, why would I have told you about the place on Spaniard's Lane at all? What would be the sense in that, then going back and covering the evidence up? And why would I have given you the scalpel handle? I'd have had to be nuts.'

He nods. 'I don't think you're that. But it might be a double bluff.'

'I wish I were that bright. Then I might be able to work out who did kill him, and why.'

He drops the handle back in the box with the ring, shuts the lid. 'Where were you this afternoon? After you came back from Southampton? I told you to go home, but your landlady, Mrs Gray, said you weren't there. And you weren't at the office either unless Miss Haward was lying.'

'She wasn't. Neither of them was. I went to Sam's. The farm. Played with my pet goat. Helped Sam stook the hay.'

'Fitting up your alibi?'

It's too much. I can't contain my temper any longer. 'Yeah, the goat will speak up for me. His name's Noah.'

'This attitude of yours isn't helpful, Mrs Lester. Not helpful at all.'

'I didn't kill Richard. Even if I'd wanted to, I wouldn't have known where to look for him. He'd said on Friday he was due to embark for France over the weekend. I'd no idea he was staying with my grandfather till Alice Beech told me two days ago. If I wanted him dead . . .' my voice breaks, but I plough on '. . . I could just have waited. Hoped the Germans would do the job for me.'

He nods. 'And did you? Want him dead, I mean?'

'How many times have I got to say it? I didn't love him, but I'm sorry he died. I never wanted that. It's not just one person's fault when a marriage fails. I have my share of the blame. I should have known when I married him, he couldn't be faithful. Don't you see, I'd have been glad if I'd heard he'd been courting Alice Beech? Then I could have started divorce proceedings myself.' I won't cry, not again. Not now, when he's looking at me with such pity. 'It horrifies me to know . . . to think of that dreadful burned body and know it's his. Surely you can understand that?'

He folds his arms, leans back in his chair. Fixes his gaze on the ceiling. 'I'll level with you, Mrs Lester. The way you've been acting, I'd be within my rights to arrest you. Obstruction of the police in their duties if nothing else.'

'But—'

'Let me finish.' It feels like a bad sign that he still doesn't look at me. 'The thing is, whatever I might believe, I have to show due diligence. Explore all the avenues. And I can't have you running about loose and contaminating the evidence until I've finished talking to the people I need to take statements from. There's this Sam Partridge to see now, and Mr Nash. And the hospital say I can't see him till the morning. So I'll make you an offer.' He brings his gaze down from the ceiling, turns it on me. 'I won't arrest you as such, but I will put you in custody overnight. The holding cell here's none too shabby. It's warm and dry and we'll feed you. Won't even lock the door if you'll give me your word not to try and leave until I say you can.'

'If you'll take my word for that, why won't you take it I won't interfere?'

'I can't,' he says. 'Not as things are. I can fudge your stay here, make it look good. But I can't square it with the paperwork if I let you go tonight.'

'I haven't got much choice, then, have I?'

Tilling lets out a long breath that seems like relief. 'Not really, no. If it's any consolation, it's the same for us both. We'll just have to take it on the chin.'

Irish is as good as her word. Nash is promoted to two pillows and allowed to sit up in bed to eat his supper. One of the side effects of the penicillin seems to be that he feels both hungry and vaguely sick at the same time, so it's helpful to find the food's an improvement on lunch at the hospital. He works his way doggedly through a plate of stewed beef and potatoes. The sooner he gets his strength back, the sooner he'll be able to go home.

By half past eight in what Nash has learned is called Red Ward, the night staff are already beginning the night routine. There are a dozen patients in the room, middle-aged men sporting various plaster casts and bandages. Nash hasn't had a chance to speak to any of them, he doesn't even know their names. It feels like being twelve again, the new boy in the dormitory at boarding school. Not knowing what to expect, hoping somewhere there'll be a friendly face. Smith call-me-Smythe has been taken elsewhere, but happily, Ted Warren, his neighbour from the Southampton ward, is next door to him here, too.

As the orderlies hustle through the business of settling everyone down for the night, Nash wants to protest. He's done nothing but sleep most of the day, and now he's wide awake. But it's no good. The routine can't be altered for one individual. He's lined up straight in his bed like everyone else, the covers turned down the regulation amount. Though it's full daylight outside, the curtains are drawn, and night-lights lit, one over every third bed. Tiny pools of gold light shine comfort into the premature gloom.

Ted is on Nash's good side this time. Perhaps ten years younger than Nash, he's a burly, dark-haired bruiser of a man who's finished up in hospital after an accident at the flour mill.

'Got a sack dropped on me head,' he'd told Nash earlier, scratching the place where his scalp has been shaved. A line of stitches like spider's legs cut across the pale flesh. 'That Corby bloke cut a hole in me head. Told me he had to do it to save me life.'

'He's supposed to be the best.'

'Cuh. Did it while I was awake, didn't he? Said he had to know where he was cutting.' He'd reached across, picked up his left hand with his right, showed how the fingers flop and curl, apparently useless. 'And I still land up like this. Same as a bloody stroke. Me leg is nearly as bad. You wait till you see me trying to walk.'

Nash hadn't known how to respond.

'Bloody Corby,' Ted said. 'Bloody sadist. Saved me life, but for what? No good to the missus now. Three kids under ten and I'll never get another job in me life.'

*

Now, though, Ted doesn't seem particularly despondent. 'Cuh,' he says. 'Tucked up for the night like a lot of bloody kids. Even me youngest won't be in bed yet.'

'Shh,' someone cautions from a bed on the other side of the room. 'People are trying to sleep.'

Ted grimaces. 'You tired?' he whispers.

'Not nearly,' Nash says in a low voice. 'I was hoping for a visitor. But if they lock us down this early every night . . .'

'Yeah. Grim. Wasn't that early on Cowen.'

'Mr Nash. Mr Warren.' It's Irish, her voice low, but it carries clearly from the half-open doorway. 'That's enough now. Off to sleep with you, Mr Warren. Mr Nash, I'll have to give you your penicillin jab at ten. Have a little doze till then.'

Time passes, so perhaps he does doze. It doesn't feel like it, he'd swear he hears every hurrying footstep, every hushed exchange in the hallway outside. Every snore from his fellow patients. Ted's the worst, despite his protestations. If it goes on like this, Nash doesn't know how he'll ever get to sleep.

At last Irish returns, an enamel kidney dish in hand. Nash can see the syringe and long needle, resigns himself to the inevitable.

'Which side?' she asks as she loosens the bedclothes.

'Left this time.' He rolls, feeling this afternoon's injection site protest.

'Sharp scratch,' she says, but he barely feels it. Even the burn of fluid as it's injected is less painful than usual. 'All done.'

He tugs the thin fabric of his trouser back into place, glad to restore his dignity. 'You're good at that. It didn't hurt at all.'

'So I should be. I was nursing before you were born.'

'Hardly,' he says. 'You're not that old.'

'Just between you and me, I'm sixty-five. They should have put me out to grass years ago.' She's been on duty since he arrived at two so she must be tired, though she doesn't seem to be in any hurry. 'Never you tell a soul, mind.'

'No one would believe me.' In the dim ward, in the silence of many sleepers, it feels almost like flirting. But the truth is, she may well have donned her uniform for the first time while he was still in nappies.

'Get away. I'm too old to be charmed by the likes of you.'

He grins. He can't help it. But he is puzzled why she should be so tender towards him. 'Now who's laying it on thick? No one's ever accused me of being a charmer before.'

'Their loss.' She skims a featherlight glance over the dressings on his face. 'Trenches?'

'Passchendaele.'

'I was there.'

That explains it. It isn't personal. He knows he's never met her before today. But there's a bond between them, a shared experience they'll never forget. 'Thank you.'

'See, I told you. Charmer.' She reaches into her pocket. 'I wasn't supposed to do this, but . . .'

'What?'

'There's a letter for you. Personal. Someone took it to Cowen when you were sleeping. It got put in the ambulance with your notes. Mr Corby-Clifford didn't want you to have it, said you shouldn't be upset, but ... you're not a child. I won't tell if you don't.'

19

Thursday, evening and night

I T'S ONE OF THE ODDEST experiences I've ever had. Once I agree to stay at the police station overnight, I'm treated almost like a guest. The holding cell's basic, but then so's the shepherd's hut on the farm. And this is warmer.

There's a bunk bed and a bentwood chair, a metal jug and basin on a shelf in the far corner, a covered bucket beneath. The walls are unplastered brick painted a shiny cream colour that's somehow reminiscent of the crust on spoiled milk. But Tilling takes my word and keeps his: the heavy metal door is left ajar, and I've permission to use the lavatory in the corridor rather than the bucket. A polite fiction pretending I could walk out at any minute if I chose. And though I hate the thought I can't, I don't try. I'm sure if I did, I'd find myself no longer treated as an awkward kind of guest, but a prisoner.

The worst of it is the isolation, the enforced idleness. I've got nothing to do but sit and think. Perhaps that was what Tilling wanted: for me to reflect on my sins, confess to something that will transform his enquiries.

I might not be able – or willing – to add anything helpful to the account of my investigation so far, but I can
still use my brain to think things through. Review what
I know. Stuck in this cell, I've got plenty of time for it.
Though Tilling's taken away my option to leave, he's left
me my bag. In it, my notebook and pencil. Through the
evening, while there's light enough, I sit cross-legged on
my bunk and make a list. A record of speculation.

First suspect: Josephine Lester. Motive: to get rid of an
inconvenient spouse. Cross her off. I know *she* didn't do it.

Next, from Tilling's point of view anyway, has got to be
Bram. I'm equally sure he's not guilty. Though he's capable, as anyone might be in theory, of killing in the heat of
the moment or by accident, he's not the man to kill in cold
blood. And it would have to have been in cold blood, for
him to have gone back after leaving Alice Beech at her door.
Searched out Richard, slaughtered him in that clearing on
the edge of Spaniard's Lane. Because I'm as certain as I can
be that it's the place where my husband died. Where his body
lay, blood soaking into the soil, until someone took it off to
the car and set fire to it.

Not Bram. Never Bram.

But my certainty that he's innocent won't be enough for
Tilling. He'll hare after motive. Opportunity. Alibi.

Motive? I suspect the sergeant will think it's the same as
mine. To get rid of a barrier to our relationship. But that's
a complete red herring. Bram had quashed any tenderness
between us as soon as Richard turned up last year.

Opportunity? Alibi?

I know, if Tilling doesn't, how sick Bram must already have been on Sunday night. How even his ordinary migraines disable him. He'd told Alice he had a headache at ten, so he'd have gone straight to the office where I'd found him the next morning. Though I wish he'd gone home, had Fan take care of him, it's not what he does when he's ill. He hides himself away, deals with the vomiting and pain alone.

Leaving aside what I know of him, the man he is, it would have been a physical impossibility for him to have gone afterwards to find Richard. And later, early on Wednesday morning when the clearing by Spaniard's Lane had been disturbed, he'd been in hospital, in a coma.

Write it down. No motive, no opportunity. Bram's not a killer.

Who then? Who?

The time gap. That's the thing that puzzles me. Assuming that meal was the lunch he'd eaten with Alice Beech, he must have been dead by eleven. And the car hadn't been set alight till 3 a.m. It's possible, of course, that the body had been in the car all the time. But I don't believe it, and the evidence doesn't support it. There was no sign of blood loss at the burn site. And the risk that someone would come by, discover the body must surely rule it out.

It has to be someone who knew Richard. Who knew about the broken-down car, the connection between them. Who saw the vehicle as the ideal means to get rid of the body.

It can't have been chance, it's too cold, too deliberate for that. Not some passing homicidal stranger. Someone who knew he'd borrowed the car that morning. The likelihood is, it's someone I've spoken to already.

Alice Beech? By her own account she's got no more of an alibi than Bram. And though she might have denied it when I spoke to her, she must have known she'd been dumped by Richard.

Her father, the colonel. There's the evidence of those burned-off eyebrows, that terrible congested chest. He could so easily have been present when the car went up in flames. Alice had said she hadn't wanted to go to him, but I've only got her word for it. And even if she hadn't run to him, she could easily have telephoned, told him what had happened. If he'd known about what Richard had done, I can easily imagine him going off to avenge her honour. He's a military man through and through, used to killing.

Would he have needed help, though?

Capstaff. I'm sure where his loyalties lie. He'd do anything his master wanted. For my money, he'd be capable of carrying out murder on his own account, too. I can believe he's got the mindset to kill. If Alice had told *him* what had happened, he might have done it for her, to protect her and spare her father from knowing she'd been shamed.

I have to stop my speculation. Or at least, stop writing it down because a policeman calls from the corridor.

'Ten o'clock, Mrs Lester. Lights out.'

The lighting in my cell goes from adequate to almost nil as the central fitting is turned off. Now there's just the thin blue glow from an emergency bulb over the bunk, a grey streak of fading daylight from the high window to remind me it's still only eight o'clock by the sun.

I put away my notebook, hopeful that tomorrow what I've written will help me persuade Tilling to look elsewhere than me or Bram for the killer. I take off my shoes, my jumper and skirt. Lie down in my underwear, pull the thin blanket up to my waist for decency's sake. Despite the open door, I haven't forgotten I'm under observation here. I'm not a guest. The policeman on night shift will check on me while I sleep, just as he's been doing all through the evening.

But when it comes to it, sleeping's what I can't do. I've never felt more awake.

In the gloom, sight denied me, my other senses sharpen. There's the carbolic smell of Jeyes Fluid they must have used to disinfect the cell at some point, the lingering scent of the fish and chip supper they brought me.

The walls are thick, but the barred window rattles in the breeze, lets in disconnected sounds from outside. An owl calls, *Tuh-whit*. Is answered, *Tuh-whoo*. A car passes on the Hundred. Somewhere around midnight, a cat yowls with unrequited desire. Inside, regular as clockwork, there's the passage of feet down the corridor, the expected pause as someone looks in or listens. I force myself to lie still, to keep my breathing even, but each time I tense, resenting the surveillance.

The thin, hard mattress is uncomfortable beneath my body. The pillow's lumpy as a bag of rocks under my head. The coarse wool blanket prickles against my bare legs. Physical discomforts I might be able to ignore. It's the other kind of feelings that keep me awake.

Emotions I can't hold at bay any longer. My continuous anxiety for Bram. Wondering how he is, whether the penicillin is as good as they say. If the porter was right, and he really has improved. If only I'd been allowed to see him for myself, or even enquire . . .

Another layer. Another reason to worry. Tilling interviewing Bram in the morning. He can't suspect him, he mustn't. I'd confess myself, rather.

Perhaps I won't have to. I know Sam will confirm I was at the farm, but perhaps Tilling won't think it's enough to prove my innocence. And I've nothing else to offer. No witnesses that I'd been there all weekend, apart from the goats. No one to confirm that my only journey back to Romsey had been on Monday morning. Even the soldiers had been gone by then.

In the end, it'll all come down to whether the sergeant believes me. I'd no reason to kill Richard. His death won't make any difference to my situation. Because it wasn't Richard who'd put an end to the relationship between Bram and me. It was Bram.

The armour cracks. Alone in the cell, I cry. And once the tears start, I can't stop them, even when the next night check comes due. I curl into a ball, turn my face away from the door. Pull the blanket up round my ears and hope the policeman won't notice.

Approach. Pause and retreat. All's quiet again. Half stifled by the blanket and the sobs that disrupt my breathing, I sit up.

Bram. Whatever happens, the man I love. No help for it, no cure. No possibility of change.

Richard. I *had* loved him once. Loved him to folly. The idea that he's gone and that the terrible burned body is his, is a horror beyond words.

But I know it must be true. Tilling said he'll have to confirm Richard's identity by checking dental records, but I'm already sure. There's the ring, and those broken bones. I remember the day it happened so well.

February 1929. Near Brading, Isle of Wight

After a mild spell at the beginning of the year, the cold had set in. The coldest winter temperatures, they said, since 1895. Though it was unusual for the Isle of Wight to have persistent snow and frost, by the end of the month it was cold enough for the Eastern Yar to freeze over where it ran through the marshes.

I'd been Richard's secretary for a year by then, his mistress for almost three months. His first wife had left him, gone back to her parents the previous summer. I'd never met her, though I'd taken her calls when she'd rung him, fobbed her off with his excuses. Passed on her tearful messages.

I should have felt guilty, but I didn't. He'd told me their marriage had been a mistake from the start. That, at least, was true. As I'd find out for myself, marriage and Richard weren't compatible. He told me she was frigid, that they hadn't slept together for years. I was foolish enough to believe him, to put the blame on her. No wonder their marriage had failed: a man like Richard couldn't be expected to be celibate. For myself, I was besotted. In those early months, I couldn't imagine not wanting him. Couldn't even guess at the pain of not being wanted by him.

I don't think anything could have stopped me then. Not common decency, not shame at stealing another woman's husband. Not the thought of my mother's history, my own miserable childhood labelled as a bastard. Not even the instinct for self-preservation. I'd flung myself headlong into the affair. It wasn't till five years later, married to Richard as soon as his wife had divorced him, that I surfaced from the madness. Realised I'd been drowning all along.

But that February day when I was twenty-eight and in love, our future together seemed to shine as bright as the ice that spread across the river, as beckoning and beautiful as the sun on the hoar frost.

There was a crowd of us from the hospital, mostly off-duty doctors and nurses, and me from the clerical staff. It was the kind of fraternisation that was frowned on by the hospital authorities, but we didn't care. We'd gathered at Silverbank, Richard's parents' home. A grand old-fashioned mansion of a place, and the old folk happy to host us, recalling long-ago house parties before the Great War.

I don't remember all their names now. All that crowd of irresponsible young women, reckless young men. Alec Corby-Clifford was there, and Oonagh, his girlfriend of the day. But as for the others, they were just noise. For me, Richard was the only one who mattered. The only one I really saw at all.

There'd been a party on the Saturday night, and we'd slept in late. When we finally came down to breakfast, it was nearly lunchtime. We ate kedgeree and boiled eggs, if our hangovers would let us, drank black coffee if they wouldn't.

Someone suggested a walk, but we voted that too boring, too tame. Someone else suggested we go skating. I think it must have been Alec, but we all fell in with it, Richard as eager as anyone.

'I used to be a champion,' he crowed. 'My skates are here somewhere.'

He pulled them out from a cupboard in the boot room, together with half a dozen other pairs. Ancient things, some of them, dating back to Victoria. We banged off the rust and cobwebs and set out.

I'd have followed him anywhere. A stretch of dodgy ice on a part-frozen river was no deterrent to me, though I'd never skated before in my life. Oh, I'd gone sliding on winter ice on Tadburn Lake with the gang, the hobnails in my boots screeching across the rough surface, scoring through to the water. Gone home after with wet feet to face a beating for playing Tom Fool. Now, though strapping what seemed like a knife blade onto my shoes and trying to walk on thin ice seemed unlikely to turn out well, I was as rash as I'd ever been, unwilling to refuse a challenge.

There weren't enough skates for us all to go on the ice at once, so there was a group of watchers on the bank as I teetered out onto the ice in Richard's wake. Struggling to keep my knees soft and my ankles firm as he directed, I managed to stay upright. Took one step, and then another, thrilled as the ice began to slide under my blade. Richard circled effortlessly round me, encouraging me. Grabbing my hands and towing me along. There was a moment of exhilarating, terrifying speed as ice sprayed from beneath my blades for a heady few seconds. Then my balance tipped, and I went arse down on the ice, all dignity lost.

The watchers cheered as Richard hauled me up, brushed me down. Planted a smacking kiss on my cold lips. 'Again,' he insisted.

Around us, the others who'd bagged skates swooped and whirled. No one was as much of a novice as me, but it didn't matter while Richard held my hands, prompted me, laughing, to try again.

All too soon I had to stop, legs turned to jelly.

'Josephine Fox,' he said as I sat down, panting, on the bank to take off my skates. My fingers wouldn't co-operate, I was shaking so hard. 'I'm proud of you. You're all heart, do you know that? Look how you're trembling. Don't you ever know when to stop?'

Every fall, every bruise, every tired muscle and awkward step was worth it in that moment. I didn't even care that Oonagh, another self-proclaimed expert, had snatched the skates from my hand and put them on, grumbling about how I'd wasted valuable skating time.

'Go back on the ice if you want,' I'd said to Richard then. 'Tutoring me, you haven't had a chance to shine.'

Another smile, another dizzying kiss and he'd gone. After my faltering efforts, his progress seemed like magic. Sweeping round in wide circles, gathering speed. Figures of eight, forwards and back.

Regardless of the cold seeping through my clothes, I'd sat mesmerised and watched him. Ridiculously proud in my turn of this man who'd claimed me as his lover.

Out on the ice, he was skating with Oonagh. Just the two of them, the rest of us watching as she matched him move for move. I didn't feel jealous, but I wished I had her expertise. Her grace. If I'd made him laugh, she was making him smile.

It was a contest now. Each of them setting the other a challenge. A sudden halt, a swooping change of direction. A spin, a jump.

There was a moment when everything seemed poised, perfect in the brilliant reflected light. A twisting leap from Oonagh, the most difficult figure either of them had tried. Richard was gathering speed for a jump in his turn when someone shouted from the bank. 'Go for it, you old rogue.'

For a heart-stopping moment he hesitated, his attention diverted. Then he launched, but his skate caught on some projection in the ice. Off balance, he fell, sprawling onto his outstretched left arm.

I couldn't have been the only one who heard the double crack of the breaking bones, loud as gunshot. Though I was first on *the ice at his side, I was the only one without medical training, so they sent me off to find a telephone and ring for help.*

I'd hated to see how much pain he was in that day. How much pain he went on suffering for weeks after that. Weeks when he couldn't work; when his temper was short. Months before he had full use of his arm. I blamed myself for telling him to go back on the ice when he was tired from teaching me. I blamed Oonagh for egging him on. And Alec Corby-Clifford for distracting him at the crucial moment.

Nash lies awake far into the night. His mind is busy with the implications raised by Jo's letter. It's lucky it's reached him tonight. Lucky it's reached him at all, come to that. If it hadn't been for Irish, so surprisingly partisan on his behalf, it would never have been delivered. He wouldn't have got the warning in time.

How many people have read it on its way to him? he wonders. Though Jo had clearly sealed the envelope, marked it 'Private', the gummed strip has been torn open, the damaged flap tucked carelessly back inside. Whoever had done it hadn't even tried to disguise the interference. More echoes of the boarding school. It seems as if patients here have no more rights to privacy than schoolboys.

If it's troubling to think of other eyes reading it, more troubling still is the news she's sent him. For the umpteenth time, he clicks the button on the tiny torch Irish lent him, doing his best to shield the narrow beam of light as he passes it over the paper.

Dear Bram,

I'm sorry but I can't visit you today after all. You know I wouldn't willingly break my promise, but I've had to agree not to see you. I'll be with you tomorrow, though, if they'll let me.

According to the porter who's going to deliver this letter, word is you're making good progress now. He's been very helpful, much more informative than the ward staff.

We're almost certain we've identified the occupant of the car. Seems it could be Richard. Remember what I said that morning about what must have happened? Turns out I was right. Sergeant Tilling is going to come and speak to you about it as soon as they'll let him in.

Please take care,

Jo.

'Mr Nash? What're you doing there?' It's one of the night orderlies, a plump little fellow smelling of cigarettes and onions. He sniggers. 'Hope you're not reading dirty magazines under the covers.'

With a ridiculous jolt of guilt, Nash clicks off the torch, thrusts it and the letter under his body. 'Sorry. Didn't realise the light would show.'

'On and off like a lighthouse all bloody night. Must be interesting.'

Nash ignores the repeated attempt to fish for details. 'What time is it, Mr . . . ? Sorry, I don't know your name.'

'Scobie. Jack Scobie.' The man doesn't bother to look at a watch. 'It's gone three. Just got back from my break, like. Mr Corby-Clifford isn't going to be happy when he hears you've been awake all night.'

'Don't tell him, then. I'll keep mum if you do.'

'Fancy a cuppa? Might help you get off.' Another snigger.

Though he doesn't want tea himself, Nash is an old enough hand at hospital routine to know Scobie might be asking because he wants a cup himself. And if it means the orderly will leave him alone for a few minutes, it'll be worth it. 'OK. Thank you.'

As soon as Scobie leaves the room, Nash retrieves the letter and Irish's penlight, tucks them away deep in the back of the locker by his bed. He feels a bit foolish, but when Scobie comes back with the tea, he's glad he took the precaution. The orderly fusses with the bedclothes, obviously searching for what Nash was looking at.

'Right, now,' Scobie says. 'Get that tea down you and then off to sleep. I'll come back and check in a couple of minutes.'

Nash gulps the scalding liquid down, settles back against his pillows and pretends to sleep. It's not long before the orderly creeps back, stands looking at Nash for a long minute before taking out his own small torch and sweeping the beam over the locker. Nash risks looking out between his lashes as Scobie fumbles in the top compartment, reaches into the washbag and between the folds of the towel. He's just made up his mind to speak up, let the orderly know he's being watched, when a voice calls from across the room. It's the man in the bed nearest the door, almost as heavily bandaged as Nash is himself. 'Mr Scobie?'

The orderly gives one more sharp look at Nash before slipping away to the other man's side. A long consultation follows, more tea is brought. All the time, Nash feigns sleep, his mind busy with speculation.

What on earth did the man think he was doing? Is he some kind of stool pigeon for Corby-Clifford or just a nosy parker on his own account? Whatever the case, it's shaken Nash. Sleep is further away than it's ever been.

He turns it all over in his head. He doesn't need to read the letter again to understand how carefully Jo's crafted it. So neutral it's almost code. The reference to murder, the warning to take care: Scobie could have read both and never realised their significance.

He shivers. That terrible corpse is Jo's husband. If it's a shock to him, how much worse must it be for her? There's no trace of it in the letter, though. No personal feelings except for regret she can't visit.

He worries she may be under suspicion. Is that why they won't let her see him? It would be a policeman's first thought. Nine times out of ten, murder is a domestic crime. But Jo . . . she's as straight as an arrow. Despite the way Richard Lester treated her, she'd never have done him harm. Tilling must surely see that. In physical terms alone, it's impossible. Lester was tall, big-boned, and though she's tough, she's slight. She could never have manhandled his corpse.

But perhaps the warning is for him. If Miss Beech has told the story of his encounter with Lester on Sunday evening, he might very well be a suspect. Tilling's got no particular trust in him; they've clashed heads too often in the past for that. Even before the business with poor George Hine last year, they'd never exactly pulled in tandem, despite both being on the same side of the law.

And things being as they are – as they *were* – he might appear to have a motive. He shifts carefully, checking Scobie's nowhere in sight. The bandage round his head is tiresome, clinging to the pillows as he tries to move, tweaking the wound beneath. Such a bloody nuisance to be ill. He hates the feeling of helplessness, of dependence. The sooner he can get out of here, the better.

He can't stop thinking of Jo, her pain. If only he'd insisted she shouldn't go with them that morning, she'd have been spared the sight of the body. The horror of it. Bad enough when they thought it was a stranger who'd died. But now she knows it was Richard, how much worse must she feel? She'd loved the man once.

It turns his stomach to think of it, but he fights the nausea down. He must get better; he must get strong. He must get out of here, do his job.

The dream of the burned man calling on him for justice hovers at the edge of his consciousness as he finally slides into sleep.

Who killed Richard Lester?

Who might have wanted the bastard dead more than he did himself?

20

Friday 9ᵗʰ June 1944, morning

DAWN HAD BEEN LIGHTENING THE sky by the time I'd dropped off. So when I wake with a dry mouth and a crick in my neck, pulled out of a deep sleep by the sound of voices, I'm disorientated. I've no idea what the time might be, or even where I am. Then it all comes flooding back. If last night I'd been philosophical about my detention, this morning I'm in a fury of impatience, ready for a fight. I have to get out of here, I have to get on with my job. Tilling can go hang with his 'take it on the chin' and promises. Open door or no open door, he'll have to arrest me if he wants me to stay any longer.

Feeling grubby and dishevelled, I dress hurriedly in yesterday's clothes. My door is still ajar, so I tiptoe quickly along to the toilet for a pee, run my face and hands under the cold tap. Fully awake, I turn towards the public areas of the police station rather than go back to my cell. The voices are louder now, partly because I'm nearer, but mostly because it's a quarrel, and everyone involved seems to be getting het up.

It's soon apparent that the quarrel's about me, so I feel justified in creeping closer to the door, listening in unashamedly.

'I told the lady Mrs Lester volunteered to stay.' I recognise PC Summers's voice.

'And I told him,' my landlady, Dot, chips in, 'that nobody told *me*. Up all night, I've been, worrying about what's happened to her.'

'Me too.' My God, that's Aggie, too. Whatever's going on? 'I was expecting her to come back to the office yesterday afternoon. I was most concerned when she didn't turn up.'

'Now then,' Tilling says. 'Let's all calm down here, shall we?'

'Not until I see Mrs Lester.' That's Dot again. I can't help smiling. She's such a terrier when she's roused.

'If she's in custody, she's entitled to a solicitor,' Aggie follows up. 'She doesn't have to say anything without proper representation.'

'She agreed,' Tilling says. I almost feel sorry for him. 'We agreed it together. Her stay was completely voluntary, we never even shut the door on her. I had to see Mr Partridge, establish her whereabouts on Sunday night.'

'What for?' That's Dot. Aggie won't have to ask, she'll have guessed.

'Ongoing police enquiry,' Tilling says. 'Can't say anything more at present.'

'And *have* you seen him?' Aggie again. She's not to be diverted.

'I did, yes. Called over there last evening.'

'Then you could have let her go, couldn't you?' Her tone is as crisp as I've ever heard it. 'Sent her home last night.'

'I didn't want her talking to Mr Nash either. Not till I—'

'Mr Nash is ill,' Aggie says. 'Very ill. He's not to be disturbed with a lot of silly questions.'

'Well, you'll be glad to hear' – Tilling sounds pleased to be making a point – 'that it seems he's not so very ill after all. I've been in touch with the hospital, and he's off the seriously ill list. Going on very nicely, they tell me. And if you ladies will excuse me, I'm off to Broadlands very soon to see him.'

'What?' I burst through the door. 'Whatever are you thinking? You can't just haul him out of hospital to suit yourself.'

The four of them turn to stare at me. PC Summers has his mouth unattractively open, while Aggie and Dot flank him in front of the desk. Tilling's closest to me, red-faced as a schoolboy caught outside Woolworths with a penny chew he hasn't paid for.

'Mrs Lester. I didn't know you were awake.'

'You know now. What's this about bringing Mr Nash to Broadlands?'

'Not me,' he says. 'The hospital. They transferred him to their annexe there yesterday. Transferred a whole lot of them if it comes to that. Making room for casualties.'

My irritation resurfaces. 'Why didn't you tell me?'

For an answer, he grins, smug at getting one over on me.

'I'm coming with you,' I insist.

That takes the smile off his face. Like a comic policeman out of a pantomime he says, 'Oh no, you're not.'

I shrug. I'm not going to play along. 'It's your choice. If you want to keep an eye on me, you'll have to take me with you. Because I'm not staying here any longer unless you've got something to charge me with.'

Out of the corner of my eye, I see Dot mime applause.

'Have you got any grounds to arrest Mrs Lester?' Aggie says.

He shakes his head. 'Not as such.'

'There you are then. Let her come with you or let her go. And I should add, of course, that whether the hospital authorities have approved your visit or not, Mr Nash has no obligation to answer your questions. He doesn't even have to see you if he doesn't want to.'

'Wind your neck in, Miss Haward. And you, Mrs Lester, you can come with me. But you'll have to wait outside till I've spoken to him. No time for mucking about, we'll have to go now, or I'll be late.'

'All right. Just let me get my bag.' It's a shame to leave Aggie and Dot in the lurch after they've been so staunch in my defence, but there's no contest. I have to take the chance to see Bram. 'Later,' I say to them as I pelt through the door at Tilling's heels. 'Meet me at the tea rooms at half past twelve. We'll catch up then.'

Out in the yard, WPC Shaw is in the driver's seat of the unmarked police car. Tilling gets into the back with me, and I don't know if it's to keep a closer eye on me, or if there's something he wants to say without the policewoman hearing.

'What did Sam tell you?' I ask him as we set off.

'You know what he said,' he answers wearily. 'That you were there with him all weekend. He told me he'd have known if you'd gone anywhere, even in the middle of the night, because that dog of his would have alerted him to anyone moving around.' He makes a face. 'I have to say, she watched me like a hawk the whole time I was there.'

Lady. I bet she did if she sensed he was hostile. But she knows me so well she'd never turn a hair if I was the one moving. 'Did you see the goats?'

'Huh.' He rolls his shoulders. 'The old man insisted on showing me round. Don't take to the creatures myself. Funny eyes.'

'Clever eyes. It's so they can see if a predator's creeping up on them.'

'Huh. Beats me why you'd want to go and stay in that poky little hut. So damn quiet, it gave me the heebie-jeebies.'

That's why I go there. It's my private space, my place away from the world. I'm happier there these days than almost anywhere else. I can't bear to think of him prying about in it. 'You went into the hut?'

'No need to look like that,' he says. 'I only popped my head round the door. Not as if there was anything to see.'

Nothing visible, of course. Just my peace of mind.

He gives another roll of his shoulders, not quite a shrug. 'Proper spartan, it looks. No accounting for taste, though I must say . . .'

'What?'

'That butter's a bit of all right.'

The tension of the last few moments lets go with a whoosh, and I laugh. 'Bribed by a pound of butter.'

'Not a pound.' He looks shocked. 'A couple of ounces, that's all. Enough for my bit of toast this morning.'

My stomach rumbles. No morning toast for me. No morning anything. My fish and chip supper seems like a long time ago.

The car turns in at the entrance to Broadlands Park and we're waved through the gate. A gravel drive curves through trees and parkland in a long S shape that offers glimpses of walled gardens and a red-brick stable block, and beyond, the yellowish square of Broadlands House itself.

When we arrive at the front of the building, another set of gates stands open to a circular forecourt of gravel that borders the imposing pillared entrance. Before the war, invited guests must have been impressed by its grandeur, but today it's swamped by the mundane, the day-to-day business of hospital life. An ambulance, doors open, stands close to the entryway, a group of nurses in attendance. No one even glances our way as we pull up.

'You wait here with Shaw,' Tilling says. 'You can go in and see Mr Nash after I've spoken to him, if they'll let you.'

I watch enviously as he goes through the portico and disappears inside the house. 'Don't you ever get tired of waiting?' I say to WPC Shaw.

'You get used to it.'

'But what do you do?' Too restless to sit in the car for even one minute more, I push open the door, stand out on the gravel.

She pulls a book out of the door pocket at her side. 'Study. Police manual. I'm swatting up for the exams. Don't want to stay an auxiliary policewoman forever.'

'I'll leave you to it, then. I'm going to take a stroll around, stretch my legs.'

'Don't be long. And stay out of trouble.'

'Born for it,' I say. 'As the sparks fly upward.'

She grins. 'I'll toot the horn when I see Sergeant Tilling coming back.'

I take a path to my left that seems to skirt round the house. As I turn the corner, there's a formal garden with topiary trees that are growing rather whiskery and an oval, stone-sided pool. I'd like to look in through the windows, see if these are the rooms which house the hospital annexe, but I can't get close enough without drawing attention to myself. A second turn brings me round to the west front, where open lawns stretch down to the river. Patients in dressing gowns and slippers are making the most of the morning sunshine, tucked into wheelchairs or strolling like me, enjoying the view. I can't help wondering where Bram is in all this bustle and splendour. What Tilling's saying to him, what answers he's giving.

I'd planned to turn again at the far corner, make my way right round the building, but as I get to the turn, I see there's an extra wing that seems to bar my way. I hesitate a minute. I'm beginning to worry I've been too long, missed Shaw's signal. I'll have to go back.

By the time I reach the gravelled forecourt again, I'm in a sort of panic, not looking where I'm going. Another ambulance draws up. I dodge out of the way, trying to see whether the police car is still there, bump into a tall man in an immaculate suit. Alec Corby-Clifford.

'Whoa, careful,' he laughs, steadying me with a hand on my arm.

'Alec.' Not the most welcome of encounters. I haven't forgiven him for his treatment of Bram, won't ever forget that awful, inarticulate cry of pain. But though Alec had been brutal, I can't deny it seems his treatment has been effective if what Tilling says about Bram's transfer to Broadlands is true. I owe Alec a great deal for that, and not just in the way of settling his bill.

Politeness would be a start. 'I hope I didn't hurt you?'

His hand is still bandaged, though much more lightly today. 'Not even a twinge. What are you doing here?'

I'd have thought he could have worked that out for himself. 'Waiting to see Mr Nash, of course. Sergeant Tilling's talking to him at the moment.'

'Ah, yes. The policeman. Seemed to think it was urgent he spoke to your employer.'

'Mm.' There's a question in his tone, but I'm not going to answer it. Not before Sergeant Tilling releases the information. Though I suppose I'll have to tell him about Richard sooner or later, before the news gets round town. They were friends, after all. 'Alec, is it true what Sergeant Tilling told me? That moving Mr Nash to Broadlands means he's getting better?'

'Improving,' Alec says. 'But he's not out of the woods yet. I'm sorry, Josephine.' He gives my arm a little shake to draw my attention. 'I know you're going to be annoyed with me, but I can't let you see Mr Nash. One visitor a day is enough in his state.'

If I was upset with him before, now I could hit him. Anxiety wars with politeness, wins hands down. 'Why not, if he's doing well?'

'He is, my dear, but we want him to continue that way, don't we? It's important he's not overtired. I gather he slept very badly last night.'

'Have you seen him already?'

'Not yet.'

'So how do you . . . ?'

'Telephone, my dear.' He's unbearably patronising. 'That's why I'm here. The night nursing staff were concerned. Thought I should give him a bit of a once-over.'

'So you might change your mind when you've seen him?'

He smiles tolerantly, as if I'm a child or a half-wit. 'I'm afraid not. Now, forgive me, I must go and turf that policeman out too.'

'But—'

'Tomorrow, Josephine. We'll see if he's fit for a visit tomorrow.'

Seething and apprehensive in equal parts, I watch him stride off. Who does he think he is with his grandiose 'we'? A proper little tinpot dictator he's turned out to be. But I have to admit, some of the blame is mine. It was probably the letter I'd sent Bram that kept him awake. I hadn't wanted to tell him about Richard that way, but I didn't think I had a choice.

He had to know before Tilling sprang it on him. I've been punished now, though. I can't bear to think another day has to pass before I can see Bram again.

Nash can't find it in himself to like Corby-Clifford. He supposes he owes him a debt of gratitude for his recovery, but that's no basis for friendly feelings. He dislikes the man's hard hands and patronising manner, however clever he might be. Resents him thoroughly for the way he'd dismissed Sergeant Tilling, scolded him like a child. Then turned to Nash and dished out more of the same.

The business of taking down his bandage and dressing is as unpleasant as before. The surgeon's own injury doesn't make him any gentler as he prods at Nash's healing wound, his gloved fingers manipulating the tissues until it seems the stitches must burst. Or any more tactful, as he turns Nash's face this way and that in the light. There are no screens to hide his scarred face from the ward and he feels as exposed and vulnerable as a snail out of its shell.

'Good,' Corby-Clifford says at last, as he strips off his rubber glove. 'The exudate's dried up, and I can't feel any further foreign material in the wound. Another twenty-four hours of penicillin should see you firmly on the road to recovery. Until then, it's bed rest for you. And I'm going to prescribe a sedative. The orderly reported you were awake all night.'

Nash curses inwardly. 'I don't need a sedative.'

'You'll do as you're told,' Corby-Clifford says with an all-boys-together smile that Nash presumes is intended to take the edge off the words. If so, it fails. 'Stay in bed, sleep as much as you can. I'll see you again tomorrow. Nurse O'Shaughnessy, a clean dressing and bandage here, please.'

The surgeon moves off, heading for Ted Warren's bed. Turns, like an afterthought, with an expression Nash can't read. 'Oh, and I'm sorry, but no more visitors for you today, Nash. You've had quite enough excitement. I told Josephine – Mrs Lester – when I ran into her outside. She was waiting to come and see you, but I had to put my foot down. Perhaps tomorrow.'

Nash feels anger rise in a hot tide. Bites down on it, on the bitter words that come with it. Only just manages to keep it in check. Whatever the surgeon said about too much excitement, it seems as if he's deliberately trying to make Nash lose his temper. The only question is why?

'Rest you back, now.' It's Irish, cool fingers on his wrist as she takes his pulse. He doesn't need her to tell him it's racing, he can feel it throbbing in his face, bounding in his chest. He lets out a long breath, shuts his eye and leans back on the pillow.

'Good man.' Her voice is pitched low, so it won't carry across to the surgeon. 'There now, give yourself a moment while I get what I need to have you all tidied up and Bristol fashion.' With what seems like a casual gesture, but which he understands as blessed kindness, she tweaks the discarded dressing back over his wound before she leaves.

I lie in wait for Sergeant Tilling. I want to talk to him before he gets back in the car. He frowns as I waylay him, looks as cross as I feel. 'Ruddy doctor,' he mutters, 'who the hell does he think he is?'

Though I've been asking myself the same question ever since Alec forbade me to see Bram, I feel obliged to defend him. 'He's doing what he thinks is best for Mr Nash.'

'He won't let you see him, you know.'

'Yes. Something you have in common.'

'Huh.' He frowns. 'Suppose I deserve that.'

'Oh, call it a truce. We need to work together unless you really think Mr Nash or I had something to do with Richard's death?'

He glances sideways at me. 'Look, I'm not going to apologise for yesterday.'

'I don't expect you to.'

'But I am sorry you can't see Mr Nash today. If it's any consolation, he seems OK. He's lost a bit of weight, but he's going to be all right.'

I swallow. 'Don't be nice to me.'

'I thought you said you wanted a truce?'

'Yes. It's just … never mind. What are we going to do next? The investigation, I mean.'

He folds his arms across his chest, stands staring moodily out across the parkland. 'Good question. We're deep in the mire here, aren't we? I suppose it's occurred to you it could have been one of the Yank soldiers from the embarkation camp who killed your husband? I know they'd mostly all left by Sunday, but there were still a few stragglers about. And if that's how it was, we don't stand a chance. They've all gone off to France now. The killer's probably dead himself.'

I had thought of it. A stranger murder. I just don't believe it. 'You can't give up.'

'We never give up on murder. The book's always open. Can't always close it though.'

'Sergeant. Sergeant Tilling.' WPC Shaw comes hurrying across the gravel towards us. 'The transceiver. A message for you. The chief constable. You've got to get back to the station straightaway.'

'That damn burglary again?'

'Yes, sir.'

He sets off at a dead run. Once again, I'm pelting after him so as not to be left behind. In the car, his mood has soured and I'm half afraid to speak. 'This burglary,' I venture. 'It must be very important?'

'So important that if I told you, I'd have to lock you up again.' He leans forward to speak to Shaw. 'Put your foot down,' he says. 'Turn the bell on too if you like.'

The shrill clangour clears our path, makes further conversation impossible. But I've still got things to say, so when we get back to the police station, and WPC Shaw draws the car to a halt in the yard, I grab hold of Tilling's sleeve.

'What?'

'You never answered my question. Am I still a suspect?'

'Oh, for God's sake. No. Let me go.'

'So what was all that fuss about last night, keeping me here?'

'Call it procedure. I was fed up with you. Not half as fed up as I'm going to be if you don't let go. You'll find yourself here tonight on a proper charge. Assaulting a police officer.'

I ignore the threat. 'What about Bram? Mr Nash?'

'No. Poor bugger, he's out of it.' He pulls free of my grip, climbs out of the car.

I follow hard on his heels. 'I can go on investigating?'

'Knock yourself out. I'll be too busy chasing after stolen goods.'

'You won't—?'

'Keep me informed,' he says. 'And for pity's sake, get out of here before the chief sees you.'

It's still only half past ten, too early for my lunch with Dot and Aggie. I need to do something purposeful, new. Something that might actually push the enquiry on. The obvious thing is go and see my grandfather, try to get an idea of Richard's life here in Romsey.

Grandfather won't like me turning up on his doorstep. But that's too bad. He'll have to put up with it for once. And if the worst comes to the worst and I can't get him to speak to me, perhaps Mags will be able to tell me what I want to know.

It's Mags who opens the door to my knock. My unmarried aunt, she's cared for Grandfather ever since Granny died. She'd been like a big sister to me, just as likely to get me into mischief as box someone's ears for hurting me.

'Josy.' She's careworn, poor Mags, a long way from that bright girl who'd played tricks on her young niece. Her straight up and down figure gets no help from a wrap-around apron in faded blue, and her mousy hair is pulled back in a fierce bun that makes her look like one of those clothes peg dolls the gypsies used to sell. She rubs her chest at the sight of me, as if the shock's given her palpitations. 'What are you doing here?'

'I came to see Grandfather. It's sort of official.'

'Official? Whatever can you mean?'

'It's about Richard. Word is, he's been staying here.'

'Well, yes, but he's gone. He went off bright and early on Sunday morning.'

I won't tell her that we think he's dead unless I have to, but ... 'Can I come in, Mags? I really do need to speak to Grandfather.'

She darts glances over her shoulder, and beyond me, out into the lane. I hate to see her looking so hunted. 'I suppose. You know he's not been well. His heart.'

I had heard. Sylvie, my uncle's French wife and the only one of the family who moves between me and Grandfather with any ease, had passed on the news back in the autumn. 'Heart failure,' she'd told me then. It had been a surprise. I'd always thought his heart must be impervious, made of steel.

'I'll try not to upset him,' I say. 'But it's me or Sergeant Tilling.'

She sighs, moves aside. I step over the threshold of my childhood home for the first time in thirty years.

The smell's the same. Damp earth, no matter how hot the weather might be, because the downstairs rooms are floored with bricks laid directly into the dirt. The faintly acrid smell of coal fires which competes with the scent of Grandfather's cigarettes, hand-rolled from Gold Flake tobacco. It's not Monday, so there's no smell of soap from a boiling copper, but as Mags shoos me into the kitchen, I see the expected stack of folded linen in a basket by the range.

'Have you heard from Mr Lester?' Mags asks in a whisper. 'Is he all right?'

'I wouldn't expect to hear from him, Mags. You must know that. I heard he had a new girlfriend.'

'Shh. Not so loud. Yes, a nice girl. Very well bred. Dad's really taken a shine to her.'

'Not like me, hey?'

Her face blotches with ugly scarlet patches. 'You should have gone back to him, Josy.'

'I don't want to discuss it, Mags. It's over, that's all. How long did he stay here?'

'He wrote to Dad in March. Said he remembered how kind we'd been last year when he got back from the POW camp and came to Romsey looking for you. Asked if we'd put him up again. He said he'd been attached to a medical unit that was training round here. Course, he didn't tell us outright, but we knew he was getting ready to go off for D-Day.' The colour in her face grows deeper. 'I don't know how you can be so stubborn. That man's a hero.'

'I've never doubted his courage. I just don't want to be married to him anymore.'

The door to the parlour swings open. 'Mags, what's she doing here? Get her out. I won't have her under my roof.'

My grandfather's voice is every bit as aggressive as it ever was, though the man in the doorway looks frailer than I imagined. He'd always been wiry, tough. Kept working well into his eighties, taking his share of shifts as a porter at the local hospital until his heart condition had forced his retirement.

'Grandfather, I need to talk to you.'

'Nothing to say.'

'It's about Richard.'

'Still nothing. Get out.'

'Won't you listen to me? It's important.'

'Nothing you've got to say matters a jot. I take more notice of a fart. Mags.' He's breathing hard now, as if he's been running.

'You'll have to go,' she says.

And because, despite everything, I don't want to give the old man another heart attack, I turn away, step back out of his sight. My aunt follows me, as if to sheepdog me off the property.

I pause in the short passageway that leads to the front door. 'Mags, I'm sorry, but I do need—'

'Give me a minute,' she says in a breathless whisper. 'Let me get him settled down again. I'll meet you down by the gate in a few.'

Beyond the cottage, the spur of lane runs down to the railway. There's a gate opening onto the railway crossing, a few acres of farmland opposite that stretch down to what they call Tadburn Lake, though I've never understood why. It's never been more than a stream from what I remember.

On this side of the crossing, there's one small field which was cut off when the railway was built. A scooped-out piece of land with the track on one side and a high bank on the other where they took out the gravel for ballasting the rails. As kids, we'd played among the mysterious humps and bumps, pretended this square enclosure of earth banks was a castle, that narrow stretch of meadow a battlefield.

I sit on the field gate, perch the way we used to, though I find it less comfortable now than I did then. At the top of the high bank, the red-brick walls of the hospital loom over the lost field. Somehow it makes it seem almost more fitting for the games we'd played, a perfect scene for a siege.

It's quite a lot more than a minute or two before Mags appears. She's carrying a small grey duffel bag in her hand. She looks flustered, and I feel sorry for her, piggy in the middle of so much hostility.

'I'll have to be quick,' she says. 'If he thinks I'm talking to you I don't know what might happen. Here, take this.' She holds out the bag.

'What is it?'

'Your husband's things. He left them behind.' She shakes it by the rope handle. 'Come on, take it.'

'You're not expecting him to come back for it?' If she isn't, I can't help wondering why not.

She narrows her eyes at me. '*You're* not expecting it,' she says. 'I can tell there's something wrong.'

I hesitate a moment, weighing it up. Tilling hasn't given me permission to reveal the facts about the body in the car, but it's all round town there was one. It won't be long before people hear who it was. I guess for most of them the death of a stranger, however horrible, will be of limited interest. Except, of course, as another scandal attached to my name.

I sigh, reach out and take the bag from her. 'You're right.'

She swallows, blinks. 'He's dead?'

'I'm sorry, Mags. I'm not allowed to say.'

'Grandfather was right. You don't care.'

'That's not true. But I can see you do.'

'Why shouldn't I?' she snaps defensively. 'I've got feelings too, you know. He was always nice to me.'

So he should have been, I think. You were, no doubt, dogsbodying for him as well as for Grandfather. But I can't say that in the face of her obvious distress. I drop the bag, reach out to touch her arm. 'I'm glad he was.'

'Oh, Josy.' The next minute, she's in my arms and I'm hugging her tight while she weeps against my shoulder. 'Was it . . . ? Did he . . . ? I suppose he was in France. I don't know what Dad's going to say.'

'Don't tell him,' I say. 'Not yet. It's not as simple as . . . Just, well, hold on. I'll explain when I can.'

She pulls free of my hug, scrubs at her face. 'I have to get back.'

'Before you go, did he have any visitors here? Did he seem worried about anything?'

She laughs, a bitter sound. 'Of course he was worried. Going off to war, and he'd been a prisoner once already. What do you think would have happened if the Nazis had got him again, knowing he'd escaped?'

'I get that. I just meant, well, something more personal, I suppose. Someone he'd had a row with, someone who'd upset him.' I see the pitfall even as I say it, but it's too late to take the words back.

'Other than you, you mean?'

I sigh. 'I deserve that. Yes, other than me.'

'No one,' she says, 'not as far as I know.'

I persist, though she's already moving away up the lane. 'And no one came here to see him? No visitors?'

'Only that nice girl Alice. He seemed very taken with her.' She stops dead in her tracks. 'Oh, no. What do I say if she comes here asking about him?'

'Tell her the truth. You don't know.'

'Well—'

'I don't imagine she will. But if she does, tell her to come and see me. I'll talk to her.'

'You won't be unkind?'

'Mags.' What does she take me for? No point in protesting though, she won't listen. She's lived with Grandfather too long. 'No. Not more than I have to.'

She casts one more uncertain look in my direction, and then hurries back up the lane to the cottage.

I stare after her, sick at heart. Watch till she vanishes from view. That one unguarded hug is all she's ever going to let me give her. No rehabilitation for this black sheep.

The duffel bag is lying on the ground at my feet where I dropped it. I pick it up, feel the squash of something soft inside. Loosening the drawstring top shows a rolled-up, dark blue sweater and a pair of hand-knitted socks. The scent of my husband's body rises overwhelmingly from the clothes, and I almost drop the bag in revulsion. I hesitate. My instinct is to leave it, hurl it away into the bushes, abandon it to whatever creatures roam the lost field. Perhaps the mice can use it for a nest, or the foxes take the socks for a plaything. But that's ridiculous. I pull the drawstring tight, sling the bag over my shoulder. I half expect it to feel heavy on my back, but it isn't. No burden at all, except on my mind.

By the time I get to the tea rooms to meet Aggie and Dot, I'm starving. They're sitting together at a table in the window, and they've got Fan Stewart with them too. They wave me over, looking as conspiratorial as Macbeth's three witches, though much more benign.

'We've ordered for you,' Dot says before I've even had the chance to sit down. 'Today's special. Egg and bacon pie.'

'We're all having the same,' Aggie puts in.

'Iced buns for afters and their biggest pot of tea.' Fan's flushed with what seems like excitement. I've never seen her so animated. It makes her look years younger than when she's in her role as Bram's sober housekeeper and I'm suddenly aware she can't be all that much older than me. 'We're celebrating,' she goes on. 'Miss Haward told us they've moved

Mr Nash to Broadlands. That's got to be good news, hasn't it? Will they let us visit, do you think?'

I turn over what Alec said about Bram not being out of the woods yet and forbidding me to visit him today. I still can't decide if that was sound clinical judgement, or pure spite. And if it was the latter, why? But Fan's looking at me with the happy colour fading from her cheeks, and I really don't want to spoil the party for no good reason.

'I'm sure they will,' I say, as cheerfully as I can. 'In a day or two. No one else can go today though, because Sergeant Tilling tired him out.'

'That awful policeman,' Fan says, with a frown. 'He's very heavy-handed these days. Arresting you, for goodness' sake. What was that all about?'

'He didn't exactly arrest me.' It's more of an effort to keep it light-hearted this time, but I don't want to go into details. Aggie's the only one who needs to know those, and I've already told her most of them. 'He'd got some bee in his bonnet about me withholding evidence. It's all sorted out now.'

'I don't know what Mr Nash would say,' she begins, just as the meal arrives. In the palaver of getting plates in front of each of us, passing salt and pepper and pouring tea, the moment passes safely away.

As we settle to the serious business of eating, I ask Dot about the news from the war. 'What with one thing and another, I haven't heard anything since yesterday lunchtime.'

She grins. 'This morning's *Daily Mail* headline says our boys are five miles beyond Bayeux already.'

'Caen's next,' Aggie says. 'And did you see that bit about Lord Louis? Dad's cock-a-hoop knowing his boss at Broadlands had such a big part in the planning.'

'Mountbatten?' I say through a mouthful of egg and bacon pie. 'Really? I thought he was just a naval man.'

'Oh, no.' Aggie's vehement. 'It was right there on the front page. When Lord Louis was Chief of Combined Operations, he ordered commando raids on the Normandy beaches to gather intelligence for the invasion. Apparently Eisenhower based his plans on what they'd found out.'

'Just like the Yanks,' Fan says. 'Let the British do the dirty work and pinch the glory.'

'Oh, come on, Fan,' I say. 'Be fair. We'd never have got this far without the Americans.'

'Course we would. Billy says we'd have been far better off without them these last months, cluttering up our roads and corrupting the children with chewing gum and chocolate.'

Another grin from Dot. 'My Land Army girls are missing the GIs,' she says. 'No parties, no nylons.'

'Exactly. Just what Billy—'

Dot cuts in smoothly. 'Another cuppa, Mrs Stewart? Miss Haward?'

I may not be a military tactician, but I recognise a diversion when I hear one. 'Don't forget me,' I say, pushing my cup forward.

'You wait your turn,' Dot says with a wink. 'Can't have two of us pouring from the same pot.'

'Ginger twins!' Fan crows, then claps her hand across her mouth.

'That's just cruel,' I say, mock-sternly. 'With hair my colour? Heaven forbid.'

'That's what they say, though, isn't it?' Fan persists. 'If two women pour from the same pot, one of them will have ginger twins.'

'You're not superstitious, surely, Mrs Stewart?' Aggie says. She shakes her head. 'Not really, but my Billy is. You'd never believe—'

My heart sinks, but it's all right. We're all soon laughing about the illogicality of men in general and Billy in particular. Despite his job – or perhaps because of it – he's always seeing omens of bad luck and impending doom. Passing on the stairs, spotting a single magpie, putting red and white flowers together in the same vase are all harbingers of death. Aggie jumps in with a story about her father, who's convinced he saw the ghost of a Roundhead soldier here in Market Place late one night. 'Whisky,' she says laconically. 'I reckon that was the only spirit abroad that night.'

Dot's contribution is about Alf's obsession with American cartoons and it falls a bit flat after that. They look at me, but what can I say about men, their unpredictability? I had a husband who wanted a wife to protect him from his mistresses? I'm in love with a man who's too obstinate to sleep with me? In the end I settle for telling them what Grandfather said this morning about taking more notice of a fart than me, watch even the strait-laced Fan dissolve into helpless giggles.

It's a much nicer meal in every way than the one I shared with Alec. The company and the food are so much better. Though the pie has been made with dried egg and the bacon is mostly absent without leave, the cook had done her best to make it look nice with a sprinkle of chives on top and generous helpings of new potatoes and cabbage salad to bulk out the portions.

My stomach's pleasantly full and my sides are aching with laughter by the time the iced buns come out. Dot's just started telling our fortunes by reading the tea leaves in our cups when Aggie lets out a shriek. 'Goodness, whatever's the time? That's Mr Simmons going back to the office.'

I stand up, lean across the table to peer out of the window. Sure enough, I see his slight figure walking down towards the Hundred.

'We'd better go,' I say. 'If I give you ten bob, Dot, can you settle the bill for us all? My treat. If it's more than that, I'll pay you back later.'

I drop the note on the table, and Aggie and I rush out of the tea rooms. The old lawyer walks so slowly we're soon closing the gap between us. As we stalk along behind him, I'm suddenly struck by a fresh fit of the giggles. After all we've said over lunch, here we are, two women in a fluster about what one kindly old man might say if we're a couple of minutes late back from lunch.

At the sound of my laughter, Simmons stops, turns. Waits for us, smiling, to catch him up. 'Ladies,' he says, tipping his hat to us as we draw level. 'How delightful to see you in such good spirits. I presume that means there's good news about Mr Nash?'

Matching my pace to his, I start to tell him about Bram's transfer to Broadlands. Aggie excuses herself, scurries on ahead. By the time Simmons and I reach the office ourselves, she's back at her desk, prim and tidy as ever, and the kettle's on for yet another cup of tea.

21

Friday, afternoon and early evening

'There,' Irish says with satisfaction as she pats Nash's bare flank. 'That's another jab done. Another twenty-four hours and you'll be finished with the course.'

Nash pulls his pyjamas up, turns onto his back. He's the only patient awake in Red Ward this afternoon. The rest are either somewhere out in the grounds, enjoying the rare sunshine, damn them, or taking an afternoon nap in their beds as he's supposed to be doing. 'Won't say I'll be sorry. But I'm grateful. I never imagined I could feel so much better so quickly.'

'It's extraordinary,' she says. 'But you've still got a fair bit of ground to make up. Can't be pulling any more tricks like yesterday's route march. You know what Mr Corby-Clifford said.'

'Route march be blowed.' He shifts irritably in the bed. 'A couple of paces from the stretcher, that's all it was.'

'Nearly didn't make it though, did you?'

He sighs. 'True. I'll be able to get out of bed tomorrow, though?'

'If the man says you can.'

'God, this inactivity drives me mad.'

'Your own fault,' she says, grinning. 'If you'd just taken the sedative as he wanted, you'd be able to dream through the day like Sleeping Beauty.'

'I've dreamt enough,' he says soberly. 'No more of that.'

'The past?' She looks sympathetic.

'My job. I'd been viewing a body the morning I collapsed.' He frowns. 'Can't get it out of my head.'

'Nasty, then?'

'Very.'

'Man of few words, aren't you?' she says. 'Hope that police-man got more out of you this morning.'

Her curiosity is transparent. He doesn't resent it, but he knows how hospitals function. Like small towns, gossip's their meat and drink. He'd fob her off, but then she'd go about her work elsewhere and he's so *bored* . . . The game will be to keep her interested without telling her anything that matters.

'Hard to tell with policemen,' he says. 'Sergeant Tilling's not a fan of mine.'

'Can't believe that.' She picks up the banter as he'd hoped she would. 'Do you want me to hide you if he comes back to haul you off to jail?'

'I don't think he'll go that far,' he says. 'But you're closer than you think. And at least I'd be allowed visitors there.'

'Your letter writer?'

'Yes.' He's not sure he wants to go down this route.

'Cough it up,' she says. 'Tell Auntie Irish.'

'Haven't you got somewhere else you should be?'

'Nowhere at all for the next ten minutes. Call it mental therapy.'

'For you or me?'

'Cheek. Get on with you.'

Knowing what will happen, he teases her by patting the bed. 'You could sit down.'

'Good God, no.' She's as scandalised as he'd guessed she'd be. He knows the idea is anathema to nurses. Only patients ever sit on beds, and then only in the approved manner and at the prescribed time of day. 'What would Florence Nightingale say? I'm easy enough on my feet.'

Joke's over. Tell or don't tell. So tempting to share.

'Mrs Lester . . . Jo. She's my assistant. The letter was about the body we found.'

'Ssss. Shouldn't have worried you with work. I thought it was a billet-doux or I wouldn't have passed it on.'

The thought of Jo writing a love letter makes him smile. 'Glad you did.'

'Worth a sleepless night?'

'Oh, yes.'

'Not just work, then?'

'No.'

'You make oysters look chatty. Want to keep talking?'

He shrugs. 'It's complicated.'

'She's married, of course.'

'That's complicated too.'

A voice calls from the hallway. 'Nurse O'Shaughnessy?'

'Yes?'

A head pops round the door. It's one of the medical orderlies. 'Sorry to disturb you. We need your help in the Long Ward.'

'Coming.' She makes a face. 'Just when it was getting interesting. Try and get some sleep now, hmm? Don't make me a liar when Mr Corby-Clifford asks.'

What else can he do but sleep? He's not even allowed to read a newspaper. But Jo's on his mind. He can't help wondering how she is. What she's doing. When Corby-Clifford will allow him to see her. And as he drifts off, the final puzzle. How does the surgeon come to be on first-name terms with her?

I'd usually go straight to the farm after work on a Friday, but I can't today. I have to stay and try and see Bram tomorrow. I ring Della at Oliver's Battery post office and ask her to get a message to Sam not to expect me tonight after all. I know he won't mind, but I do.

By the time I've washed the smell of fish and chips and Jeyes Fluid out of my hair back at Dot's, it's six o'clock. I've shoved the duffel bag Mags gave me right to the back of my wardrobe, unopened. I can't face it. I don't want to think about Richard anymore tonight. I change out of my stale work clothes into a favourite old pair of corduroy trousers, worn soft and thin in the wash, and an Aertex shirt Dot picked up in a jumble sale. Dot and Alf won't mind that I'm scruffy, though the land girls Dot cooks for each evening will probably make snide comments. But I don't care. There's trout and new peas for supper tonight and I'm looking forward to it.

Dot's out in the back garden, picking the peas when there's a knock at the front door.

'I'll get it,' I shout as I run downstairs. We seldom use the front door, so I have to wrestle the bolts back before I pull it open.

I'm faced with an enormous bunch of flowers. Not the sort picked from the garden that Dot fills the vases with around the house, but a proper florist's bouquet. Long-stemmed red roses and white carnations, swaddled in drifts of baby's breath and fern. Carrying them is Alec Corby-Clifford. I'm completely taken aback.

'What? Alec . . . ? What's this?'

'A peace offering. I know I upset you this morning.'

'Yes, well . . . There was no need.' I'm aware I'm not being very gracious, but I don't feel all that kindly towards him. And flowers, however extravagant, aren't going to change my mind.

'Won't you take them?' he says with a deprecating little laugh. 'Or am I still in your bad books?'

What can I say to that? *Yes, you are*? But it's because of him Bram's getting better. I owe him politeness for that.

'Well, thank you.' I let him put the bouquet into my hands, though it's awkwardly top-heavy to hold. The only way that works is to cradle it in my arms as if it's a baby.

'Who is it, love?' Dot calls.

'Um . . .' I turn, find her standing right beside me. 'Mr Corby-Clifford brought me flowers.' I'm still completely baffled by the gesture, the fact that he's turned up here at all. Who can have told him where I live?

'Who's a lucky girl, then?' she says, positively twinkling at Alec. 'What gorgeous roses. Haven't seen any like that since before the war.'

'They are lovely.' Under her watchful gaze, I concede that much. 'You really shouldn't have, Alec.'

'My pleasure.'

'Well, thanks,' I say again, hoping he'll take it as a goodbye. To make it clear, I juggle one hand free of the flowers, reach to shut the door.

'Whatever are you thinking?' Dot says. 'Don't leave the poor man on the doorstep. Come on in, Mr Corby-Clifford. Jo, be careful with those flowers, you'll drop them. Here, give them to me.'

I'm glad to relinquish the bouquet, but I'm less happy she's invited Alec in. Before I can do or say anything to prevent it, he's over the threshold, looking perfectly at ease. Can he really not have noticed my lack of warmth?

'Take Mr Corby-Clifford through to the parlour,' Dot prompts. 'It's tidy in there.'

There's no escape. I open the parlour door. It's *always* tidy in there. Once Pa Gray's domain, since his death a couple of years ago it's only used for best. Alec wanders in, prowls across to the bay window and stands looking out.

Dot glances at me, then back at him, her brow wrinkled. I can see she's puzzled by my lack of enthusiasm, the tension between Alec and me. But now he's in, she'd never let him go without offering hospitality.

'Can I get you a cup of tea? Or there's a nice drop of elderflower wine if you'd care for it.'

'You make it yourself?' Alec asks.

'Every year,' she says. 'Sunshine in a glass, my old dad used to call it.'

'What a delightful thought,' he says, turning a smile on her that could have melted chocolate, if there had been any to hand. 'How can I possibly resist?'

Dot blushes, patters away to the kitchen. At least she won't be so long if it's only wine she's got to pour, rather than making tea.

Once she's out of earshot, I go across to where he's standing. 'Alec, what is all this about?'

'I told you. I wanted to make it up with you for this morning.'

I shrug. 'It wasn't personal, was it? You were doing what you thought was best for Bram. Mr Nash.'

'Of course. You know how it is. Sometimes we have to make difficult decisions in the patient's best interest.'

That pompous 'we' again. 'Richard used to say something like that.'

'Ah, yes, Richard. Have you heard from the old rogue?'

'No.' It's on the tip of my tongue to tell him, but I'd better not. 'I wouldn't expect to.'

Dot comes back. I'm relieved to see the tray she carries has three glasses on it, rather than two. I hope it's because she's picked up something of my reluctance to be alone in Alec's company. 'Here, Mr Corby-Clifford, Jo. I thought we'd toast our boys over there in France.'

Alec takes a glass, holds it up to the light. 'You're right,' he says to Dot. 'It is a pretty colour.'

Cynically, I wonder what he'll make of the taste. I like it, but I imagine it's much sweeter than his sophisticated palate would usually prefer.

'A toast, then,' he says. 'Luck to the forces of right, and a swift victory.'

'Amen to that,' Dot says fervently, but I don't join in. There's something about the way Alec's chosen his words that makes me uneasy. I get a distinct feeling he's not whole-heartedly in support of the invasion.

There's another awkward moment of silence before Dot rushes to fill it. 'Now then, sit down, Mr Corby-Clifford. No need to stand on ceremony in this house. Any friend of Jo's . . .'

I'm desperately hoping he'll refuse, say he has to go, but he takes the chair she indicates, the seat of honour, old Pa Gray's Windsor armchair. At least she hasn't pushed him towards the couch. She perches there herself, pats the seat beside her. 'Come on, Jo. Sit down. Don't be rude to Mr Corby-Clifford when he's brought you those lovely flowers.'

Ill at ease, I sit. I'm surprised Dot's being so determined to make this into a social occasion. I'd expect her to be on tenterhooks to get on with preparations for supper.

'Now, Mr Corby-Clifford, how's Mr Nash doing? I know Jo's very grateful to you for taking him into your care.' She looks at his bandaged hand. 'Especially when you're wounded yourself.'

'He's making progress,' Alec says austerely. 'Though it will be a while before he's fully back on his feet.'

'Jo said you and she were old friends?'

That's going it pretty rich, I think. I'd said nothing about being *friends*. Just that I'd known him years ago. The elder-flower wine is sticky on my lips, too sweet today, too inno-cent for the memories she's conjuring up, though Alec seems happy enough to answer.

'Oh yes,' he says. 'Josephine and I have been friends for many years. Her husband and I were colleagues on the Isle of Wight. She may have told you, he and I tried to do our bit over at Dunkirk. Didn't quite work out. We were separated, lost touch after that.'

'You didn't know he was back in England?'

He shakes his head, but I'm not convinced. When I'd first seen him at the hospital, he'd asked if I was with Richard. He didn't sound like a man who thought his friend was still in a POW camp.

'And you too,' Dot burbles on. 'You managed to escape as well?'

I'd be interested to hear that story, but he shakes his head again. 'I didn't come here to bore you with war stories, Mrs Gray. What I wanted—'

'We wouldn't be bored, would we, Jo?'

'Of course not.' But I'm pretty sure Alec won't take the bait. He's definitely evasive about that period of his life. In the wee small hours of the night, I've been thinking what might have happened between Richard and him. Could he have abandoned Richard and escaped? Is that why he's shifty about it?

'What I really came for' – he turns those cool, water-grey eyes my way – 'apart from bringing the flowers, of course, was to ask you to dine with me tonight, Josephine.'

For all sorts of reasons, Wednesday lunchtime's experience is not one I'm keen to repeat. 'I don't think so, Alec. I'm sorry. It's been a difficult week and I'm very tired.'

'All the more reason to have a break, surely? Do you good to get away from your problems for a few hours.'

'Perhaps another time.'

He grins. 'Perhaps I won't ask another time. I maybe won't get another chance. Had you thought of that?'

It's the same old argument that Richard used. A bit more subtle, but still a kind of emotional blackmail. *Be nice to me, I'm off to war.*

'I'll have to risk it.' In reality, I wouldn't be heartbroken if he didn't ask again.

'Mrs Gray, I appeal to you,' he says. 'Can't you convince Josephine to take pity on a lonely soul and spend a few hours with me?'

Lonely soul? What a lot of nonsense. Another repeat performance, this time of the game he'd played on Wednesday, with the waiter. Banking on my reluctance to be rude to a bystander to get me to do what he wants. I'm seething, but it works, because I don't up and slap his smug face as I'd like to.

Dot looks wary. 'Well, now, I'd have to say if Jo doesn't want to do something I'm not sure anyone can persuade her otherwise.'

He sighs, gazes at me with an expression I can't entirely read. 'There's nothing I can do to change your mind? The promise of an hour with Mr Nash tomorrow?'

I stare. Everything goes still inside me. Is this a threat? Is he implying he'll stop me seeing Bram if I don't go out with him?

'I was hoping that would happen anyway.' Despite my outrage, I do my best to keep my voice level.

'Of course,' he says blandly. 'All things being equal, I'd hope so too. Come on, Josephine. Give a little.'

'Tell you what,' Dot breaks in, 'what about this for an idea? Why don't you stay and have supper with us, Mr Corby-Clifford? Give Jo a chance to relax. Then perhaps you and she can go off for a drink somewhere afterwards.'

His face lightens. 'Why, that sounds like a perfect solution. If you're sure it won't put too much of a strain on the household budget.'

Dot chuckles. 'It's not a problem in this house. My nephew, Alf—'

I nudge her, hard, in the ribs.

'Ow, Jo,' she protests, casting a fractious glance my way. 'What was that for?'

'Sorry,' I mutter, shaking my head. 'I must just have . . .' I don't finish because there's no excuse. I just hope I've given her time to think about what she says. It wouldn't be a good idea to let Alec know about Alf's foraging.

'What was I saying?' she says, focusing on Alec once more. 'Oh, yes. Alf's working an extra shift tonight, so he won't be back for supper. There'll be more than enough to go round. Trout and new peas from the garden. I was outside picking them when you called.'

'Perfect. I'll agree on one condition.'

Dot raises her eyebrows. 'Oh, yes?'

'That you'll let me come out in the garden with you and help pick the peas.' His smile this time is impish. 'I used to love doing that at home when I was a boy. Peas never taste so good as when you eat them straight from the pod.'

'As long as you don't eat more than you pick.'

Wouldn't matter if he did, I think. The way she's acting, he could eat the whole lot and she'd think it was his due. I must have made a sound because she looks my way again.

'Why don't you go and get changed, Jo?' she says. 'While Mr Corby-Clifford and I are in the garden.'

'Alec,' he breaks in before I can reply. 'Do call me Alec, please. And I hope you won't mind if I call you Dot.'

'I'll leave you two to it.' I stand up, disgusted. 'Perhaps you'd be better off taking Dot out tonight, Alec. You seem to be getting on like a house on fire.'

She shakes her head at me. 'It's not like you to be silly, Jo.'

I clatter upstairs, fuming. I hate the feeling that I've been backed into a corner, but like a child who's been shamed for bad behaviour, I know it's true. I have been behaving abominably rudely. It's my own fault that Dot's felt she had to step in to smooth things over. If I'd been a bit more civil, I wouldn't be stuck with having to share his company this evening. Or, a demon thought prompts me, if I'd just shut the door in his face in the first place, Dot would never have known he was there.

When I get to my room, I just manage not to slam the door behind me. I pace out my irritation, as angry with myself for being childish as I am with either Alec or Dot. I can hear their voices floating in from the garden, his cultivated baritone punctuating her more homely commentary. I have to restrain myself from going over to the window to see what they're doing, listen to what they're saying. I've got problems enough up here.

The first is what I'm going to wear. I've never been much of a one to worry about clothes, though when I was married to Richard, I had wardrobes full of stuff he'd bought me or persuaded me to buy. Something for every occasion: sleek dresses for evenings, fashionable ensembles for daytime wear. I'd left all but the bare minimum behind when I'd moved out, resolved to be self-sufficient. I'd never drawn on the allowance he'd kept paying into my bank account every month, either. I wasn't going to have him say he was still supporting me. But it meant I hadn't had money to splash around on fancy stuff. And since the war, and clothes couponing, we've all been the same, buying for utility rather than frivolity. Which all boils down to the fact I've got nothing suitable for a night on the town with an elegant chap like Alec.

Not that it matters. I'm not trying to impress him. I just don't want to let myself down. Opening the wardrobe, I rattle past blouses I've had for donkey's years, a few newer shirts I've bought for work. Jumpers Dot's knitted. Skirts, mostly serviceable black or navy, though there's one in an ill-advised tartan Dot talked me into buying from a jumble sale. The demon thought whispers in my ear: *Wear that one, it'll definitely put him off.*

I give myself a good talking-to. I'm letting my imagination run away with me. It's plain ego to suppose Alec's got designs on me. He might flirt – look at the way he is with Dot – but he still thinks Richard's on the scene. I'm probably in for an evening of point-scoring, but I can deal with that. Even enjoy it if I come out on top.

Right at the back of the wardrobe, behind my winter coat, there's a blouse I haven't worn in years. Emerald-green silk with a kind of twill to the surface, it has a dull gleam that's sophisticated enough for evening wear. It used to be a favourite, which was why I'd kept it, even though Richard had given it to me.

I've nothing so good in the way of a skirt, but there's one, relatively new, that should pass muster. A pencil skirt in black crêpe that I bought for my undercover role last year, when I was trying to be a different kind of woman altogether than Josy Fox.

22

Friday, evening

B Y THE TIME SUPPER IS on the table, I've managed to
shelve my hostility and ego. At the beginning, there's
a cynical kind of pleasure in watching how Alec oper-
ates. Remembering how he always did like to be the centre of
attention: his blond good looks and smooth manners making
him the golden boy of any group. Since he's got Dot eating out
of his hand already, he spends the meal concentrating on Joan
and Betty, the two land girls. Joan, the chatty one, succumbs at
first glance, talks through most of the meal ignoring her food
for the pleasure of flirting with Alec. Betty just stares. She's such
easy prey for a man like Alec. A wink and a smile, and she's
bedazzled. Never much of a talker, tonight she's dumbstruck.

After a while, I start to feel uncomfortable on her behalf.
One more of his high-octane smiles, another sly touch of
the hand as he fills her water glass or hands her the cruet,
and she'll be in love. With a sense of trepidation, I set out
to divert his attention. Better that she winds up this evening
cross with me rather than heartbroken.

Dot's just served the pudding, a mousse she's made with a precious hoarded tin of mandarins, orange jelly and evaporated milk, when Joan asks him when he'll be going to France.

'I don't know,' he says, putting down his spoon with what looks suspiciously like relief. 'Having to wait for my wretched hand to heal to the army's satisfaction is a bore. It means my original placement is void, because the chaps I'd been meant to go with left on Wednesday.'

'You're not actually in the army, though, are you? Not if you're swanning around in that suit.' Joan giggles. 'Could they really make you go?'

'I was seconded,' he says, 'rather than enlisted. But I can't tell you how impatient I am to get away. To go where I'm needed.'

Another giggle from Joan. 'But surely, you're needed here, Mr Corby-Clifford?'

He raises his eyebrows in mock disapproval. 'I told you to call me Alec.'

'Yes, well, *Alec*. Jo has told us all about how you saved Mr Nash.'

He looks at me in real surprise. 'Really?'

'Really not,' I say. 'I mentioned you'd agreed to see him.'

'Jo,' Joan squeals in protest. 'You fibber. I heard you telling Dot how grateful you were.'

'Telling *me*,' Dot breaks in. 'In a private conversation if I remember rightly. You'd no call to go listening in, Joan. I've had cause to speak to you about that before.'

Joan flushes, drops her gaze.

274

'Ladies, ladies.' Alec's tone is smooth, conciliatory, but I notice he looks smug. 'No need to fight over details. I've been glad to do what I can for Mr Nash while I've been held up here. Him and a couple of others at the Mountbatten Annexe. Patients of mine before I stepped down in preparation for going away.'

It seems like a good moment for me to chip in, provide a much-needed distraction. 'If you're finished, Alec, we could perhaps go now? Find somewhere to have that drink. I don't want to be too late back tonight.'

He gets up with suspicious enthusiasm. 'If Dot and these other delightful young ladies will excuse us?'

'Of course,' Dot says, though I think both Betty and Joan would like to disagree. 'Off you go. Enjoy the rest of your evening.'

'I'm sure we shall. Josephine, do you need anything before we go?'

'I'll fetch a coat on the way out.' A niggle of irritation makes me ask him the same question.

'I'll just wash my hands if I may?'

A suppressed giggle from Joan as I stand waiting by the door. Dot frowns at her. Despite my earlier reluctance, there's a part of me that's glad to be getting out. I don't fancy the endless churning over Alec's appeal that's certain to happen as soon as he's out of the door.

Dot gets up from the table, comes across to me. 'Look, I'm sorry if I was a bit . . . you know . . . meddlesome, earlier. But it won't do you any harm to have some fun for once.'

'All right. I meant it about being tired. I won't be late.'

She leans forward, kisses me on the cheek. 'You do whatever you want,' she says. 'Key'll be in the usual place.'

I don't get a chance for another denial because Alec's calling from the hallway. 'Josephine?'

One last glance over my shoulder. Joan sticks her tongue out sulkily at me while Betty reaches across to Alec's bowl with her spoon, scoops up a heaping mouthful. Dot pats my arm. 'Off you go.'

Outside, the air's damp and fresh, and for once, it's not raining, though I'm glad of the jacket I picked up on my way out. Like a proper gentleman, Alec takes the outside position on the pavement, offers me his arm. A moment's hesitation, then I accept.

'That's better,' Alec says, drawing me closer. 'Much cosier.'

A bit too cosy, I think. I fight, as surreptitiously as I may, to re-establish a little distance between us. There's still enough light to be able to walk without having to watch my feet overmuch, and I've no desire to let him think I need to lean against him like some kind of wilting blossom. Even if my best shoes are a bit tighter than I remember, I can still stand on my own two feet.

Everything this evening seems to be conspiring to set the stage for the kind of romantic encounter that happens in cheesy films. As we walk down Botley Road, we're heading almost directly into the sunset. There's a line of clear lemon light low down, while tatters of indigo cloud backlit with gold and pink scud across an aquamarine sky. Unwilling as I am to let Alec's flirtatious behaviour go any further, I have to admit to feeling more mellow than I was before supper.

'What a beautiful sky,' I say. 'Do you think it's going to be fine tomorrow?'

'Who cares?' Alec murmurs, leaning in against me. 'The question is, have I told you how beautiful *you* are tonight? And your hair, so pretty, loose like that.'

Secretly, I have to admit I'm pleased with my rediscovery of the green silk blouse. And, I suppose, with the opportunity to wear it. But no one with ginger hair and a nose like mine can ever be called beautiful. 'Don't need to lay it on so thick, Alec. I'm not one of your new conquests.'

He laughs. 'Whatever do you mean?'

'You know very well. You had Dot on your side from the moment she saw the flowers, and Joan couldn't stop flirting with you. And poor Betty was eating you up with her eyes all through supper.'

Another laugh. 'Looks as if that one spends altogether too much time eating. A bit of distraction should prove beneficial.'

'That's unkind.'

I feel him shrug. 'But true. Anyway, I've done my duty, dining *à la maison*, being nice to all your friends. Don't I deserve my reward now?'

'I don't think there's anything particularly heroic about eating Dot's cooking. And you didn't have to flirt with anyone.'

'So austere,' he says. 'You're not jealous, Josephine?'

'You're right. I'm not. Where shall we go for this drink?'

'Where would you suggest? You must be much more expert about the pubs of Romsey than me.'

'The only experts about the pubs of Romsey are the drunks.'

'There do seem to be rather a lot. Pubs, I mean.'

'A lot of both. There's the Crown coming up, and the Bishop Blaize. Then the Sawyer's Arms and the Sceptre, the King's Head, the Red Lion, the Phoenix, the Dolphin Hotel, and the Tudor Rose. And that's all before the White Horse. Take your pick.'

'Umm. The Red Lion, I think. A nice, old, traditional name.'

'OK.' I smile to myself. It's definitely an old building, but if he's thinking in terms of Tudor beams and inglenook fireplaces, he's in for a disappointment. It's gas lighting and spittoons, and its position next to the jam factory means its clientele is mostly drawn from the workers there. None the worse for that. It'll be the perfect antidote to his sentimental mood.

'Mr Nash?'

'Yes, Scobie?' The settling-down routine again. The time's gone so slowly this evening that Nash is almost glad of the early preparations for sleep. Though he's no more tired than he'd been last night, the enforced dark will at least give him a sense of privacy, a chance to think his own thoughts. Or at a pinch, he could cave and take the despised sedative

Corby-Clifford prescribed and sleep the night away. Against regulations, Irish has left the little pot with the tablet on his locker, allowing him to decide if and when to take it.

'Your job.' The man's fussing around, tidying or perhaps being nosy like last night. 'Coroner. What is it exactly you do? You investigate deaths, don't you?'

'Up to a point. Not every death, of course. Only those where the cause is unexplained or there's a question of identity.'

'You cut up the bodies, like?'

'Thankfully, not. I leave that to my medical colleagues.'

'Must be interesting.'

'It has its moments.'

'Only . . .' The man's repositioned Nash's water jug twice already, an obvious ploy.

'Yes?'

'They're saying this car that caught fire the other night, there was a body in it. Is that true? Is that why the copper came to see you this morning?'

Nash is silent a moment, thinking it through. Is this just morbid curiosity, or is there something more behind it? He's very conscious of the proximity here at Broadlands to the site of the fire. And that he's in the equivocal position of being one of the last people who'd seen Richard Lester alive and heading this way. 'There is an ongoing investigation,' he says cautiously. 'But I'm afraid I'm not really at liberty to discuss it. Unless . . . do you think you might know something about it? Not just gossip, I mean.' He knows at once the word was ill-chosen.

Scobie sets down the jug with a bang. 'Gossip? What do you think I am, some old lady in a tea shop?'

'I meant . . . Look, if you have got information about what happened on Sunday night, you need to tell someone. I'd be happy to hear, but . . .' he gestures to the bed '. . . I'm a bit helpless at the moment. You'd be much better to talk to Sergeant Tilling at Romsey police station.'

'I'll think about it.' Scobie picks up the little pot, rattles the tablet within it. 'Right now, my job is to see you get this sleeping pill down you. Dunno what Irish was thinking of, leaving it lying around on the locker. Against all the rules.'

'She said I could take it if I needed it.'

'You take it now.' Scobie tips the pill into Nash's hand. Holds out his glass. 'Come on.'

Reluctant, Nash puts the pill to his mouth, takes a sip of water.

'All gone?' Scobie says.

Nash nods. 'Yes.'

'Good. Soon be out for the count.'

'Scobie . . . I meant what I said about telling someone what you know.'

'Goodnight, Mr Nash. Sleep well.' He gives one last fierce twitch to the bedclothes to straighten them and walks away.

Nash sighs, spits out the half-dissolved tablet. It's left a bitter taste in his mouth, but he doesn't think he'll be sleeping much tonight. Wondering what the man knows, wishing he'd encouraged him to speak. This damn illness, it's made him slow. He's lost his edge, his instinct.

23

Friday, evening

THE RED LION IS NOT a success. From the moment we walk into the bar parlour, it's apparent Alec doesn't see the funny side. It's quiet enough here, though the noises coming through from the smoking room suggest there's a lively gathering going on in there. The only other customers in this part of the pub are a couple of elderly men, sitting at a table in one corner playing cribbage. They look up briefly at our entrance, nod a greeting, then proceed to ignore us completely.

'Good God, Josephine,' Alec mutters. 'Don't you think . . . ?'

'Half of bitter, please,' I say. 'I'll sit over there.'

There is a settle flanking the unlit fireplace. If I'd chosen one of the single seats available, a mishmash set of Windsor armchairs, I think Alec would have walked out at once. He eyes the settle. I can almost see him weighing up the possibilities.

'A half, you say?'

'Please.' While he goes to the bar, I move across to my chosen spot. By the time he gets back with the two drinks,

I'm installed in one corner of the settle, my jacket folded up on the faded cushion beside me. Keep it pleasant, I think, keep it light. Just got to get through the next hour or so . . .

He hands me my glass and I take a sip. Though the surroundings are what Alec no doubt thinks of as primitive, the beer's good. 'Nice,' I say appreciatively.

'Nice?' He plonks down on the seat beside me, as close as he can get without actually sitting on my coat. 'Very funny, Josephine.'

'Try it.'

He takes a long swallow, maybe a third of his pint disappearing in one go. 'Hmm.' It's grudging. 'You can't really want to stay here?'

'Don't be such a snob.' A smile, to take the sting out of the insult. 'Better to have good beer and basic surroundings than bad beer in luxury, surely?'

'Luxury?' He looks around. 'Simple comfort would be good enough. We'd be far better to go back to my hotel.'

Another smile, but no comment. That's exactly what I want to avoid. He takes a second long pull at his beer.

'Do you realise,' he says, 'my glass is stamped "VR".'

'A proper antique. I hope you feel honoured.'

'Josephine. Hasn't the joke gone far enough?'

A sip of my drink. 'Joke?'

'This.' He traces a semicircle in the air with his glass to indicate our surroundings. 'You letting me choose this place.'

'It's not a joke, Alec, it's real life. This is Romsey, not the West End. There are a lot of pubs, but no one ever said they were posh.'

'I suppose I asked for that. And you're right, it is good beer. But just the one, hey?'

'Plenty for me.' I've still got most of my drink left, and I'm intending to eke it out for as long as I can.

There's no table, so we have to nurse our glasses or put them on the floor. Despite my jibes at Alec about not needing to be posh, that's taking mucking in with the locals a bit too far even for me.

'Here, give it to me,' Alec says. He stands, pushes a dusty-looking trophy along an even dustier-looking shelf above the hearth, and sets down the glasses. He moves my jacket to the far end of the settle and sits, takes my hand in his own. It's the bandaged one, and I don't like to resist in case I hurt him. 'Now then, my lovely. Do say you've forgiven me for this morning.'

It's a mistake on his part. A surprising miscalcula-tion to remind me of that, though I'd be willing to bet he doesn't make many of those. Because if I'd begun to feel a little more relaxed in the company of this softer version of himself, now I remember. It's not so much his veto of my visit to Bram this morning, though I'm fairly sure that wasn't done solely out of care for his patient's welfare, as knowing how ruthless he can be. In a reversal of the classic story, his Mr Hyde is benevolent. It's when he's Dr Jekyll, he's an unkind bastard.

'As long as you don't stop me seeing him again tomorrow,' I say.

He turns my hand over in his. I feel oddly vulnerable as he begins to trace the lines of my palm. 'A strong, clear life-line,' he says. 'That's good. But your love-line, that's a different story. Very suggestive. All these feathery little breaks incline me to wonder—'

'Alec,' I protest, snatching my hand away. 'You surely can't believe in palmistry?'

He grins, rests his head against the high back of the settle. 'Not in palmistry, no. But I'm not a fool. I can make deductions from known data.' He turns his face towards me, a sly mischief once more in his expression.

He's waiting for me to say *What deductions?* I suppose, but I know it's a trap. I can't think of a witty response that will steer us away from the danger zone. In fact, I can't think of any response at all. I must hesitate too long, because he slips an arm round my shoulders, gives me a little shake. 'Josephine?'

'Sorry, yes?'

'Surely I haven't offended you again? It was such a delicate little hint. I don't remember you being so sensitive in the past.'

'Delicate or not, don't do it, Alec.'

He doesn't ask *Do what?* He knows perfectly well. 'You're not such a prude as all that, surely?'

'A prude?'

He captures my hand again, lifts it to his lips. His eyes on mine, I feel his tongue flick voluptuously across my knuckles.

'I remember you, Josephine, how you used to be. Marriage wasn't all that sacred to you then. After all, you were with Richard a long time before he made an honest woman of you.'

I try to pull my hand away, but even with the encumbering bandage, he manages to keep a firm hold.

'And now' – he raises his eyebrows – 'it seems you're still not above a little dalliance on the side. It's common knowledge you're having an affair with Nash.'

I wrench my hand free. This time I don't care if I hurt him. 'Listening to gossip, Alec? I'd have thought you would have been above that. Really, if you want us to stay friends, I wouldn't say anything more.'

'Friends? Are we friends, Josephine? I'd have said acquaintances. A mutually beneficial alliance, each using the other for what we can get out of them. You, wanting me to save your lover. Me? Well, I always did fancy you. Where's the harm?'

'What about Richard? You don't care about him?'

He laughs. 'How would he ever find out? I shan't tell him. And you, you don't even know where he is.'

Oh, I know, I think. I'm only glad Alec doesn't. If I'd told him what had happened to Richard, I wouldn't have even that thread of defence.

'Is it Nash who's holding you back?' he says. 'Don't make me regret I helped him.'

This time it's an open threat. 'You're saying I have to sleep with you because you helped Mr Nash?'

He shrugs. 'I'm suggesting a way you could pay me, my dear.'

The thought nauseates me, but I keep my voice low, try not to let the disgust bleed through. 'You'd do that? You'd press me to have sex with you even though you must know I don't want to?'

'Don't be naive, darling,' he says. 'It doesn't become you. A little pain, a little reluctance just adds spice to the dish.'

'Right.' I let out a long breath. Inside, I'm incandescent with rage. Aching with fear. What happens if I say no? Bram's in his care, his power . . . Would I go that far? Do it for him, to protect him? 'This payment,' I say, making a last-ditch attempt to pretend I still think he's joking, 'would it be a one-off, or will it come in instalments?'

He hugs me close, laughs. A great belly laugh of victory that has the cribbage players looking across in disapproval. 'You know, the thing I like most about you, Josephine, is your sense of humour. Why don't we see how it goes? If the dish turns out to be tasty, you might be glad to pay on the never-never.'

'You know, Alec, you're making a mistake.'

'How's that, my lovely?' He's still chuckling.

'Well, you've as good as told me that if I don't please you . . . if I'm boring enough in bed, I'll get away with a single payment.'

Another chuckle. 'Dear girl, you won't be boring. Not with me. I won't allow it.'

For me, the joke's well and truly over. Now I have to find a way out of the mess I've got myself in. The bar parlour seems suddenly claustrophobic. I need to move, to escape. I shake off his arm, stand up abruptly. Pick up my drink, pour it down my throat in one long draught.

'What a swallow,' he says admiringly. 'And you thought you might be boring?'

I blink at the boldness of it. Pretend a kind of brazenness of my own. 'Come on, Alec. Let's get out of here.'

'It will be my absolute pleasure.' His smile is so smug I almost break then. Tell him how he disgusts me. I can't believe the ego that makes him think I'll accept his offer, but he's going to be faced with reality soon. In my heart of hearts I know even for Bram, I won't do it. What Alec's proposing is rape in all but name.

I've no idea how I'm going to get away from him. I don't underestimate him, his capacity for ruthlessness. He's dangerous, and not just to me. Somehow, I have to make sure Bram is safe. I could stay here, raise an almighty fuss, but I don't fancy the publicity. It'd be all round town before morning. Alec's got a point about gossip, what people say about me. My reputation is not stainless. And it would be my word against his. I know how that goes, especially since the crib players would be bound to say we'd appeared on friendly, even intimate terms until now.

There'll be a chance, perhaps, to turn things round before we get back to the White Horse. And if not, I'll make my stand there. They're too discreet in an establishment like that to let tittle-tattle about their patrons get out.

Chivalrously, he helps me on with my jacket. But the fingers that go under the collar to stroke my neck are anything but chivalrous in intent.

It's quiet on the street tonight. The sky's clear now, and there's a bit of a moon, so it's not entirely dark. Alec's not content with offering me an arm this time. Instead, he slides his good hand under my jacket and around my waist, his palm hot through the thin silk of my blouse. His fingers move restlessly against my breast in a vicious exploration that's nothing like a caress. I shudder, I can't help myself, and the cool night air and my fear grant him a reaction he takes as eagerness.

'Ah, dear girl,' he murmurs. His fingers pinch my nipple hard. 'We're two of a kind, you and me. We'll have such fun.'

We pass my uncle Tom's greengrocer's shop. There's no chink of light coming from the upper windows, though I can see the sash is up to let the night air in. If I screamed, would Tom come down to see what was going on? Or Sylvie, perhaps? I imagine them up in their amazing black and white sitting room, imagine myself sitting safe with them, one of Tom's giant Martinis in my hand.

But I don't scream. Somehow the thought of dealing with their partisan concern is as daunting as raising a kerfuffle in the pub. I keep walking, doing my best to evade his probing fingers, trying desperately to think how I'm going to get away.

We cross over by the Cornmarket. The entrance to the hotel is just up ahead when he stops suddenly, pushes me into a doorway. He's hard against me, his hips grinding into my belly, mouth on mine in a savage kiss. I struggle, but he's very strong. After a moment, I realise he's enjoying the struggle. It's what he wants. He wasn't kidding when he said my reluctance would add spice for him.

I force myself to stop fighting. I can feel his surprise as I go limp against him. He draws back, looks down at me. With his back to what little light there is in the sky, I can only see the glint of his eyes. The rest of his expression is lost. But I know my face will be better illuminated, and I take care not to show my true feelings.

'That's more like it,' he murmurs. 'Now, how are we going to smuggle you into the hotel? I somehow don't think they'll approve of me taking you up to my room openly.'

'Especially since you've made such a mess of my hair and clothes.' I match my tone to his, breathless, a little complacent. 'I must look as if I've been dragged through a hedge backwards.'

He makes a satisfied little sound in his throat. 'Mm. You look delicious. Rumpled and ready to be thoroughly screwed,' he says. 'Even that dim cow on reception couldn't miss it.'

'Tell you what,' I say, inventing furiously, 'why don't you go ahead and check in? If you collect your key and go up to your room, I can slip round the back. I know where the kitchen entrance is, and the backstairs to the rooms. Give me a few minutes, and I'll find my way up to you without anyone being the wiser.'

'You will?'

'What do you think?' I glance coyly up at him. 'After all this?'

'You'll want my room number.'

'Oh, I know it,' I say. 'I took special note of it when I first came to the hotel looking for you.'

'You sly little vixen,' he says. I can practically hear his ego purr. 'All that show of reluctance.'

'Kiss me,' I say, steeling myself for another invasion of his tongue in my mouth. It's all I can do not to show my revulsion, but I have to convince him. Though he likes a little spice, I think. I pull away, nip his lower lip hard between my teeth.

'Vixen,' he repeats, smiling as he dabs away a dark smear of blood with his finger. 'You just wait, my girl.'

'Not too long,' I say with what I hope he'll interpret as an eager smile. My heart's thumping away in my chest so erratically I'm surprised he doesn't feel it. It all rides on him believing me. 'Come on.' I pat his arm encouragingly. 'Hurry up, Alec.'

He nods, strides off towards the hotel entrance. The moment he's out of sight I take off. How long have I got before he realises he's been duped?

24

Friday, late evening

NASH COMES OUT OF A troubled doze to the sound of someone choking. Disorientated at first, he can't think where he is or what's happening. The choking sounds grow louder, and a rhythmic banging starts up. He looks towards the sound. His neighbour, Ted Warren, is having some kind of fit. Moving his head to see across to his blind side, Nash looks around. There's no one but himself awake in the room, and no nurse or medical orderly handily standing by.

'Ted?'

But the man can't answer. Nash slides cautiously out of bed. It'll do no one any good if he collapses before he can get help. Once on his feet, he's surprised to realise he feels none of yesterday's dizziness. In fact, he feels quite strong. Almost normal.

He goes to Warren. He's lying on his back, the horrid choking sounds seeming more staccato, irregular. He knows he ought to clear the man's airway, turn him onto his side, but he can't manage to do either. Warren's jaw is clamped shut, and he's too rigid, too heavy for Nash to move. Where are the damn nurses?

He hurries to the door and out into the hallway. Dim lighting shows a corridor yawning emptily on either side of the Red Ward door, no clues which way to go to get help. 'Nurse!' he calls. And when there's no response, calls again with more force. '*Nurse!*'

Scobie appears from a door down the hallway to the left. He plods forward, an irritable expression on his face. 'Mr Nash. You shouldn't be out of bed.'

'You need to come. Ted Warren's having a fit.'

Scobie tuts, takes his arm. 'Let's get you back to bed.'

Nash shakes him off. 'For goodness' sake, man. Leave me be, I'm fine. You need to see to Ted. Can't you hear?'

Scobie cocks his head. The banging reaches a crescendo. 'Oh, oh.' He hurries off, Nash following.

Inside the room, Scobie's pulling at Ted's bedclothes. He untucks the bottom sheet, and with a heave of his wrists uses the material to turn Ted onto his side the way a housewife turns out a roly-poly.

'The bell,' he pants to Nash. 'Pull the bell, for God's sake.'

If he'd known there was a bell, Nash thinks fleetingly, he'd have used it in the first place. 'Where is it?'

'Far side of the fireplace. Quick.'

Nash scoots round a bed, tripping over a pair of slippers and rattling a urine bottle against the side of a locker. The bell rope is well in shadow, but he finds it at last, heaves vigor-ously on it. 'What else?'

'Hand me that towel. That's right.' The orderly's up on his knees on the bare mattress at Ted's back, keeping him on his side despite the spasms that still rock the unconscious man. He takes the towel, wipes the blood and foam from Warren's mouth. 'Now get yourself back to bed. Don't want any more emergencies tonight.'

Another time, Nash might have resented the blunt direc-tion, but his strength has run out with shocking sudden-ness, and he's glad to do as he's been told. In any case, he'd only be in the way. In response to the bell, two nurses have joined Scobie now. Nash pulls the bedclothes up round his shoulders, settles back against the pillows. Turning his head deliberately away from their busy ministrations, he gives the stricken man what privacy he can.

While he can choose not to see what's going on, he can't help but hear. Muttered discussions of *grand mal* and *status epilepticus*, brain damage and paraldehyde enemas. By now there are other wakeful patients in the ward, a groundswell of grumbling at the disturbance. And it's only – he looks at his watch – quarter past ten. It's going to be a long, long night. Perhaps he should have taken that sedative after all. Just sheer bloody-mindedness not to have done it because Corby-Clifford had prescribed it.

And what would have happened to Ted then? a voice in his head murmurs. A bit of lost sleep? It really doesn't matter.

His neighbour's breathing is less chokingly audible now, but the rhythmic banging continues. Muffled curses, and a powerful chemical stink like vinegar begins to invade the room, overriding the smell of urine-soaked sheets and Lifebuoy soap. It takes Nash back to the wards in France and Sidcup, to men with much worse head injuries than his, struck down with uncontrollable fitting like Ted's.

Despite everything, he must have dozed a little, because the next thing he knows, Scobie is putting a mug of tea down on his locker.

'Wha—what time is it?' The ward's silent again.

'Just after eleven. Still trying to get things straight.' In the dim light, Nash sees Scobie cast an assessing, almost sly glance his way. 'You seemed awful restless, mumbling and carrying on. Thought you'd have everyone awake again, so I brought you a cuppa.'

The dream – half-dream – comes back to Nash. With a groan he wonders if the hallucinations have begun again, but his skin is cool, almost cold, and his brain feels quite clear.

Jo. Half-hidden in deep shadow. She's upset about something, worried. Somehow, it's France, and she's trying to reach him through deep trenches of mud. Or is it blood? The stink of rot is in his nostrils, and he calls to her. Go back. Don't risk it. Stay safe.

'Sorry. Hope I didn't—'

'No, you're all right.' Scobie lingers, the way he had earlier in the evening. What's it all about? Nash thinks. Surely the man can't want to talk at this time of night? Resigned, he boosts himself up on the pillows, rubs a hand across his face. Perhaps it won't take too long.

'Thanks for the tea. How's Ted?'

Scobie shakes his head. 'Not so good. Sister Meadowes has called Mr Corby-Clifford in.'

'At this time of night?' He's surprised to think the surgeon would be so altruistic, especially as he's supposed to be on the sick list himself.

'Any bloody time of night,' Scobie grumbles. 'Midnight or three o'clock in the morning, it's all the same to him, seemingly. Caught him sneaking around more than once this last week. Even when he hasn't been asked to come in.'

'Perhaps he's got a girlfriend on the staff.'

Scobie pulls a face. 'Boyfriend down in the park's more like it. One of the soldiers. I saw them together, very friendly. Must have been saying their fond farewells, I reckon.'

The man seems to have a positive weakness for scandal of any kind, Nash thinks, though he can't imagine why the orderly would suppose he'd be interested in Corby-Clifford's sex life. 'That kind of thing . . . my view is, live and let live.'

'You're missing the point, mate. Never mind. You get back to sleep now, before Mr High-and-Mighty comes in and catches you or we'll both be in trouble. Oh, and I've put that pill down the lavvy. Thought I'd better get rid of the evidence, like.'

The beat of my heels echoes the stutter of my heart as I hurry away from Market Place. I'm not sure where I'm going except away. Anywhere, so long as I get away from Alec's hands and mouth, his assumptions about me.

My eyes blur with tears. I'm not a prude, and I didn't think I was naive, but I feel ashamed, dirty. I misread him so completely, the way he turned from flirtation to outright menace in the blink of an eye . . .

That he could think . . . that he could *imagine* I'd be willing to sell myself. That he'd gloat about forcing me, enjoying it . . .

A sudden great flare of anger bursts through the fear. How dare he? How dare he think I'd play his filthy game? Let him use my love for Bram to coerce me?

I pull up short. Bram. What might Alec do to Bram?

His threat was explicit. I'm sick with self-disgust. I'm worse than Alec. Running away, saving my own skin, when Bram's in danger.

I turn back. I don't know what I'm going to do. Only that I have to do something. I can't slink home and leave Alec free to . . .

Tilling. If I went to the police station and told him, would he believe me? Even if he did, what could he do? Alec hasn't actually done anything more than frighten me. He'd just say I'd led him on, and I had. I know it was so I could put him off guard and get away, but he'd have the pub regulars on his side, not to mention my tarnished reputation.

And as for my fears for Bram . . . I can hear Sergeant Tilling laughing at the very idea. A reputable man like Alec Corby-Clifford? An eminent surgeon, sworn to do good? Not a hope in hell he'd believe me. That anyone would.

Back in Market Place, I'm torn. I've no sense of how long it's been since I watched him walk into the hotel. A quarter of an hour? Twenty minutes? Long enough, at any rate, for him to have realised I'm not going to show up.

I should leave. Every instinct but one screams it. And that one won't let me go. I need to keep watch.

I find myself a shadowy corner in the lee of the Cornmarket, where I can see the hotel's front door and coach way. I don't know what I'm waiting for, but I know I have to stay.

He'll be so angry. Frustrated. The best I can hope for is that he's written me off in disgust. The worst . . . that he'll come looking for me, wanting to pay me back for tricking him. He'll see it as humiliation, need to punish me.

The brave thing would be to go across to the hotel. To walk in, ask for him at reception. Brazen it out, tell him that I couldn't find a way in after all, pretend I'm disappointed. I'm almost sure the hotel staff wouldn't let me to go up to his room, so I'd be safe enough, at least tonight. But I'm not brave. I can't persuade myself to do it. And every minute that passes makes it that much less likely he'll believe me.

What if he's out here somewhere already? Every sound, every movement makes me jump. I'm shivering with chill, a combination of the night air and fright. I think longingly of Dot's warm kitchen. I'd be so much safer there. She wouldn't give me away if she knew what Alec is really like.

And that one instinct which is keeping me here is because I know what Alec's really like. Him coming after me isn't the worst thing that could happen. That's if he carries out his threat to get back at me by making Bram his target.

It's my fault that Bram's in Alec's sights, vulnerable to his sadism. And it is sadism, not just a surgeon's ruthless efficiency. Alec enjoys giving pain. I've seen it, felt it. Heard it. That cry of Bram's when Alec first examined him still plays in my head.

As time ticks by, I start to worry that I'm too late. That's he's already left the hotel. That he might be on his way to the hospital annexe to hurt Bram.

I try to tell myself it's ridiculous. That even he wouldn't expect to get away with some kind of midnight revenge on a patient. But it would be so easy. An urgent procedure, a changed prescription. It goes round and round in my head. He's got such power . . .

Later, I'll tell myself that I was about to take my courage in my hands, go over to the hotel, when the door opens and Alec steps out. I think it's true, but I'm not sure. I don't know if it would have made any difference if I had. At this moment, as he crosses the road towards me, all I can think is that he's seen me. And how much more afraid of him I am than I've been telling myself I was. I shrink back, but there's no need. He moves purposefully past the shopfront that's sheltering me and disappears from my view in the direction of Bell Street.

South, I think. Towards the bypass, and Broadlands? I dash across to the hotel, tumble in through the door. The receptionist looks up, surprised. Recognises me with a smile.

'Good evening, Mrs Lester. I'm so sorry, but if you're looking for Mr Corby-Clifford, I'm afraid you've just missed him. He's been called out to see someone at the hospital wing at Broadlands. It sounded rather urgent.'

I'm dumb. It's my worst nightmare.

'I offered to telephone for a taxi,' she goes on, 'but he wouldn't wait. He seemed rather upset.'

'Thanks.' I'm halfway back through the door when she calls after me. She'll probably put me down as upset too.

'Would you like to leave a message for him?'

'No need. I'll catch up with him soon.'

It has to be soon, I think. Adrenaline and dread are pouring through me, bringing a terrible sense of foreboding. I mustn't be too late.

I hurry down Bell Street but there's no sign of Alec. Into Banning Street, the close-packed terraces making the roadway seem very dark. Ahead, at last, I spot a figure. Please, let it be him.

Yes.

I see his distinctive outline silhouetted against the lighter spaces of the bypass beyond. He crosses the footbridge over the stream, moves quickly across the stretch of green beyond.

Careful not to alert him to my presence, I hang back as he pauses to scan the road for traffic.

Everything is so quiet I'm worried he'll hear my laboured breathing. The sound of his footsteps carries clearly to me as he crosses towards the Broadlands gate. I daren't step forward yet, the green verge and road offer no cover to hide me if I do. My heart hammering with anxiety, I wait till I hear the squeal of iron hinges as Alec goes into the park.

I daren't delay a moment longer. I dart forward, cross bridge and green and road in one careless rush, less concerned about passing vehicles than that Alec doesn't see me.

How to get into the park without that betraying screech of iron on iron? The gates across the main entrance are firmly shut, but the small pedestrian gate which Alec must have used is helpfully ajar. I edge my way round, moving it as little as possible. A squeak, no more. If he hears it, perhaps he'll think it's an owl.

I've lost sight of him again. The trees along the drive offer me plenty of cover, but I'm uneasily aware that it's the same for him, too. If he's realised he's being followed, he could be lying in wait somewhere in the shadows.

Speed or stealth? I do my best to remember what Alf showed me the other night about moving unseen through the landscape. Keep on the grass, near the trees but not under or between them. The shadows are best if I want to move fast.

If Alf were here now, he'd probably still think I was making enough noise for a herd of elephants. God, it would be good if he were, but with Tilling's warning, I know he's taken his foraging over towards Baddesley the last few nights.

I can do it if I have to.

I can do it alone.

I grow rash, cut corners as I move towards the dark bulk of Broadlands House. I need to catch up with Alec, but there's no sign of him. I don't know what I'll do if I've lost him.

The trees give me cover enough to get close to the front of the house without risk of being seen. Just as well, because there's a woman in the uniform of a senior nurse standing in the entrance. She seems to be waiting for something. My heart skips a beat. Or someone? Perhaps I've beaten Alec to it after all. I close my eyes, try to calm my breathing. Count to ten . . .

'Mr Corby-Clifford.' The woman's voice is pitched low, but it carries quite clearly to where I'm hiding. I open my eyes with a start. Alec's walking across the gravel towards the nurse, making so little noise I haven't heard a thing. Alf would be proud of him.

'Sister.' His voice makes me shiver. 'I came as fast as I could. How is Warren now?'

'Very poor, I'm afraid.' They move into the portico, and I don't catch any more of what they say. Somewhat relieved, I settle again to wait. I feel sorry for Warren, whoever he might be. But I'm profoundly glad it's him and not Bram who's needing Alec's attentions.

Nash lies wakeful in the quiet ward. Warren's breathing is slow and regular now, each exhalation sending another gust of paraldehyde-tainted breath his way. Even without that, he doubts he could sleep. Scobie's hints, which had seemed like nosiness and tittle-tattle, are nagging at the back of his mind. He should have tried harder to persuade the orderly to tell him more. At the very least, he could have asked which nights he'd seen Corby-Clifford, and when. If Sunday had been one of the occasions, either might have seen something that relates to Richard Lester's death.

Nash tries to put it together in his head, but he's blocked by knowing so little. If only he could have talked to Jo, asked her the questions that are going round in his head now. What time had Richard Lester died? He knows the man was alive and well shortly after nine when Alice Beech and he had set out for Romsey. And the fire hadn't started till three, so where might he have been till then? If he'd been alive, what might he have done? Where could he have gone?

He'd been supposed to go to the docks by midnight to embark, so the fact he was still in Romsey suggests he must have been dead by then, anyway . . .

Nash suddenly becomes aware of voices out in the hallway. Corby-Clifford's clipped tones are immediately recognisable. The other belongs to Sister Meadowes, the night sister. Neither will be pleased if they find him awake. He turns his face away from the nightlight burning over Ted Warren's bed, slows his breathing to a level he hopes will pass muster to convince them he's sleeping.

'Mr Corby-Clifford, sir. Sister.' Scobie must have been waiting for them in the hallway.

'Anything to report?'

'No, sir. All quiet. Mr Warren hasn't had any more fits.'

'Right. Let's take a look.'

They're in the room now. Nash keeps as still as he can, hoping Corby-Clifford will stay on the far side of Ted's bed. But as before, the close confines of the ward make him an inevitable eavesdropper to what's going on.

'Warren,' Corby-Clifford calls sharply, but there's no audible response. 'Hmm. I'll need him on his back. Just roll him for me, Scobie.'

The rustle of bedclothes, a grunt from Scobie. The muffled thump of a heavy body flopping helplessly.

'Patella hammer, Sister.'

A soundless pause.

'Pin.'

Another silent moment.

'No response?' Sister Meadowes asks.

'Not a flicker.'

'The paraldehyde?'

'Filthy stuff, but it doesn't suppress reflexes. Torch.'

Silence.

'Hmm, hmm. Pupils both blown, unreactive. Let's have him back on his side.'

More effortful noises.

'Will he need further surgery, do you think?' Sister Meadowes says. 'Perhaps we should transfer him back to the RSH.'

'Do more harm than good in his state. I want him in a room of his own, though. The sooner the better, before the sedative wears off.' He yawns. 'Absolute quiet will be essential.'

'I think we might contrive something if we clear the bottom linen room. There's space enough in there for a bed, though there aren't any windows.'

'Perfect, dark is good.'

'If you'll excuse me, then, I'll go and get it organised. Scobie, you'd better take your break when you've seen Mr Corby-Clifford out.'

'Thank you, Sister.'

Nash listens intently but hears only one set of footsteps leaving.

'That's Nash in the next bed, isn't it?' There's Corby-Clifford again, sounding very close.

'Yes, sir. He was the one alerted us to Mr Warren's condition.'

'Tuh. He should have been sleeping. Didn't he take his sedative?'

Nash tries not to tense, waiting for Scobie's answer. Thinks about faking a snore. Rejects it.

'Yes, sir. Gave it to him myself. Looks like he's spark out now, anyway.'

'You think? Well, I'll review it tomorrow.' Another cracking yawn. 'I'll get on my way.'

'If I could just speak to you for a moment, sir?'

'What? What do you want?' Corby-Clifford sounds irritable. Nash can't blame him for that.

'It's a private matter, sir. I'd rather not talk about it here.'

'Look, man, it's late. Spit it out. If you've got haemorrhoids or a dose of the clap—'

'Nothing like that. It's you I'm thinking of, see. Your reputation.'

In the cover of the shadows, Nash frowns. What game is Scobie playing now?

'What are you talking about?'

'I'm trying *not* to talk about it in here, but if you insist. Thing is, Sunday night I happened to see—'

Christ, Nash thinks. *Sunday* night . . .

A scuffle. 'Hold your tongue.'

It's blackmail, and by the sound of Corby-Clifford's panicky response, there's something to blackmail him about. He has to put a stop to this, pronto. He shifts, pretending to wake up. But it's too late. The two men are already out of the door.

For the second time tonight, Nash gets out of bed. Hunts for his slippers. He'll have to do something. Find someone. But instead, someone finds him.

'Mr Nash.'

He jerks upright. Sister Meadowes.

'What do you think you're doing out of bed? I knew you weren't asleep. Back you get.'

She does that same trick Irish is so good at, hoisting him into bed without his help or volition.

'Now then.' She holds out a medicine glass with half an inch of colourless fluid in the bottom. 'Take this.'

'What is it?'

'Chloral hydrate. It will help you sleep.'

'I don't want—'

'Take it, or I'll call Mr Corby-Clifford back to prescribe a sedative I can give by injection. I know you can't have swallowed that tablet, whatever Mr Scobie might have thought.'

He hesitates. If she calls the surgeon back, it'll interrupt his conversation with Scobie. That would only be for the good. But a craven voice in his head is urging discretion. If Corby-Clifford comes back, realises he's been awake, listening . . . There's no telling what knock-out concoction he might prescribe.

'Go on. Take it.'

He swallows half the dose, grimacing at the bitter taste.

'All of it.'

Reluctantly, he complies. 'Sister, I'm worried—'

'That's why you need the chloral. You must sleep.'

He tries again. 'Scobie and Mr Corby-Clifford seemed to be having an argument. He seemed very annoyed. Mr Corby-Clifford, I mean.'

She chuckles. 'No need to worry about that. That'll be Scobie on one of his crusades. Silly man, what a time to pick. He's got a bee in his bonnet about Mr Corby-Clifford taking some instruments from our store the other night. I've told him, it's nothing for him to concern himself with.'

Could that be it? Just Scobie being officious? 'But—'

'But me no buts. Now, settle down. You'll be glad of the chloral, because we're going to be in and out of here for a while, getting Mr Warren off to a room of his own. And don't be in any doubt but that we'll be keeping an eye on you, too.'

It seems an age before Alec comes out again. I'm on tenterhooks, wondering what he's doing. Should I follow him in? I don't even know where Bram is. I can hardly stand guard over his bed. They'd chuck me out as a loony. I debate it. It might be worth it if it meant they might call Tilling . . .

But I don't. Once again, I stay at a distance, ashamed of my lack of spine. I'd pray, except I don't believe in it. I'm no use at all.

Voices. Footsteps. Alec. Not the sister with him this time, though. A stout little man in the white jacket of a medical orderly is trotting along a pace or two in front. Unlikely as it might seem, it's the orderly who appears to be taking the lead, Alec following.

Another decision to make. Leave or wait? Follow them? Driven by the same instinct that's brought me this far, insisting I need to keep tabs on Alec, I follow.

They set out along another gravel path, and though Alec's still moving silently as a cat, the other man's footsteps are self-importantly loud in the night. There's not much risk of losing them. I can afford to stay further back.

The path they've taken leads away from the house, skirting the formal garden before it strikes out into the park. Trees border the left-hand side of the path, tall evergreens whose dropped needles make a pillowing layer underfoot.

An easy task for me to stalk along parallel with them in the concealing shadow. I'd love to hear what they're saying, but I daren't get any closer.

A roofline appears. Not four square like the main house, this is a single storey with a pitched roof. Set so it must offer an unobstructed view south across the parkland, the building makes up for its lack of height with length. A part-glazed roof and fancy columns at the end nearest me make it look like a cross between a Greek temple and one of Wills' tomato houses.

The footsteps stop, and as I continue to creep forward, I hear Alec's voice.

'What is this place?'

'The Orangery, sir.' That must be the orderly. 'It's nice and private, like, for a smoke of an evening. Or a bit of a chat, of course. I often come down here on my break. Bit of shelter under the porch, even if the weather's bad. I can watch the comings and goings. Foxes and badgers, you'd be surprised what I get to see.'

'For God's sake, Scobie, I'm not interested in your wildlife musings. Say what you've got to say and let me get off to bed.' Alec sounds as if he's on the verge of losing his temper, but there's something else too, a hint of bluster that puzzles me. But even that's not so much of a mystery as the fact he's here at all.

'Not just wildlife, sir. It's quiet now the soldiers have gone, but there were lots of interesting things to see when they were here. Know what I mean?'

'I've no *idea* what you mean.'

The two men have moved into the Greek-seeming portico, and I edge closer to keep them in view. Scobie – if that's his name – pulls a pack of cigarettes out of his pocket, offers Alec one. He waves them away irritably.

'Well, sir. Just as a for instance, take last Sunday evening. Nine o'clock or thereabouts, I happened to see you in the treatment room. We'd only just replaced the missing stock from last week, and there you were, at it again. Wasn't as if we'd called you out or nothing. We'd had a quiet evening.'

Sunday evening, I think. Alec was here at nine on Sunday evening? An awful suspicion begins to slither into my consciousness.

Alec laughs. There's relief in the sound. 'You're after me for borrowing a few bits and pieces ready for my trip to France? Come on, man. You surely can't think anyone would be interested in that. If I hadn't been injured, I'd be out there on the battlefield by now.'

'No, sir. It's not about the instruments, though it's true we're awful short ourselves. It was after that. I saw you again out in the garden. Taking the air, maybe.'

'That's a crime now? This is ridiculous. You're just wasting my time.' Alec turns abruptly away from the orderly as if he's about to leave. Though his voice has the same mocking quality as before, I get a glimpse of his face. He's far from amused.

'There was a man,' Scobie goes on as Alec paces behind him. 'A soldier, tall chap. He came up from the park in a hell of a hurry. But you seemed to know him. Very friendly, you looked. Went off together to the stables, very chummy.'

God. The suspicion grows. A tall man, in uniform. In a hurry . . . Could it have been Richard? Could he have come this far?

'What of it?' No amusement now. A chill that makes me cold through to my bones, though Scobie doesn't seem to feel it.

'Buggery is against the law, sir.'

'You think I'm a queer? A nancy boy?' Another laugh.

'Just saying, sir.'

'That's all you've got? Seeing me meet a friend?'

Scobie sighs. 'I had to go back to the ward, then. But later . . .' he picks a shred of tobacco from his lip '. . . I saw you again. Proper night for it, it was. There you were, strolling up through the park at three o'clock with a great grin on your face. Though I bet that hand hurt, didn't it?'

I don't know if Scobie had worked it out. If he'd realised how damning his evidence was. Whether he was accusing Alec not just of sexual misconduct, but murder too. Because that's where my suspicions have brought me.

The evidence is damning. With a sense of inevitability so strong I don't know how I didn't put my doubts about Alec together before now, I'm convinced. Alec is Richard's killer.

My head swims and I can't seem to breathe. For a moment it feels as if the universe is poised on a pinhead. Topple and fall, or go on?

'What do you want?' Alec says.

'Sensible man,' Scobie says. 'I've got you bang to rights, no point making a fuss. Reckon we can come to an agreement, don't you? Something for our mutual benefit?'

'Cash for silence? How much?'

'Two hundred and fifty now, fifty a month after.'

'That's a bit steep.'

Scobie shrugs. 'Worth it, though, if you don't want it to get about. Be a bit of a pity if I happened to let it slip, accidental like, one day. Especially since that Nash chap is on my ward.'

I think that's the threat which galvanises Alec. Before I can move, shout a warning even, he attacks, fingers digging into Scobie's neck. Horrified, I see the little man claw at Alec's hands, trying to break his hold. I look round wildly. I can't stand and watch; I have to do something.

But even as I move forward, Scobie crumples to the ground. He gives a kind of convulsive shudder, and then lies still.

I don't know what I'm thinking. I can't be thinking at all because I don't run. Don't scream for help. Like a rabbit mesmerised by the stoat's dance, I stand clear of my hiding place.

'Alec.'

'Josephine. How unexpected. What are you doing here? I thought you'd run away.' His voice is slurred, almost sexual as he pushes Scobie's body with a foot. Not quite a kick, but something like. There's no reaction. The medical orderly doesn't stir.

Still in a daze, I hear myself say, 'What happened, Alec? Surely you can't have killed him?'

Alec makes an amused little sound in his throat, almost a chuckle. 'Oh, I've killed him. A little expert knowledge is all it takes. A few seconds compression on the right nerves. Quick and silent, nothing so crude as strangulation.'

'And . . . What Scobie said about Sunday night . . . did you kill Richard too?'

'Of course.' He smiles, takes a step towards me. 'Different method, same result. You've been a bit slow, Josephine, haven't you? You'd never have guessed if it hadn't been for this carrion.' This time it is a kick.

'I suppose not.'

'The question is, what am I going to do with you now?' Another step.

I back away.

'It's true,' he goes on, 'that I wanted to kill you earlier, when you didn't keep your promise. But now . . .' he frowns '. . . I've lost my appetite for you, somehow.'

I can hear the words, but they don't seem to add up. I suppose I must still be in shock, because I can't seem to realise what's happening, feel the danger I'm in. I've heard it said that in a civilised society we're so unused to violence, we don't respond quickly enough when it happens. Like sheep at an abattoir, we go meekly to the slaughter. That's why they have to train civilians before they send them off as soldiers. 'Why did you do it?'

'Go off you? Perhaps killing's more fun.'

Another step forward for him, one back for me. A slow dance to death, I find myself thinking. 'And . . . Richard?'

'A long story, my lovely. Not sure you'll be around long enough to hear it. Now, wouldn't you like to take a chance? For your poor Mr Nash's sake, if nothing else. It's not far through to the house. Why don't you just . . . *Run!*'

It's the worst thing I could do, I know it. The chase will only excite him. But his tone, that last word acts like a trigger. And like a gun, I explode.

I do run, gravel spurting under my feet. I'm panting with terror before I've taken a dozen steps, though I've no sense for a moment that he's pursuing me. I might make it . . .

Then I hear him laugh, much closer than he's any right to be. A hand grabs at my shoulder, pulls me round in a skidding halt.

'Alec—'

His hands reach for my throat. 'Josephine. Oh, dear, Josephine.'

There's no pain. No time for that. The world goes black. My last thought, my only thought as I fall is *Bram*.

Thanks to the chloral, Nash sleeps through the hustle and bustle of moving Ted Wallace's bed from the ward. Sleeps on through the annoyance and concern when Scobie fails to return from his break. Short of a pair of hands because of Scobie's absence, the remaining nurses are happy to leave him to it, one less patient to worry about.

25

Saturday 10ᵗʰ June 1944, early morning

WHEN THE BLACKNESS RECEDES, MY limbs are cramped. I try to stretch, but I can't. I'm lying on my side, my right shoulder and hip, the right side of my face pressed hard against a cold surface. There's the sour taste of vomit in my mouth and my throat feels bruised and swollen.

I open my eyes. A dusty grey expanse presents itself to my view. By raising my head a painful inch, I can see it's a stone floor. I'm lying on a cold grey stone floor in a cold grey light that speaks of early morning. I struggle to sit up, but my wrists are bound behind my back, my ankles tied. In some way the bonds must be linked, because when I try to straighten my legs, the movement drags on my wrists. For a few frantic moments, I fight, but it's useless, a waste of energy. The ties are just getting tighter and tighter. I let myself flop. Think, I need to think . . .

There's a sound that chills me more than the stone flags I'm lying on. A human chuckle.

I'm not alone.

'Wh—what?'

'Back in the land of the living, Josephine?'

Alec, of course. Who else?

'I must admit, I was beginning to wonder if I'd gone too far. That commando trick is very useful, but you were out much longer than I expected.'

Footsteps approach. Tan brogues appear in my view as hard hands take hold of me, haul me upright, prop me into a painful, half-sitting, half-kneeling position against a wall. Renewed perspective lets me see the space I'm in from one extreme end: massive, impressive, empty, smelling vaguely of earth and damp. I must be inside the Orangery. A blank wall at my shoulder stretches away to my left, floor-to-ceiling windows face me. But between me and them – and, for that matter, the two doors in the cross-wall to my right – Alec squats on his haunches like some elegant but poisonous toad.

'What are you going to do with me, Alec?'

'A very good question. Just what I was asking myself. You are a bit of a nuisance, my lovely.' He laughs. 'Though actually, not so very lovely right now. You should see yourself.'

I don't need a mirror to tell me my hair's come out of the combs, and there's a button off my good green blouse. My skirt is filthy with dirt from the floor, and it feels suspiciously damp. I must have wet myself when I blacked out. I swallow, try to match my tone with his, echo his apparent nonchalance. 'I'd rather not.'

He leans forward, picks a clump of cobwebs from my hair. The touch of his hand makes me shiver.

'Cold hands.' Another laugh. 'I'm sorry, but you know what they say. *Cold hands, warm heart.* That must be why I haven't killed you yet.' He stands, brushes his fingertips together to clean them before pulling fastidiously at the knees of his trousers to restore the crease.

'What have you done with Scobie?' It feels unsafe to remind him, but I have to know. My only hope is to talk my way through this. Or him, out of it.

'That stupid little man? Don't worry about him,' he says with a smile. 'I borrowed a wheelchair from the annexe, popped him in the river. With a bit of luck, he won't surface till he gets to Southampton.'

The more he speaks, the more deranged he sounds. I don't know if this is the real Alec revealing himself, or if he's having some kind of breakdown in front of my eyes. 'That . . . should give you time to get away before anyone realises.'

'My idea exactly. I think the best thing would be for me to make my way across the Channel. Talk my way onto one of the transports. Should be easy enough, they're desperate for surgeons.' Another of those mad little laughs. 'Perhaps I could take Richard's place.'

'You'd . . . work with the army?'

He cocks his head, looks consideringly at me. 'I might, if I thought you wouldn't give me away. But I don't think I can rely on that, can I? Not even after all I've done for your Mr Nash.'

'I told you I was grateful for that.'

'Not grateful enough.' With a sudden dart of his hand, he grabs a handful of my hair, drags my head painfully towards him. 'Unless you'd like to reconsider?'

My heart stutters in fear. If I say yes, would it give me a chance to lull him, get away? But even for that, I can't. 'No.'

A huge tug tears hair from my scalp, brings involuntary tears to my eyes. Then he pushes me away in disgust. 'You bitch,' he says. 'As if I'd want you now. Stinking of piss and vomit, snot running down your face. Give me credit for some taste.'

He flicks a clump of my hair from his fingers, paces across to the window. 'The thing is,' he says in a musing kind of voice that makes me think he's speaking to himself rather than me, 'this bloody invasion's upset all my plans. Germany's supposed to win this time. I've been banking on it. That's what Richard didn't understand. Not even at the beginning.'

'He didn't?'

'He was so bloody sanctimonious. I mean, it wasn't just me. They offered the way out for both of us.' He turns from the window, contempt on his face. 'His morals were fluid enough when it came to women. You know that.'

'Was this . . . after Dunkirk?'

'It was an adventure,' he says plaintively. 'A quest. We weren't supposed to get caught. I don't care what Richard said, he was shitting himself too. They could have shot us, you know. I thought they would. So when they offered a gentleman's agreement . . . well, it was obvious, wasn't it? Especially when I didn't disagree with them, not fundamentally.'

There's a silence I don't know how to break. The idea that he's in sympathy with Nazi doctrine is distasteful, but I suppose I shouldn't be surprised. His cruelty, his sense of superiority, even his damned appearance fit so well with their ideals.

'We had a row,' he says at last, and I can't tell if he's talking about 1940 or now. 'Richard and me. A ridiculous argument about principles. I ask you, what do they matter when your life's on the line? You'd say anything, wouldn't you? Do anything.'

Not anything, I think. I know that now. And there's a part of me, scared as I am, that's glad to know Richard wouldn't either.

'He wouldn't have it,' Alec goes on. 'I told him, I wasn't going to rot in a POW camp for years when I could get out so easily. I only had to give my word and they sent me home.'

'But Richard stayed?'

'Oh, yes. St Richard stayed, incarcerated for his faith.' He laughs. 'Proper little martyr. Never thought I'd see him again. Certainly wouldn't have credited him with the gumption to escape. And then I had to run into him like that. What were the odds? Another hour or two and he'd have been gone, not a whit the wiser.'

'This was . . . Sunday?'

'He accused me of being a spy. *Me*. I told him; it was nothing like that. Nothing so sordid. All I had to do when I got back was speak up for the advantages of the German system.

Use my influence. I could do that with a perfectly clear conscience. Then when the Reich triumphed, I'd be ready, waiting to take up my proper position.'

'He didn't see it like that?'

'He was as bloody stiff-necked as you. No wonder you
couldn't get on.' He draws a deep breath, seems to focus. The
edge of madness retreats behind the cool facade I'm used to,
and he's all business again.

'Now, I think what we'll do is this. I'm going to stroll over
to the wards, put in an appearance. See what they're saying
about Scobie.'

'And me?'

'There's the rub. What *am* I going to do with you?' He stalks
towards me, reaching into his jacket pocket. When he brings
out his hand, I see he has a knife. Not a modern scalpel this
time. With a frisson of fear, I recognise the long, fixed blade
of the kind of surgical instrument they'd used in the 1920s.

I don't think I've ever been more scared in my life. Not in
the Blitz, not even when Ruth's brother had held me hostage
three years ago. He'd had a gun, but I'd never really believed
he'd use it. Alec . . . I've seen the result of his work with a
scalpel. The blood. I feel light-headed. Try not to show it.

'Pretty little thing, isn't it?' he says. 'So sharp you don't feel
the first cut. Now then, hold still. It really is in your interest
not to struggle.'

*All over Romsey, telephones begin to ring. First, Dot, embar-
rassed. A call to the White Horse. No, Mr Corby-Clifford*

isn't available. He was called out to an emergency late last night and hasn't yet returned. No, Mrs Lester isn't there either. There are undertones of shocked disapproval that Mrs Gray should think such irregularities might go on in their hotel.

Next, Dot, furious, to the police station. Jumping to conclusions, insisting on speaking to Sergeant Tilling. Accusing him of locking Mrs Lester up again. Too worried to be easily mollified when he tells her he hasn't done anything of the sort.

And again, Dot, forcing herself to seem calm, to the office of Nash, Simmons and Bing. Aggie, puzzled to be asked. Mrs Lester isn't in yet. It's still early.

Aggie to Fan Stewart. No sign, no news. Why would Mrs Lester be there? When the story's told, she's anxious too. She rings Sylvie Fox. No, Jo's not with them. The sense of alarm gains momentum. Where can she be?

Aggie and Dot. Two frightened women at the police station. Dot's feeling guilty. She knows Jo hadn't wanted to go out with Corby-Clifford last night. As Tilling tries to calm them, the phone rings. It's Mountbatten Annexe. The water bailiff has just fished a body out of the river.

Breakfast comes and goes, and Nash sleeps on, porridge congealing in the bowl at his bedside. It's almost nine before he comes to, groggy as hell and with a thumping headache. He blinks, trying to focus on his surroundings. All the patients are already up, beds tidily made. There's a space next to him where Ted Wallace should be, and the sight of the empty place brings back the events of the night.

He struggles to sit up. Drinks thirstily from the glass of water on his bedside locker. Beyond the quiet of the semi-deserted ward, there seems to be some kind of fuss going on. Raised voices. An argument?

He swings his legs out of bed, cursing the chloral for making him so muzzy. He has to find a lavatory. Out in the hall, turn right. Unoccupied, thank God. The relief of his bladder and splashing his face and neck with chilly water brings him back to some semblance of normality. Whatever they say, he thinks, yawning, he won't be taking any more of that muck tonight.

In the hallway again, he can hear someone crying. A woman. He wonders about Ted, if the worst has happened. But it's anxiety he hears in the buzz of voices acting as counterpoint to the sound of tears, not condolence. He pulls his dressing gown more securely round himself, sets out to investigate the source of the fuss. He's sick of being passive while events move round him. Sick of not knowing what's going on.

Beyond, in the main entrance hall, surprises come in quick succession. The first is seeing Sergeant Tilling bending over the weeping figure of Sister Meadowes, who's huddled on an incongruously placed chair. He can't imagine what's upset her so much. Or why she's still here so long after the end of her shift. A crowd of onlookers account for the buzz of sound: nurses, medical orderlies, patients in dressing gowns and slippers all milling about together. It's a mark of the confusion that no one takes notice of him or tries for the moment to hustle him back to bed.

As he gets closer, there's a second shock. At the back of the throng, by the main door, he sees Aggie Haward. What in hell is she doing here? As if his thought has reached her, she turns her head, spots him. Face grim, she nods her head in acknowledgement. Whatever it is that's brought her, it's not good news.

No time to find out. An impressive figure sweeps in from the portico. He recognises the Matron-in-charge of the RSH hospitals, and though he doesn't think he ever managed to say anything to her, he dimly remembers her speaking to him on her morning rounds.

She claps her hands. 'Silence.' She doesn't raise her voice, but it carries across the space with absolute clarity. 'This is a hospital, not a side show to a circus. Nurses, orderlies, about your business. Get these patients back to their wards. You' – she points to one flinching nurse – 'take Sister Meadowes to the nurses' sitting room at once.'

The area begins to clear. Matron crosses to Sergeant Tilling. Aggie Haward, dauntless as ever, follows. Despite the general order for patients to leave, Nash is determined. He's going nowhere until he finds out why they are here.

But it seems there's not going to be a row about it. As the three of them confer, Irish arrives at his side with a wheelchair and blanket. Rather than the expected instruction to get back to bed, she gestures to the wheelchair, deals the third shock. 'You're exempt from the edict,' she says. 'They want you to stay. But I think you'd better sit down.'

Full of misgivings, he does as she asks. If they're not insisting on treating him as a patient with that irritating, half-patronising concern that's excluded him from any kind of decision so far, something serious must be going on.

'What's all this about?' he says as Irish tucks the blanket round his legs.

'You'll find out soon enough. Here they come.'

'We need to consult you, Mr Nash.' Sergeant Tilling gestures to a half-open door, where Aggie and the matron are waiting. 'We can use the office there.'

A fragment of Nash's anxiety lifts briefly at the word 'consult'. That sounds like work. Something to do with this morning's fuss, perhaps, though it doesn't entirely explain Aggie's presence. Under Matron's eagle eye, Irish manoeuvres the wheelchair into the office, prepares to leave.

'Stay, O'Shaughnessy.' It's a curt command. 'I'm here to represent the hospital, Mr Nash. This is all most irregular, but I'm persuaded there's no alternative. Shut the door, Sergeant. Sit down, and your associate, Miss ... whatever your name is. We need to get this *consultation* over with as quickly as possible. Mr Nash must be allowed to rest.'

Tilling hunches in his chair, looks uncomfortable. 'I'm sorry to have to call on you, Mr Nash, but we're in a right pickle. Missing persons, suspicious death, the works.'

He picks out the element most likely to concern him. 'A death?'

'One of the orderlies here. The water bailiff fished him out of the river this morning. Chap called Scobie.'

'*Scobie*?'

'You knew him?'

'Yes.' He takes a deep breath. 'You're telling me he's dead? Drowned?'

Tilling shakes his head. 'Not drowned, we don't think. There are bruises on his neck, here and here.' He indicates a place on either side of his throat, close to his collarbone. 'We tried artificial respiration but there was no water coming out of his lungs. We'll have to wait for the post-mortem, but I'd guess he was dead before he went into the river.'

'Another murder?'

Tilling shrugs. 'Looks like it.'

'You'll need a witness statement from me, then.'

'You?' Tilling looks puzzled. 'Why ever . . . ? I want you to look at the body, but—'

'I'm probably one of the last people to have seen him alive. Heard him, anyway.'

'What?'

'You haven't talked to Sister Meadowes?'

'She's not making much sense at the moment,' Tilling says with disgust. 'I thought nurses were supposed to have clear heads.'

Out of the corner of his eye, Nash sees Matron draw herself up as if to speak, cuts in sharply before she can take over.

'Tell me, when *was* Scobie last seen? It's important.'

'Meadowes says she sent him off for his break around midnight. He was due back by one, but he didn't turn up.'

Nash blows out a deep breath. 'Then you need to be looking for a man called Corby-Clifford. A surgeon who's been attached to the annexe here. He was with Scobie at midnight or just after. And, God help me, I heard Scobie threatening him with blackmail.'

'Mr Nash?' It's Aggie, but Tilling holds up his hand to silence her.

His gaze fixed on Nash, he says, 'Why didn't you—?'

'They drugged me,' Nash says bitterly. 'Well meaning, of course. All for my own good. I tried to tell Sister Meadowes what I'd heard, but she dismissed it. Said it was some silly misunderstanding about missing instruments. But I thought at the time it was more serious than that.'

'This is utter nonsense,' Matron protests. 'It's true that the inventory came up with a deficit, but you cannot seriously suppose Mr Corby-Clifford had anything to do with Scobie's death.'

'I can most seriously suppose that he did,' Nash says. 'I know what I heard.'

'But that's fantastic,' the senior nurse goes on. 'He's a most respected man.'

'Matron, please,' Tilling breaks in. 'I must ask you to leave this to me. Now, Mr Nash?'

Nash rubs his hand across his face. 'Truth is, I missed it, Tilling. Twice last evening Scobie tried to tell me something and I didn't respond as he wanted. The first time was about the body in the car.'

'How did he know about that? We haven't released the information to the public yet.'

'You know what gossip's like in Romsey. Hospitals are even worse. That was the problem when Scobie first spoke to me. I called it gossip and he was offended. I told him he needed to speak to you if he thought he'd seen something, but he didn't seem keen. I thought it must be trivial, then the second time, he was talking specifically about Corby-Clifford. Said he'd seen the man hanging around at night.'

'Sunday?'

'Yes. I didn't know it then. I just thought Scobie was scandalmongering. He'd got this idea Corby-Clifford was indulging in indecent relationships with soldiers from the camp. I didn't think it was any of my business, so I brushed him off. It wasn't until I overheard him talking to the surgeon—'

'Mr Nash.' Aggie again.

'Hang on a minute, Aggie,' Nash says. 'I just need to finish. They were right next to me in the room. I was supposed to be asleep. Corby-Clifford had been called in to see a patient, and after, Scobie started to make insinuations about what he'd seen. That was when he said it was Sunday. They left the ward then and I tried to follow them, but Sister Meadowes caught me, made me take a sedative. I should have tried harder to make her listen. If Scobie was dead by one, Tilling, it's a ridiculously small window of opportunity. You need to get hold of Corby-Clifford.'

'*Mr Nash.*'

'What is it, Aggie?'

'Mrs Lester went out with Alec Corby-Clifford yesterday evening. Dot told me she hadn't really wanted to go, but he'd brought her flowers and everything, so Dot persuaded her. Mrs Lester said she wouldn't be long, but she hasn't come home. Dot thought ... well, she was worried, so she rang round trying to find her this morning. When she got in touch with me, we thought perhaps Sergeant Tilling had locked her up again, but ...'

'What?' Nash exclaims.

'It's a long story,' Tilling says. 'No time for it now. The thing is, Nash, no one's seen her since last night.'

Missing persons, Tilling had said, right at the beginning. And he'd ignored it. Oh, God, *Jo* ...

'She was with Corby-Clifford then?'

'Not actually with him then. We're not sure what had happened, because they were definitely together earlier on. The receptionist at the hotel said she'd gone rushing into the hotel a couple of minutes after he'd been called out. Seemed upset to learn he'd gone. Dashed out after him.'

'She went looking for him?' Nash says through gritted teeth.

'That's what the receptionist thought.'

Nash has no doubt she would have gone after Corby-Clifford if something had happened to make her suspicious of the surgeon. She's always more likely to run into danger than away from it.

'He came here,' he says slowly. 'And I listened to him being blackmailed, did nothing. Now Scobie's dead. You need to find him, Tilling. And Jo. You have to find her.'

26

Saturday, late morning

I'M TRUSSED UP, NAKED AS a chicken ready for roasting underneath the blanket Alec has wrapped me in. He'd derived unholy delight from slicing off my blouse and skirt with slow deliberation, the knife razor-sharp against my shrinking skin. He'd taken my shoes and stockings too, and if it hadn't been for the impossibility of getting me to stay in the wheelchair he'd used to get rid of Scobie's body, bound as I was, he'd probably have left me hog-tied in my undies. In the end, though, he'd had to admit defeat, cut the bandages he'd tied me with in the first place. He'd used strips of my clothing instead to strap me into the chair: wrists, ankles, even a band round my waist. Though I tried everything I could to hinder him, the knife made it an uneven contest. When he was done, I was bleeding from a dozen cuts, even more helpless than before.

'Don't trust you where I can't see you,' he'd said as he gagged me, swathed my head in the remnants of the bandages. Tucked the blanket round so nothing showed but my

329

bare feet and a few unrecognisable inches of my face. 'This way I can keep you close. That's the beauty of it, you see? No one's going to take any notice of a patient in a wheelchair.'

I'm not sure why he hasn't just killed me. I suppose he must think he has a use for me. I try not to think what it might be, though thankfully, he doesn't seem interested in what my body has to offer anymore. It's as if he's playing a game, tormenting me the way a cat will toy with a mouse before killing it. Or perhaps it's simpler than that: he needs me as a witness to his cleverness.

Whatever his reason, I try and tell myself it's his mistake. As he bumps the wheelchair along the gravel path to the house, I hold on to the idea that while I'm alive, there's still a chance, however remote, that I can get out of this. Under cover of the blanket, I work my wrists against their bonds. The silk from my blouse is tough, but it gives a little as I pull, the blanket acting in my favour now to conceal my efforts.

As we get closer to the house, I see there are several cars parked on the forecourt. One has the crest of the hospital on the door, another looks like Tilling's black police vehicle. My heart quickens. Could Alec's plans have gone awry after all? Do they know about Scobie already?

A group of patients in dressing gowns and slippers are standing about, while a harassed-looking nurse and medical orderly seem to be trying to get them to go back inside.

'What the hell?' Alec mutters.

I strain my whole body against my bonds, try to call out.

'Quiet,' he says, and I feel a sharp pricking in my back. 'One more sound out of you and you'll be dead before anyone knows it.'

There's a young man who's broken away from the group of patients coming towards us. The pressure on the knife-point increases momentarily and then withdraws. I don't know what Alec's done with the knife, but I know it won't be far away.

'What's happening?' Alec hails the young man. 'Some kind of flap on?'

The young man shrugs. 'One of the night staff chucked himself in the river last night. They're trying to make all the patients go back to bed so they can talk to us. Talk all they like, it's nothing to do with me. I'm off. I'm gasping for a smoke.'

'Me, too,' Alec laughs. 'Thanks for the info. Think we'll make ourselves scarce.' He turns the chair with a sickening wrench, starts back the way we've come.

The young man walks with us for a minute, then cuts away onto the grass bordering the path. 'I'm going down this way,' he says. 'There's a good place for a bit of peace and quiet down through the woods just here. Don't mind if you want to come along.'

'I'll have to stay on the path with this one.' Alec slaps my shoulder with his hand. 'You carry on. We'll be OK.'

'Take my advice, then. Steer clear of the Orangery,' the young man calls. 'It's always the first bloody place they look for smokers.'

*

'Aren't you jumping to conclusions?' Tilling says. 'We don't know Mrs Lester's with him.'

'I don't believe in coincidences,' Nash says, throwing the blanket off his legs and standing up. 'She's with him, or he knows where she is.'

Alive, he thinks. She has to be alive. He can't let himself believe anything else.

Tilling shakes his head. 'I'll do what I can, Mr Nash, but I'll be honest, I don't know where to start. I've only got half a dozen men and there's thousands of acres here for him to hide in. Always assuming he's not gone back to town or left the area altogether.'

'As long as you start somewhere,' Nash urges. 'Just do it. Aggie, see if you can get hold of Alf. If anyone can find their tracks, he can. Tilling, you should send someone to ask the estate workers for help. They'll know all the places to look. If you give me a minute to get dressed, we can go and see where the body was found.'

'Mr Nash—' Irish protests.

'You won't stop me,' he says. 'You can come with me or stay here. It's up to you.'

She studies him a moment. 'I'll come,' she says. 'Someone's got to look after you.'

When he's dressed, pulling the clothes he was wearing when he was admitted over his pyjamas, Irish stoops down and ties his shoelaces, hands him a stick. 'There now,' she says. 'Stubborn is as stubborn does. Let's hope it doesn't set you back too far.'

He manages the ghost of a smile. 'Well, at least I won't have to face Corby-Clifford if it does.'

'You really think he's your man?' she asks as they walk through to the main entrance. 'He's a mean bastard sure enough, but to kill poor old Scobie over a bit of a scandal . . . ?'

'I'll reserve judgement about that,' he says, though it's not true. He's already made up his mind. The sick feeling of apprehension in his gut tells him Corby-Clifford is guilty of more than indecency. 'At the very least, he's got questions to answer. And maybe for more than Scobie.'

'The body in the car?'

'Possibly.' The implications are enormous, but he can't let himself be distracted. Not while Jo is in danger. What he needs now is a cool head and clear thinking if he's to be of any help to her.

Outside, he feels almost disorientated to be out in the open after his week confined between hospital walls. The air is damp and cool on his skin and the sky seems oddly bright despite an overcast of cloud that threatens yet more rain.

'Where's your sergeant got to?' Irish asks. 'It's to be hoped he's got the posse organised.'

'If he hasn't, Aggie Haward will have done it. My secretary doesn't let the grass grow under her feet.'

'Don't send her out on the search, though, if you don't want us to have another patient on our hands. She's a poor colour. Looks like cardiac to me.'

He frowns, remembering how Aggie gets winded coming up the stairs to his office. What a fool he is, he's never thought of it in terms of illness. Another blind spot in his armour. There's so much he'll have to change once he gets fit, gets back to the office.

'Thanks for the tip. I'll ask her to stay on here, co-ordinate the search.'

But it seems Aggie's assumed that role already as she bustles up to him. He notices, as he might not have done without Irish's comment, that her lips are bluish, and there's a wheeze somewhere in the depths of her breathing. 'Alf's on his way,' she says. 'And Sergeant Tilling is instructing the search teams. A man on the staff in the private wing is going to investigate the buildings around the house.' She shakes her head. 'Seems there's a whole warren of icehouses and machinery rooms. There's even a tunnel under the lawn.'

'I can't imagine Corby-Clifford would know about those.'

'Better to be thorough,' she says primly.

'Of course. You'll stay here, Aggie? Co-ordinate our efforts.'

'If you think that's for the best. I'm so sorry, Mr Nash. About Mrs Lester, I mean.'

'Yes. Now, where's Tilling?'

'Round the other side of the house. He wanted to look at the riverbank.'

'I'll show you,' Irish says. 'It's this way.'

An almost-luminous green sweep of lawn runs from the west portico down to the water. Here, the River Test curves round in a soft arc framed on either side by artfully placed trees. It's a beautiful, calming view, though none of the benches which offer the observer a place to rest are occupied today. Matron's edict, Nash supposes, and is grateful. If they're to have any hope of tracking where Corby-Clifford may have gone, the fewer feet trampling about, the better. But at least there's hope there will be tracks, with the ground so soft from all the rain.

By the framing clump of trees to the left of the lush green, Nash sees Tilling beckoning to him from the river's edge. There's a grey-haired man in an old brown mackintosh with him, a long-legged terrier at his feet. The dog seems as engaged by what the two men are discussing as they are themselves.

Stepping carefully, Nash makes his way across to them. Though there's grass underfoot here, just beyond the trees he can see there's a stony path which comes down from the upper levels of the garden before turning abruptly downstream.

'There you are,' Tilling says. 'Wilson here is the water bailiff. He's the one who found Scobie's body.'

'It was here? So close to the house?'

'No, no, my dear,' Wilson says. He lifts the thumb stick he's been leaning on, points it downstream. 'That was down along that way a quarter of a mile or more. But I reckon this is where he went in.' He jabs the base of the stick down near the edge of the riverbank, where a narrow scrape has broken through the grass and moss to the wet earth beneath. A cautious examination shows an impression of a patterned tread in the mud. Not a footprint, but what looks like the mark of a bicycle tyre. Parallel to the mark, perhaps fifteen inches beyond, a clump of reeds lies crushed.

'You didn't find any signs of a scuffle?'

'Not a thing. Reckon the poor wight must'a been dead when your man brought him here.'

Nash looks at the marks again. 'He used a wheelchair, by the looks of it.'

'Perfect for moving a body,' Tilling puts in. 'Even a dead one. Who would have given it a second thought if they'd seen Corby-Clifford with a wheelchair?'

'I'm not so sure about that. It's well out of character for him. In any case, wouldn't it have looked strange at that time of night?'

'He must have hit lucky because no one did see him.'

Except Jo, Nash thinks. What if she saw him?

'Suppose he thought it was worth the risk,' Tilling goes on.

'Yes. He's a chancer, all right.' Nash turns, looks back towards the house. It would be possible, even in daylight, to keep out of sight under the trees. And by night, anyone standing here would be practically invisible so long as he took care not to get himself outlined against the pale water.

'Reckon he must'a come down the path,' Wilson says, pointing up the slope. 'Nothing to see on the ground 'cept right by the water there.'

'And if we follow the path downstream?'

'You'll come to the footbridge where the body fetched up. If he hadn'a got hung up underneath, there'da been nothing else to stop him till he got out to sea.'

'There's no point in us going that way if you want to view the body,' Tilling says with a touch of asperity. 'It's not there anymore. He should have been left in situ for you, of course, but they brought him back to the house, tried to resuscitate him before they even let us know.'

'That's right.' Wilson seems unimpressed by Tilling's criticism. 'Could'a been able to save him.'

'And if we go up the path?'

'It's the formal garden on your left,' Irish puts in. She's been silent so long Nash has almost forgotten she's there. 'The Orangery is on the right. That might be worth a try. Scobie used to like to go there for a smoke.'

'Fair enough,' Nash says. 'We can take a look at the footbridge afterwards.'

The slope's steep enough, or his legs are sufficiently weak that the climb makes his calves ache fiercely. He pushes on despite Irish's concerned glances, grateful nonetheless when they reach level ground at the top. Looking round, he sees they're almost equidistant between the main house on one side and a long, low building in matching yellow brick on the other.

'That's the Orangery?' he says.

Irish nods assent.

'Right.' Nash is about to head that way when he hears the sound of a familiar two-stroke engine. He pulls up short. He could swear it's Jo's Cyc-Auto. A spurt of hope flares in his chest. Perhaps he's been wrong all along and she's . . .

But the moment the bicycle comes into view, his hopes are dashed. It's not Jo, but Alf, still in the navy dungarees he wears for his job. The boy abandons the bike, races towards them.

'I know it's a cheek using Jo's bike,' Alf pants. 'But I wanted to get here quick as I could. Didn't think she'd mind.' He shifts uneasily, casting furtive glances at the water bailiff and the policeman.

The boy's poaching activities are bound to make him feel awkward in this company, Nash thinks. But there's no help for it. He needs him, needs all of them. 'I'm sure she wouldn't,' he says as he sets off towards the yellow brick building. 'Don't worry about it. We're all on the same side trying to get the job done, aren't we, gentlemen?'

Tilling gives a curt nod, and the water bailiff grins. 'No reason we can't all be friends while it's daylight, I reckon.'

'We're looking for anything that might show what happened last night,' Nash tells the boy. 'The man they took out of the river was with Corby-Clifford around midnight, but he didn't turn up at one when he was supposed to get back from his break. Mr Wilson's found the place his body went into the water, but it's not where he was killed. If we can find that, all to the good. But the priority now is trying to track him down. Find him, and find Jo.'

'You think Corby-Clifford's got her?' Alf looks grim.

'I do.' Nash can only hope so. Because it's the one thing that accounts for her disappearance, her continued absence.

And if she's not with Corby-Clifford as some kind of hostage, he's terribly afraid she's dead. He tries not to show his distress.

'The last time anyone saw Jo, she was looking for him. The hotel receptionist told Sergeant Tilling she seemed upset. We don't know why, but if she'd thought something was wrong, she wouldn't just have walked away. She'd have gone after him.'

To the north of the Orangery, Nash sees the trees grow close to the building, a strip of woodland that runs back towards the house. 'If you could have a hunt through there?' he says to Alf.

'Gotcha.' The boy slips away beneath the trees.

Tilling's already scrutinising the ground in front of the building, while Wilson sets off with his dog along the southern side, stopping to peer into each set of windows as he goes.

'Looks like a proper favourite with the smokers,' Tilling calls. 'Footprints and fag ends everywhere. Not sure we'll get anything useful from this lot.'

Behind the columns at the front of the Orangery, there's a covered area. In the centre, the statue of a naked figure looks dispassionately out across the park. A door on either side of the androgyne youth gives access to the building itself.

Nash goes to the left-hand door, tries the handle, but it won't budge.

'It'll be locked,' Irish calls. 'It always is.'

Undaunted, he tries the right-hand door handle. It rattles in its seating, and Nash can see the paint round the lock is chipped.

He turns the handle again, summons up what strength he has and barges against the door with his shoulder. It gives reluctantly, allows enough access for him to slip inside.

The long run of windows to the south and glazed roof panels at the far end mean that light floods a space which is empty of almost everything but dust. Even on an overcast day like this, it's bright enough to show that the thick layer powdering the floor has recently been disturbed.

Footprints, a muddle of them here by the door, a clearer trail across to one window. Wheel marks, too, the track of narrow tyres set about fifteen inches apart.

'Tilling,' Nash calls urgently.

As the sergeant comes in, the movement of air sets something fluttering in the corner by the door that wouldn't open, a brief glitter which catches Nash's eye. Careful not to compromise the evidence in the grime, he moves towards the place.

Here, in what seems like the only dim corner of the building, the dust is smeared across a wide patch of floor. Nash crouches to look, notices a sprinkle of fibres spread across the flagstones: black, green, and white fragments of what looks like cloth. And there, as he breathes, that flutter of bright movement higher up. A dozen copper threads snagged in a cobweb.

Jo's hair.

Damn integrity of evidence. He leans forward, captures the threads. Winds them round his finger. Notes the roots are still attached.

'She was here,' he says dully as he straightens up.

'What?' Tilling hustles over.

'She was here,' Nash repeats. 'They both were. This is her hair. And those are a man's footprints. But there are none small enough for Jo's.'

Tilling bends effortfully over the meagre fibres on the floor. 'That doesn't make sense.'

'It does if he carried her,' Nash says from a place that threatens to sink him fathoms deep in despair. 'Or put her in a damn wheelchair.' Like Scobie, he thinks, but can't bear to say it.

'Mr Nash, Mr Nash,' Alf calls from outside. 'She was here. Jo was here.'

Nash slips outside, leaving Tilling to his deliberations. 'What is it, Alf?'

'This. I found it on the ground just in the bushes there.' The boy holds out a curved tortoiseshell comb Nash has seen Jo wear.

'Yes.' Nash takes it, smooths away a trace of leaf mould from between the teeth. Slides it into his pocket. 'There are signs inside,' he tells the boy. 'They must have both been there.'

Tilling emerges from the Orangery. 'I'll need to get someone over here,' he says, as he hurries off towards the house. 'Secure the place till we can examine it properly.'

'Yes.' It's all Nash can manage to do to acknowledge what Tilling has said. The only thing that matters is finding Jo. Where has Corby-Clifford taken her?

He walks away from the Orangery's elaborate facade, impatiently scanning to find a place where he can get a clear view of the countryside around. Back towards the house, he can see Tilling beckoning to one of his officers. Half a dozen figures, searchers or hospital staff, are moving purposefully about. However much he wants to, he can't be everywhere at once. He has to trust they'll follow it up if they find any sign that Corby-Clifford's gone that way.

But instinct argues against it. Corby-Clifford will want to go away from habitation, places where people might be.

Jo, oh, Jo. He rubs his thumb against the strands of hair wrapped round his finger. It's life or death. He can't get it wrong.

South, beyond the ha-ha, there's nowhere to hide. The wide stretches of parkland are empty of anything but a few cows and landscaped trees that are too isolated to provide cover. If Corby-Clifford goes that way, he'll be as conspicuous as a peacock in a hen house.

It has to be the woodland path down towards the river. An intolerable sense of urgency begins to heckle in his blood. *Hurry, hurry, hurry . . .*

'This way,' he says. 'Quick as we can. If he's still got the wheelchair,' *if he's still got Jo*, 'he'll have gone this way.'

Almost as soon as the young man is out of sight between the trees, Alec begins to mutter to himself. At first, I can't make out what he's saying, but as the volume increases, I realise it's the same thing over and over. *What to do, what to do? Where shall I go?*

It sounds like madness, but at least he's so preoccupied he's paying no attention to me. The tie on my left wrist is beginning to loosen, and the way the wheelchair bumps over the uneven stony path helps to disguise my efforts as I twist and strain against the stubborn fabric.

We come to the bottom of the woodland garden before I finally manage to work my wrist free of its tethering strip of silk. There's still tree cover all around but every now and then I've caught a glimpse of open pasture beyond the ditch that divides the grazing land from the gardens. Alec hesitates.

'Which way?' he mutters. 'How do I get out of this fucking place?'

He lets go of the wheelchair handles, walks a few steps away, heading for a footbridge over the ditch which gives access to the park.

Now's my chance. If only I could ...

I redouble my efforts to free myself, but my ankles and right wrist won't budge and the loop he's made from my stockings is unyielding round my waist. As I buck and strain, the wheelchair starts to move. He can't have put the brake on. Reckless in an attempt to escape, I push the blanket away from my head, claw at the gag. I can't get it off, but I manage to pull it down. If I scream, will anyone hear?

'Ah, no, you bitch.' The knife is in Alec's hand again as he lunges towards me. 'One sound, that's all. Just give me an excuse—'

'If you want to get away from here,' I whisper, 'I can show you.'

343

'Another trick?' he snarls, murder in his eyes.

I make myself stay absolutely still as the knife point bores into my chest. His other hand twists the gag round my neck, cutting off my oxygen. 'No,' I manage to croak. 'I don't mind helping you to escape.'

'You expect me to believe that?'

'Why not? It's true.' I will him to believe it, though it is a lie. The first out-and-out lie I've told him, despite everything.

'You're more grateful that husband of yours is dead than that Nash is alive? You *are* a bitch.' As if he's forgotten he killed Richard himself, the fabric round my neck tightens even further.

'I can't tell you . . . how . . . if you kill me,' I gasp.

It feels like an age that he stands over me, apparently debating what to do. The pressure against my windpipe doesn't ease. The buzzing in my ears and greyness in my vision warns me if I don't do something soon it'll be too late. Make a plan, count to three, risk a fight. Do anything I can to get out of his hands. The wheelchair brake is still not on. If I throw my weight it'll move, maybe even topple. If I could just get the breath to scream someone might hear. Someone might come . . . Even if not, it'd be better to die fighting than go like a lamb to the slaughter.

The countdown's at two or two and a half, when the pressure on my neck releases. The knife's still sharp against my chest, and I can feel a new trickle of blood from the cut, but at least I can breathe.

'Show me.'

344

I've got to try and avoid him gagging me again. I can't bear the thought of having that nauseating fabric stuffed back into my mouth. Only give him enough direction for the next turn. 'Towards the river,' I say between ragged breaths. 'Go straight ahead.'

It's a guess, really, based on the old map I pored over with Aggie. I remember her talking about walking along by the river, something about Spaniard's Lane. I just have to hope things haven't changed since 1911.

Now he's the one in a quandary. He'll have to move the knife from my chest if he's to push the chair. He'll need both hands for that. It's going to hold him up when he's eager for speed.

'You could untie me,' I say. 'Let me walk. We'd get on much faster.'

There's another long pause while he thinks it through. Long enough that I'm beginning to hope he'll take me up on it. Though I'm not looking forward to having to walk far in my bare feet, it wouldn't be a first. I'd gone barefoot as often as not when I was a child. At any rate, it'd be worth it not to be tethered and helpless in this chair.

Then, suddenly, out of nowhere, a long-legged white terrier appears, barking joyously around Alec's feet.

'What the . . . ?' He kicks out, and the terrier skips away as if it's the most delightful game.

Behind us, a voice calls, 'Gwyn, Gwyn!'

The terrier pauses in its dance, then sets off back along the path. Now it's stopped barking it's clear there are footsteps approaching. Someone – more than one person – is coming this way. In a hurry, too.

'Alec, cut me loose.' I tug at my right wrist but it's too late. He grabs the chair and begins to run helter-skelter down the path. With only my left hand free, I'm thrown from side to side as the wheelchair skitters and skids. The crunch of the tyres on the stony surface of the path and the sound of Alec's running feet, not so cat-like now, all but obliterate every other noise. The gleam of water warns me we're getting close to the river. Just ahead, if the map's still true, the path divides. Right will take us upstream, back towards the house. A split second's debate and then, 'Left,' I scream, infected by his panic. 'Turn left.'

He jerks the chair round in a slew of small stones that jars the breath from my lungs and brings the chair briefly to a halt.

There's a shout from behind. 'There they are.'

I can't look back, can't see who might be coming, but any pursuit must be bad news for Alec. And now it's apparent there's someone running down the path from the right, too. A wrenching glance over my shoulder as he sets the chair in motion again gives me the briefest glimpse of WPC Shaw converging on our path.

'No, no, no . . .' Alec forces the wheelchair on along the downstream footpath. He doesn't seem to realise he can't hope to outrun his pursuers like this. Even worse, when the park vista opens up in front of us, he must see, as I do, figures in the landscape coming towards us. Farmworkers, by the look of it, and a long way off yet, but alerted by the commotion, they start to run too. They'll cut us off for sure. Almost sobbing, Alec pulls up short, stands at bay.

'Bastard, bastard, *bitch* . . .'

I ready myself to evade the knife at my throat or between my shoulder blades as best I can. Cornered, facing inevitable capture, this is the moment Alec will kill me.

I don't expect what happens next. There is a thump at my back, but it's acceleration, not the knife. An almighty shove which throws me off balance, propels the wheelchair onto the riverbank. Drops it, on top of me, into the water.

Still attached to the chair, all I manage is one startled gasp before the icy water envelops me. I sink like a stone. It's deep, much deeper than I would have imagined and the current drags at my body. There's no hope I can get myself free. This is it, then. Not the knife after all. I'm going to drown.

The headlong dash down the path as they sighted Corby-Clifford has all but exhausted Nash. Much as he tries, his debilitated body can't fulfil the demands of his will. At the bottom of the slope, he has to stop. He bends, hands on thighs, paralysed in the grip of a ferocious stitch, trying to calm his laboured breathing. Though Irish stays at his side, Alf and Wilson, even Tilling, thundering down from behind, are ahead when it happens.

A shout makes him straighten. Corby-Clifford thrusts the chair forward before taking off, running blindly out into the expanse of parkland. But even as Nash hears Tilling shout orders to the pursuers, his attention is all for what's happening on the riverbank. Like a nightmare, he sees the chair tip into the water. A flash of a hand raised as it falls, a muffled cry. It's Jo.

Running feet all around him. Nash couldn't care less who catches Corby-Clifford, or even if he's caught at all.

Jo.

She can swim, he knows. Why hasn't she surfaced?

Wilson's peering down into the water. 'She's trapped,' he calls.

Another splash. Alf's in the river. Nash starts uncertainly forward.

'No.' A tug from Irish drops him to his knees. 'Stay here. I know what to do.'

A sob escapes his throat. He can't do nothing, watch her die. He struggles to his feet, panting.

The melee on the bank has turned into something more like a chain gang. Irish is in the water now too, her white nurse's cap floating away like some bizarre kind of swan's wing. She takes a deep breath, ducks beneath the surface. Alf is shouting 'a knife, a knife', while Wilson is hanging head first over the water, reaching down with his stick, trying to hook onto the chair.

Nash pulls the penknife from his pocket. So little to contribute, but it's all he can manage. 'Here,' he shouts to Alf, lobbing the knife as soon as he gets his attention.

As the boy vanishes beneath the surface, Irish's head lifts above the water in a bizarre kind of seesaw act. Another deep breath and she's gone: a third hostage to the river god.

It's impossible to see what's happening beneath the surface. All the activity has stirred up the silt, turned the water opaque. Too long. It's taking far too long. Nash is in an agony of suspense. What's going on?

'Once more,' Irish gasps in air before she ducks down again. 'It'll be all right.'

A swirl in the water. Wilson drops his stick, reaches out his hands. Alf, bedraggled and gasping, is pulling something up. Pulling someone . . . Irish, on the other side, equally breathless, equally engaged in supporting a body, is helping him haul it to the surface.

He can't see. It's Jo, but . . . she seems limp in their arms, lifeless, as Wilson and a policewoman who's appeared out of nowhere heave her onto the bank, dump her unceremoniously onto her back in the grass.

'For the love of Mike, put her on her side,' Irish yells from the water. 'Don't any of you know anything about artificial respiration?'

'I do,' Nash says, stumbling forward. But thank God, it isn't necessary. As the policewoman rolls Jo onto her side she coughs, brings up a great flood of water. He drags off his jacket, kneels beside her to tuck it round her heaving shoulders. Away in the periphery of his vision, he sees Wilson help Irish from the water, wrap his old mac round her. Her immaculate white uniform is filthy with river mud and her grey hair straggles in rat's tails over her face, but to Nash she seems as transcendent as any hero from legend.

'You breathed her alive,' he says as she hurries over.

She waves it aside, harangues the growing crowd of bystanders. 'Ach, what are you thinking? The lot of you useless gawkers and gobaloonies. Someone run up to the annexe, we need blankets and a stretcher. Tell Matron, one for a bed in the women's ward, a chair for Mr Nash and two hot baths.' She grins as Alf draggles over. 'Someone give the boy a coat, he's shivering fit to bust himself.'

'I'm sorry, Mr Nash,' he says. 'I lost your knife.'

He can't speak. Tears choke him.

On the ground, Jo stirs. 'Bram?' she says. 'What the hell are you doing here?'

27

Saturday, afternoon

I SAW A PICTURE ONCE OF a Roman mosaic. It had a border of octopuses and fish, mermen blowing trumpets, a boy riding a dolphin. But the centre of it had been damaged, ploughed out or burned, I can't remember what they said had happened. Only a few disconnected patches of tesserae had remained in the middle portion, fragmentary images archaeologists had to try to decipher. A picture of Poseidon, they imagined, magnificent in a chariot pulled by foaming white sea horses.

It hardly matters what it was, but it's how I feel now. My mind's full of disconnected images, sensations that won't join up to make sense of what happened this morning after I went into the water. I can't decide what was real, and what imagination, my life flashing before my eyes.

The shock of cold water on my skin. The sinuous dance of vivid green weed. Being dragged deeper down, pressed into the soft river silt by the weight of the wheelchair. The horror of knowing I couldn't get free.

Alf, sawing at my bonds. Aggie's voice, talking about water fairies. A woman in white, breathing air from her lungs into mine, the strange rush and choke as I struggled against her before I realised what she was trying to do.

Hard hands dragging at me, tearing, bruising. The river's reluctance to give me up, the blessed rush of air . . .

Lying in the grass, retching, hands wrapping me in coarse woollen cloth that smelled of Bram.

The man himself. Haggard, exhausted, tears running down his face.

Even less than that of the journey back to the annexe. Jolting on a stretcher, vomiting again and again. Rough towels rubbing my skin almost raw, a sudden delicious oblivion of warmth as I sank into bed surrounded by hot-water bottles.

When I wake, my first thoughts are of Bram. Where is he? Where am I? I'm starving . . .

Above my head, there's a square of finely decorated ceiling that suggests some kind of fancy boudoir. Walls, a deep royal blue, show in a strip beneath the cornice, are covered lower down by panels of some kind of board. I shove myself up in the bed, trying to make out where I am. A glimpse of three beds, then the disconnected pieces scatter, swirl giddily in my head as I move, and the scent of the river rises in a warm fug from my skin. My gorge rises, and I'm almost sick again.

'Awake, then,' a husky voice greets me. It's the woman in the bed next to mine. Her face seems oddly familiar, but somehow, I can't quite place her. 'A bit late to introduce ourselves, Mrs Lester. I'm Margery O'Shaughnessy. They call me Irish.'

It's the voice that does it. 'It was you,' I say, sitting bolt upright. 'You were the one who saved me.'

'Ah, no,' she says. 'Not just me. Took a whole gang of us, so it did.'

'But you're hurt?' The thought that she might have come to harm because of me is appalling.

She grins. 'Not a bit of it. Just cold, that's all. Matron decreed I should be warded overnight like you.'

'Overnight?' Shocked, I struggle to sit up. 'I've slept right through?'

'Easy now. You've been asleep a long while, but it's still Saturday.'

'How am I ever going to thank you?'

'Take care of that good man of yours when he gets out of here. That'll do for me.'

'Bram?' The best man I know but . . . 'He's not my—'

'You didn't get sight of him when we pulled you out?'

The swirl of disconnected pieces shows me his face again, rips at me afresh. 'Where is he? Is he all right? He shouldn't have been out there.'

'True enough, he shouldn't. But there was no stopping him when he knew you were in danger.'

'He'll be all right?' I insist.

'Sure, and he'll be fine in a day or two.'

I push the covers back, slide my legs out of bed. My shoulders and back ache, and there are chafed red marks

353

round my ankles and wrists, but I don't get the swirling nausea as I move this time. 'Will they let me see him?'

'Not like that.' Another grin.

The hospital nightie they've put me in is a violent pink cotton with sprigs of yellow flowers. It flaps round my body, and I can feel a draught that lets me know it's slit up the back, so my behind is hanging out in the breeze. 'Where can I find a dressing gown?'

She sighs. 'You'll get me the sack.'

'Please?'

'Linen cupboard. The door over there. Bottom shelf. See if you can find something for your feet, too.'

There's a stash of dressing gowns, blue striped towelling pale with laundering. As large as the nightie, the one I pick is fit to wrap round me twice. It's heavy, too, but it covers me up. I roll back the sleeves, ferret around in the cupboard till I find a pile of thick white socks.

'Theatre socks,' Irish says, laughing, when I emerge. 'If the sight of you doesn't cheer him up, nothing will.'

'Where is he?'

'The sack for sure.' She sighs again, but I know she's not serious or she wouldn't have helped me get this far. 'Straight out of the door here, down to the end. Turn right. Third door on the right.'

I scoot across to her bed, kiss her on the cheek. Her skin is soft, papery-thin, and I see she must be older than I'd first thought. The courage of the woman. I owe her much more than a kiss.

'Dear girl,' she says, her cheeks reddening. 'You'll do.'

No one sees me as I shuffle along the corridors, my thick socks soundless on the carpeted floors. The double width doors to the room where Bram is are open, and I see him at once. He's sleeping, propped up against his pillows in a bed next to the window. He looks so worn and thin my breath catches in my throat.

I hesitate. I probably should go away again, leave him to rest. It seems somehow like an invasion of his privacy to watch him sleeping like this, just as it had done back in his office on Monday morning.

Monday . . . Less than a week, but it feels like a lifetime. Despite the thick folds of the dressing gown, I shiver. Regret tears at me. I've survived, but Richard wasn't so lucky. I can't help thinking what Alec said, taunting me. That I was more grateful he'd killed Richard than that he'd saved Bram.

Another shiver. It's so far from true. Without his intervention, Bram might easily have died. If he had, I don't think I'd have fought so hard this morning. Knife or river, I'd have been ready to die.

But Richard? His death hasn't put out the moon and stars for me as Bram's would have done. I'd have been happy never to see him again, even better pleased if he'd agreed to dissolve our marriage, but I'd still much rather he was alive to thwart me than that his death has made me free.

'Jo?' Bram's voice brings me out of the morass of my thoughts. 'Come here where I can see you.'

*

Ever since Nash has known the body in the car was Richard Lester's, he's been trying to think what he'll say to Jo when he sees her. It seems as if it should be the first thing he addresses, but now she's here, he still doesn't have the words he needs.

Jo, paler than she should be, bundled up in a hospital dressing gown three sizes too big for her, inexpressibly dear. Jo, almost lost. It's a scalding shame to him that she was saved by no effort of his. He'd failed her when she needed him most.

She perches on the chair at his bedside, takes his hand. 'If we were cats,' she says, 'I don't think either of us would have any of our nine lives left.'

'And I'd be as grey as a badger,' he says, picking up her cue, 'or as bald as a coot with worry.'

She looks at him judiciously. 'No,' she says. 'Still the same old Bram.'

It's enough. He knows he doesn't have to find the words right now. It won't matter if he never finds them, or if they're the wrong ones. The only response he needs slips easily from his tongue. 'Still the same old Jo.'

28

Monday 12ᵗʰ June 1944, morning

I'D BEEN DISCHARGED FROM THE annexe on Sunday
morning, arriving home in Mercer's taxi to a greeting
from Dot that was half apologetic, half relieved and
wholly, overwhelmingly kind. An off-lay chicken had been
sacrificed for Sunday lunch and though I'd had to pay a for-
feit for its life by answering Joan and Betty's excited questions between mouthfuls, the meal felt like a celebration.
Like Irish, Alf had shrugged off my thanks for his part in my
rescue, and I was left feeling pretty silly at the girls' admiring
banter. I'd done nothing brave, just caused a lot of trouble
for everyone.

News from Allied Forces in France is good, but Germany
hasn't given up. After months without air raids, the south
of England's being hit again. Rumours about unmanned
rockets, Hitler's vengeance. Will it never end?

Bram's still in hospital. They're insisting he rest, but they
let me visit him again before I left. Seems he should be home
by the end of the week, though it will be some time yet before

he can come back to work. Irish, on the other hand, is already back on duty, demonstrating an iron constitution that puts me in awe. If she can get back to work so quickly, I must be able to manage it too.

On Sunday afternoon, I set out to see Alice Beech. The news about the body in the car had been made public, though so far Tilling had kept Richard's identity secret. I was glad of that for my own sake, but I knew it wouldn't be long before it was common knowledge. It wouldn't just be Joan and Betty then. Half the town would be watching me, asking questions. Waiting to see my reaction. But at least it was some kind of respite. I had a chance to tell Alice before she heard it on the grapevine.

I'd sorted through the duffel bag Mags had given me, found nothing very remarkable. Some casual clothes, a paperback copy of *My Man Jeeves*, and a few letters Alice had written him. I'd no desire to read them. She should have them back; know he'd valued them enough to keep. There must be other stuff somewhere, bags he'd packed ready to take to France, but I've no idea where they might be. If they were in the car when it went up in flames, they're lost forever. Pretty much the same applies if they've been put on a transport on its way to France. Not that it matters, I've no use for his possessions. I've given Dot everything except the letters: she's a mistress of make do and mend, nothing will go to waste.

When I arrived at the cherry-red door, armed only with the packet of letters, I knew I'd be unwelcome enough without the news I was bringing. Alice reacted much as I expected, hostility first, then when I told her about Richard, disbelief and anger. How could I possibly know? I was just being cruel. But when I finally got her to understand it was true, she collapsed in floods of weeping, the letters clasped to her bosom, as if she saw herself as a heroine from an old-time novel.

But I had no right to criticise. Her grief was real, much more heartfelt than anything I could lay claim to. Though I was pretty certain Richard would never have gone back to her, that the quarrel in Lee Lane would have marked the end of their relationship even if he'd survived, I didn't say so. If it consoled her to think she'd been his one true love, at least she'd never have to find out he was a liar. She begged me for a photograph of him, but I couldn't give what I didn't have, and her weeping edged into a hysteria that frightened me. I was afraid of what she might do, so I called her father. Capstaff turned up twenty minutes later, kept Mercer's taxi waiting outside while he gathered her up with astonishing tenderness. For me, he had nothing but hostility: echoing all the blame, all the contempt I felt for myself. It left me shaken, added another sleepless night to my score. But I consoled myself. The worst was surely over.

So, on Monday morning, 10 a.m. on the dot, I turn up at the police station ready to give my formal statement. I'm a little apprehensive, but not expecting anything worse than embarrassment and a rap on the knuckles from Sergeant Tilling for having acted stupidly on Friday night. Though I still don't think I could have done anything else. I'm sure he wouldn't have believed me about Alec before it all got out of control. And then it was too late.

WPC Shaw is at the desk. She puts down the book she's reading, greets me with a smile. 'How are you feeling?'

'I'm fine.'

'You're looking better.'

I think of how I'd been the last time she'd seen me. Like a drowned rat, vomiting up half the River Test. 'So I should hope.'

'Sergeant Tilling said to show you straight through to his office.' She opens the door to the corridor, and though I'd be able to find my own way, she comes with me.

'Thanks. Constable Shaw, I—' I don't get a chance to finish. There's a shout from the direction of the cells.

'Josephine, Josephine. I need to speak to you. I need to explain.'

My God. It's Alec. I'd never have come if I'd known. The idea I'm under the same roof as him turns my knees loose as a puppet's. 'What's going on?' I whisper to WPC Shaw. 'Why's Alec still here?'

She puts a finger to her lips. Too late, I think. It would have been better to have told me to keep quiet *before* he heard me. As it is, he's still shouting my name, demanding to see me as she hurries me into Tilling's office.

'Bloody fellow.' The sergeant gets up from his desk to greet me, sighing heavily. 'Sorry, Mrs Lester. Sit down. Didn't mean to give you a shock.'

Another shout. 'Josephine!'

'Shut the door, Shaw,' Tilling snaps. 'I'm sick of listening to him.'

I take the offered seat. 'I didn't know Mr Corby-Clifford was still here.'

'He's due to be transferred to Winchester jail this afternoon. I'll be glad to see the back of him. He's either sulking, refusing to say a word, or screaming the place down. Can't get a statement out of him, keeps saying the only person he'll talk to is you. If you'll believe it, he won't even have a solicitor, says they're all in a conspiracy against him.'

'Can I get you something?' WPC Shaw asks. 'Some water? A cup of tea?'

'Tea,' Tilling decides for me. 'I need to ask Mrs Lester a favour.'

A cold certainty creeps over me. 'You want me to talk to him?' I'd crumple, weeping like Alice, but I can't let the side down. Dot and Aggie would probably tell me not to do it, and Bram would hate it if he knew. But I think, now it's my turn to show I can be brave. I have to go through with it.

'We'll have him secured,' Tilling says. 'He won't be able to hurt you.'

That's a matter of opinion, I think. Alec might not be able to do me physical harm, but the idea of sitting in a room with him, seeing his face, hearing his voice makes me feel sick. What can he possibly want to say to me?

I saw him commit murder, nearly died myself because of it. I know I'll have to give evidence about it one day at his trial, but there's every chance he'll never be brought to book for Richard's killing. We only have hearsay for that: what Bram and I had heard Scobie insinuate, what he'd said to me outside the Orangery. Without physical evidence to tie him to Richard's death, it won't be enough to convict him. It's on my conscience that the only evidence we might have had, I'd destroyed. Wiped that scalpel handle in full knowledge of what I was doing. Not that I'm going to tell Tilling that. So perhaps it's only right I should see him, listen to what he has to say. I owe Richard – and Tilling – that much.

'All right.'

Tilling beams with what seems suspiciously like relief. 'Good girl. Give us a couple of minutes to get him set up, and then we'll take you through.'

I accept the tea WPC Shaw brings me but though my throat is dry I can't make myself want to drink it. Outside, I can hear muffled sounds coming from the cells. Loud demands from Alec to see me alone, Tilling's brusque responses. Scuffling footsteps in the corridor, and someone cursing. I jump as a shoulder bumps heavily against Tilling's door, glad that Constable Shaw is still with me. The cup of tea trembles in my cold hands.

'Will you be all right?' she asks softly. 'You don't have to do it.'

'Yeah, I do. Best get it over with.' I put down the tea, stand up. I'm glad I put on my best business suit this morning, intent on convincing Aggie and Mr Simmons that I'm fit for work. I put my hands to my hair, check it hasn't started to come loose from the French pleat I tidied it into this morning.

Tilling comes back into the room, breathing heavily. 'It's like this, Mrs Lester. Corby-Clifford's in the interview room. He's cuffed, and I'll be standing by in the corridor just outside the room. He's insisting he won't talk unless he's alone with you, but I've told him the door won't be shut. First hint of nonsense from him and it's all over. He'll be back in his cell till they come for him from Winchester. They certainly won't allow any privileges there, so he knows this is his only chance.'

'OK.'

'You want out of there, you just call, whether he's said his piece or not.'

'Yes.' Call now, I think. Get me out of here now.

'Come on then.'

It's a bare little room not much different to the cell I'd spent the night in. The same cream-painted brick walls, the same basic eye for furnishing. No bunk, of course. Instead, there's a table, two chairs, one tiny window. Notices on the walls, etiquette for the prisoner. NO SPITTING, NO SMOKING, NO SWEARING. A full ashtray on the table belies at least one of these commands.

Alec is sitting in the chair furthest from the door. It gives me a sense of security but no joy to see his wrists are handcuffed on either side of the chair's back support. The chain of the cuffs is too short to let him stand up, so he can't readily move, his own weight effectively anchoring him in place.

They've taken his jacket and tie, but he's wearing the same shirt and trousers as he was on Friday. He's a bit the worse for wear, but his natural elegance means he's nothing like as dishevelled as I was after a night in the cells. He doesn't even look all that tired.

Tilling ushers me to the chair across from Alec, so I'm facing him with only the flimsy barrier of the table between us. 'The door stays open,' the sergeant says, ostensibly to me, though it's clear he's speaking to Alec. 'Any move out of this one, any worries, you call me. I'll be just outside.'

I nod, unable for the moment to speak. Alec stares at Tilling with undisguised hostility, waiting for him to leave the room. Then his face softens, and he leans forward eagerly in his chair. His voice is low, imploring, full of the old careless charm.

'Josephine, I'm so glad to see you. I was so afraid . . . It was an accident; I didn't mean harm to come to you. You must believe me.'

I think of the bumps and bruises, the chafed marks round my wrists and ankles. The dozen or more superficial cuts on my body, the deeper one over my heart where the knife point drilled in as he'd threatened to kill me. My muscles still ache from my efforts to escape, and my throat is sore from vomiting. 'You'll excuse me if I don't find that very easy to do, Alec.'

He sighs. 'I was angry with you, frustrated. I thought we were . . . you know what I thought.'

'That I'd come across, give you sex as payment.'

He winces. 'Such an ugly way of putting it, Josephine. I thought we were *sympatico*, adults capable of playing grown-up games. I admit, I may have been a little rough.'

'And Scobie? What sort of game were you playing with him?'

'That was entirely your fault,' he says, his voice hardening. 'If I hadn't been so angry with you, I could have dealt with him quite calmly. He touched a raw nerve talking about Nash like that.'

'Bram? What have you got against him?'

He laughs, a harsh sound. 'How can you ask? One of the Untermensch, cuckolding my best friend.'

'That's pretty rich, coming from you. Your best friend? You *killed* Richard.'

'Self-defence.' He shrugs. 'It was very sad. A few minutes either way and we'd never have met. He'd still be around to stand in your way.'

'I'd rather he was.'

'You don't fool me. You'll be back in Nash's bed as soon as he can get it up.'

'I don't have to listen to this.' I push out of my chair, ready to leave.

'No, Josephine, please.' In another of his mercurial mood changes, he puts little-boy appeal into his tone. 'I'm sorry, I shouldn't have said that. But please, don't leave. I need you to understand. If Richard hadn't threatened me . . .'

I think of Tilling, listening outside in the corridor, hoping for Alec's confession. I think of Alice Beech, broken in bits by Richard's death. I think of Richard himself. He deserves justice. Though Alec won't tell it straight, the truth will be in the story, inescapable. I sit down again.

'All right. Tell me what happened.'

*

Sunday 4ᵗʰ June 1944, evening and night

Alec Corby-Clifford stands smoking in the formal garden to the south of Broadlands House. He's going to miss this place, this view. A house like this is very much to his taste, pity it's wasted on the wrong people. Characteristic of the British aristocracy to let the riff-raff in. Such sentimentality.

He grins to himself, acknowledging the irony. If it wasn't for the riff-raff, he wouldn't have an excuse to be here himself. It's been very convenient. A pleasant interlude with side benefits: his routine workload lifted; all he's had to do is give his opinion on a few of the more interesting cases admitted to the hospital. That chap Warren, for one. He's done well since the decompression of his head injury. Fascinating how burr hole surgery can be done with so little anaesthesia. He'd love to experiment further, explore that delicious paradox between the brain's function as the seat of feeling and its own comparative insensitivity to pain. An idea he'll pursue once he's safely away. The Reich are keen to advance medical knowledge, he knows, and he's kept his promise, done his part. They owe him a place safely out of range of Hitler's vengeance on Britain. This footling invasion doesn't stand a chance in the face of Germany's might.

He wonders whether his last message got through. He's heard nothing, but he has to trust to the network. He'll slip away as planned. Once he's in France, he can soon make himself known to the right people. The empfehlung, *his letter of introduction, is safely stitched into his shoe. He's had another modest haul of equipment and drugs from the stores this evening. Pity that old fusser Scobie caught him at it. Not that he cares. Another few days and he'll be gone. And when it comes down to it, who's going to take an orderly's word over his?*

He yawns, stretches. Better get back to the hotel. He'll be in good time for a nightcap before he turns in.

He drops his cigarette, grinds it out. Picks up his bag. One last look round and . . .

'Hey! Hey there, wait a minute!' a voice shouts breathlessly from the twilight gloom. He pauses. There's someone running up from the bottom of the park, a man in the uniform of an RAMC officer. There must be an emergency of some kind. He'd thought all the troops had left, but perhaps not. He frowns. Just bored enough not to turn his back and walk away, he calls out, 'What's going on?'

'I need help,' the newcomer pants.

'What—?' Astonished, Corby-Clifford recognises the man. Richard Lester. The last person he'd have expected . . . certainly the last he wants to meet right now. This could be a disaster.

'Alec? Alec Corby-Clifford? What the hell are you doing here?'

'Never mind about that. What's the emergency?'

'What? Oh . . . I was looking for someone to give me a lift down to the docks. I'm supposed to be . . .' He hesitates, looks flustered.

'Embarking?' Corby-Clifford queries. 'Don't worry, your secret's safe with me.'

'Look, don't muck about. The camp is empty, I just thought there might be someone up here?'

'Don't look at me, old man. I don't go until Wednesday.'

'You do?' Lester looks confused. 'I mean . . . you don't? Well, I suppose that's all right. You've no access to transport, by any chance?'

'Shanks's pony,' Corby-Clifford says, thinking furiously. 'Just about to walk back into town. Come with me, why don't you? Maybe you'll find someone there who—'

'I've got a bloody car. Down in the lane. Bastard thing ran out of petrol.'

'Ah, well, if that's the problem . . . I know where we can get you some fuel.' In his night-time prowling, Corby-Clifford has noted many things that might one day be of use. 'Come with me.'

He leads the way to the stables. At one end, away from the horses dozing in their boxes, there's a room that's used to house all manner of tools and equipment, including a petrol-driven generator. And with it, like the well-organised folk they are, someone has stashed a can of fuel. 'Here you are.' He shakes the can, hears it slosh. 'Must be half full. That should be enough to get you into town.'

Lester hesitates. 'What if someone needs it?'

'Do you want to get to the docks tonight or not?'

'I've got to get there.'

'Well, then. If you're worried, why don't I come with you to the car, then I'll bring the can back? I'll let someone know what's happened in the morning, they'll be able to get it refilled.'

'You're a pal.' Lester looks uncomfortable. 'Look, Alec, I—'

'Come on, old man. Don't let's mess about. Time's a-wasting. I'll just put this here.' He drops his bag into a corner, fiddles with the catch a moment before covering it with a sack. 'No need to carry the whole kit and caboodle when we're in a hurry.'

'This way.' Lester hurries off past the end of the house and into the park.

Corby-Clifford follows on his heels, petrol can in hand. Waiting for the right moment, the right opportunity. 'You seem to know your way about, old man?'

Lester snorts. 'Not the foggiest. But I can retrace my steps all right. You?'

'No idea. You know me, I've always been an urban soul. I just hope you don't get us lost.'

'Trust me.'

'That's just it though, isn't it? Can I trust you, old man?'

Lester slows, comes to a halt. 'How did you get back to England, Alec? Did you take their deal? I hope not, because it looks like you might have chosen the wrong side after all.'

'Don't you worry about me,' he responds. 'I'm all right. You just concentrate on being Hawkeye the pathfinder.'

A moment when the other man stares at him, frowning. Is this the crunch point? But then Lester shrugs. 'Ah, leave it for now,' he says. 'I've got to get on.' He sets off running, heading south.

The moon is waxing towards full, giving enough light to make speed possible. It's an eerie journey, and as Corby-Clifford follows Lester across the wide pastures, he feels *nakedly exposed. It would have been so much better if their way had led into the belt of woodland that runs almost parallel with their course. Towards the end of their journey, there are clear indications on the ground of where the troops have been camped, but there's no sign now of human life. He estimates they've gone almost a mile as the crow flies when they reach a blessed corner of woodland.*

'Just through here,' Lester says. 'Then we'll be out on the lane. The car's not far.'

'Hold on a minute.' Corby-Clifford senses it's now or never. There's only one way to guarantee his old friend won't talk about this meeting later. He exaggerates his breathlessness, banking that Richard Lester won't push on ahead without the can of fuel. He puts it down close to his feet in a litter of leaves, bends as if to catch his breath. 'I'm not used to all this route marching.'

'Should have let me carry the can,' Lester says, his tone mocking. 'Old man.'

As soon as he's in range, Corby-Clifford straightens up. In his hand, he has the scalpel he pulled out of his bag before they left the stables. As Lester reaches out for the fuel can, Corby-Clifford slashes the instrument viciously at his old friend, aiming for his unprotected neck. The strike misses its intended mark but lays open the other man's cheek to the bone.

'W-what?' Lester's surprise is almost comical. He presses his hand against the welling cut. Corby-Clifford slashes again, forcing the scalpel deep into the flesh of Lester's raised

arm. *The blade bites deep, even through the wool sleeve. But now it sticks, breaks. Corby-Clifford leaps back, ready to defend himself, but there's no need. He's hit the brachial artery with this second blow, and blood pumps from the wound.*

'What have you done?' Lester says.

'Sorry, old man.' Corby-Clifford steps back out of range of blood and reaching hand, watches as Lester scrabbles to stop the flow. 'Afraid you do have to carry the can. I'm almost home free. Can't risk exposure at this stage.'

Lester falls to his knees. 'Help me . . .' But his voice is feeble already. It won't take long now.

He waits until it's over. Time enough to make his plans. He could leave the body where it is, trust to fate it won't be found any time soon. It's tempting, but fate has already served him one dirty trick tonight, better not give it the opportunity to hand out another. The petrol? What a bonfire it would make if he poured it over Lester's mangy corpse and set light to it. But he mustn't be hasty. He has to think it through.

The sound of a vehicle approaches. He freezes. A diesel engine, something heavier than a car. Military, most likely. Though he hasn't got Lester's innate sense of direction, he's fairly sure it's travelling away from Romsey. How sadly ironic. If Lester had caught up with that, he'd have been safely away to the docks. The engine noise passes, fades, disappears. He's safe. But it's given him an idea. The best idea. Lester's car. How much better if the body's found there, burned to a crisp. It might almost be ruled an accident.

Another thrum of an engine. He settles to wait. Give it another hour or so, make sure everyone's settled down for the night before he moves the body.

'I went to sleep,' Alec says, sounding aggrieved. 'Would you believe it? I fell asleep, and when I woke up it was two o'clock. I was shocked. Just as well I didn't have anyone waiting up for me. The hotel staff were used to me being called out, they're very discreet.'

I feel foolish. If only I'd thought to ask the right questions sooner. I'd been so distracted by Bram's illness, I'd only seen Alec as a means to get the precious penicillin. Yet he should have been an obvious suspect, with his connection to Richard. If I'd had more detachment, Scobie might still be alive. On the other hand, Bram might be dead . . .

'You put the body in the car?'

'Ticklish business, that. He was getting a bit stiff by then. But I managed it. Got him all set up nicely. A splash or two of petrol, and up she goes.'

'Is that how you hurt your hand?'

He grimaces. 'Wasn't quite quick enough. Hurt like a bastard. Thought I could take care of it myself, but it was too awkward. Had to go along to the hospital. Told them a tale about having to deal with a log that had fallen out of an open fire. They were most sympathetic. Worst of it was it screwed my plans to get away.'

'And then you met me.'

'That was the damnedest thing. I'd seen neither you nor Richard for years, and then you both turn up within twenty-four hours. Fate must really have had it in for me.'

'You know, if you'd just walked away that morning, I'd never have known you were there. You'd have got away scot-free.'

He shrugs. 'I was . . . intrigued. I thought how delicious it would be if I could get you to sleep with me without knowing I'd killed Richard. And of course, when you told me about your job, it seemed like I'd had a lucky break after all. I could keep an eye on you, on the investigation. I thought if it came to the crunch, you might even put in a good word for me.'

'Is that why you agreed to help Bram?'

'It pained me, but I thought it might be useful to have you grateful to me.'

I shudder. 'The thing that puzzles me . . .'

'Only one thing, Josephine? You never even looked at me for the killing.'

I suppose that's fair enough. Whether I would have worked it out, given time, I'll never know. I'd been too wrapped up in personal anxieties to think it through. 'The place where you killed Richard, Alec. My friend Alf found it on Tuesday night, took me to see it. Then the next day it was gone. Why did you leave it so late to clear it up?'

'Put it down to human frailty. I meant to do it on Monday night, but I was exhausted. My hand hurt like the devil, so I took a couple of painkillers, went out like a light. Tuesday, I was on hot coals all day in case someone found the place. I'd realised I'd lost the scalpel handle by then. I've been told you picked it up.'

'Yes.'

Conscious of Tilling listening, I'm not going to tell him he'd missed finding it on Tuesday, too. There's something speculative in his expression.

'No prints on it though.' He grins with sly satisfaction.

I meet his eyes as steadily as I can. Let him think what he likes. It wasn't to protect *him* I'd wiped it. 'I believe not.'

'To cut a long story short, I had to wait till the small hours before it got dark enough to risk going back. Bloody moon didn't set till gone three. Then I pinched a fork from the gardeners' shed, went down and raked over the ground. All a bit of a rush, and much more difficult than I thought it'd be with this bloody hand. But I did have a bit of luck, finding that badger. I thought, if I'd left any traces, they'd think the blood had come from that.'

More luck than he realises, I think. Alf and I hadn't left Spaniard's Lane till getting on for three. A few minutes either way, and we'd have seen him. 'You know, Alec, I think I would have worked it out. I'd started to remember how ruthless you could be when anyone annoyed you. That time Richard broke his arm on the ice, that was your fault. You distracted him just as he was about to jump. I suppose you were cross because he was skating with Oonagh. Then there was the way you spoke to Bram the other day, the way you treated him. You did what I'd asked, but you made sure he suffered for it. The other thing . . . I couldn't help wondering why you were so reluctant to tell how you'd got home from France. It seemed dodgy to me. You were quick enough to boast about everything else. I thought if you'd had some miraculous escape, you'd have wanted to tell everyone about it.'

'Hindsight, Josephine,' he says with a certain degree of truth. 'I'm tired of this. If you won't call for Tilling, I will.'

'I don't need to call,' I say as I stand up. 'I can just walk out. Goodbye, Alec. See you in court. And that good word? Don't bank on that. It isn't going to happen.'

'Josephine!' he shouts as I leave the room. 'Scobie's death is on you. Don't you ever forget it.'

Epilogue

Thursday 29ᵗʰ June 1944,
morning – three weeks after D-Day

T HE LETTER THAT CAME THIS morning has thrown
me completely. On good thick paper that's a rar-
ity these days, the letterhead shows it's come from
a solicitor on the Isle of Wight. It proffers condolences on
the untimely decease of my late husband, Richard Marshall
Lester, and informs me he has left his whole estate, including Silverbank, the big house by the Yar, to me. In delicate
phraseology, it urges me to contact Jonathan Hardy at my
earliest convenience.

It had never occurred to me that I would inherit Richard's
property. It's been so long since I've thought of myself as
married to him that I'd never considered what being his
widow – such a horrid word, it always makes me think of
spiders – would mean. If I'd thought of it at all, I suppose I
imagined he'd have made a new will once we separated, left
his property to someone who hadn't betrayed him. But when
I call the solicitor from the telephone box in Botley Road, he

tells me it *is* a new will, made as so many soldiers do, on the eve of going off to war.

He probes: such gentle, tactfully worded questioning that he puts me in mind of our own Mr Simmons. In the end, it boils down to asking whether I'll go to the Island to deal with the settlement of my husband's affairs. And if so, when? The phrase 'at my earliest convenience' hangs unspoken between us, and I'm grateful when the operator announces our three minutes is up. When she asks if I want a further three, I say no, tell Mr Hardy I'll be in touch when I've spoken to my employer.

The letter weighs heavy on my mind as I walk to work. Bram's been back in the office for almost a week, and that's been another circumspect, delicate situation. After that one unguarded meeting on the afternoon of my dip in the River Test, we've been as wary as ever of each other, afraid – at least on my part – of stepping on forbidden ground. I've been longing to ask what happens next for us, while he, I'm almost sure, has been holding back because of Richard's death. But I can't put things off any longer. For good or ill, I have to know now.

I'm late to work, last to arrive in the office this morning. Aggie is in the kitchen, making tea. She raises her eyebrows at me, but there's none of the old disdain.

'Is he in?' I ask.

She nods.

'Busy?'

'Not that I know of. The tea's for him.' I can see the effort she's making not to ask questions.

'I'll take it up. I have to talk to him.'

She nods again. 'About bloody time.'

I don't think I've ever heard her swear before. 'Aggie!'

She doesn't look at me as she puts two cups of tea on a tray, set out as precisely as ever with a lacy doily and a plate of digestive biscuits. And then, to my absolute astonishment, she hugs me, a fierce quick embrace that's over before I can react.

'Aggie . . . ?'

'I'll see you aren't disturbed,' she says in a half-strangled voice as she thrusts the tray into my hands. 'Just . . . don't waste any more time.'

I make my way up the narrow stairs, doing my best not to slop tea into the saucers. At the top, I pause to catch my breath before knocking.

'Come in.'

I juggle the tray and the door handle. Bram's sitting at his desk, looking over some papers, fountain pen in hand. He's still thinner than he ought to be, and there are new lines on his face I don't believe will ever go away, but the miracle of his recovery is enough to be grateful for. 'I've brought some tea.'

He smiles. 'Very civil of you.' He lays down his pen, pushes the papers aside so I can put down the tray.

'Are you busy?'

'Not very.' He nods towards the teacups. 'Are you going to join me?'

'If I may. I . . . we need to talk, Bram.'

'You'd better sit down.' A muscle flicks at the corner of his jaw. I hate it that he seems to feel the need to brace himself for what's coming, but Aggie is right. We shouldn't waste any more time.

I take the client's chair facing him across the desk. The last thing I want is this barrier between us, but I don't know how to get beyond it. It reminds me too vividly of that last session with Alec, only now it's convention that's holding Bram and me back.

'I've had a letter,' I say, pulling it out of my pocket. Smoothing out the extra creases I made to fit it in. 'About Richard's estate. He's left everything to me.'

He nods. 'Of course. You were his wife.' There's such sadness in his face, I want to shout the denial.

'Not in any way that counts.' I take a deep breath. 'A long time ago, I paid you half a crown to act as my solicitor.'

He smiles again, but it doesn't touch the sadness. 'Yes. But I gave it back to you. I couldn't do it then, Jo, and I can't now. It's too complicated. You'll have to ask Simmons.'

'I know. What I remember is why you refused me then. You said it was because you didn't know what was going on in my head.'

'Did I? You've got a better memory than I have.'

'Is it still like that? You don't know what I'm thinking?'

'Not a clue.' He picks up his pen, twists it end over end between his fingers.

I gather my courage. 'When you were ill, unconscious, the nurses told me you might be able to hear what people said to you. I don't know if it's true?'

He nods, the pen turning, turning. 'Yes.'

379

'I sat by your bedside and held your hand. Told you I loved you. I do, Bram. I love you.'

The pen stops moving. There's a long silence that feels like forever.

'It's all right,' I gabble. 'Don't look like that. I had to tell you, had to be sure you knew, but . . . I'll go away, go back to the Island. I don't want to be an embarrassment to you.'

He looks stricken. 'Not that. Never that. But you're so vulnerable with all that's happened. I can't take advantage of that. Of you.'

And still he sits on the far side of that damn desk.

'What if I say I want you to take advantage of me?'

A sudden flash of real humour lightens his expression. 'It seems you're as clueless as me, doesn't it?' He opens his desk drawer, takes out something small. Puts it down on the desk between us.

I know he learned to make things out of metal in the trenches long ago, a hobby he still practices. Last year, he'd refashioned the mask that hides his scars. This . . . a tiny silver fox, sitting pert on the desk, is as perfectly lifelike as anything less than an inch high could possibly be. Pointed ears and nose, tail wrapped snugly round its feet. Captivated, I pick it up. 'It's so clever.'

'I made it years ago,' he says. 'When you first came back to Romsey. It's you.'

'Me?'

'In a way.' He looks me straight in the eye for the first time. 'It was because of you. I wasn't ready to commit anything to a relationship back then. But you stole me. Body and soul, if I have one. Heart.'

'Bram . . .'

'I'd always thought I'd never let anyone get close. That life was too fragile, too unpredictable. But I made this, too, back then, so I suppose . . .' He pushes something else over the desktop towards me. 'I suppose I was waiting for the right time to give it to you.'

It's a circlet of silver, its surface engraved with what looks like the twisting stems of a briar. A ring. I daren't touch it.

He stands, comes round the desk towards me. 'I can't do marriage, Jo. You know how I feel about that. It wouldn't be right, anyway, not now. But if you'd accept the ring, wear it, you'd make me very happy.'

I rise from my seat, practically leap into his arms. They go tight around me, hold me close, but no closer than my arms around him. The sound of his heartbeat is in my ears, the scent of his skin in my nose. It ought to be velvet midnight, not nine thirty in the morning. There ought to be music and champagne, not the distant sound of a telephone ringing, two cups of tea going cold. But it doesn't matter. I don't need romance if I have this.

'I'll wear it,' I say, 'if you'll leave the little fox out on your desk. Don't hide her away.'

I feel, rather than hear him laugh. 'It's a deal.'

No need for declarations. This is enough, these moments, meshed in each other's arms. These kisses, enough.

Time passes. At some point I tell him I'll have to go to the Island, arrange for Silverbank to be sold.

'You'll come back?' he murmurs into my hair.

'Oh, I'll be back, Bram. I promise. This is where I want to be.'

Acknowledgements

I CAN'T BELIEVE IT'S TIME FOR me to thank my lovely writing support group again! Once, it seemed like a wild dream to think of having one novel published, and now, number three is a reality. Each and everyone of you made a real difference to the process of writing *A Conflict of Interests*.

Firstly, many thanks to my agent, Rowan Lawton, and Eleanor Lawlor at The Soho Agency. The editorial team at Bonnier, especially Kelly Smith, my hugely supportive editor, Ciara Corrigan, Eleanor Stammeijer and Sandra Ferguson, and to everyone who works behind the scenes in getting my work on the bookshelves. We may not have met, but I really appreciate all you do!

As a writer, I spend so many solitary hours at the keyboard that I'd be lost without the wider writing community for its support and encouragement. For both of these, and for much more, including bracing commentary to keep me on track – thanks go to current Chandlers Ford Writers members Anne Summerfield, Adelaide Morris, Corinne Pebody, John Barfield and Jan Moring. Taverners writers, especially Claire Fuller, Judith Heneghan, Susmita Bhattacharya,

Amanda Oosthuizen and Louise Taylor played their part in welcoming me to their group despite my intermittent attendance at their meetings. Dovetail Writers still let me lead them in their extraordinary writing endeavours, and as ever, my involvement with students and colleagues at the University of Winchester has been inspirational.

Special mention once again to Rebecca Fletcher, writer and freelance journalist – thank you so much for your help and support. You are amazing!

As ever, thanks go to my family: I love you all to the moon and back! My older son Will and his partner, Abbie, and my brand-new granddaughter, Margot; and my younger son Phil, his wife, Kat, and Danny, my grandson – I just wish we could see much more of all of you. Phil has played a special part in discussing the twists and turns of the plot for *A Conflict of Interests* – I owe you so much for your patience and eagle eye for inconsistencies. Love and apologies in equal measure go to Kat and Danny for letting us talk and talk and . . . then talk some more!

Finally, all my love to Nick, my husband, who endures endless late meals and appeals for cups of coffee with superhuman forbearance. You know I couldn't have done anything at all without you.

Find me on Twitter (@ClaireGradidge) or online at www. chandlersfordwriters.wordpress.com/chandlers-ford-writers

Return to where it all began . . .

THE
UNEXPECTED
RETURN
OF
JOSEPHINE
FOX

Winner of the 2019 Richard and Judy Search for
a Bestseller competition

'Jo Fox, a very modern woman in wartime England. Getting
to know her was a delight. More please, Claire Gradidge'

RICHARD MADELEY

'Feisty, determined, and brave – I loved Josephine ('Jo') Fox.
What a debut from a marvellous new author'

JUDY FINNIGAN

'A complete delight, the story sings with authenticity . . .
unputdownable'

CAZ FREAR

Available now

Prologue

14ᵗʰ/15ᵗʰ April 1941, the skies over southern England

BOMBER'S MOON. FROM TWENTY THOUSAND feet, the Solent shines like a mermaid's tail, showing the way to the city so plainly the blackout is useless. There's no mistaking the boatyards, the aircraft factories, the docks. The first Junkers follow the water, set down their payload as simple as laying eggs.

Targets lose their definition as the fires spread. The city answers back, ack-ack guns pouring defiance into the sky. Caught in a stream of tracer, one bomber jinks wildly, turns for home. Engine stuttering smoke, it jettisons its load ten miles off target, sees a dark spot light up like Christmas.

Unknowing, the aircraft has seven deaths on its tally sheet when a Beaufighter brings it down barely a minute later. But tomorrow, when the Heavy Rescue Crew digs the last casualty out of what's left of the little Hampshire pub on the outskirts of Romsey, there will be an extra body to carry to the makeshift mortuary. Not seven shrouded corpses, but eight: eight unlawful deaths for the town's coroner to investigate.

1

The same night, on the ground

I<small>T'S MIDNIGHT WHEN THE TRAIN</small> leaves London. I'd arrived much too early, had to wait until the carriages filled up and the labyrinthine processes of wartime travel set us on our way. Now, in the blacked-out, blue-lit, third-class compartment my fellow travellers are sleeping, stiff upper lip in the face of danger. *If it ain't got your name on it . . .*

But I can't sleep. It isn't the bombs, I'm used to them. It's the thought of what lies ahead.

Romsey.

So long ago.

I'd promised myself I'd never go back. If they didn't want me, I'd show them. I'd never set foot in the place again. That's how you think at fourteen, when your life's crashing down around you. And though it's ridiculous to feel the same when you're almost forty, I do. I'm nervous, but I don't have a choice. If I want to know the truth, I've got to go back.

I peer out through a crack in the blind. Before the war, this moonlit landscape would have been peaceful, eerily beautiful, but tonight the distant wail of air raid sirens seeps into the carriage, dogging our journey and sending us cross-country, miles out of our way. I watch the repeated flare of incendiaries in the distance, see the dark huddled towns spring to light, watch the slow-motion fall of bombs. Glimpses, like at the pictures; except this is life and death.

Not far now.

As dawn breaks, the train is still stopping more often than it moves. If my suitcase weren't so heavy, I could walk from here.

But I wait, and at last we struggle into Romsey station. It hasn't changed a bit. The stationmaster's still waiting by the exit, alert for tips and fare-dodgers. Old Bunny Burnage studies my ticket, barely glances at my face. I don't think he recognises me, but I can't help remembering all the times he'd caught us playing near the railway tracks.

When we laid pennies on the line for the express to flatten. The whole gang of us, messing about, daring each other to play 'last across'. Looking for trouble and finding it.

'Penny'll derail the express,' Billy says.

'Nah. Him'll get cutten in half.' That's Bert.

'Bollocks. Look here.' Abe pulls something from his pocket, holds it out. We look, because Abe is the leader, and what he says, goes. 'It'll just get flattened, like this. And hot, if it isn't pushed off.'

'That's treason.' Jem fingers the squashed irregular shape. 'My dad says—'

'My dad's a copper, my da-ad is,' we taunt him.

'Dad says you can get yer head chopped off for spoiling a coin. Put in the Tower of London with the spies and shot.'

'Liar, liar, pants on fire,' I chant. 'Can't get shot and beheaded.'

'Can too, Carrotty-head.'

'They can't kill you twice, you bloody chicken.'

Spitting mad, I run to where the rail is singing already with the train on its way. The only girl in the gang, I have to prove myself every time. As I set down my penny, they scarper. Bunny Burnage is pounding towards me, cutting off my escape as the express screams past in a shawl of smoke, the rush of it nearly knocking me over. Just in time, I grab the penny. Shove it in my pocket, fingers tingling with heat, ear stinging with the stationmaster's blow as I stumble away.

'Josephine Fox!' he shouts. 'Should have known. Serve you right if you'd been killed. I'd tell your father if anyone knew who he was. Hop it, you little bastard, and don't come back.'

So I'd hopped, and while the penny and the slap had cooled before I'd even caught up with the gang, the stationmaster's contempt stung much longer. In a way it still rankles, so now when he touches his cap and calls me madam, I want to laugh, dare him to call me bastard to my grown-up face.

I push my suitcase forward. 'I'd like to leave this here for the time being.'

'No noxious substances, no perishable goods, no livestock.'

'None of those.'

'That'll be thruppence.' He hands me a pink ticket. 'No claim without a ticket.' He licks the back of the counterfoil, sticks it to the corner of the case. 'Southern Railway wishes to make it clear that the company takes no responsibility for loss or damage caused by war operations.'

I can't help smiling. 'Safe enough in Romsey, surely?'

'Begging your pardon, madam, but that's all you know. We had a tip and run raider come over last night, flattened the Cricketers' Arms. Still digging them out last I heard, dead as doornails, the whole lot.'

'The old place in Green Lane? That's bad.'

'You know it?' He peers closely at me as I turn away. 'Hang on a minute. You got the look of—'

I pretend not to hear, keep on walking.

Don't miss the second intriguing case for Josephine Fox

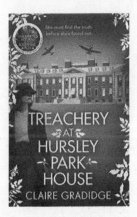

DECEMBER 1942. As the war rages on, the accidental death of a young man is almost unremarkable. Except this young man was patrolling the grounds of Hursley Park House, where teams are designing crucial modifications to the Spitfire – and he was found clutching part of a blueprint.

JANUARY 1943. Josephine Fox is given a code name and a mission as she is seconded to Hursley: uncover the network responsible for information leaks to the enemy. And when the dead man's father visits Bram Nash convinced that his son was innocent of espionage and the victim of murder, her friend is also drawn into the investigation.

But as Jo and Bram circle closer to the truth, danger is closing in around them . . .

Available now